Dawn of Darkness

The Knights of Ezazeruth Trilogy

Thomas R. Gaskin

British Library Cataloguing in Publication Data. A catalogue record for this book is available from the British Library

www.thomasrgaskin.com

ISBN: 978-1-78507-163-8

www.newgeneration-publishing.com

 New Generation Publishing

ACKNOWLEDGEMENTS

Big thanks to everyone who has helped me create my second book as well as to all those who have read and enjoyed the first.

To my family who have been so supportive. You're all truly great.

To my number one fan Luci, thanks for your support.

To Matt for your help in designing my website.

Jon, again you have again created an amazing cover, thank you.

To Graham, for your methodical skills in copy editing my manuscript.

Jen, you're amazing! Thanks for your proofreading skills and support. Lots of big hugs.

My good friend and beta reader Paul, I'd be lost without you.

To Julia, thanks for your support in Germany.

To Santi, for creating my video.

I am dyslexic, so this book also goes out to all those with learning difficulties. It's a hard world to exist in but exist in it we do, and great things we can still achieve.

Dedicated to my wonderful family.

My brother and sister.

My mum and dad.

And last but never least to my children and beautiful wife.

Part Three

Chapter One
Gaining Allies

Two glowing yellow eyes stared at Framlar as he ate, just visible through the black veil. They held many stories, none of which were pleasant or friendly, but filled with pain and the sadistic pleasure that the creature loved. But Framlar was unfazed by its presence, sitting down and scoffing as much as he could fit into his mouth, with chunks of chicken and drops of wine all over his big, black, bushy beard; he delighted himself with every bite. (Whereas those below him had to starve under his iron-fisted reign.) But he never drank water with his meals (or ever, for that matter) – always wine, constantly red wine. Because of this, he was unfit and often tired.

There was a sudden murmur from the corner, as one of his five brides whimpered as they knelt shackled together with their heads bowed; this was their usual custom, but they were now trembling with fear in the presence of the creature before them. For all the horrors they had seen, they had never seen anything quite like this before.

Framlar chucked a chicken thigh at her to keep her quiet. She moaned as it hit her, yet she forced herself to be calm.

"So, what do you want?" said Framlar between bites of bread, his fingers greasy.

"We want you to help us defeat Camia!" said the cursed voice from behind the shadowy veil. It was calm and sophisticated. As the creature spoke, its lips were moist as they rubbed together.

"HA, HA!" Framlar boomed with mockery.

"Why do you laugh?" said the sinister voice, not recognising the ridicule.

"Because of what you just said." Framlar wiped away tears of laughter from his eyes with a cloth that had been resting on his stomach.

The figure waited patiently for an explanation, but Framlar was not intimidated by this mysterious foe that he had not met until this day. He had met many creatures and beasts, and this was just another to add to his collection in the dungeon. He kept peering at his commander, who poked his head through the drapes behind the beast, wondering when to pounce and capture it.

Looking up at it, as it stared back at him unwearyingly, Framlar dropped his food and sat back, making himself comfortable as if he was going to explain something frankly.

"Camia is more than most military powers. It has the best-trained soldiers in the world – most are hand-picked – they're put through the most vigorous training course in all of Ezazeruth, which is updated every year. Those who do pass are fighting machines and are trained experts at their trade; they obey orders to the full and never retreat, and don't even get me started on their Knight Hawks!" he said viciously, as if he held a personal vendetta against them.

"Who?"

"The Knight Hawks, the Camions' Shadow Ops. They live in the darkness. Camion soldiers are good, but the Hawks are supreme." The creature let out a crude and deep laugh. "We tried it once!" Framlar said, banging his fist on the table. "Never again. They *always* win, so don't come into my domain and mock me!"

"Maybe not this time?" said the quiet voice of the demon.

Framlar looked up intently. "What do you propose?"

"I have the means and you have the wants. I can provide you with an army that will devour the Camions – all I ask is for your allegiance?"

"Allegiance to what?"

"The control of the world!"

Framlar let out a crude, unpleasant smile and began to boom with scornful laughter, his huge stomach vibrating with every guffaw.

"You consider yourself to be powerful?" he mocked. He knew of all the powers and small armies within the known world, but the creature before him was not one he knew, and therefore, he thought, posed no threat. But the creature sighed and looked at the floor; then its arm swiftly pulled apart its robe, revealing its body, showing its long tail wrapped around itself as if to keep it hidden, its skin glittering turquoise in the firelight. The long arm caught the commander by his throat, and he was brought through the drapes and into the room. It raised him to the demon's eye level, with his legs kicking off the floor. The commander, dark-skinned, tall and strong, punched the demon in the head, yet it had no effect. But as he caught its yellow eyes, he went very still, as if it were showing him the horrors it had committed. Then, as if the commander's neck were made like a twig, the creature snapped it and let the body slump to the floor.

"The Ninsks are under your control, are they not?" said the demon as it pulled the cloak back around itself and watched calmly before Framlar's fascinated gaze.

"In a manner of speaking."

"Explain."

"They answer to another, but *they* are under my control."

"Good, then get them to join in my – *our* venture, allow them to let my units cross the land undeterred, and I will happily let you rise in our glory."

"If your army is so powerful, why don't you just charge across the Rogan Defence Line?"

"You know how strong the Ninsks are – it would be my undoing."

"Indeed."

"So, we have an agreement?"

Framlar just smiled, but it was all the confirmation that the creature wanted. Pulling down its veil, revealing pearly-white fangs, and a long, narrow, scaled head that glittered turquoise in the dim candlelight, it joined in with Framlar's crude laughter.

***

"The gates are open," said Blar, crouching low and holding his spear, whilst looking on nervously at the back of his fearsome leader, who had not moved in a while. Blar wore little – just a rag with a huge animal skin over his shoulders, a bone knife strapped to his waist. He was not prepared for war, but was subjected to it under his oath – now the biggest regret of his life.

Before them sat a dark and eerie city. The Acropolis stood out, with giant braziers lining it, blazing away. It looked as though the building was hovering in the darkness, with the rest of the city being so darn quiet.

Zweld, the leader, looked on at the city of Cam with malicious intent in his eyes. After his brothers had been killed three weeks earlier on a rocky outcrop, he had mustered his armies and marched on the city. He was not really sure what to expect, but when anger clouds one's eyes, their judgement is affected. But serendipity had worked in his favour and, looking upon what appeared to be an empty metropolis, he plotted his retribution.

"Let's move," he said hoarsely, his hands still shaking with anger. And, emerging from the trees, several thousand Emiros advanced on the city, obscured by a dark cloud following them across the plains surrounding Cam.

Chapter Two
The Shadow upon the Hill

"Bored!" Andreas said to Pausanias. "Here we are, the best soldiers in the land, and we're babysitting a princess whilst the rest of the country fights!" Pausanias rubbed his forehead on hearing the same moan from his younger brother for the third time that day. They had been at Ambenol for nearly two months now, ever since the Three-Thirty-Third had escorted them there, and Andreas had done little else other than moan. "I mean, come on! We should be fighting the Black, not sitting on the same balcony each day looking out to nothing."

"Will you shut up?!" shouted Pausanias, finally having had enough of his sulking. "Our orders are to protect Princess Undrea, and you will obey them to the letter!"

Andreas huffed.

But Pausanias looked at him and sighed. He knew how difficult it was – Andreas was much younger than he was, and did not know how to cope with his emotions as well as he did. He also had just passed the gruesome Knight Hawks' tests, meaning he was keen to get stuck in to Shadow Ops missions. Pausanias was already a Knight Hawk. At the age of twenty-eight, he was a legend amongst them, calm, collected and the best swordsman since his father – a Hawk who had mysteriously disappeared ten years previously, having brought his sons up to know what he knew, teaching them the Agam Var'k fighting system. Pausanias was one of his proudest creations, being adept at everything he needed to know; but before his disappearance, he had not had enough time to pass it on to Andreas. Pausanias tried his best to fill the void.

Taking a breath, Pausanias tried to compose himself, feeling guilty for shouting at his little brother. Ever since his father's disappearance, Andreas hadn't coped well, and it often tested Pausanias's patience. The Knight Hawks had trained him to endure brutal interrogators, but his brother's moaning pushed him beyond the edge of his fortitude.

"Want to do some practice?" Pausanias said cheerfully.

"No! I want to fight for real. When the time does come to fight someone with a sword, I'm going to be so used to not running them through, that instead I will fend off the blade, step back and say 'your go'."

Pausanias laughed. "We will have our time, little brother. Let it be a lucky day for the enemy, for each day we don't meet, they live a little longer."

"Ha! That's true, and something I would drink to."

Pausanias leant on the pommel of his sword, which was attached to his thigh. It was clear he favoured swords, with four broken-back Seaxes of varying lengths spread around his person. Sitting next to the wall he also had his Malorga, a mechanical crossbow that all Hawks came equipped with – a highly powerful, accurate weapon, which at maximum velocity would split a man's torso in half from a hundred paces. However, due to Andreas's 'freaky' skills with a bow, he stuck with that. Although Pausanias tried to teach him what he knew about duelling, Andreas just did not want to know, being too impatient. He had his skill and he was happy with that.

Pausanias leant on the battlements and looked at the town below. Surrounded by a crescent wall, the town was built into a large hill, with several hundred houses compacted inside. On top of the hill was a smaller version of the Acropolis of Cam, with a long flight of steps running up to it from the town. There, Lord Malisten lived in all his glory, caring little for anyone other than himself. He was the richest man in Camia after the King, and wanted his own palace with his own rule, and so he had Ambenol built just for him. He had his own army within the walls and charged a fortune in taxes, but Ambenol was a tranquil and well-kept metropolis, and the rich living within the walls were happy to pay, as no beggars lay in the streets, and they got any law they wanted passed to suit them.

Sticking out from the back of the Acropolis was a long tower stretching high into the sky, giving a view all around. Undrea sat inside it, looking out of the window.

Looking up to check on her for the hundredth time that morning, Pausanias grew worried, for he could not see her clearly, and preferred to be there with her, his oath and duty bound to make sure she was safe – but she ordered him to leave her be.

He started to tremble with worry, and so shook his head clear. He wanted Andreas to leave him so he could practice the Agam Var'k, a slow dance where his arms and legs would mimic fighting stances to tune up his muscle memory. Whenever he did it, all Andreas could do was mock him.

"If we're attacked, there is nowhere to run – we're cornered here," Pausanias said, trying to make conversation as he looked at the defences, and distracting his mind from his thoughts.

"Uh-hm," said Andreas, resting his chin on his hands as he leant against the parapet. Seeing one of the giant crossbows that lined the wall, he started playing with it, aiming at a bird and making sounds of firing it.

"Stop playing with that damn thing!" Pausanias said sharply.

"I think you're just jealous that you can't hit a beetle from twenty paces!" said Andreas, still peering through the sight.

"Father taught us to be warriors, not to brag. To use your skills – not to become bored and play with a weapon, but to respect it!"

Andreas huffed and stood next to his brother, looking out at the landscape, trying to see what he was seeing.

There was a moment's silence, and the corners of Pausanias's mouth curled into a smile as a gentle breeze passed by, with no annoying moans.

"HA!" shouted Andreas, breaking the tranquillity.

"What now?" Pausanias said, rubbing his forehead again.

"That guard just fell over." He pointed to one of the garrison soldiers, being helped out by the others.

"You're so childish."

Andreas maintained his smirk. Picking up his longbow, which had been leaning on a bench, and taking a tin of beeswax and a cloth, he started rubbing the beeswax into the fine wood.

"If you keep doing that without using it, you'll damage it."

"Stick to your sword, big brother. I know my bow and I don't need you to tell me how to maintain it!!" Andreas said calmly as he ran his cloth delicately along the yew-tree wood.

"Very well, although I would not mock me too much. I'm a master with a sword, remember? At the age of just seventeen, I beat five Kings' guards —"

" — with one wooden sword – yes, I know, and so does everybody else who fights and lives within Camia, heck, Ezazeruth! But remember that Father also said not to be too big-headed."

Pausanias chewed his lip. Andreas, despite being younger and more irritating, always knew how to end a conversation with him.

He continued to fix his gaze on the horizon, and took in a deep breath with his arms folded. As he gazed out, it looked as if the hills were moving, but it was just the heat vapour in the distance. But yet again he was distracted by his brother, as the cloth squeaked whilst he was rubbing his bow.

"Why don't you go for a walk? I could do with some time alone and you could do with letting off some steam. Go down to the town and back."

Andreas sighed heavily. Getting up, he leant his bow against the wall, picked up his helmet and turned to walk along the white, arched bridges leading from the balcony to the steps.

"Well, well, here we are," Pausanias said, closing his eyes and enjoying the near-silence – just the sounds of the wind hitting against his face and of an eagle calling out in the distance as it circled the ground for its prey. He loved the quiet – not just the absence of his brother and his moaning, but in general; the growing world was always filled with noises, everyone in a big rush to get everywhere and move on. It was nice to stop for a moment and take in the natural world, and in that moment he felt like the calmest person there was.

As he opened his eyes he saw Andreas making his way down the long stone steps leading towards the town, walking like a sulking child, dragging his heels.

But as he looked out upon the hills again, he saw shadows that he thought were cast down from the clouds above, creating darkness upon them. As he squinted, though, he realised something was amiss – there were no clouds. He watched on for a moment, trying to work out what the dark shade was, but it was heading his way, and fast.

"Oh, no … Andreas!" he yelled down to his brother.

Andreas looked up sharply, seeing Pausanias point to the approaching army swarming across the land. Seeing it, he raced up to join him.

"Where did they come from?" he said, panting.

"I don't know, but we need to get the town ready!" Turning, Pausanias faced his younger brother directly. "Sound the alarm! Get men to arms!"

"Yes, Sir," he said in an official-sounding manner, recognising his older brother's authoritative tone. He ran down the battlements towards a horn that rang out into the town.

On hearing the sound of the horn, Undrea put down her bag of purple powder and ran to the window. Looking out, she gasped as she saw the approaching horde, then ran back into the room.

"Oh, no – where is it?" she said to herself.

She started moving plates and scrolls, making more of a mess than there already was in the small room.

Becoming frustrated, she started throwing things out of the window to clear some space. Then, looking in the corner, she found the horsehair tail that General Drorkon had given her. Clutching it at her breast, she closed her eyes and concentrated.

"Where are you?"

Running down the long flight of steps, Pausanias and Andreas were almost jumping, taking three or four steps at a time. As they got to the wall, Pausanias directed where he wanted the garrison to be, whilst Andreas followed enthusiastically. Being members of the eminent Knight Hawks, they had both donned their dark helmets. Pausanias was a sergeant, and had two rust-coloured feathers fixed to the back of his helmet like fins on a fish, whereas Andreas just had the single crest. And the slits in the helmet for their eyes and mouth were covered by a black piece of fabric, meaning no one could see their faces, almost as if they were demons with no face to show. They were not allowed to go anywhere in public without them, but the distinguishing feature about the Knight Hawks was not their helmets, it was their swords – both had them strapped to their backs with a Hawk for a hilt, and two ruby-red eyes nestled into the guard.

"Every soldier to the walls!!!" Pausanias bellowed at the garrison.

Screaming, the inhabitants ran to their houses and locked themselves inside, with the wall lined with soldiers, oval shields on their left arms and tall, thin spears to their right, gallantly dressed in fine suits of armour that glistened in the sunlight. These soldiers were few but well equipped and trained, with Lord Malisten paying for what was needed, although they were still grossly outmatched by the advancing horde.

Just then, Lord Malisten appeared, running down the long stairway. He held an elaborately decorative sword, which was also very ancient and probably no longer fit for use.

"Man the walls! Stop the beasts!" he bellowed in his forthright tone. He looked as though he had just woken up, as he wore nightclothes and an undone dressing gown, the tassels waving about as he ran.

"They already have their orders, my Lord," said Pausanias.

Lord Malisten nodded with worry. "Yes, good, good, ermm, what ... ermm."

"Yes, my Lord?"

Lowering his voice, he stepped closer to Pausanias. "What should we do now?"

Pausanias kept his voice low. "Well, you say some words of inspiration to the men, and then you turn and run back up those steps and protect Undrea."

"Oh yes, right, yes, good!"

He stood on the spot as he thought things through, everyone looking at him.

"Oh, and, my Lord?"

"Yes?" he said, startled, looking back up.

"Say something along the lines of, *fight for now, fight for justice, fight these filthy rekons into the ground!*"

A smile appeared on the lord's face. "Yes, that, that is good – thank you."

"Any time, Sir ..."

The lord stood there, still not knowing what to do or say.

"... It may be a good time to say it now, Sir?"

"Oh, yes, OK. FIGHT, FIGHT, MY MEN," he said with a raised fist, and then, losing himself with fear as he saw the Black approach, he turned and ran back up the stairway towards the tower.

"He's an odd one," Andreas said, looking on.

"Yes, he is, but he is out of the way and that's what we need."

"He could have taken the women and children with him, though?" Andreas said, observing the houses near the wall, knowing that they would be cowering inside.

"No – he's an aristocrat, a completely different social class to the rest of us. He probably doesn't even know they exist."

They watched him clamber up the steps, his unfit state causing him to stop for breath every few paces.

"Anyway, to business," Pausanias said, turning and rubbing his hands together. "It looks like your lust for blood is about to be fulfilled, little brother. I hope you're ready!"

Andreas didn't answer – he was too distracted, counting how many arrows he had in his quiver and checking that they were pulling without snagging.

"There's someone approaching!" came a shout from a lieutenant above the gate.

Pausanias ran over to the officer, who pointed towards a lone rider heading their way, a glint of sunlight reflecting from his helmet.

"Who is it?"

"I don't know – I think he's Camion!"

Pausanias squinted. As the surreptitious figure came into view it became clear who it was. "It's General Drakator!" he said, with a slight laugh. "Funny, we could do with him."

Drakator was riding a huge, white horse and was well in front of the advancing enemy, who were now less than two leagues away from the fortress.

"Open the gates! Let the general in!" Pausanias barked at the men below.

Drakator trotted in but did not acknowledge anyone. Dismounting, he ran up to the battlements as the guards below hastily tried to close the gate, the view of the creatures causing them to shiver. He wasn't clad in as much armour as he usually was – just a large belt with guards on his arms and shins, showing off his raw, muscular physique.

"It's good to see you, General," said Andreas, although Pausanias knew that he would not reply, and he didn't. Drakator was a mute, but was the general to all the infantry units. It was an honour for Pausanias to be standing with him right then, and, as he gazed out, a smile appeared behind the face guard of his helmet.

Drakator walked straight past them towards the most forward point of the fort's battlements, and stood looking at the approaching horde.

Drawing his sword, which was a large single blade with a purple tinge to the steel and hilt, he stood with his hands by his sides, waiting for the army to approach.

As the Black got nearer, their howls were audible in the hills, making the garrison shudder and look at each other with worry; they had heard the rumours of recent attacks, but now they were seeing them for real.

But the Knight Hawks stood still, either side of Drakator, each of them looking out vacantly.

The Black army stopped just out of arrow range from the fort as they created a semicircle around it, the creatures taunting the garrison with their weapons and vile shrieks. It worked. Pausanias looked around and noted their fear, some stepping back slightly, their eyes wide and hands shaking. He, though, was calm, as was his brother; in fact, Andreas was edging forward slightly, eager to start fighting. This worried Pausanias – he seemed too eager to kill.

"Stand your ground!" he said hoarsely to the men. "You're soldiers of Camia – you *will* protect this fort." Noting his calm and composed appearance, they obeyed.

Drakator still had not moved, but maintained his posture of looking at the Black, as if waiting for something.

The creatures before them numbered over five thousand, and one thing made Pausanias worry – where had they come from? For he feared that this may be a splinter group that may have come from Cam; *is Cam destroyed?* He tried to bury the thought at the back of his mind and concentrate on the here and now.

Things turned even worse, though, when the creatures parted out of the way for siege engines to be brought forward, towed by a long line of larger creatures built from nothing but muscle, hauling the machines towards the town. There was a battering ram and several catapults. Groups of archers clustered around them.

A large monster clad in armour stepped up onto a rock so it was visible to all. Pausanias couldn't see its face – it was covered in black, spiked armour, with skulls of its victims on the spikes. The creature was just huge in comparison with anything else he had seen, with a torso like that of a boar and a howl that matched a Gracker – it was fearsome. Raising a mace into the air as if it weighed nothing at all, it howled at its army; then, as one, the horde charged towards the town.

Pausanias just stood with his left hand under his right armpit and right arm up to his lip in front of the fabric of his helmet; he concentrated. But his concentration was cut short when he saw Drakator's sword thrust in front of his face, then someone shouted, *"Shield me!"*

Pausanias looked around, wondering who had said it, but the guards just looked out, fear still gripping them. He thought it was one of them making a prayer to their chosen god, but there it was again: "*Shield me!*" It seemed to be coming from Drakator, but it couldn't be – he was a mute. So he looked at his brother, who also had noticed the words, and was looking his way.

Again: "*Shield me!*" But this time there was more conviction in the tone.

"*Shield me!*"

The voice was also not that of a man or woman, but like a distant echo from a demon.

"*Shield me!!*" Drakator shouted.

Pausanias went to walk forward to find out what was going on, but suddenly fell backwards as a bolt of lightning struck the sword in front of him. Suddenly, as if the sword were drawing all the wind towards them, everything around him changed. Dirt and leaves blew fiercely; his cloak flapped around and kept getting in the way of his view; the garrison crouched down and held onto the battlements as if they were going to be blown away.

As he looked up, Pausanias saw that the cloudless sky had turned dark, with ripples of purple lightning behind it and fierce rumbles of thunder.

"*Shield me!!*" Drakator bellowed again, even louder.

"General … Drakator!!" Pausanias shouted, wondering what was going on, fear gripping him for the first time that he could remember.

"*SHIELD MEEE!!*" Drakator let out one continual scream. With both arms out, he stood like a cross with his sword in his right hand. The cascading thunderstorm then erupted before Pausanias's eyes, all channelling into the sword – it glowed in a fierce purple, creating its own light in the darkness produced by the cloud.

From the creatures' point of view, they saw purple thunder erupting in front of them to one point at the centre of the wall above the gate. The once bright day was now shrouded in near-darkness, with the only source of light being the thunder. And from it, a purple shield emerged, growing in its intensity like a bubble over the town.

"Fire!!" shouted the clad Golesh, fearing the strange phenomenon, and every arrow and rock was fired at the strange object before them.

As it kept growing – the thunder feeding its intensity – it got nearer to the creatures, so near that some of them threw their spears into it; some even tried attacking it and got sucked in. But anything that went towards the shield was absorbed, and did not pass through or bounce off, but disappeared as if taken into another dimension.

Drakator stopped his crying out – his grey eyes vacant, blue veins protruding all around his face and body, his skin tight as if he had been drained of everything. The shield-bubble stood motionless where it was, and inside was like a giant room. A bird chirped, creating an echo; the one noise that could not be heard was the wind, and everything was still.

The garrison looked around, completely perplexed as to what was going on – as everyone was, except for one person. Undrea stood in her tower looking down, playing with Havovatch's Gracker tooth around her neck as she watched the scene unfold.

Drakator started to shake, trying to maintain his posture as if fighting against a force of evil within him. With his arms outstretched, the thunder now stopped, and he slowly brought his arms towards his chest with great resistance. As he did so, the bubble shrank quickly towards him until it became a small orb, hovering within his grasp at his chest, and he looked at the mystical orb floating before him. He could hold it no longer.

He threw out his arms as violently as he could, and every arrow, boulder, spear and sword, and even the odd creature that had got sucked in, went shooting back out towards the horde.

The Black had little time to move, and any that did were tripped up by, or became tangled with, their own brethren. The boulders came crashing down and carried on rolling over the Golesh with more force than they had been thrown with; the spears shot straight through armour and bodies and kept going. Within seconds the army was reduced to less than half of what it had been.

Drakator lay slumped on the ground, unconscious. Pausanias pulled himself over, a loud ringing in his ears. He looked out in disbelief at the army in disarray, trying to work out what had just happened.

The creatures picked themselves back up; then, realising that there were still enough of them to take on the town, without instruction they started howling and charged.

"Prepare to defend!" Pausanias shouted, trying to haul Drakator to his feet, but he was out cold.

"You two!" he shouted at the closest guards, who were crouching down and holding their ears. "Get the general somewhere safe and return to the wall with haste!" But they looked at each other as if to say *did you hear him?* Looking back, Pausanias deliberately pointed to Drakator and the bottom of the stairway. Sluggishly, they did as instructed.

"Stand your ground! Protect the town at all costs!" Pausanias shouted as he rallied the men.

Then he began to wonder, where was his brother?

Looking around he could not see him anywhere, but was distracted by the cries from the Black, which were nearly upon them.

The creatures' shouts were unsettling, but also obscured the charging cavalry from behind them.

Pausanias saw the charge, and knew instantly that victory was theirs. Drawing his sword and placing one hand on the battlements, he leapt over, landing gracefully at the base of the wall, and charged at the creatures.

Chapter Three
The Hawks' Quest

The sun shone brightly as it always did in Camia, highlighting the greenness of the world. Scattered over the rolling hills near the western border, before the Plains of Fernara, a cavalry regiment sat along the landscape in a dishevelled, rushed encampment. Columns of tents had been erected in a disorganised manner with few standing watch, and men quarrelling in their drunken state.

But their noise was drowned out by the constant shouting emanating from the large tent in the centre.

"YOU CALL YOURSELF A GENERAL?!"

"Watch your tongue, Malffay – I outrank you!"

"Try saying that with a sword in your hand, coward! You wouldn't even know what to do with it!"

Malffay strode out into the open, keen to get away before he did something rash.

But his general was not yet done. Pushing his way through the tent flaps, Sarka chased after his first officer.

"I am not yet done with you! One click of my fingers and you'll be dead!"

"Ha! I would love to see any of these rekons try!"

Malffay mockingly drew his sword and started dancing and parrying around the men. Most were accustomed to his temper, and so ignored him as they continued their own doings.

"See! None of these cretins has it in them to take me on. This is *your* army, General," he shouted, pointing his sword at Sarka. "Cowards!"

"I gave you a job to do, and you failed!"

"I won't apologise for any insolence, *General*!" He kept saying "General" as if it were a joke. "I told you – they vanished!"

"I did not think even *you* would sink so low as to believe in childish antics – you rode after them, you *saw* them!"

"Aye, I did, but as I said, when they went over the crest of that hill," he said, pointing to the rise to the west, "we followed and they vanished. No evidence of them was seen, not even hoof prints on the ground!"

"Three thousand horses do not just disappear off the face of the earth, Malffay. Maybe you're not cut out for the position I put you in."

Malffay pointed to his commander's insignia of an oak leaf on his shoulders. "Want them? Come and take them," he hissed.

Sarka said nothing and stood uncomfortably.

"Just as I thought – a coward to lead a regiment. How Camion!"

"You're too mad for your own good."

Malffay laughed as he swaggered away.

Sarka stood firm watching him, keen to gain some credibility in front of his men. "I want someone made an example of over this!" he snarled.

Malffay turned and smiled, looking at the closest person to him – a young lad, not much older than twenty. He still had a young face, with smooth, pale skin and innocent eyes; his naivety had got the better of him, with the promise of wealth and power easily persuading him to betray his country – even his family.

Before anyone suspected what was about to happen, Malffay slashed heavily, cutting through his helmet and skull, leaving his head rolling on the ground before his body slumped after it.

Most looked on, shocked; even Sarka winced slightly. Malffay again laughed and staggered off in his strutting, confident way, pulling a waterskin from his belt and downing the contents, but Sarka was sure it was not water.

"Clear this mess up!" he said to a sentry, before going back into his tent. But the men stood around, clearly in shock; no one wanted to go near the body.

Once inside, Sarka threw his helmet at a stone statue of himself, which was chipped by the impact.

He rubbed his face hard in regretful reflection of his promotion of Malffay, but he knew he had no one else who could better him in a fight – he was too strong and skilled, even more so when he was drunk. He had been too careless in selecting his men, paying off as many as he could who would happily betray their country for coin and power. He just wished he'd vetted them more thoroughly than he had done. Fortunately for him, he had got rid of all the noble and honourable warriors in his regiment, but the thought made him rub his jaw, which still cracked after a sergeant had struck him in the face. But he laughed at the thought of the man who was now in the infantry, and he spat on the floor at the vermin who walked on foot instead of riding on horseback.

Suddenly he was taken out of his trance by a hissing noise coming from a box sitting next to him.

He stood looking fearful at it and made no attempt to move, his heart missing a beat. But the hissing grew in its intensity, and he saw the edges around the lid glowing as the noise became more frantic and loud.

He wandered over slowly to the box, which sat on a table at waist height, square in shape and made of varnished wood, yet showing its age with rough edges, chips and scrapes. Markings were etched around the exterior – not Camion, not anything Ezazeruth had seen for more than an age.

Slowly he rested his hands either side of the lid and lifted it. He stood mesmerised, looking into the dazzling glow of different shades of orange and pink. It then dimmed and he looked through, fearful of the response. He had opened it many times before, ever since it was given to him by a dark and shady character, but had never seen it so bright; his master was clearly more agitated that day.

"How may I be of service, my Lord?" he said, trembling, wary of how the one thing he feared most in the world was going to react.

The voice that came out was harsh in tone and echoed around the confines of the tent. "You are failing me, human. I still sense great power coming from your land; we will soon be leaving towards you and yet a threat still exists."

Sarka tried to compose himself. "A-apologies, there have been some … complications, but I still do not know of this power you speak of … my scouts —"

"YOU-ARE-NOT-WORKING-HARD-ENOUGH!" The voice barked quickly and the glow turned purple, with flames before his eyes. Sarka tried to hold back from crying, he was so scared.

"We will continue to endeavour in our course, but I assure you, few stand in opposition to you now – you are no match for anything in Ezazeruth!"

There was a cruel and deep laughter from the box. "Your instructions were to eradicate ALL opposition. We will be on your land before the season is over. You have until then to kill everything that stands in our way!"

The light vanished before Sarka could blink. Falling to the floor, he tried to take some deep breaths as he hyperventilated. He looked at his hands, trembling beyond his control.

When he had calmed down, about an hour later, he schemed hard to better the situation, and to work out who this power was. Yet he realised that his army was too small – he needed more men.

***

An hour passed and Pausanias was walking through the carnage of trampled bodies. His sword was dripping with black blood as he looked for anything left alive, which soon met its end as his sword was thrust into its heart.

The garrison had come out too – not to fight, just through mere fascination about the rumours. They had done no fighting at all – there was no need – and they counted themselves lucky that despite them being outnumbered, no Camion had died that day.

Pausanias knelt down to look at one of the creatures, with one arm missing, black blood covering the ground where it had died. He looked at its vile face, its skin of bluish grey, its long, pointed ears, its bottom set of teeth sticking upwards over its top lip – it was a savage thing. Riddled with scars like writing on a parchment, with wounds held together by plates of metal, screws and nails stuck into its bones, it was a crude beast that he believed could only have come from the Shadow World.

He now knew two things about them, though. One: pain was not something that seemed to bother them; and two: they could be killed.

Looking up, he saw Andreas approaching, holding his head and staggering like a drunk.

"Where the hell have you been?" he said standing up and walking towards him.

"I remember a loud noise and a flash," he said, dazed, as if no one would believe him, "and a bright purple light. The next thing I know, I'm waking up, looking at the sky." He clearly looked puzzled, as if he were trying to work out a dream.

"Ha! You fell backwards and got knocked unconscious? Wait until the other Hawks hear this."

Andreas hissed at him through his gritted teeth. "How many did you kill?"

"Five, six maybe?"

"Liar!" he said sulkily, annoyed that he had missed all the action.

For the first time since being there, Pausanias smiled, as his anger had been vented and he felt whole again, and ready for a few weeks more of his brother.

"Where do you think they came from?" Andreas said, assessing the creatures.

"I don't know, but the Defences may have been overrun ..."

General Drorkon returned to Ambenol with a splinter group of his cohort, as they returned from chasing down a few retreating creatures. But then, joining them from the south, came a small scouting group.

"Report!" he said as they slowed to a canter.

"General, the Elite of Camia are leaving the city. They are taking every soldier with them. Imara is leading the army."

"Where are they going?"

"I don't know, Sir."

"Keep on them. I need to know everything!"

"Yes, Sir."

The scouts reined in their mounts and galloped back the way he had come.

Plinth, a very large man, approached; he was Drorkon's second in command.

"What do you think she's doing?"

Then Drorkon thought back to the meeting at the Gathered Council, and a terrible thought struck him. "Maybe ...? No, she can't have?"

"Can't have what, Sir?"

"When I was at the Gathered Council, Lord Fennel suggested taking the rich and all the military in Cam and putting them in a forest to keep them safe."

"Which forest?"

Drorkon thought for a moment.

"Bysing Forest. There is an old fort in the centre, and it's not too far. Imara will house herself there, with the troops spread around the forest."

"She will use the entire military of Cam for her own gain," said Plinth wryly.

"General!" came a cheerful cry, before he could answer.

Greeting them was Undrea, running through the battlefield towards them. The sight was unusual, with her pearlescent white toga flapping against her thin frame in the breeze, whilst surrounding her was the blood and death of the Black. She grasped his hands and they touched foreheads, a sign that they were old and dear friends.

"You got my message," she said sweetly, her radiant smile lighting up her face. For a moment, Drorkon was taken back to a memory of another woman with such a smile.

"I did, my Lady. We came as soon as we could. I trust you're well?"

"Yes, although, as you know, I have not spoken to Havovatch in some time. I worry for him."

"As do I. Come, my dear, we must find out where he is, and with you being here, you can help me."

"Very well."

"Plinth, bring my chest to the tower immediately!" he shouted over his shoulder.

"Yes, General."

With Undrea on his arm, Drorkon escorted her back to her tower. Just then, two Knight Hawks approached them. One broad and strong with swords all about his person, the other tall and slim with a bow and a quiver of arrows.

"My Lady," said the taller, broad one. "You were instructed to stay in your tower. We cannot protect you if you wander out."

"Come, gentlemen," Drorkon said pleasantly, "she came out to see me. Surely this time you can let it go?"

The two Hawks bowed their heads in respect.

"General, Drakator is in there … he did something, Sir."

"Is he OK?"

"Unconscious, Sir, but he created some kind of … spell." Pausanias's voice wobbled with fear as he spoke.

"Whatever you saw, Hawk, it came in your favour."

"Yes, Sir." Although his voice showed regret about not knowing more, he was a soldier of steel and muscle; anything he could not explain terrified him.

"Sir," added Andreas.

Drorkon stopped walking away, clearly becoming irritated by their questions, but smiled and turned back.

"Yes, Hawk? But please make it quick!"

"Where did these things come from? Is Cam overrun?"

For the first time, Drorkon looked around and realised he had a point – where had they come from? The scout mentioned nothing about the Black on his travels, but he did realise that the Defences may have been overrun.

"I don't know. Come, my Lady."

The general and the Princess carried on towards the tower leaving the brothers to stand in the middle of the battlefield.

Sitting on two giant rocks, Pausanias and Andreas looked around. Andreas kept sticking his finger up the side of his helmet, scratching at an itch.

"I suppose, this once, we can take them off," said Pausanias as he removed his helmet and ran his hand through his hair, combing the sweat out.

"I don't believe it – I missed all this?" Andreas said, fanning his arms around the battlefield. They were in the dead centre of it, with bodies aplenty.

"Your time will come, little brother. You shouldn't be so eager to kill."

"It's different when these things are attacking our world."

A sudden clap of thunder made them both jump. Looking up, they saw a man approaching, dressed in white clothes adorned with purple patterns. They couldn't take their eyes away, nor could they move.

"What's going on?" Andreas grunted as he tried desperately to move his arms.

The stranger continued to head towards them, but no one else seemed to see him. As a soldier wandered by, towing his horse, the man passed through it, as if he were a ghost.

"Good day, gentlemen," he said in a kindly voice.

At first, the two Hawks were too dumbstruck to reply.

"Please – I mean you no harm."

"Who are you? What have you done to us?" Pausanias said through gritted teeth, trying desperately in vain to free himself.

"Worry not, young Hawk. I am a messenger and I bring word."

"What words do you bring that will liberate us from this spell?"

"Not yet," he said, holding his hand up. "You're the best of your trade: if I release you, you may harm me."

"How?" said Pausanias.

"Your weapons are more special than you think."

The two stared silently up at him.

"Hawks, your paths have been laid out for you. Follow them." Andreas's eyes moved around as if he were looking for the path. "Metaphorically speaking, that is, young Hawk."

"How will we know what our paths are?" Pausanias said hoarsely, as he kept trying to fight the spell.

"Go with the general."

"But we need to protect the Princess!" Andreas said sharply.

"What, and be stuck on the same balcony all day long? I don't think so. You have talents needed elsewhere. Besides, she will be well cared for here."

"Why should we trust you?" said Pausanias.

"Your father is trying to get back to you. But you must go with the general."

"How do you know our father? What's going on?" Pausanias shouted.

The man put his hands out to calm Pausanias's abrupt questions, for even though a spell held him down, he moved slightly at the mention of his father. "Your father said one word to you before he left: *Redemption*."

The two looked at each other.

"How do you know that?" shouted Andreas. "Our father went missing years ago!"

"Yes, he did, but I know this word to be the bond of your family's legacy: follow the general, and you shall get your Redemption."

The two hawks were filled with questions they wanted to blurt out, but just then there was another thunderclap, and the two fell forward as their constraints were released. On all fours, they looked at each other.

"No one knows of our word – no one!" Andreas had tears forming in his eyes, and looked desperately at Pausanias for counsel.

Pausanias looked at where the stranger had stood, just a small burnt patch in the grass. Gritting his teeth, he swallowed, and tried to come to a decision.

***

"You don't like to keep yourself tidy?" Drorkon said, looking around at the mess in Undrea's room.

"I have had more pressing matters on my mind," she said, smiling, and clearing a space in the centre.

But standing in the room, Drorkon sensed something very familiar to him indeed. Pacing over to her desk, which stood below the window, he looked at a bundle of small bags with ties at the top. Picking one up, he undid the tie and smelt the powder within. He looked at Undrea sharply.

"This is dangerous stuff. How did you come by it?"

Undrea grew uncomfortable. "I was bored, and Lord Malisten had someone find them for me."

"What could you possibly want with Igaror? It's horrifically volatile."

"Just practising, my Master," she said innocently, trying to smile.

"There are many spells and charms you could have worked with that would have been far safer than this. If this had touched a spark it would have blown the whole tower apart!"

"I know, I know, but I need to learn something different. If I don't, all I know is the basic stuff."

Drorkon relaxed somewhat, remembering how enthusiastic he had been at her age.

"Fine, but this comes with me," he said, collecting the pouches up and placing them in his bag. Undrea sighed as she watched him take it all.

Just then, Plinth entered, carrying a huge wooden box with unusual markings etched into the wood, markings that very few in Ezazeruth would understand – in fact, the only two who would were standing in that room. It looked heavy, yet Plinth stood back straight, waiting to be told where to put it.

"Just there, commander – thank you."

As Plinth left, Drorkon closed the door and locked it as Undrea put two stools either side of the chest. Sitting down, they looked at each other.

"Will you be OK this time?"

"I have learnt much of the Phalism Link since our last session, Master."

Drorkon smiled, knowing that his best student had done her homework. She closed her eyes and put her hands together as if in prayer.

He sat opposite her and went to adopt the same position, and slowly, he lifted the lid of the chest. A loud howling noise came out, with a purple and orange glow lighting up the room. And in their minds, they saw images of what may come to be.

After some time, the spell broke and they both fell backwards in a cold sweat, panting heavily. As they leant back, a blue light disappeared from their eyes, vanishing in the black abyss of their pupils.

Undrea pulled up a goblet and a jug with trembling hands; she filled the goblet with water and drank desperately.

Drorkon breathed slowly, trying to get his breath back.

"Are you OK?"

"Yes. There was much to see."

"Indeed, I am just trying to interpret it now," he said, still breathing heavily.

"Master?" she said anxiously.

He looked down at her, knowing that what he saw, she saw too.

"I saw a city in ruin. A large city – it was burning," she said, her face wrought with horror, "and an empty wall upon a shoreline."

"Do not worry yourself. These are visions of what *could* happen. By seeing these, we have a chance to stop it."

"I don't remember much else – it all happened too quickly, just like a dream. It seemed so real, but now, I remember little."

Drorkon did not tell her, but one image that did linger in his mind was a death charge by the Two-Twenty-Eighth, his flag waving in the wind as arrows rained down upon his regiment charging at a wall of spears.

"Yes … it did." He shook his head and cleared his throat. What else do you remember?" he said, pulling out a quill, some ink and parchment.

She looked at him as if she didn't want to say it. "A tall, monstrous creature, strong, savage … it was shrouded in a white haze."

"Yes, I remember." He said pointing at her with the quill as he recollected the memory.

"What does that mean?"

"Well, white usually signifies good, or at least good intentions."

"OK. I also remember my two Hawks, they were there too."

"What were they doing?"

She looked at him incredulously. "Following you."

"OK ..." he said, letting it ring out.

"Anything else?"

"Yes, a man, tall and strong with a Hawk helmet and three crests upon the back. I didn't see his face."

"Yes, I remember now – the crest would mean he was the commander of the Knight Hawks, but that is Thiamos, and the man was certainly not him."

"So who is he?"

"I'm not sure, but there is something vaguely familiar about him."

Drorkon put several exclamation marks next to "Commander of the Knight Hawks".

"Anything more?"

"Yes." She looked at the floor and pulled her arms around herself, as if a chill had suddenly entered the room. "I saw ... a black demon," she swallowed, "with dark red eyes, tall and strong, sitting upon a throne." Her voice was trembling as she spoke. Every time she thought of the demon a shock went through her, as if her soul was becoming detached from her.

Drorkon frowned. "Yes – that, my dear, was Agorath." Then he asked himself, "But why would he be sitting on a throne?" He clenched the quill in his fist and leaned on his arm, creasing his face as he tried to understand it.

"Maybe it's what he wants?" said Undrea. "To rule the throne of Ezazeruth."

"Hmmm – I don't think so. There is no throne of Ezazeruth, and, come to think of it, it's not a throne I recognise."

"I don't know."

"Let me think on that one." He scribbled down the comments, along with some notes of his own.

"Anything else?"

As she desperately sought to remember, it all started to vanish from her mind, leaving a dark void. "No, it's all gone." She began to break down, fearing that her memory had failed her.

Drorkon got up and wrapped his arm around her. "It will be OK. I still remember much," he said, although he didn't. "We will stop this now," he added, like a father trying to reassure his daughter.

Undrea nodded and wiped away her tears.

"One thing that is sticking in my mind", said Drorkon, "is to follow the Hawk."

"The Hawk? My Hawks?" she sniffled, "Surely we need to solve the mystery of where that horde lying at our gates came from?"

"Indeed, but you have to remember that *they* told us these visions for a reason. By following them, we may find out where the horde came from."

There was a sudden sound outside their window, and there, sitting on the sill, was a hawk.

"What does that mean?"

"It means I must follow it."

He went to leave, but not before placing his hands on her shoulders and looking deep into her eyes. "You are well protected here, Undrea. Do not leave – you *must* not! If the Black find you they will kill you. If any other countries find you they will hold you to ransom – you are a princess. And at the moment, there is no one who can protect you outside of these gates."

Her eyes flashed at a locked cupboard in the corner, but she returned to his stern gaze, and nodded.

Drorkon smiled sympathetically and pushed a piece of her hair out the way of her face. "My brightest student, I am so proud of what you have accomplished."

Undrea smiled back, thankful for the man who had taken her father's place and raised her. But as Drorkon looked into her eyes, he saw a blue light quickly disappear; and, fearing what it could mean, ignored it, hoping that it was just his imagination.

He paced towards the door and pulled the lock back. Standing outside was Plinth, as if he knew what they were doing and was making sure they were uninterrupted.

"General?" said Undrea before he left.

He turned to meet her still worried face.

"I didn't see Havovatch."

Chapter Four
Sipping Tea

Fandorazz was happy – well, as happy as he could be. Sipping herbal tea from his finely crafted cup, he sat upright in his chair with one leg slung across the other, the Camion Scroll between his hands. The past month's hard work was slowly coming to an end, and he was doing what he always did when work was complete – he sat, ignored what was going on outside, and drank tea for hours whilst learning of other matters in the city, letting his mind grow calm as the heavy burden of his workload became a distant memory.

Around the tent, pitched at the top of the Defences, were all sorts of possessions of his. He had paid a high price for couriers to bring them to him, helping him to feel more at home, although he was glad he wasn't, as he knew that being there would restore him to his previous self.

The inside of his tent was very neat, with a rug covering the floor. His now completed matchstick castle sat in the corner – now a mighty structure, with huge towers and turrets, standing taller than a man – and there was a folded-down desk to one side for him to draw and write memos. He couldn't get his family portrait sent down, due to its size, so he had an artist create a small copy in perfect detail, as if someone had shrunk the large portrait down. It was so well detailed it looked better than the original, and sat in a plain wooden frame on his table.

Fandorazz frowned as he read an article in the paper on the subject of "Important Matters", about the rich being evacuated from the city and the call for all soldiers to return to Cam. Upon reading it, he remembered that he had received an urgent scroll and wondered if it had something to do with this.

Picking it up, he pulled the ribbon off and unravelled the scroll, with the following written on the front in blue ink:

For the addressee only – urgent – must read and respond.

He frowned. He had not received anything so official in quite some time. Turning the scroll over, he read, and his eyes went wide with horror.

Fandorazz of the House of Vimeon.

You must return with haste to the capital at the request of Duchess Imara – Chief and Queen of our land.

Your fortune is to be handed over to the benefit of the state, with three per cent being given to the lower classes to arrange their own security.

The rest will be given to Her Majesty in order to safeguard the rich.

Failure to do so will result in death.

Yours faithfully, the Upper Class Representatives.

Reading it several times to see if it were really true, Fandorazz struggled to take it in, trying to work out how such an order could have been passed. But he was taken out of his trance as horns and bells rang out. They echoed violently and were clearly not to be ignored.

Dropping the scroll on the table, he stepped outside and saw soldiers arming themselves and running down to the wall. Looking up at the horizon, he saw a sight of dread. Ships were sailing towards them – not a great many, but enough to give cause for grave concern.

Captain Seer approached him. "Your ideas will now be put to the test, Architect," he said. "Put this on!" He handed him a steel helmet and a short sword.

"What do you expect me to do with these?" Fandorazz said with distaste, looking down at them, as if he did not know what they were. ·

"You will learn soon enough. I cannot afford any men to protect you – you must fight for your own safety." Captain Seer ran off and began barking orders for regiments to muster on the Defences. He was now in his element and knew exactly what needed to be done.

Adrenalin was starting to set in as Fandorazz realised the reality of what was happening. He had never been in any conflict before, he had never even been in a fight before, and now he was expected to fight for life or death …?

Shakily, he put on the helmet, strapped the sword around his waist, then followed Captain Seer.

He went down the dip of the hill that led to the wall. Looking north, the wall was shining bronze and looked like part of the sea as the infantrymen moved about like waves in their columns. There were lines of soldiers pulling their rounded shields to their left and holding their spears up.

All regiments, regardless of their speciality, were given garrison roles and stood defensively, with archers in their green tunics at the rear and in the towers. Infantry regiments in blue mixed with cavalry regiments in black. The sight was impressive, with watch towers of varying heights all the way along to the end, the tree trunks which had been spiked and placed in the sea during the low tide stuck out like another phalanx line, pointing at the approaching ships as waves past over them. Catapults of all shapes and sizes lined the cliff's edge and, behind the archers, engineers in red stood by. There must have been at least ten thousand soldiers from Camia at the Defences, but he knew there would have been far more if the Banners had been there with them. Ever since they had left nearly four weeks earlier, he could not understand the logic behind it, and had felt an emptiness in him.

But the moment was cut short as he again looked at the threat from ships as they approached quickly. Something was amiss, though. Captain Seer called Fandorazz to him. "I think some of them are ours," he said, squinting with his ageing eyesight.

"Only one, Captain!" a young officer with a good eye pointed out. "I think it is being chased."

"We cannot use the catapults, then – we may hit one of our own," Fandorazz said.

"If we cannot fend them off, then we will deal with them the infantry way," said Captain Seer, drawing his sword and nodding to his officers. They all ran to their positions and made ready for the attack, with the infantry units starting their chant – beating the pommels of their swords or the shafts of their spears against their shields and shouting "HAR-HAR-HAR".

The ships came clearly into view upon the crystal ocean. The lead ship appeared to be Camion. It was wide and galleon-shaped, with huge white sails billowing out like giant pillows, pushing the vessel through the water, the prow carving its way through the waves, with white foam forming around its sides. It was travelling swiftly, with every sail open. Standing on the deck and hanging from the rigging were dozens of men, firing arrows at their pursuers. The ships following could only be described as deadly. Long, narrow and covered in spikes, they were menacing. Their prows had huge spikes at the front to puncture the hulls of ships. They were black, with tall masts billowing torn black sails, but in spite of the damage they still seemed to move with speed and agility. Gaining on the galleon, they didn't relent despite getting close to land.

As they approached the coastline, the Black's ships clustered together to avoid the giant rocks as they approached the opening to the cove. They had no choice, with the coastline littered with giant, jagged boulders sticking out over the waves like horns on an alligator's back, if they hit them they would be obliterated. Some of the rocks were three or four times bigger than the vessels. The waves crashed against them, with white spray and foam flying into the air. The sea around the rocks became choppy with the vessels tossing uncontrollably on the ebb and flow of the waves.

Fandorazz stood aghast, his heart booming inside his chest as he watched the onslaught. He knew that the galleon wouldn't be able to navigate through the logs with the speed it was going at, and it didn't even slow down as it hurtled towards the Defences with hundreds of spiked logs facing its way.

The galleon didn't bother to slow down for the logs and plunged straight into them, breaking them like matchsticks. But it created a free path behind as the Black ships followed. Creatures hung off the nets and ropes with their weapons in the air, howling at the galleon and the defenders upon the walls.

The logs started to slow the ship down, with chunks being punctured from its hull. It quickly took on water and started to list. Instantly, a small raft was hoisted down beside the vessel, with four figures inside. As soon as the raft hit the sea, two of the figures started rowing frantically, with some of the crew above screaming for help at the helpless Camions on the wall. Most of the ship's crew were at the back, firing arrows at the Black ships, but they were all but obliterated as the lead ship ploughed into the back, demolishing the stern and taking the crew with it. Creatures jumped from their vessel, several feet into the air and onto the sinking galleon, killing the crew indiscriminately, their screams sending shudders and fury through the garrison upon the wall as they watched on.

"Fire!" screamed Seer, anger getting the better of him.

The silent wall was awoken by the catapults, as the sounds of wood clonking together and ropes being unwound echoed. Rocks hurtled through the air, rotating slowly; most crashed into the sea, but some hit their marks, puncturing the decks of the Black ships and sending shards of wood upwards. But it didn't stop their gain, and the small fleet carried on charging towards the wall.

"It's the King!" shouted an officer standing on the parapet, gazing out at the approaching raft.

Fandorazz squinted again, and could just see King Colomune, looking scared as he shouted and hit the sailors as they rowed, desperately out of time with each other as they kept looking at the Black ships approaching.

"Prepare to get the King onto land, whatever the cost!" shouted Seer as he went to the front of the phalanx.

The galleon was now little more than the mast sticking out from the surface of the sea. Leaning to one side, the vessel's body was completely submerged, with flotsam floating around it. The long Black ships carried on past like savage animals, as if the galleon was a dead creature stripped of its flesh.

"Make way for the King!" a voice shouted as the boat met the bottom of the steep wall rising diagonally out of the sea. Several ropes were flung over to them. Atken, the king's butler was there, grabbing the ropes and trying to tie them around the frantic King Colomune, who was panicking beyond reason. Eventually, taking a breath, Atken slapped him across the face to stop his endless babbling. He then managed to get the rope around Colomune and he was hoisted up the wall, half running and half panicking as he looked behind him at the Black ships. Atken was clinging to him as he whispered into his ear, trying to calm him, but it made little difference.

The sailors in the boat waited idle in the low tide for the ropes to be thrown back down to them, but they didn't appear. All they could see were the tops of the helmets and spears of the garrison behind the parapet. They screamed for their lives as the Black ships approached, one steadying itself on a course towards them, their deafening cries cut short in an instant as the crude vessel smashed into the wall. Its speed was so great that it rose up the incline and beached itself on the parapet, crushing several soldiers. The creatures plunged onto the battlements, most meeting the Camion spears that were pointing their way. Hails of arrows began to rain down on the vessel from the archers. But the creatures were undeterred and flung themselves off the ship and into the phalanx lines. The Camions, holding their spears cumbersomely upwards in tight rows, struggled to let go and draw their swords, and many soldiers were cut down before the creatures were set upon by the infantry.

With the other ships ramming the walls all the way along the Defences, similar skirmishes broke out. The catapults continued to pummel rocks at the ships, causing heavy damage, but the ships carried on towards the wall. The last one at the rear slowed down, though; oars appeared either side of the vessel, and it was rowed back out of the cove and into the open water.

Standing at the south edge of the phalanx, Fandorazz watched on, mesmerised by the chaos. He had never seen a fight before, let alone a battle. The trained infantry's war cries sent a shock through him as they bellowed with all their breath at the creatures. Yet the beasts seemed undeterred and kept trying in vain to break through the phalanx. Seeing the creatures was unsettling to him – he wasn't even sure who he was defending Camia against, and, holding his drawing book close to him, his bottom lip trembling, he just watched. The creatures were like nothing he had ever seen before. The only word he could use to describe them was an "abomination".

His heart skipped a beat when he saw several large creatures standing on the deck, picking up some much smaller ones and hurling them over the phalanx. They landed awkwardly but showed no signs of being injured, and turned to hack away at the backline of the Camions. The archers panicked and fired at them, hitting several Camions in the back as they did. But Fandorazz was stricken, as one of the creatures landed before him and charged his way.

At first walking backwards quickly, he dropped his book and drew his sword, but the scabbard came with it. He clearly showed his ineptness at using it.

The small creature – a short, elf-like thing with huge, pointed ears bigger than its face – held a hatchet and a club. It swung them madly at Fandorazz, who shakily pulled the sword free and slashed back, just as he would beat a tramp away from him. But the club hit his hand and pain surged up his arm, along with anger. Fury suddenly flowed through his veins as if he had drunk it. Snarling through his teeth, he shouted and cut his sword in a crossing motion, the heavy weapon suddenly feeling light in his grasp. The creature recognised his anger, went wide-eyed and started stepping backwards.

Fandorazz hit the axe away and quickly brought the sword around again, cutting through its skull and neck and embedding it into its torso. Blood gushed up, ruining his expensive, tailored suit. Yet he stood there holding the blade, propping up the body and breathing heavily. Fandorazz suddenly came out of his hate-fuelled trance, looked at what he had done, and was not too sure what to make of it. He stood poised, just staring, wondering if he had done right or wrong. But he didn't think for much longer, as a blackness overcame him and the last thing he saw was the ground coming his way.

The battle soon came to an end, with the archers peppering the vessels. Some creatures who knew their fate dived into the water and swam out to the ship sitting idle in the open sea, either waiting for survivors or merely indulging in watching on – no one knew.

The battle was a hollow victory for the Camions, with many soldiers dead or injured. They had not been prepared for what had come, with men crushed under the vessel, some still screaming for help, as they hit the wall, and the creatures' erratic fighting style. Despite their size and number, the Camions had been outmatched. If it had not been for Fandorazz's measures, the outcome of the battle may well have been defeat, or the loss staggeringly greater.

No cheers were cried out, for the beasts swam away with most of the soldiers watching on in shock, the shock realisation of looking pure evil in the eye.

Out of the way of the settling madness, a creature clung to the wall, just peering above the parapet at the disorganised rabble of the Camion military, probably out of morbid fascination. As it studied its surroundings, a curt, satisfied smile appeared on its face, as if it had seen something the Camions had overlooked. And, falling down into the water, it swam off to the idle ship.

***

Fandorazz woke to the smell of smoke and the clinking of metal. There was weight upon him and he struggled to pull it off, but it was far too heavy for his strength to compensate for it.

"Help me!" he croaked with a dry mouth, as if he had eaten sand, his face buried into the ground with a pounding headache.

Clearing his throat, he tried to shout. "Help me!"

It took some time, but he felt the weight removed and he sat upright. Someone took his helmet off him, revealing a heavy dent in the side. A battlefield surgeon knelt in front of him and dabbed the side of his head with a wet rag.

"How are you feeling, soldier?"

Fandorazz was dazed and did not answer, seeing only swaying shapes before him.

"How many fingers am I holding up?"

Fandorazz tried to squint and correct his vision, but saw several fingers as his head spun.

"OK – what colour is my tunic?" said the surgeon, getting no replies from his patient.

Fandorazz could only see his outline, unable to see his detailed features.

"Purple?"

"Good. Do you know who you are, or where we are?"

It suddenly occurred to him that he was in a battle, and he gazed out along the wall to see that the black narrow ships lining the wall were ablaze, with thick plumes of smoke lifting high into the air as if the wood were dipped in oil. And, to his amazement, to one side was a column of soldiers, all ready to march west, with dozens of fallen men lying on the ground with their cloaks over them. The newly built Defences were deserted; there was an eerie feeling.

"Soldier! I need to know how you are feeling!" the surgeon pressed, getting irritated with Fandorazz's distraction.

"Despite the throbbing and unforgettable pain in my head, I actually feel quite good."

He wasn't lying – fighting for the first time in his life had given him a buzz.

He kept looking around, trying to understand what was going on. He saw Captain Seer speaking with King Colomune, and thought it best to get to them, so he pushed away from the surgeon and approached them. The surgeon shrugged, packed his things up and walked away.

The King's expression was solemn; Fandorazz had never seen him like this before. His head was bowed, and from what he could make out in his face was that he was severely depressed.

"My King." He bowed. "I trust your quest went well?"

Colomune said nothing. Captain Seer turned to Fandorazz. "There has been a … complication."

"Oh?"

"They were led into a trap; few survived."

Fandorazz stood shocked, and looked out at the waters when only a few weeks earlier, many vessels held thousands of men and woman.

"But *all* the armies in Ezazeruth were there! How many made it back?"

"Just the King."

King Colomune said nothing. He had tears rolling down his face and into his now shaggy thick beard, the words seeming to make the torment he was going through even worse. He was almost in shock, as if everything was supposed to have fitted into place but it hadn't, and he was waking up to the reality of what he had done.

"Where do we go from here?" Fandorazz asked the captain.

Captain Seer looked at his King, who had not changed his expression, and suddenly all decisions were upon him.

"Well, I have orders to take everyone back to Cam."

"*Why?*"

"Those are my orders. I do not question them, Architect."

"But your King is now here – he can tell you to stay."

Captain Seer looked at Colomune. "My Liege?"

But he said nothing.

Captain Seer turned back to Fandorazz. "The King is in no state to talk at this moment, and therefore I will carry out my orders."

"If you leave now, Captain, the last defence of this world will be left empty for the Black to simply moor up and attack. You cannot do this!"

The captain shrugged.

Fandorazz pushed past him, grabbed Colomune by his shoulders and stared intently into his eyes.

"My King!" he forced. But there was no reply, so he shook him. "COLOMUNE!" he shouted.

He looked up slowly.

"Colomune, I have lost loved ones too, but your actions now could affect the course of the future – you *need* to command the captain to stay!"

For a moment it looked as if Colomune was going to do just that, but unbeknownst to Fandorazz, Colomune's thoughts had returned to him, of people giving him ideas, ideas that he thought had been good. And now tens of thousands of men were lying at the bottom of the ocean because of him. And so his eyes sank back down and the words fell on deaf ears.

Seeing Fandorazz touching the King, several soldiers approached and pulled him away.

Captain Seer turned as well, leaving Fandorazz alone.

"So, this is it?" he shouted after them. "This is what you are going to do? Leave this world defenceless for the Black to conquer?"

But Captain Seer did not turn back. He gave the command to march, and the last garrison of the Defences, of Camia and the world, departed and headed west.

Fandorazz looked along the superb defence wall, now deserted, and then out to sea, and was struck by the most real feeling of fear, a fear he had never known before.

"Well, we are not all that mighty now, are we?"

Fandorazz turned to see Hembel standing there. He hadn't seen him in days, ever since he had stormed off in a tantrum. "Hembel? Where have you been? Are you OK?"

"Like you would care?"

He walked, ominously holding a sword – his grip tight, showing the whites of his knuckles. His gaze was fixed upon Fandorazz, as if he was about to commit a terrible act. Suddenly, his gaze flicked out at the deserted Defences.

"Ha! I don't know how you do it?" he said, shaking his head.

"Do what? What is the matter with you? I thought you were my friend?"

Hembel spat before Fandorazz's feet. "I was never a friend of yours, I was always your rival, a man caught in your shadow. I was seeking desperately to honour my house, but you simply walked over me as if I were not there. You were so arrogant, walking past everyone as if they were below you. The death of your family was the best thing that could have happened to you!"

With his new-found confidence for violence, Fandorazz immediately struck out at Hembel, sending him to the floor.

"DON'T-YOU-DARE-DISGRACE-MY-FAMILY!"

Hembel turned around onto his back and wiped blood away from the corner of his mouth with a curt grin. "Ha! You've finally found it in you to fight?"

"If you detest everything I am, then why did you stand by me for so many years?"

"To try to get your gift, you thick rekon – to find out how you thought, to become you!"

Hembel stood up and clutched his hand around the grip of his sword. "I failed at that, but this opportunity is too much to give away."

Raising his sword, Hembel lunged forward and slashed out at Fandorazz, who tried to draw his own, but again the scabbard came up with it and he looked up alarmed as Hembel's blade came towards him.

Falling back, the blade just missed his face, but he finally managed to draw his sword.

Knocking his blows away from him, he outmatched Hembel, but could not bring himself to hurt him. Using the sole of his boot, he kicked him back.

"You're drunk, man. Calm yourself and return home!"

"Argghhh!" Hembel cried out as he parried again. Raising his sword, he brought it down to cave in Fandorazz's head, but missed. He tried again, but Fandorazz merely disengaged. Hembel stood looking ready for his next move, but was hit from behind and fell to the floor.

Groga, Fandorazz's old friend from the quarry, stood there holding a stone hammer, "I never liked that weaselly rekon!" he spat.

"I don't know what came over him." Fandorazz bent down before his slumbering body, but did not reach out to touch him.

"Probably madness. Fear of this dark tide can cause the mood of any man to change beyond what they are capable of withstanding."

Fandorazz got up and walked down the hill, holstering his blade back into his scabbard. Folding his arms, he gazed out. "All this work for nothing, such skill in labour, time, effort … to be abandoned as it once was."

"What now?" Groga said, holding the hammer behind his neck as they both looked at the beautiful sunset falling before them.

"Well, what *can* anyone do? This is it – the time of freedom and democracy within this world has ended. The Black will come, they will attack and no soul will stand here to stop them."

Groga frowned. "You think we had freedom and democracy before this?"

Fandorazz was high-born, and knew little about the troubles of the poor or working-class. It was in that moment that he took them into consideration for the first time.

"We have a king, Razz," said Groga. "There is no democracy here."

"We can vote in other matters."

"Few. You must know that whoever is the wealthiest will get their way."

Fandorazz was about to say *that cannot be true*, but stopped when several thoughts struck him at once, where he had seen just that.

Groga sighed heavily and sat on a rock. Fandorazz joined him and the two old friends sat calmly, looking at the horizon.

"I can't leave, Grog, but two men against an army? It's not enough."

"Maybe we could get the locals to help us?"

"No – most have fled to Cam for better protection. We need an army: people who know how to fight."

Groga frowned, "Maybe …?"

Fandorazz looked up at him. "Maybe what?"

> Stone, rock, granite & might, the land we come from shall give a fright.
>
> Towering valleys, sun ever shone, the stone of our valley will be ours alone.
>
> The Clup'ta strong, heavy and worn, we worship the rock that burdens our home.
>
> Strong & fierce, never to retreat, we are the Clup'ta, and will not be beat.
>
> The Forbidden Passage is our sacred home, for you to enter will bring death and bone.
>
> We are the Clup'ta, for we shall never meet, and if we shall, RUN! RUN! And retreat.

"… Good!" Fandorazz said sardonically after a moment's silence.

"Don't patronise me – you know I would not say anything unless it had meaning."

"And what is the meaning of this … crude poem?"

"I am a stone mason! And there is no stone mason alive worth his salt who does not know that song. It is said that there is a mysterious foe, one that does not want to reveal itself to the world, all we know of them is that they are *Stone Men*."

"Men made of stone?" Fandorazz said, raising an eyebrow.

"No! Men who live surrounded by stone. They worship it, they respect it and they're called the Clup'ta. They live within the Forbidden Passage and they *may* be able to help us."

"Why them?"

"I know of no others and I dread of thinking of them, but if no army shall defend this wall, then let's create one, because my town is the first thing the vermin shall strike when they return."

"How far is the stone valley?"

Groga puffed his cheeks. "Several weeks."

"Several weeks! We don't have that long. What if the Black arrive tomorrow?"

"Then what's your plan?"

Fandorazz said nothing, realising that he didn't have any other options.

"Look, we can both head back to Cam, or Ambenol, and seek shelter. But if we get the Clup'ta, they will march against the Black whether they are here now or tomorrow."

"Fine." Fandorazz sighed.

Lifting his stone hammer, Groga went to set off, but Fandorazz looked at his tent, with all his meaningful possessions inside.

"One second," he said, pacing down to it.

He emerged shortly afterwards, just clutching the small drawing of his family he held in a frame. He and Groga set off on a mission, neither of them knowing what its outcome might be.

Chapter Five
Dread

Buskull had not moved in hours. He sat reflectively against the wall of the cave cell. If anyone who knew him looked at him at that moment, they dared not approach. With the enraged look he possessed and his muscles constantly flexed, he looked as though he could defeat an army of ghouls single-handedly.

Feera and Hilclop had done little apart from pacing around. They were just as quiet; all three sat separately with their own thoughts, depressed by watching their captain's death, helpless to stop it.

Their cell was a carving in a long tunnel leading underground, with bars fixed into the floor and ceiling. Apart from a few torches lining the wall, it was relatively dark, with just the two guards standing with their backs to them; they were tall and broad, dressed from head to foot in armour.

Hilclop sneered into the darkness. He didn't know what made him speak – maybe it was the anger building up inside him, maybe it was the darkness taking over his soul, maybe it was fear?

"I hate him."

Feera shot him a look. "Who?"

"Havovatch. He brought me here – I didn't want to come. I want to get out." He stood up and grabbed hold of the bars. "I want to get out!" he screamed, his voice sounding like that of a whining child.

Feera stood up next to him, placing a hand on his shoulder, but Hilclop abruptly shrugged it off.

"Oi!" Feera said sternly.

"Leave me alone!"

"Shut up!" shouted one of the guards, before hitting Hilclop's hand with his spear as he clutched the bars.

"Ow!" Hilclop withdrew his hand. It wasn't broken; it wasn't even bruised. But he pulled his other hand back to form a fist and looked at the guard. Feera shot forward and threw him to the back of the cell. Pushing Hilclop's injured hand against his stomach and pinning the other against the wall, he then got up close to his face.

"That captain you so easily insult was one of the bravest and greatest men I've ever met. Now, you grow a damn pair and shut up!"

Hilclop whimpered.

Feera let go and sat back down to his thoughts on the other side of the cell. All the while, Buskull had not moved and just sat with his back against the wall, his giant legs stretched out before him, the firelight reflecting off his eyes.

The uncomfortable silence returned.

A while passed and the guards were replaced. They exchanged a quick chat at the end of the tunnel, one laughing as they swapped over. The new guards stood as the others had done, as if soulless men inside mental armour.

Buskull's eyes thinned – he felt angry, very angry. He couldn't relax, but he didn't know what to do. For all his experience, he didn't think he could lead a unit. He didn't even know how to get out. His anger was so strong that his senses stopped working and for the first time in years, he felt blind. He couldn't map out what was around him. So he sat there, quiet and alone with his thoughts of watching his captain die being replaced before him in the darkness. It didn't matter what anyone said to him – he had failed his captain, the biggest mistake and regret of his life.

But then he heard something. Singing. Distant and gentle, it was full of harmony. He looked at Feera and Hilclop, who sat there, not moving. He looked around curiously, the first time he had moved since being put in the cell. The singing grew louder, but it was soft, spoken in a way that could relax anyone in any state of mind. And it did. Buskull started to get a tingling sensation across his body; darkness formed around his eyes as if he could fall asleep. But he kept them open, and there, appearing from around the corner of the tunnel, was a woman, glowing white with a purple haze shrouded around her. She smiled upon seeing him – a smile that told of many happy memories. Tears formed in Buskull's eyes.

"Ellisiot," he said softly, almost as if his breath had been taken away.

The apparition passed through the bars as if she were a ghost. Her eyes fixed on his; she did not look away. As she got nearer, she bent down and slowly reached out to touch his face; he felt it, her gentle hands, her delicate and smooth skin.

"Ellisiot," he said again, closing his eyes and beginning to cry, as a pain he had burdened himself with for over seventy years started to come out.

The apparition hugged her arms around him, holding his head at her breast and resting her head on top of his. *"Shhh,"* she said softly as she stroked him.

Buskull wanted to reach up and wrap his giant arms around her petite body, but, not wanting to fall for this mirage, he gripped the earth, knowing that this could not be anything other than a dream.

With her hands behind his neck, she pulled back and gazed up into his eyes.

"I love you," she said gently. *"Your children love you."* At the mention of them, he broke down more. *"It's time you let us go. Go now – you are a warrior. Fight the Black; save the world so that others will not end up like us. We are fine, and we will one day be reunited."*

She smiled, and a tear appeared in her eyes as she looked upon her love.

Buskull's tears intensified, as he shot his arms out, grabbed her and hugged her close. Despite her being a ghost, he felt warmth in her; he felt her body. Ellisiot broke down and hugged him tightly, her nose sniffling. *"I miss you, my love,"* she said sweetly as her body began to dissipate.

"No, no!" he shouted as he felt her body disappear within his grasp. Sucking a lungful of air, he screamed, his hoarse voice echoing down the tunnel, out of the cave and into the city, and the apparition left. "NO!!!!!"

Sand and dust fell from the walls; the guards jumped and pointed their spears at him. Any noise from outside went deathly silent. Hilclop and Feera jumped up and stood with their backs pressed against the bars – they were both trembling, fearful of the man in the cell with them. For all the loyalty that Feera held, at that moment he wanted to be nowhere near Buskull. Like a mad dog, he didn't know what Buskull was doing or what he could do.

Buskull sat there with his hands buried into his face as he tried to hold on to his wife, clenching his fists and squeezing his eyes shut. He gritted his teeth. His face was wet from crying, yet he could feel it was not just his own tears, he felt Ellisiot's upon his face too.

A moment passed, and the sound of rushing steps filled the tunnel as two dozen Xiphos knights ran in.

"What the heck was that?"

"Him, the giant – he just shouted. I've got ringing in my ears," one guard shouted, not realising how loudly he was speaking.

Buskull had his head bowed forward, his eyes still shut as he held on to the memory of Ellisiot's voice. His head kept jolting as he cried.

"Idiot – he's woken up half the city."

"I didn't even know a man could shout that loudly," said a younger-looking soldier, yet much older than the unit in the cell.

"Clearly you've not heard of the brilliance of the Algermatum?" said one of the guards.

"Who?"

"The first thing you have to know about the Algermatum ..." began the guard as they all left the tunnel. The original two guards returned to their positions, although they kept sticking their fingers in their ears due to the constant ringing. Feera and Hilclop glanced at each other and sat down together, as far away from Buskull as they could get.

It must have been a couple of hours later, when two more guards arrived. Again, they walked to the end of the tunnel and exchanged a few words, this time for much longer than before. When the new guards returned, they gazed long and hard at Buskull. They stood up straight and faced the wall. And just then, as quick as an arrow being fired, Buskull launched up and, without effort, bent the bars apart. Before the guards could turn he leant out, grabbed them by their cuirasses and threw them into each other, so hard that their armour was dented heavily, killing them both.

Feera and Hilclop jumped to their feet looking at him, not really knowing what to do, but Buskull went through the bars and paced quietly down the cave towards the entrance.

"*Don their uniforms!*" he whispered back harshly, still with fierce rage in his voice.

Feera started to remove the helmet and armour, his hands trembling as he put it on Hilclop, who was clearly scared by the ordeal, with his eyes wide open and frozen in his posture. He didn't know what to do, in fear of reprisal; after watching what the Xiphos commander had done to his captain, he feared what would happen to him.

"Hilclop," said Feera, trying to get his attention; but he just stared ahead, too afraid to move. Feera slapped him across the face, not hard enough to make a noise but enough to wake him from his trance.

"Look at me." He did, his eyes a little more focused. "We're getting out of here – Buskull *will* get us out of here!"

He nodded, although he was still quiet.

The dents in the Xiphos armour were large, but their previous owners were so broad in stature that the armour hung off Feera and Hilclop with plenty of room to spare, clearly showing that they were not its owners. But they were struck by surprise when the armour began to compress around their bodies. Hilclop panicked and grasped the armour below his neck, trying to rip it off. Buskull ran back to see what the noise was.

"It's strangling me!" he shouted, his voice echoing down the cave. Feera too was struck by surprise, and, tensing up, he frantically tried to loosen the straps in an effort to remove the cuirass.

But it stopped. Buskull took a torch from the wall and approached. The dents had vanished and the metal seemed to have fitted comfortably onto the armour's new owners.

"Wow," said Buskull, stunned – even he did not know a spell that could do that. Suddenly, they heard muffled voices from the entrance to the cave. Buskull turned back to the unit. "Quick! Pick up their spears – we need to get out of here!"

Hilclop and Feera retrieved the weapons. Feera bound Buskull loosely with a rope and, walking on either side of him, they escorted him out of the cave. Despite wearing full armour, which was very different from what they had previously worn, they felt comfortable as well as protected. The armour was light and did not rub or itch. They felt they could manoeuvre easily without being restricted. Bending down, jumping, holding their arms high – it all seemed as easy as if wearing nothing.

Outside was dark, with an eerie city before them, almost as if it were in mourning – which seemed strange considering it was a Camion captain who had died by the hand of their leader, but Feera wondered if the thoughts of the people were different from the thoughts of their leader. *Maybe they did not want solitude any more,* he thought.

Standing in the middle of a plaza, the unit looked to Buskull, who appeared to be sniffing the air, following some scent they could not smell. Next to them stood a huge white statue of a warrior, standing tall and dignified. Below, carved into the plinth, were figures following him as if he were a destined leader, and scriptures carved around the edges in a language neither could decipher.

The city was white, with white floors and white buildings, flat roofs, all different heights, spread across the uneven terrain. It reminded them in many ways of Cam. Off in the distance was a huge lake, painted silver by the moons above. But they couldn't understand where they were; they were climbing a mountain and yet it was warm, the air thick.

"Strange how this army seems to have a better lifestyle than the other two?" Hilclop whispered.

But he was shushed.

The only sounds around them were the coughing of a guard in the distance, the wind blowing a wooden window protector against the wall, and a bird flying overhead.

Buskull then moved towards a shadowy area where no buildings stood. As they drew into the shadows and their eyes adjusted to the dark, they saw a group of tents. The tents were at the highest point in the city as if looking over it, and just beyond them was a wall, though not a big wall – maybe twelve feet high – with just the one arch-shaped, gateless hole in the centre.

Proceeding towards the tent on their left, into which Havovatch's body had been taken, Feera pulled Hilclop to attention outside as Buskull entered alone.

He ignored Havovatch's body lying on a table to the right. He saw what he wanted: his rare battle-axe, hanging on a hook in front of him; a noise within his ears, which no one else could hear, told him where it was. Around the tent were other ceremonial weapons, as if they had been claimed as trophies – maybe from other warriors who had entered their domain – with Hilclop's and Feera's weapons and uniforms laid out along a table to one side.

There was a pile of sacks in the corner. Picking one up, Buskull put all their equipment inside and retrieved his axe. He slung it over his shoulder and went to leave, but as he stood at the exit from the tent, he sucked in a breath of air and looked over at Havovatch's lifeless body.

He was drawn to him and walked over slowly, his eyes full of sorrow, as if looking down at his own child.

Letting out a heavy sigh, he placed his hands on the table and buried his chin into his chest, his eyes shut tightly. Opening them again, he placed one of his big hands on Havovatch's chest, near the huge wound that had killed him, and closed his eyes.

"May the Grey Knight of the soul guide you to the everlasting light," he said, quietly but croakily.

But when he opened his eyes, he frowned as he noticed something. As he looked down at his hand, he saw that Havovatch's chest was rising.

Bending down and placing his ear by Havovatch's mouth he felt a puff of air blow against his skin, but ever so slight. He checked Havovatch's pulse and his heart was beating. Looking at the wound he could clearly see inside Havovatch's body and knew that it was more than a fatal blow. He stood back and looked over his body, confusion doubling in his mind. Was this what he was truly seeing? He felt that he must be mad. But whatever he saw, he knew he could not leave his body there and so went to pick it up; but just as he placed his hands under him to do so, a change came in the atmosphere.

Slowly, a white orb appeared above Havovatch's body and a voice spoke to Buskull in a language he had long since wanted to remember.

Buskull, Sêmena al forta, brim letiya mi.

Buskull absent-mindedly nodded, the glow of the orb highlighting the tears around his eyes. He swallowed and took in the words that had been said to him.

Picking up his sack, he went to leave, but picked up Havovatch's helmet and sword as he did. Just as he went to push through the tent flaps, he took one more look back to make sure he was not going insane.

"Let's go!" he said to the others as he walked out, and they paced after him.

"I heard speaking. Who was in there?" said Hilclop, louder than he meant to.

"I'll tell you later, now hush!"

Buskull did not walk subtly, his natural sense had returned and he knew where to go and where the guards were. They ran towards a mountainous ridge in the near distance, with the thin white wall snaking over the hills surrounding the city. They headed towards the arch, which appeared to be the entrance – but there were no gates. A group of knights stood in full armour, chatting and smoking; there were about six of them clustered around a fire kiln. Buskull produced his axe from the sack and ran, with Feera and Hilclop trying to keep up.

He covered ground quickly and made little noise.

The guards did not see him coming; he crashed into them before they could shout out, sending four of them flying heavily against a wall and knocking them out. The other two got up and drew their swords, but Buskull hit them with the sack, sending one flying over the wall. He picked up the other in his hand and squeezed his throat; his body went limp in his grasp.

He had created more noise than he had intended to, with raised voices coming from behind them, but he felt better.

"Come on!" he shouted.

Unbeknownst to them, a pair of dark eyes watched from the shadows. Seeing them flee, it started to emerge just as two sentries came running towards the scene. The sentries had spotted the bodies and turned to call out, one producing a horn.

The surreptitious figure emerged from the shadows, tall and strong. It charged quickly at the soldiers.

They did not see it coming. Going for the one with the horn first, it struck him across the face with its long arm, then headbutted the next, knocking them both unconscious.

Smiling sadistically as if pleased with its violence, it turned, strolled casually out of the gate, and followed the unit.

Having gone through to the other side of the wall, the unit were shocked to see that the wall was no longer there, and neither was the city. What lay before them was nothing more than a barren wasteland, dark and sinister, somewhere no one would want to go.

They continued to run, though, desperate to try to find a way down the mountain before the Xiphos started hunting them down. But there was just a cliff of rock before them, and blackness to their right. Feera looked up to see if they could climb the rock face. But there was no way of doing so – it was just a sheer cliff.

"Where do we go?" asked Feera, starved of breath from running in full armour.

Then Hilclop pointed. "Over there!"

He pointed to a glow before them, coming from around the corner.

They ran towards it breathlessly. As they turned the corner, they stood before a vortex in the side of the mountain, swirling in all shades of blue. The light illuminated their amazement, for neither of them had seen such a thing before. Swirling it looked like a tunnel but to where, neither knew. Buskull, at first, was slightly hesitant about approaching – not knowing of the magic before him, he grew wary of the unknown. But a cry came from the direction they had come from. With a deep breath, he entered. Feera followed, their bodies consumed by the swirling mass.

Hilclop stood still, went to walk forward, but then turned around, too scared to bring himself to go in. In fear of what might happen next, he spent a few moments walking to and from the vortex, his mind telling him to go through but his body refusing.

"They've escaped!" came a shout, and the loud sound of metal clinking together was approaching.

"Oh, sod this!"

In a moment of moral fibre or just plain fear, he ran head-on into the vortex and vanished.

Watching from the shadows, the figure emerged again, its eyes narrowing as it watched the unit disappear. The city then erupted with noise as a huge horn from the tower in the centre was blown.

The figure smiled, and nonchalantly walked towards the swirling blue.

It was suddenly very cold, colder than Hilclop could cope with. Lying with his face planted into the snow, he looked up and saw Buskull and Feera looking down at him quizzically.

"Took your time. We were thinking of going without you," Feera jibed.

"They're coming!" he panted.

Feera and Buskull exchanged a look.

"Keep their uniforms on – we need to move," Buskull said, before producing a rope from the sack. They tied it to themselves and made their way back down the path.

Going down was much easier than climbing up, but it started to wreak havoc on their knees, with the burden of the equipment they wore and the constant trudging as they descended.

A few days later, they had left the harsh winds and cold temperatures behind and were now venturing on flat green ground. Their pace slowed as they made their way towards the Three-Thirty-Third's camp which they clearly saw as they had descended. They had discarded the Xiphos's uniform and donned their own.

Fleeing in fear, the unit had spent little time resting, constantly watching over their shoulders to see if the Xiphos were chasing them down.

As the ground levelled out, Buskull suddenly stopped again, for the thirteenth time that morning, and looked around, sniffing the air.

"What now?" Hilclop said, exasperated.

"I think ..." He frowned hard, then shook his head. "... nothing."

And they continued down the path towards the Three-Thirty-Third.

As they continued, behind them, off in the distance, a shadow appeared as a creature jumped from one rock to another, tracking them down. It stayed upwind from them and used the rocks to move rather than the earth, leaving no sign of its presence.

After half a day's walk, Buskull and the unit came into full sight of the Three-Thirty-Third's camp, which had transformed hugely from what they had seen several days previously.

A spiked palisade pointing outwards was now surrounding the camp, with six-foot-long pikes dug into a huge mound of earth encircling it. Several layers thick, it would be nearly impossible for any army or assassin to penetrate. Inside the makeshift camp were several small shelters for officers' meetings and physicians. Within, soldiers were lined up in columns as they practised phalanx manoeuvres or sword drills, the gruff chants of the officers ringing out for each drill. Their ranks were, after all, swelled with new recruits, and they had to get them ready for war. Most of the new recruits were distinguishable by their lack of equipment – they had no armour, wooden clubs for swords, and long branches for spears; some even had barrel lids for their shields. They had left Cam too soon to get what they needed to escort Princess Undrea to Ambenol, leaving a large infantry unit vastly under-equipped. Although, their long branches appeared strong and were spiked at the end, maybe they could repel a cavalry charge, but little else.

Acting Captain Jadge was standing with several other officers on a rise, arms folded and observing everything going on, when the unit approached the camp. Seeing them, they almost didn't believe it, and ran over to them.

"Where's Havovatch … where's our captain?" Jadge said hurriedly.

Buskull was the only one who could bring himself to speak: "He's … dead. We failed."

Jadge's face dropped and looked up at the peak of the mountains, as he tried to comprehend what he was hearing.

"You are now in command of the Three-Thirty-Third," said Buskull, "and we need to get out of here … now!"

Jadge nodded after a moment's thought, as Buskull and the others passed him and walked into the camp.

Buskull heard Metiya before he saw him, bellowing with his authoritative but fatherly tone, shouting commands. Buskull knew he was teaching sword drills.

"CARVE, CUT, SLICE, JAB! No! No, you stupid rekon, if you can't do it properly, don't do it at all!"

Following the voice, Buskull saw the lines of soldiers with Ferith amongst them. Standing at the edge of a line in just his white jersey and dark trousers, he swung his own sabre in the same way as the others. He was picking it up well – better than the recruits, anyway.

Metiya noticed his presence, and Buskull opened his mouth to speak, but ended up just giving a nod and kept walking; he was not sure where to, but he kept going.

"Go, boy!" said Metiya to Ferith.

Ferith gave a nod of thanks to him, as if Metiya had instilled wisdom into him during his stay. Picking up his satchel and jacket, he left the camp heading east.

Chapter Six
Training

Marching in a column of over eight thousand men, the Three-Thirty-Third stretched across the terrain in shades of blue and bronze, the sun glinting off their spearheads as they held them upright. If anyone looked upon them they dared not approach, what with recent rumours of a mysterious black army attacking the world and a strange army far from home. It was more than enough to make the locals grow wary, and at a distance, they watched the dust cloud of sand as it was kicked up into the air.

Buskull, however, had been sent ahead with Hilclop and Feera as a scouting unit. After their failure to summon the Xiphos, Hilclop's development as a soldier and their witnessing the death of their captain, Jadge thought it was important that they stayed together to see it through to the end. And, with the regiment at their backs, they covered less ground than when they had been alone; they were lucky to make ten miles a day.

Buskull was very much a different leader to Havovatch. Although he possessed much experience, he was not used to having the responsibility of making decisions. This time, though, he knew he had to. He was constantly checking the welfare of his two men, making sure their weapons were suitable, their uniforms were well kept; he even checked their feet at the end of each day to make sure they weren't blistered, although this was more for Hilclop's benefit than Feera's.

One of the most important roles on Buskull's agenda, though, was getting Hilclop up to the standard of a competent soldier, and, for what he had in mind, above average. He gave him responsibilities, such as climbing trees or high rises to see if he could see anything ahead – although his senses could tell – he also got him to count how many steps they made at certain intervals, so he could calculate how far they had travelled. When they took a break, Hilclop had to do fifty push-ups. Feera would kick his elbows in and push down on his backside with his boot – if he got it wrong he had to start again. Hilclop was becoming more than irritated by it, and on several occasions he was ready to snap. But as he looked up at Buskull's features, his sinister eyes, his toned body, any strength he had to challenge him evaporated. But this is what Buskull wanted. It was the beginning of him changing, becoming mentally harder, physically stronger, the time when he would release the soul of his boyhood past to allow a new one to enter.

After a couple of nights, Hilclop lay sprawled out on the ground, almost unconscious with exhaustion as his chest rose and fell with his heavy breathing. Feera sat striking two rocks together to get a spark into some kindling, and Buskull had just emerged from the forest. "Got two today," he said, raising two dead coneys in his grasp.

"Well, you will be eating them raw if I cannot get this damned fire going," Feera said sharply, before throwing the stones onto the floor and rubbing his face.

Buskull leant down, picked them up in one huge hand and put the other on Feera's shoulder.

"We did all we could – there was nothing different that could have been done. Now, you're a soldier." He handed him the stones back. "Havovatch would have wanted nothing other than for you to stay as one."

Feera pursed his lips and nodded, and again began striking the stones.

As Hilclop started to drift off into a world of his own, Buskull approached and gave him a kick.

"Stand up!" he said sharply.

Hilclop forced open one eyelid. Feeling an ominous situation about to unfold, he looked at Feera, thinking he had done something wrong.

"Stand up!" Buskull demanded again.

Hilclop closed his eyes and took in another breath. Then, mustering all his energy, he tried to lift his sore and aching body, wincing as he sat up and tried to get to his feet.

"You think that hurts? Try lasting your third week in training," jibed Feera.

Hilclop glared at him and pushed himself to his feet, swaying slightly in his almost delirious state.

Buskull turned, walked a few paces to his bag and pulled out a wooden sword. It was new and appeared to be something Buskull had made over recent days, probably when the other two were sleeping.

"Under the rules of war," he began, "if you have signed up to the Camion military, you're invested straight into any regiment, missing out your training. However, if you had done your training correctly, you would now be halfway through becoming one of the best soldiers in the world. Yet, here you are on a mission to save the world with little skill and ability."

Buskull spoke very matter-of-factly, pointing out not Hilclop's errors, but his position.

"Draw your sword," he said, taking a defensive stance with his. Hilclop did so, hesitantly, as Feera made himself comfortable watching on, his now small fire starting to illuminate their camp in the evening dusk. None of them knew it, but the glow was reflected in two eyes in the shadows of the bushes.

Hilclop stood square, his feet shoulder-width apart and his sword held loosely by his side.

Within the blink of an eye, Buskull hit him in the shoulder with the flat of the wooden blade. It was quick, so quick that Hilclop only just saw it coming and had no time to react.

"Ow!" he said, withdrawing and rubbing his aching arm.

"You think that hurts?" Buskull said rhetorically, and hit him again on the leg.

"Argh, stop it!" he shouted in his pathetic, whiny voice.

"You want me to stop? Then stop me!" Buskull shouted, before lunging forward.

Hilclop did not raise his sword, but stepped back. Eyes wide, he just kept walking backwards across the camp, too scared to engage.

"Raise your sword!" shouted Feera with amusement.

Hilclop held it up to stop Buskull's next attack, but was swatted away.

"Come on, boy!" Buskull shouted. "If I were trying to kill you, you would be lying on the floor in several pieces by now. Grit your teeth, build up your rage and attack me!"

A sudden image appeared in Hilclop's mind – one he would long remember, one that would burn a frightening and deep void into his memory. Crouching low and holding the sword parallel, he slashed at Buskull's legs with his blade. Buskull moved back just in time to prevent his legs getting cut. Feera's jaw dropped with shock. Hilclop lunged up and threw his sword in a crossing motion, causing Buskull to step back even quicker. Feera got up onto one knee, this was getting exciting!

Buskull assessed the distance he had been pushed back. "Good!" he said, pacing around as Hilclop held an unusual fighting stance that would leave him vulnerable in several places.

"You're holding the sword in your right hand, are you not? Then place your right foot forward!" Hilclop did so. "Put the weight on your back leg. If I slice forward, don't move your back leg as your body stays where it is – move the leg that is in front."

Hilclop did so as Buskull slashed the sword at his face. Moving his right leg back caused his face to merely move back out of its path.

"Good! Very good!"

Hilclop smiled and dropped his guard to look at Feera, who smacked the flat of his hand against his face as Hilclop was hit by the pommel of Buskull's sword.

It was pitch black where Hilclop woke up, staring at the thousands of stars and two of the three moons above.

"Which one do you think is bigger?" he said out loud to himself.

"Huh?" said Feera.

Lying on the ground, he noticed a blanket had been wrapped around him, and he looked up to see Feera and Buskull eating rabbit stew.

"What happened?" he said, getting up and holding his head.

"You didn't listen," said Buskull. "Tomorrow, we'll try again, but remember, boy, in battle there are no second chances ... to be honest, I don't know how you've survived this long with what we have been through."

Hilclop staggered over to the small cauldron, with a divine smell emanating from the bubbling stew. Hilclop knew that Buskull had found some herbs nearby, it added to the flavour. Taking his bowl, he filled it and sat down, sipping at the hot meal.

"When will the pain stop?" he asked, already fed up with the swaying shapes.

"Don't wait for it to stop!" said Feera. "Embrace it, accept it, for you will experience far more in your lifetime." Feera rubbed his knuckles, reminded of a past injury that still irritated him.

They sat in silence for some time with their own thoughts.

"Chaps?" said Buskull, breaking the tense silence. "How are we?"

"My head hurts," said Hilclop.

"No you rekon, I mean emotionally."

"... I have a heavy heart," said Feera distantly – Buskull knew he wanted to talk about it, "after Mercury ... now our captain. After *everything* we did, what was the point?"

"We did all we could. It was the hate of another man that did this, not us."

"He did not have to die," said Feera, staring into the fire and poking it with a stick. "He's younger than me – he didn't deserve that!"

Buskull set his bowl down. Leaning on his knees by his elbows, he grasped his hands together and took in a deep breath.

"Things may not always be as they seem, chaps. Tomorrow is another day. We're still here and that means that Grash has a plan for us. Let's see it through."

He received vacant nods from the other two. Knowing that it was time and experience that would help, more than words of wisdom, he got up and walked over to a small stream to clean his bowl.

As Buskull returned, he stood tall and proud over the small camp.

"Turn in for the night, gents. We will be up early tomorrow to keep ahead of the Three-Thirty-Third. And Hilclop," – he looked up at him expectantly – "you'll be working harder."

Feera grinned and turned over, wrapping his blanket over himself. But something caught his eye. As he looked into the bushes he saw a face with two piercing eyes, and although he wanted to shout out he could not, for fear gripped him as he stared at the crude, unpleasant, growling creature.

Chapter Seven
Wrisscrass

"Your fault!"

"Was not!"

"Was too!"

"Was not!"

"Was too!"

"Was —" Pausanias stopped as he looked around and noticed the Two-Twenty-Eighth looking at them.

"Look," he said lowering his voice to his little brother, "we both agreed we would leave, and General Drorkon said he would stick up for us and explain it to the commander."

"No! *You* said we should leave. I bashed my head, remember – how was I supposed to think clearly?" Andreas looked away as if that was it, he had said his bit and it wasn't going to be argued.

Pausanias drew in a sharp breath and puffed it out, wishing he received a bit more support from his brother. "How you passed the Hawks' tests, I have no idea!"

"Still did better than you in bits."

"I did mine eight years ago – it was tougher then."

"Any excuse."

"Look! Will you —" then, on noticing the turning of more heads from the cavalry unit, Pausanias calmed himself. Thinking it was better just to be quiet, he said nothing.

"I don't like this thing," said Andreas, after a while assessing his mount. "And, man, don't these things get itchy?" he added, placing a finger up his helmet to scratch behind his ear again.

"You'll get used to it, but you know the rules: we're not allowed to remove them. And don't keep scratching, you'll get a sore."

"Yeah, but I don't understand why."

Pausanias sighed. "Part of our reputation is that no one sees our faces – people think that we're not human. If you remove your helmet then everyone will see your face. It takes a lifetime to build a reputation and a moment to destroy it. Anyway, I thought you were told all this during induction?"

Andreas just shrugged. "Meh!"

Pausanias couldn't understand why his brother was the way he was. Always complaining, never seeing things from a point of view other than his own. Always needing everything explained to him like a child. If it were not for the fact he was such a good shot with a bow, he didn't know what use he was in the Knight Hawks, or the military for that matter.

"Anyway, what's wrong with your mount?"

"It's moving."

"They generally do."

"Yeah, well, I don't like it. I keep feeling like I'm going to fall off."

"Let's just hope you don't need to start galloping."

Andreas shot him an alarmed stare. "You don't think we will need to, do you?" he said, lowering his voice.

"What's the matter, little brother? Scared of a little speed?"

Andreas went very quiet and did not answer back to his jibe. Instead, he clutched his reins tighter and hooked his legs around the horse's waist. Acting very precariously, he longed for the journey to be over.

"I would be less worried about going for a ride," said Pausanias, "and more concerned about what the commander is going to do when he finds out we left our post."

"Do you think he'll be angry?"

"What do you think?" Pausanias said sharply, "for the fact that it was the *Princess*, of all people, that we left behind, I think he's going to be livid."

Andreas became fidgety, not knowing what to do with his arms. "I can't take this – let's go back," he pleaded.

Pausanias sighed. "I know – I've felt like I've got a rope tugging at me ever since we left." He frowned behind his helmet as he thought of why they had left.

"But that guy, how did he know our word? How did he know *us*?" moaned Andreas. He shivered. "I don't like it."

They exchanged a look.

"We should go back," said Pausanias.

Andreas nodded.

As they reined in their mounts, the Two-Twenty-Eighth passed them, and they looked behind at the distance they had covered.

"You know," said Pausanias, "it's only been three days since we left. I know where we are, and it takes much longer than three days to get here from Ambenol."

He chewed his lip as he tried to work it out, had he counted his days wrong? Andreas, as always, was not paying attention, and Pausanias's words were left hanging in the air.

Looking at the landscape behind them, they knew it would take days to get back to Ambenol. They felt that they had made a bad decision, and finally realised the consequences of their actions.

"C'mon," said Pausanias, as he pushed his mount back the way they had come. But just then, within the blink of an eye, there was a thunderclap, and, walking towards them in white robes, surrounded by a purple haze, was the stranger they had met at Ambenol.

"Greetings," he said cheerfully.

This time there was no spell holding them down. Reacting to what they thought was a threat, Pausanias drew his sword and braced himself as Andreas fixed a long, thick arrow with a barbed head to his bowstring, aiming it between the stranger's eyes.

The stranger placed his hands up to show he was no threat.

"You have no reason to harm me."

"Last time we met, you took control of us. What do you think we're going to do now – hug?"

"Save the world," the stranger shrugged. "You have come this far, gentlemen – don't turn back now. As I said, Undrea will be fine; and more importantly, so will your father. He needs you, he taught you well and he's trying to get back to you. Stay with the general and follow your path."

"It's not just Undrea we're concerned about, and what do you know of our father!" shouted Andreas.

"Things have a strange way of working out, gentlemen. I know your time is precious, so I will leave you with this: *Redemption*. Your father's word."

The brothers looked at each other again. But before they could turn back to the stranger, there was another thunderclap and he'd disappeared.

"What are we going to do, Pausanias?" pleaded Andreas, almost sobbing with worry between their father and their duty.

Pausanias drew in a breath as he looked back at where the man had been – it was as before, just a burnt patch of grass on the ground. He realised now that this was all on him – he had the responsibility to look after his brother. The decision was easy: follow his duty and return to Ambenol, and he went to say just that. But when he opened his mouth, the love for his father took over.

"Come, let's keep going."

Turning their mounts, they followed behind the Two-Twenty-Eighth. There was only one feeling that helped Pausanias in a time like this: anger. And he summoned as much of it as he could by thinking of his father's disappearance, and the more he thought about it the less worried he became.

*****

Breathing heavier and heavier, his heart booming inside his chest. Feera tried secretly to reach over for his swords behind him, but feared that if he did so, the creature would jump out and kill him before he could get to them.

Buskull, sensing his erratic behaviour, looked up and saw the eyes shrouded in the darkness.

"To guard!" he shouted, grabbing his axe and jumping over Feera towards the shadow. The eyes disappeared.

Throwing his huge, heavy arm into the bush, Buskull hauled the creature out and threw it into the camp. It landed awkwardly but did not get up to fight – it casually turned over onto its back and looked up at the unit bearing down on it. It was huge, almost as big as Buskull, with a strong, toned body, wearing just rags. It had gashes in its back and arms as if it had been tortured.

"Who're you?" shouted Hilclop, pointing his sword close to the creature's throat, gaining more confidence with every passing day. Buskull pulled him back, though, knowing that he was holding his sword too close and the strong-looking beast could have disarmed him. But it didn't, and looked up at them passively.

"He asked you a question!" said Buskull.

But the creature just smiled.

"Hang on! I know you," said Feera.

Buskull looked up at him. "Who ... what is it ... he ... it?"

"I fought him at Haval, on the walls."

"What a brilliant mind you have, human," spat the creature with sour breath and a harsh voice.

Feera sneered back at him, his knuckles turning white as he gripped his sword.

"Why are you following us? Another assassin?" asked Buskull.

"I think that my assassin days are done, Giant."

Before the other two could blink, Buskull bore down on the creature, stamping hard on its stomach. But the creature barely flinched; it gritted its jaw as if taking the pain, then smiled again.

"You can't hurt me, Giant, so don't even think about it!"

Buskull dropped his axe, bent down and picked the creature up, throwing it against a large rock. He held his forearm under its chin, making it difficult for the creature to breathe. Now toe-to-toe with Buskull, it still remained passive, despite being nearly the same size as him and seemingly just as strong.

"Give me one reason why I shouldn't break your neck!" Buskull hissed.

"I'll give you several," said the creature between clenches teeth.

Buskull sneered, happy to snap its neck like a twig, but the mystery of why this creature was hunting them, but not killing them, was too much to leave unanswered.

Pulling away, he let the creature fall to the floor, and it sat on all fours, rubbing its neck.

"Give me some food and water, and I will tell you all that you want to know."

Hilclop let out a laugh, but Buskull walked over to his canteen and cow's stomach. Filling the canteen with stew, he put it and the water on the floor before the creature. The creature pulled itself forward and disgustingly stuck its face into the stew, then gulped the water. The whole time the unit looked on, curious as to why their enemy was in their camp and not fighting them.

When it had finished, it belched and sat back against the rock face, looking up at the unit.

"You're one short. Where's the bronze man with the blue crest?"

"That is not of your concern. Now tell us why you are here before I cut your stomach open and retrieve the meal we gave you," demanded Buskull.

The creature did not look stricken by the threat, but kept its grin.

"Very well. Unfortunately, I failed in a mission from my master to kill you all, a master who is not very forgiving. I now have no life. As you can see, I have cut the trophies from my hair and punished my body; I have changed who I am, for I want to live, but I cannot be a beast of the Black any more."

"So, you thought you'd come into our camp?"

"You are the only humans I have met. To go elsewhere would be suicide."

"Coming here is suicide," Feera pointed out.

"I don't think so."

"Oh, why not?" hissed Buskull.

"For you are human, and one emotion you have that I don't is compassion. If you were going to kill me, you would have already have done it by now."

Buskull lifted up his axe to gauge the creature's reaction, but it didn't even flinch.

"What is your name, beast?"

"Wrisscrass."

"You want to follow us?"

"Ha! If that's what you want to call it? I will fight by your side, and then, when this is all over, I will make my own way in the world."

"That won't happen. I don't believe that you will just give yourself up willingly to fight against your own."

"I am the enemy of my own. There are more around than you know, and although I may be bound by breed, I am not by blood. I will happily kill anything to live."

"A quality we fortunately don't have as humans," said Feera proudly.

"Maybe that's why you are always at war with each other, no? Instead of killing those who need to die?"

There was a long silence as Feera chewed on the remark, and could not help but think that there was truth to that.

Buskull stomped over and heaved Wrisscrass to his feet, making him turn to face the rock. Pulling rope from behind his belt, he tied his wrists tightly and looped the rope above his elbows – a technique he had learnt from the Knight Hawks – making it impossible to get out of.

Sitting him down, he stepped back, not taking his eyes off the beast, who still held a grin.

"I will take the first watch. Feera, you take the second. Sorry, Hilclop, but he is too dangerous for you to watch alone. Go to sleep."

Chapter Eight
Rivers of Blood

Wrisscrass walked confidently, surrounded by the unit, with his arms tied in front of him. Feera walked behind him, glaring intently. The numbing pains in Wrisscrass's arms from the tight bonds did not bother him in the slightest – pain was little bother to one of his species.

Buskull was questioning every sense he had as to why he was still there, but killing an unarmed man – if he could be called that – just seemed too cold, and would bring him down to their level.

Hilclop was a changed person, too, from the one he had been before their journey had begun. He was doing well in his training and often his mind slipped off into a dream, dreaming about himself as a warrior of invincibility, taking on armies by himself and leaving without a scratch – much like Drakator. Then again, his imagination did place his face in Drakator's armour.

"So, you 'av a boy in your unit? I do wonder how you lot killed so many of my kin," Wrisscrass mocked, looking Hilclop up and down. "He's so puny, I could snap him like a twig."

"Silence!" shouted Feera, giving him a shove, but Wrisscrass still maintained his grin.

Hilclop glared at him but said nothing; in truth, he was not too sure what to say.

Suddenly, Buskull raised a clenched fist into the air and they all stopped and dropped to one knee, silently examining what was going on – apart from Wrisscrass, who stood there, sensing something; a curt smile crossed his face.

Buskull's senses told him something was coming, but he did not know what. Whatever it was, though, it was terribly ominous. The path curved around a corner and he gazed intently. He kept low, waiting for whatever or whoever it was to appear, and then they did. A little girl hobbled vacantly towards them, her toga torn and stained with human blood and dirt. Buskull, showing no reaction, ran to her and, almost as if she accepted her fate, she sank into his arms and stared up into his eyes. His eyes began to water as he felt the mental pain she had recently been subjected to.

"Buskull!" shouted Feera, the sound of steel ringing out as he quickly drew his sword, and the wicked smile on Wrisscrass's face widened.

They saw a group of nine Golesh shambling towards them; but Buskull was too engrossed with the poor girl in his arms to notice. Almost as if seeing a face from his past, he gently brushed the hair out of her face and wiped the tears from her eyes, whispering *"It'll be OK."*

"'ello, chums!" said Wrisscrass, strutting towards the group of Golesh. "Out for a stroll, are we?" he said, casually.

Hilclop drew near Feera, who gritted his teeth in regret over having not killed Wrisscrass when they had had the chance.

The Golesh approached Wrisscrass, and, seeing his bonds, they approached without caution.

"Give us a 'and with these, would ya?" he said nonchalantly, raising his hands.

One of them cut through with a single swipe of its sword, the others surrounding him, ready to attack the unit.

"Ta, chum," Wrisscrass said, looking down at the feeble creature, and smiled. Then, without warning, he rammed his forehead straight into its skull, blood splattering everywhere. Grabbing its sword, he turned quickly and cut clean through the next one's neck. The rest of the Golesh company were so confused to see one of their own fighting them that they did not know what was going on, with some even looking into the trees, thinking they were being ambushed. Dropping the now broken weapon, Wrisscrass made easy work of the rest of the company with his brute strength and bare hands, howling as he tore off limbs and repeatedly smashed another's head against a rock. The fight was just carnage, whilst Feera and Hilclop sneered on, although, they showed their concern about Wrisscrass walking around free, but, after witnessing his brutality, they dared not take a step towards him. With corpses littering the ground Wrisscrass went about turning them over, looting whatever he thought he could use.

He pulled the jerkin off one of the corpses and tried to don it, but it was far too small, with none of the creatures matching his stature. He also took a belt and several knives. It was almost as if he had planned the attack, killing them in such a way that left him with what he wanted without them being tarnished.

He smiled back at the unit. "See! Told ya, I'm on your side," he said, holding up a collection of knives. "Cor!!" he said, admiring them with a huge grin.

Buskull looked up and saw what had happened, but not one of them said anything; they were still trying to work out if he really was, after all, their enemy.

He wasn't much differently dressed with no top on and still wearing his dark trousers, however, he was armed from head to foot. Large knives placed inside his boot with the handle sticking out, with several other knives and daggers strapped around his arms and thigh. It appeared he wanted smaller weapons which seemed odd to Feera, for he looked big enough to wield a larger weapon. Still, Wrisscrass stood happily admiring the arsenal around him, he looked like a kid in a toy shop whose parents had bought him everything he wanted. But something caught his eye, and his expression changed to one of glad surprise. "It cannot be," he said, looking at one of the dead Golesh. Kicking it over with little dignity, it revealed a set of long knives which were joined together by a handle and had a long piece of metal with a ring at the end, for their owner to feed their arms through. Picking them up in his grip, he admired them. "HA, HA, HA! I have not seen these beauties in a very long time – fangerlores!"

"Keep your eye on him, Hilclop," said Feera, staring down the road at Wrisscrass as he pleasured himself with his loot. He looked over Buskull's shoulder at the traumatised girl. She became more aware of what was around her and started to hyperventilate, her eyes wide as if she had seen horrors too dreadful to contemplate. Buskull fixed his large hand on her head and looked intently into her eyes, speaking in a tongue she did not know; even Feera looked at him in alarm, wondering what he was saying.

"Belia, terridesium."

She calmed visibly on hearing the softly spoken words; her breathing returned to normal and her eyes closed as if she were falling asleep. But as she started to doze, she spoke quietly. "My city," she said slowly, in an innocent voice, "it is under attack … creatures, hideous creatures, they killed my mum … I don't know what happened to my father; they killed everyone in the streets, horns rang out, soldiers tried to stop them, but there were too many."

Buskull fixed his gaze on her intently. "When was this?" he asked, his voice deeper than Feera or Hilclop had heard, almost possessed with hatred. The little girl did not say anything, but with a shaky hand she pointed back down the path that she had come from. Buskull picked her up and took her into the edge of the forest; he lowered her gently onto a thick patch of moss, and she started to snooze. Breaking several fern branches off without taking his eyes off the girl, he gently covered her to keep her warm. Then, bending down by her side, he placed a hand on her forehead. She slept like a child should, her eyes closed as she was possessed by the pleasant dreams that Buskull created with his words. Bending lower, he whispered into her ear, "I *will* be back for you. Do not move!"

Returning to the others, he had his battle-axe drawn and his face intent. "Hilclop, run – get the regiment." Hilclop stood poised for a second. "*RUN!*" he roared, as loud as his war cry, and Hilclop half fell over with shock. Scrambling to his feet, he sprinted back to the Three-Thirty-Third.

Feera suddenly noticed that Wrisscrass was with them, standing aloof with his weapons, he saw him tensing his arms, lusting for the battle to come. Feera stood ready next to Buskull. "Should we leave the girl?" he asked.

"She will be fine – I sense no more trouble here." He looked further down the road. "Feera …" he said.

Feera looked up at him; his voice was soft and spoke of trepidation.

"You do not have to come with me for this. Wait for the Three-Thirty-Third!"

"You know that won't happen."

"Then try to keep up."

Buskull launched forward, leaving heavy bootprints in the ground. Feera trailed behind, Wrisscrass joining him, but Buskull did not object.

Hilclop was long since out of breath, fuelled on adrenalin, panic and fear as well as other emotions as he ran towards the Three-Thirty-Third in the distance. He could just see them, along with the dust kicked up by the long column.

Not knowing what message to give, but knowing that it was important, he rushed forward and soon came into view of the blue and bronze. He shouted and waved his arms frantically; the astute scouts saw him and the order was passed down the column to summon the captain. Jadge ran down, as did other officers, and approached Hilclop, who fell to his knees before them, desperately trying to speak. Jadge hauled him up by his shoulders.

"What is it? Where are Buskull and Feera? Speak!"

"Buskull-needs-help, attack-on-a-town-nearby, it's-a-massacre!" he said in one long breath, before collapsing back to the ground.

Jadge immediately turned to the column. "PREPARE!!"

The Three-Thirty-Third went from a vertical column stretching down the road to a horizontal one, and marched with haste over the fields, officers bringing up their units. The call for combat rang out, and words of encouragement were shouted out from officers: "This is what you have been waiting for."

They did not pull into phalanx position yet, but marched hard and fast to warm up towards the now notable black smoke behind the trees ahead of them.

Buskull and Feera did not have far to go. The small canyon they had left behind dipped down into an open valley, and at the bottom was a large city, devastated by fire, smoke … and the Golesh. Audible from within the walls were cries from those being slaughtered, tortured and raped, as creatures howled with delight.

Buskull ran through the shattered gates before him, half hanging off their giant hinges with the city's garrison littering the floor. He could sense the beasts within the city – there were thousands, tens of thousands of them – but their scent was distinctly different from what he knew of them. Running into a wide street, the floor the same orangey white as the walls, with low houses and flat roofs, he looked left and right and took a moment to sense where he was needed first. Wrisscrass stood behind, his fist clenched with his fangerlores in hand, readying himself. With an almost animal prowess he crouched low, looking intently between the buildings. He almost seemed professional in what he was doing. Feera was still puzzled by his attitude, but in light of the situation, he let it lie.

Buskull closed his eyes and his senses created an imaginary map in his head. Singling out the humans within the city – what was left of the populace was nearly spent – he ran to where he needed to be, which was everywhere.

They immediately came into contact with the Golesh, hands filled with the spoils from their victims' houses. Before they could react to a threat, their bodies were cut in two by sweeping blows from Buskull's axe. Feera stayed behind him and took many out with his own skill, but Wrisscrass laid into them with equally brutal actions, as he had done with the previous users of his new equipment. Soon the street was clear and they ventured further in, knowing their path behind was now blocked and there was no turning back; but only Feera was thinking about that. Women and children were still screaming as they fought their way towards the noises; one woman, battered and cut, was being pinned down with her toga over her face and a Golesh ravaging her.

Buskull pulled the unsuspecting Golesh up by its belt and threw it into a wall so hard that there was but a spatter of black blood from the impact of its body.

Feera shouted at the women and children running hysterically around. "CAMION MILITARY, TAKE COVER!"

The woman pulled her toga back over her naked body and ran back into the adjacent house, barring the door.

Feera and Buskull carried on into the carnage to find the same thing going on in every street, alley and thoroughfare. All met the same fate, as they did not expect the two warriors coming at them, and wherever they were, Wrisscrass was with them.

Enraged more when he came into contact with fleeing children, Buskull shouted for them to run, and met their pursuers with little respect. He heard them approaching – their sadistic laughs, their malicious shrieks – as they loomed out of the dense black smoke. But Buskull emerged too, frowning and gritting his teeth like a snarling hound. He held his axe firmly and shouted with his monstrous war cry, so loud that it cleared the smoke around him and filled the streets with an almost physical sense of fear. Shrieks stopped in the city, as all turned in the direction of his war cry to hear what it was – like a lion making its mark, or in Buskull's case, making his stand. He called them to him; this was his fight and he was going to take them with him, *all* of them.

Feera stood back, stricken. He had seen a lot from Buskull recently, but this was on a different level. Instead of joining in, he guided the remaining children into a house and watched on whilst Buskull fought as dozens of Golesh rounded the corner of the street to investigate the noise. Wrisscrass stood by his side and, with his crude weapons, he joined in what looked like a game for him, as his dominance and strength equalled Buskull's, though both were fuelled by different emotions.

Then horns rang out. Running to a gap between two houses, Feera looked west and saw that at the top of the hills surrounding the city – now lined with blue and bronze – the Three-Thirty-Third had arrived. As they advanced towards the city, he knew that Buskull's time was not yet up, and shouted for the children to barricade themselves as he stood outside with his two swords to protect them.

Hilclop, now reeling on his reserves of energy, was paced well behind the regiment. The Three-Thirty-Third, fresh on vigour, built up from months of frustration, waiting to fight the Black, were finally having a real chance to let it out.

Once on top of the hill, the regiment wasted no time in becoming a disorganised rabble, and started running for the three gates on their side of the city, which were all broken and open to anyone. There was no need for phalanx manoeuvres or specific formations. They were fighting within a compact city, and the last of the populace needed them. Spears thrown over shields, swords raised high into the air, arrows notched to bowstrings, they quickly found their enemy and went into bloody conflict with the Golesh, which were outmatched by the trained and clad heavy infantry.

Buskull and Feera worked together, leaving an impressive amount of bodies littering the cobbled streets, whilst Wrisscrass was jumping from walls and rooftops at anything that appeared, and which soon met its end. The Golesh became fewer in number, and their attack now turned into defence as they ran for their lives.

The unit soon came into contact with their own regiment, and the west side of the city was quickly seized. Any women and children were escorted out of the city, and fled into the valley above to meet the Three-Thirty-Third's battlefield surgeons, and scouts who would defend them. What was left of the city's soldiers – although very few in number – were told to fall back in reserve and regain their breath as the Three-Thirty-Third took hold of the city. With the odds turning in their favour, the Golesh could do little to stop them; with close quarters fighting and the tenacious efforts of the Three-Thirty-Third, they quickly killed off the Golesh, leaving the streets paved with black armour and blood.

An hour had passed, and much of the city was taken, but still thousands of Golesh (who by now had rallied against their enemy) were not pillaging any more but regrouping to fight again, with the east side still strictly under their control.

But, off in the distance, more horns rang out and the Camion soldiers recognised them.

"Ha, ha!" shouted Andreas, with his fist in the air, clutching his bow. "I'm coming, you filthy rekons!"

Pausanias was already ahead of him, with Drakator paced in front, approaching the gates. Andreas didn't like it, though, and, as he pushed his stirrups into his mount's side, the horse jolted; he lost his balance and fell off. The Two-Twenty-Eighth, despite being in packed, neat ranks, swerved around him as he lay looking up at the sky, feeling numb.

With the Two-Twenty-Eighth's flags loosened to flap in the wind and tell their enemy who they were, they valiantly made their way to the city. Officers rode out in front of their commands – their posture perfectly square, holding their swords upright, with Drorkon setting an example by leading the charge, and Pausanias and Drakator before him. The hills were covered in stampeding cavalry, leaving long trails of churned-up dirt.

As Drakator approached the gates of the city, he looked up to see Golesh archers taking positions on the parapet. He let out a deafening shriek, like an echo of a demon's voice. The Golesh in his view fell to their knees, clutching their large, sensitive ears. As he approached the gate, he jumped from his saddle high into the air, as if an invisible giant had picked him up and dropped him on the battlements. Pausanias looked on, amazed. As Drakator landed, he rolled along the ground to break his fall. He jumped up and, drawing his swords simultaneously, he was a blur as he sliced through the first few creatures with ease. He quickly undid the clasps holding his cloak to his armour and threw it into a creature, which ended up being wrapped around as it tried hysterically to free itself.

Below him, Pausanias charged through the keep and jumped from his horse. He too preferred not to fight on horseback, and, jumping against several Golesh to break his fall, he worked his way up the steps to Drakator. Just below, the Two-Twenty-Eighth galloped into the city, running down the Golesh horde, their battle cries ringing out.

Drakator worked his way along the north wall as Pausanias went south. As much as Pausanias tried not to make it a competition, he couldn't help it; although the number of bodies Drakator left showed he was clearly the victor.

From either side, the Three-Thirty-Third made their way towards them. Drakator fought as the tales had said, almost as if he had eyes all around him. He matched every thrust and parry that came his way. With his two short swords he cut through everything, headbutted several, kicked, punched and used every limb he had. The Golesh in the city were now surrounded and appeared to scramble, some fleeing, others seeking refuge in houses as the odds turned against them. Some went out of the city to meet the cavalry, not caring what their fate might be, but were mowed down by the brute force of the horse lords.

On horseback, the Two-Twenty-Eighth quickly enveloped the city and soon met with the Three-Thirty-Third, and it was then that the Golesh were fighting for survival.

Buskull ran after a group of creatures that were trying desperately to get away from him, their eyes wide with terror as one by one he caught up with them. There was no camaraderie amongst them, as they tried to trip each other up so that they could get away. But Buskull stopped when he heard screaming coming from another direction, screaming from a woman.

The entire street was covered in dense smoke from the burning buildings. Soldiers were still running through the streets in search of another kill, and some stricken Golesh appeared, but clearly looking to find a way out rather than fight.

Buskull knew they were no threat any more, but was intent on finding the source of the screaming. As he ran down several alleyways it got louder, and he then came into view of a thin woman crouched down by the side of a burning house. Her long, brown hair was a mess; she was sweating and stricken. He did not know what she was screaming at – she just crouched down, looking at the floor of a burning house.

He approached hesitantly, his eyes trying to escape the sight of the fire raging around him, but his sense of duty and honour overpowered his fear.

"What's the matter?" he said, hoarsely.

The woman looked up. She was almost shocked to see the man before her, for she had never seen anyone so large in her life, and was unsure whether he was part of the Camion army that had appeared or one of the creatures.

"*What's the matter?*" Buskull demanded more forcefully, trying to get past her shock.

"My daughter – she's trapped!"

Buskull looked down to where she was and saw a terrified girl, her body hidden under the house. As they had tried to flee the cellar, it was apparent it had partially come down on her as her mother had tried to pull her out.

He dropped his axe and, taking hold of the structure of the house by beams sticking out from the first floor, he pushed. It moved only slightly, and his strength was not enough. Again, he tried to move it off the young girl, with the mother stroking her hair and telling her all would be OK. But it would not budge.

He started to breathe heavily with exhaustion, as his body could not muster the strength to lift the structure. It was just too heavy, even for him.

Turning, he met Sergeant Metiya. "Sergeant! Get as many men over here as you can, *now!*"

He left immediately to find some.

Buskull looked down at the little girl.

"Mummy, my feet hurt."

"I know darling. It will be OK – we will help you."

"No! You don't understand. They are burning – it is getting worse."

Buskull's face turned desperate, then angry. Something pulsated through him and his posture changed; his teeth snarled as a rage he could not remember experiencing in a long time surged through his veins. Gritting his teeth, he took hold of the house again, his feet braced, his arms firm; and, with a cry louder than he had ever shouted before, he pushed, digging his feet into the stone floor, making it crack.

The house moved up, his shout echoing through the city. The debris was raised off the girl and the mother pulled her clear, the deed done. Buskull let go, unable to move out of the way with the burning building landing on top of him. No part of him was seen, just huge lumps of wood and brick smouldering where he stood.

Just then, Metiya returned with a body of men.

"He is under there – get him out!" the mother screamed as she held the girl in her arms, and covered her mouth in shock.

The house was swarmed by soldiers, keen to save their comrade despite the flames. They removed their cloaks and started beating at them, some lifting beams whilst others searched for water.

But every beam removed revealed no part of Buskull, and, as time moved on, the flames intensified.

Chapter Nine
Alone

Nearly two weeks on, Fandorazz and Groga were approaching the Plains of Fernara. Exhausted and stressed, the architect and mason dragged their heels in the unbearable heat as the sun shone down mockingly upon them. Fandorazz had not walked like this since he had moved with his family to their new lives, with his dream of designing a city. But, along his journey, he was plagued with memories of the events leading up to their deaths. To distract him from the mental torment he tried to think of the happy memories of time spent with them, but all thoughts lead down the same path and he was again solemn.

Blistered and sore, their feet pushed on through the pain, knowing how important the mission was. Groga, though, was tired, and he showed it. He was a large man with a strong frame, carrying his stone hammer over his shoulder like a bindle. But he was not built for endless walking, and it affected his temper.

"Darn and blast!" he shouted as his blisters rubbed against his feet.

Fandorazz wished to say something, but he wasn't really too sure as to what.

"You OK?" he said, nervously. Yet his kind words were met with contempt.

"What do you think?!"

Fandorazz shifted uneasily. But Groga took in a breath.

"I'm sorry – I shouldn't have lashed out like that."

Fandorazz sighed and stretched. They both fell into a heap on the ground, and Groga removed his boots. He poured water onto a cloth and dabbed at the pockets of flesh falling away from his feet. Fandorazz just closed his eyes and contemplated his life. He had never been an adventurer, and it felt too surreal to think that now he was one.

Fortunately, they fell into the shade of a forest looming behind them as they got their breath back.

"Well, not far to go, I hope?" said Fandorazz.

"We're almost halfway," Groga said plainly.

Fandorazz shook his head and rubbed his face. "I can't do this, Grog. This is not who I am. My head hurts, I feel dizzy. I am not cut out for this."

"Neither am I. If I were, I would be in the infantry. But we need to do this – otherwise, who else will?"

"The Black could already be here by now," said Fandorazz with exasperation, looking east, not knowing what to think. "I mean: look at us." He stood, frustrated, again rubbing his hands across his face. "We're on a mission to seek out a dangerous horde of *Stone Men*; we have no idea if they will even listen to us, and the Defences are without a garrison. Camia has seemingly forsaken everyone but the rich, and as for us two, the only people who seem to give a damn in this world, we're not even halfway and yet we're battered and tired."

"What do you want me to do?" Groga shouted, opening his arms. "I don't like it any more than you do, but we have to do something!"

"We would have been better trying to train the locals into militia," Fandorazz said, kicking a group of white pebbles stacked neatly on the ground. Then, as he looked out at the terrain, he frowned, realising that there were several small stacks of white pebbles spread before him – they certainly weren't part of the natural landscape.

"Look – if we can get the Clup'ta to help us, then we will have a *huge* advantage."

Fandorazz turned. "Of course – you're right." He went and sat back down next to his friend. Groga had opened a flask and offered it to him. They sat in silence for a while, as Fandorazz looked at the white markers and wondered what they were. But they both jumped when there was a sudden rustling from the trees behind. They launched to their feet and spun around to see eight Camion infantrymen bursting out from the trees, spears in hand.

Fandorazz had his hand gripped on the hilt of his sword, but released it and showed the palms of his hands instead. "What is the meaning of this?" he said in his noble pronunciation, hoping that speaking as a member of the higher class would gain him an advantage.

"Stand firm, Mister," said the captain of the unit, somewhat taken aback by the stranger before him. "I must ask who you are and what business you have here." The captain tried to speak in an official manner but was clearly hesitant, not knowing who the higher-born before him was.

Fandorazz knew he was one of the Noble and had some authority over them. "Captain, I believe?" he said rhetorically, in his formal tone. Putting his hands behind his back, he walked forward, looking the rest of the men up and down as if everything they were doing was wrong. Recognising the manner in which he spoke, they withdrew slightly and pointed their spears at Groga rather than at him.

"We are Camions. This is my trusted friend, Groga, stonemason from Brinth." Upon hearing the word "friend", the unit pulled their spears up, keen to try not to offend the higher-born. "And I am Lord Fandorazz from the House of —"

"Did you say Fandorazz?" interrupted the captain.

"Yes?" he said with some trepidation, his confidence wavering somewhat.

"Good – we were worried that you had perished."

"What do you need of me?"

"You are on the list to be protected. Duchess Imara also wanted your expertise on helping with defences around the forest."

"Well, you can send the Duchess my best regards, for I am currently on another assignment – I cannot return to Cam."

"You don't have to, my Lord. All the higher people of Cam are within *this* forest," he said, gesturing behind him.

Fandorazz looked over the captain's shoulder and saw movement from within. He stood, startled. "What's going on? I thought all the troops had returned to Cam?"

"Yes, we had, and soon as we got there we began escorting the higher classes into this forest. They will be hidden and surrounded by the Camion military."

"But … that's outrageous – what about the civilians within the city?"

"An unfortunate sacrifice for our … higher people," said the captain in a way that showed he did not agree, but was bound by his oath and honour to serve the crown.

Fandorazz shook his head and raised his hand matter-of-factly. "I cannot come with you, Captain. We have other pressing matters."

"Apologies, my Lord, but I don't think you are aware of the new system?"

"*What new system?*" he spat.

"Queen Imara – as she has now appointed herself – and King Fennel are now in charge, because of the ill health of the King, and they have established martial law. All people in the higher levels are to be protected within the forest – no questions. So we will escort you into the forest, where you will do your job!"

"But this is absurd."

The soldiers approached. Groga lifted his stone axe, causing the infantrymen to return to guard again.

"No! No!" Fandorazz put his hand on top of his axe and lowered it. Stepping before him, he looked into his friend's eyes.

"I will come willingly. Do not hurt him."

"We have no quarrel with him, but the edge of the forest is for the Camion higher class only. If he enters it, he will be killed."

Fandorazz, feeling hopeless, bowed his head in shame for being a Camion. He put his hand on Groga's shoulder and smiled, a tear forming in his eye.

"Don't worry, Drozz," said Groga. "As long as there's breath in my body, I won't let the Defences fall."

They shook hands for a long moment, Fandorazz feeling anger about everything being outside his control. The unit of soldiers clustered around him, and he was led into the confines of the forest, Groga watching on helplessly.

**

The cavern was deep underground, with naturally formed balconies and caves etched into the rock, almost as if the ground had once been liquid with bubbles forming and then it had suddenly solidified, leaving huge, sphere-shaped rooms and corridors.

No torches were needed in the shadow, for although sunlight did not reach the cavern, dotted along the ceiling were turquoise stones illuminating the rooms – a natural phenomenon releasing a calm feeling to all who entered. In the centre of the labyrinth was the largest room, spanning the size of Rowlg Arena, with the balconies and tunnels surrounding the cavern. In the centre of the warren, the floor rose with a flat platform for all to see. No one of the known world knew how it had come to be, for it was certain that it was natural, for man would not have the tools or genius to create something so beautiful; and so it was made as the land of peace for the Knights of Ezazeruth, to meet and discuss what needed to be – no blood was allowed to touch its almost sacred floors.

No one would dare venture near, for the entrance – a giant mouth in the earth leading down – was surrounded by the Hirithul Marshes, almost impossible for anyone to navigate through unless they were a member of the Knights of Ezazeruth. Some wondered how it had been found at all; some said that a calming voice had attracted those with a good heart, others that it was just chance. Whatever the truth was, no one who didn't need to know of it ever found it.

After centuries of an eerie silence, with just the company of the swirling blue crystals in the ceiling, noises suddenly began to echo through the tunnels. And, entering the great hall in the centre, the Knights of Ezazeruth appeared. Meeting old friends and acquaintances they had not seen in a millennia, the Oistos and the Ippikós all merged together, and a joyous and cathartic meeting ensued – all gripping forearms, hugging and cheering.

"It's good to see you, Avron – you look good for an old man," Garvelia said sweetly, seeing him for the first time in a long time, so long she did not wish to remember.

Smiling, Avron held out his mighty arms and took Garvelia into his embrace. Hugging tightly, they wished not to let go. After a while, when the moment seemed as though it had gone further than just friends, they parted, to the admiring gaze of the soldiers looking up at them on the platform. Avron held his arms up and spun on the spot to see everyone. "It has been too long, my friends, but the time has come." He boomed, his voice echoing down the cavern. "A time when we may shed these skins we've endured for so long. I know what happened to us was beyond tragic, but for the sake of the innocent, we must protect this world."

There was a tremendous cheer of agreement that echoed through the tunnels, making it sound as if there were thrice as many as there were.

Making themselves comfortable, the knights sat down and talked as they all waited to see if the Xiphos would join them.

"Do you think Duruck will come?" Avron said, lowering his voice and grinning to his men as he and Garvelia made their way through the crowd.

"I don't know."

"The worrying thing is, neither do I."

He stopped to shake hands with a sergeant he remembered well from the Oistos. They talked and joked for a moment before he carried on walking down the tunnel. The rest of their journey was quiet, as they knew that what they wanted to discuss could not be talked about with prying ears around. Coming to a darkened corridor, Garvelia lifted her sword and hit the pommel against the wall. The darkness was illuminated as carvings appeared in front of her A mixture of red, green and blue lines formed a picture as if an invisible artist was there drawing it before them. An arch appeared with three warriors standing on a peak. Avron and Garvelia watched and smiled as they shared a memory. When the drawing had completed, it then set into the stone, the colour disappearing and replaced with black lines. Then, what looked like a doorway appeared. After a long moment of looking at the magic before them, Avron placed the flat of his hand on the wall. He felt the stone as if he were looking for something, somewhere. Then, he stopped. Pulling his sword out he hit the pommel against it. The hollow sound belied its appearance, it was wood disguised as rock. He pulled the debris away, pulled out a key and pushed it into a small hole in the centre. There was no sound of bolts unlocking, the door just pushed inwards revealing a room which suddenly lit up as if it opened to the outside. As they entered, the two commanders looked upon a room they had not seen in two thousand years.

"For some reason, I expected it to be different," said Garvelia as she walked around a large, triangular table in the centre, patterns adorning the table top.

"As did I," said Avron as he picked up a very old quill, which fell apart at his touch

Garvelia pulled back a very large, green chair and sat down. "You know, I missed this so much that I had an exact replica made for me at home." She shifted. "It still wasn't as comfortable as this one, though."

Avron grinned. "I think we both have done similar things," he said as he pulled his chair back and ran his hand gently down the side. But their stares moved to the vacant chair next to them.

Chapter Ten
Retribution

As Buskull slept, he smelt the unmistakable smell of burning. As he woke and opened his eyes, he saw that the room was a haze of smoke.

Pulling himself up quickly, he looked around the room and noticed he was alone. His wife had let him sleep in again – he hated it when she did that, but she knew he needed his rest and was too stubborn to admit it. He stood up and looked around to see what was causing the smoke. But as he passed each room, he could not tell; then he looked through the window and saw the fields were on fire. "Ellisiot!" he shouted out to alert her, but he heard nothing.

He ran outside. The entire plantation of crops was on fire. "Ellisiot! Bayer! Crem!" he shouted again, looking desperately for his wife and children; but there was nothing – just the eerie silence of no one around and the roaring flames from the blaze of his life's work.

The city of Minta became quiet as peace was restored. A few hundred Golesh creatures had been captured after the battle, and herded into the main plaza at the centre of the city. They sat in columns on their knees with their hands behind their necks. All their weapons had been confiscated, and there were constant patrols by cavalry and foot soldiers. Archers wandered past them slowly with arrows already notched to their bows, surveying them, ready for any movement. To make sure they understood who was in charge, the bodies of their dead were piled up on the other side of the plaza; the pile soon became a very large one as a constant feed was collected from around the city. One or two officers suggested burning the corpses, but General Drorkon said no, warning that any more smoke could act as a beacon if any more creatures were about.

The lord of the city was found dead in his villa, where most of the garrison was also found, having suffered the same fate. The rest of the garrison was down to a few hundred from the thousands that had guarded the huge trading city. They were told to relax as the Camions took over – but they could not, with their homes destroyed, their loved ones missing and their city in disarray (not to mention Camions seemingly taking control); they began the big clean-up operation in the hope of finding their families.

The city walls were patrolled by the Three-Thirty-Third. Anything that could be salvaged was made use of. Barrels were found and filled with arrows or spears along the walls. The markets, and anything that could catch fire near the walls, were pulled down. Any weapons were collected for inspection. Very quickly, the city had been turned into Cam, with the protocols being followed. Every drill the Camion military had rehearsed for so long was being put into effect, and Drorkon, showing his serious side, became the self-appointed governor until the city was restored.

As Pausanias paced down the road, his arms covered in black blood and his longest Seax in his hand, he saw Andreas approaching, looking more than miserable. His hands were dug firmly into his pockets; he stared at the ground and kicked stones as if they were in his way.

"How you doing, little brother?" said Pausanias, a little puzzled by his behaviour.

"What do you think? Another battle and I didn't fire anything."

"What? Nothing?"

"No! I ... I ..." Andreas through his arms into the air as he admitted his humiliation. "I fell off my horse, or was thrown off would be more correct. I knew those things didn't like me..." although his words were not heard as Pausanias tried in vain not to laugh. "How many did you get?"

"Three."

"Liar."

"Your time will come, little brother." He said trying to hold back his giggling.

"You keep saying that. How long do I have to wait? Why do bad things happen to good soldiers?"

Just then, Drakator appeared; he approached Pausanias as if he had been looking for him. Pausanias produced a rag, wiped the blood from the sword and sheathed it. Then they both saluted their general. Drakator, however, didn't respond. He walked with purpose, and, standing to the side of Pausanias, he held his shoulder and pushed his other hand into the lower lumber of his back, making Pausanias stand up straight. He then stood back and gave a nod, and continued to walk down the street.

"What just happened?" said Pausanias, still in the same position as he tried to work out what he had just done.

"I think … I *think* …" Andreas said with deliberate intention, "he was telling you to keep your back straight during combat." A very smug grin appeared on his face, and Pausanias looked towards Drakator as he walked down the street, not feeling amused.

"That darn blue dot again!" Drorkon said to himself as he shook his head clear. Ever since he saw it in Undrea's eyes he couldn't let it go, almost like it was haunting him and he had to work it out. But he already knew what it was, he just didn't want to accept it. Fortunately, he was distracted upon seeing Captain Jadge sitting on a barrel and squeezing closed a wound on his leg as a battlefield surgeon tried, without much success, to stitch it, as he was constantly moving around, barking out orders.

Drorkon approached him. "Captain Jadge – report!"

Jadge paused, as the last time he had seen the general he had done something to him which had made him desert and forget a month of his life.

"Captain!" Drorkon said, firmly recognising his alarm and keen not to go over old ground.

"Sir!" Jadge saluted in the Camion manner, with a clenched fist to the heart and a straight hand to the side of his forehead. "We had reports of the city being under attack, Sir. We advanced from the west."

"Very good. Lucky too – this place has suffered a great loss, but it would have been far greater if it had not been for your actions."

"Thank you, Sir. What would you have of us now?"

"Well, firstly, I want you to sit down so that this surgeon can fix your wound." Jadge looked down at the surgeon as if he had just realised for the first time that he was there. "You have other officers who can take over for now. When the surgeon has finished and is happy for you to continue, then you can do more. Do you have any engineers in your regiment?"

"No, Sir – all soldiers," he said proudly.

Drorkon huffed as he looked around the men. "There must be some who know some skills in labouring and building, have word passed down for any men who have worked in the trade to come forward, we have work we need to do!"

"Yes, Sir. Can I ask how you have come to be so far away from Camia, though?"

"It is none of your concern, Captain. Until it is said otherwise, I am the senior officer of this city. Now, where is the unit? I need to speak with them all immediately."

"Buskull and the others have not yet been accounted for. I will send word to find them."

Drorkon showed him the palm of his hand. "No – I will find them. I need a walk anyway."

He left briskly, but thought it strange that he had said Buskull and the others – not Havovatch. But, after the battle, his mind was too distracted to read anything into it.

"Pssst!"

Feera heard. Looking behind him, he could see that a door was ajar, with Wrisscrass's face peering at him. As he approached, Wrisscrass pulled the door open further, allowing him to enter. Inside the room, Feera saw two unconscious Camion soldiers slumped against each other, and bent down to check that they were OK.

"Just sleeping," said Wrisscrass, as he peered out of a window, whilst staying in the shadows.

"What did you do to them?"

"Well, they would have killed me, so I knocked their heads together ... had to be patient and wait for you."

"We have gathered up your lot and put them in the plaza – I will take you there now!" said Feera, standing up and heading for the door.

"I'm not anything to do with these vile Catashes!" said Wrisscrass, with fierce resentment.

"I don't care – many people have died here because of them."

"Hello?! I helped save them. I took more down than your giant – he ran off somewhere, leaving me to fight 'em alone."

"How could you turn on your own kind?" said Feera, with disgust at his lack of respect for his kin.

"You do it! Look at the wars you have fought over the centuries. How many humans have *you* killed? And as I said, I'm not one of them!"

"Then what are you?"

"Something far worse," he said with a wicked grin.

Feera looked on incredulously.

"What do I have to do to prove myself to you humans?"

"Die!"

Wrisscrass knew he was not getting anywhere. He relaxed his arms; Feera stripped him of his weapons and tied his arms behind his back.

"Make sure you keep those safe! They're good tools," said Wrisscrass, looking at his arsenal collected in the corner of the room, which had now grown larger from the spoils of the corpses in the city. As he was escorted out of the door, he kept his eyes on them, hoping to see them again.

Drorkon passed through the streets, waving his hand tiredly at the many salutes he kept receiving from the Camion soldiers. He looked intently for the unit, stopping any officers to ask if they had seen them. But as he rounded one corner, he heard noises – shouting – and followed them. Rounding the bend, he came to a gathering of men standing around the rubble of what had once been a large house, with a petite young woman cradling a young girl, watching on as the soldiers cleared the debris. Drorkon cocked his head and walked over to the group, for he felt his presence was needed. Sergeant Metiya stood barking out orders; stripped of his armour and covered in soot, dust and sweat, he was at the centre of the group, orchestrating the incident. "Heave! One-two-three, Heave!" There were huge clouds of vapour steaming off the timbers as a chain of soldiers threw buckets onto the smouldering wood.

Then there was a shout, which made everyone stop. "I see something!" Metiya pushed his way through the mob as he assessed the findings. "It's him! Move quickly!" he bellowed.

Suddenly there was a commotion and the general rushed forward.

"The beam won't budge, Sergeant!"

As Drorkon pushed his way through the crowd, he looked down through the debris at Buskull, lying unconscious with a huge beam across his body. He was covered in soot and did not look like he once had done, the mighty warrior who could not be brought down – now he looked so … so human.

"Try again!" he shouted, discreetly rotating his wrist as he then whispered another word. There was a crunch as the beam snapped in half before the soldiers' eyes. At first they jumped, but then they carried on, thinking it had just broken under the stress of the weight.

The beam, which had now been pulled out, was in two parts, with Buskull lying on the floor, free to be picked up. It took several of the larger soldiers to lift him out – it was a huge struggle.

The soldiers parted out of the way with exhaustion as Buskull's body was laid down on the floor, his right arm severely burnt, with red, scorched muscle visible.

"He's still alive, Sergeant, but only just," said a surgeon who had rushed in.

Drorkon pushed his way through and stared down upon him. Quickly putting his hand on his forehead, he muttered some words and a green glow emanated between his hand and Buskull's head. Buskull's breathing resumed normally, although he was still unconscious; the soldiers looked at each other in disbelief.

"Sergeant, get him somewhere cool and tend to his arm."

"Yes, Sir." In his veteran and almost grandfatherly way, Metiya ordered the men to make a stretcher from the beams of the house that were still intact, but prove an adequate size for Buskull.

The woman who was holding the little girl approached Drorkon. "Excuse me?"

"Yes, little lady?" he said tiredly.

"I am a training physician. He saved my daughter. Please let me help him. There's a small apothecary just down the street – he can be looked after there."

"Very well – we can do with all the help we can find right now."

As the soldiers around him began to move, a glimmer of light reflected from the flames caught Drorkon's eye. Crouching down, he pulled out a burnt satchel. *It must have been Buskull's*, he thought. Picking it up, he was surprised at how heavy it was. It was so badly burnt that the embers were still eating away at the leather. As he held it up, a book fell out of one of the burning holes, then a bottle of what appeared to be wine. He hastily kicked out, just breaking the fall with his boot to stop it from smashing. But it was still heavy, and he could hear a metallic noise as two metal items clinked together. He undid the string at the top and pulled it open, and saw a captain's helmet, with its blue crest badly burnt, and a Kopis sword. He brushed the flakes of ash off and looked at it hard, wondering which captain it had belonged to.

That afternoon, General Drorkon left the apothecary, leaving Buskull to recover in the indoor shade. The kind woman he had met showed she was more skilled than she had let on, and used all the ointments required to heal Buskull's burns. Although he was still unconscious, Drorkon knew he was well cared for. He just hoped he would make it, for his loss would be a huge blow, with the coming conflict in mind; yet he relaxed in the knowledge that he didn't see him in the Phalism Link.

As Drorkon wandered around the west side of the city, he saw that the fires had now been brought under control, with human chains from the Three-Thirty-Third and Two-Twenty-Eighth passing buckets of water from the fountains dotted around the city to the buildings that had been set alight. Civilians who were found dead had white sheets laid over them as their bodies lined the streets, to assess how many were lost. The injured were sitting up in the shade and being tended to, yet looking on at the number of corpses nearby sent them into shock. The proficiency of the Camions in keeping working until everything was done shocked them too, for Camions were not liked in much of the world – they were known as savages – but to save a city and then carry on working to restore it showed the populace a different side of them. Here and there, though, there were still sneers and signs of resentment.

Drorkon ignored them and carried on, with his hands clasped behind his back. At every street corner, useful items were being piled up, ready to be taken to where they were needed – mainly piles of wood, pieces of equipment, food, buckets, weapons and scrap metal for melting down to be reused. But, in all the conflicts he had had to endure, he had never seen such savagery in a city. Usually he would fight out on the plains against another army or two, but as he continued his walk he was brought back to a time almost long since forgotten. A time when blood had trickled down the cobbled streets, a mixture of black and red … suddenly he was overcome with flashbacks. *Thick blood ran in tributaries, then rivers, so many dead, all ages and all sizes.* "How can anything do this?" said Drorkon solemnly as he watched on, wishing to die. Just as suddenly, he came back to reality after the repressed images had surfaced. After steadying himself on a wall for a moment, he quickly sneaked into an alley. Grabbing his flask, his hands shaking, he gulped down the contents, trying to gain control of himself. He took in a deep breath and looked into space for a moment. Before him was just the inner brickwork exposed from a damaged building, yet, again, images of terror were flashing before his eyes, terror from his past. Families fleeing hand in hand, men fighting in vain to save their loved ones. The sounds and smells were all there. Drorkon fell to the floor and clasped his hands over his ears. He didn't want war anymore, he couldn't take it, "too much blood," he sobbed out loud, "too much death!" Then, the small blue light appeared again, brighter than before. "No!" he said out loud, "it's too powerful!"

The images vanished and he came back to reality. Looking up he saw two woman staring at him incredulously. Dragging himself to his feet, he turned and, emerged through the other side of the alleyway. He carried on walking as if nothing untoward had happened. Grunting he cleared his throat and tried to act normal again although his hands were trembling somewhat. But he was glad for a distraction. Approaching him out of the smoke came Hilclop, carrying a girl in his arms.

"Recruit!" he addressed him, hastily, and ran towards him.

Hilclop gave a long stare, with his irritation clearly showing. He thought himself a soldier, not a recruit, but technically he was the latter. But he had learnt a few things in recent days, and one of them was to keep quiet.

"Who's this?"

"She alerted us to the attack. Buskull hid her. I stayed with her after alerting the Three-Thirty-Third."

Drorkon looked down at him with admiration. "Good man," he said respectfully. The beam of a smile that Hilclop shot him showed his gratitude, for he saw true respect in Drorkon's eyes, something he had never seen before this day.

But then they started upon hearing a cry from a soldier running towards them. He was from the town's garrison, and at first Hilclop and Drorkon braced themselves, thinking he was going to attack them. But he grabbed the girl from Hilclop's arms, laid her on the ground, and wept as he held her tightly. Realising that it was her father, Drorkon motioned for Hilclop to step to one side and let them have their moment.

Just then, Feera approached from around a corner, dusting his hands off as if he had just performed an unpleasant task. Patting Hilclop on the back with a smile, he was covered in black blood and soot, his tunic torn and several scratch marks and grazes on his arms and legs; there was one long, bloodied scratch along his right cheek which would definitely leave a scar.

"Gentlemen, I am very glad to see you both alive!" said Drorkon.

"As we are you, Sir. Please tell us, have you seen Buskull? I cannot find him anywhere."

"He has been injured, but is recovering. I will take you to him."

Drorkon turned to make his way as the two looked at each other to try to gauge each other's reactions – the thought of Buskull being injured did not seem possible. Just then, Drakator appeared. He gave a nod at Drorkon and stood with his hands on his hips.

"Before we go, where is Havovatch? I must speak with him urgently!"

"Erm ... Sir, I regret to inform you ... he's dead," said Feera remorsefully.

Drorkon looked at Feera for a long moment, the deep furrows of his eyebrows frowning as if what he had said just could not be true.

"Dead! How?" he shouted, forgetting himself at the shock of the news.

Feera did not know what to say, and stood with his mouth hanging open as he looked between Drorkon and Hilclop for the right words to use.

"WHAT'S HAPPENED, SOLDIER?!" Drorkon bellowed, stepping closer.

Feera, slightly taken aback by his sudden belligerence, tried to find the right words to explain. "We found the Xiphos, Sir, but they were not willing in accepting their oath. Their commander duelled with Havovatch, but he was far greater in skill ... well ... he died ... Sir." Seeing the general's face plastered with confusion, Feera pressed on. "We escaped and made contact with the Three-Thirty-Third. And now we're here; the unit appears to be just me and Hilclop now."

Drorkon's face filled with rage. With his hands by his sides, he clenched his fists so tightly he began to shake. He turned to Drakator.

"You know what to do!"

Drakator gave a nod and left, walking towards the west gate, the peaks of the Northern Mountains visible in the distance.

***

The soldier walked along the floor, ragged and tired. Like a drunk, he struggled to stand up as he pushed himself along the rough terrain of the woods. His eyes showed he had not slept in days, his uniform was worn and frayed, and his trousers were torn at the knees and stained with blood from the multiple times he had tripped and fallen over. Looming before him was the fort in the middle of Bysing Wood, with generals on guard all around it. They noticed his absent demeanour and allowed him to enter unchallenged; he walked like a ghost as if passing through a wall, the generals walking around him as if he were not there.

As the doors were opened for him, he entered partial darkness, just illuminated by candlelight, making his mind long for sleep. He walked down the long corridor, but propped himself against the wall for a moment – breathing, darkness clouding his eyes; this was it – he was about to sleep and went to fall to the floor. But a light appeared in front of him. Opening his crusty, heavy eyes he thought he had entered the world of Internal Light, but there was a voice. The voice kept speaking, but it was a murmur to him; then it became harsher, and he felt wet as something was thrown at him. The young man could taste something sweet, and, as he regained consciousness, he realised it was wine. Coming into full awareness of everything around him, he looked up at Queen Imara looking down, very unamused.

"Well! Are you just going to just stand there or are you going to do your duty?"

The young soldier took in a deep breath and hauled himself to his full height.

"Apologies, Ma'am."

Stepping into the warm and well-lit room, he blinked as he took in his surroundings. Queen Imara was slouched into a chair. Sitting to her right was King Fennel, perched with his hands on his lap, watching his Queen expectantly as if waiting for her to notice him.

"What news do you bring?" the Queen demanded, not looking up as she refilled her goblet, a bowl of grapes next to it. The soldier was so tired, he took in what she said but couldn't find the words he needed to answer her questions.

Imara sighed. "Do I have to claim *your* head as well?"

"No, my Queen."

"Then, what news do you bring?"

Suddenly, he saw a glimmer of recollection – a bronze helmet and black uniform. He was looking up at a cavalry scout, with one word coming from behind his the hole in the scout's faceguard.

"*Dead*, my Queen."

"All of them?" she said, aghast.

"Yes, my Queen – over three hundred."

"Ha! Serves them right for leaving their posts. Still, we're safe here – that's all that matters," she said nonchalantly.

"They just want to get home, my Queen. There is news that Cam has been overrun."

"Your duties are to me!" she said sharply.

"… yes, my Queen."

"Is there any news on the Birdmen?"

"Birdmen?"

Imara sighed, "You know, those dark, dishevelled vermin …"

"Knight Hawks?" Fennel said, nodding, with a smile.

"If I want your counsel I'll ask for it!" she said sharply. Fennel returned to his silent demeanour.

"They have all gone, my Queen. Commander Thiamos has also left."

"Ha! We're better off without him. I knew he couldn't stomach it. He was weak."

The officer stood swaying before her as she carried on sipping her wine and eating her grapes. Then she stopped and looked up at him. "Yes? Is there anything else?"

"No, well … yes, my Queen, may I please rest? I need to sleep."

"Yes, you can rest, once you have inspected all the men along the border of our trees," she said with delight.

"Yes, my Queen." The soldier staggered back outside, but as the door closed, Imara heard a body slump to the floor.

From afar, Fandorazz stood watching the fort, his frown growing deeper with each passing day. Anger pulsated through him. His entire fortune had been taken from him for "the good of the land", although, as he looked at the fort, he knew that it was all in there. But how long it would last him he did not know, for only last night a family camped next to him had been informed that the money for protecting them had run out, and they had been escorted to the outskirts of the forest. They were on their own once they'd left. It seemed that whatever money anyone had was taken from them, with Imara apparently just making up a figure of how much time they could afford to stay there, and one by one everyone was being banished. What he couldn't understand was why, for once the rich were gone there was no one left to protect – no one, that is, except Imara herself. And, looking at the empty tents dotting the area, he worried how many had perished.

Bored and returning to severe depression, Fandorazz fought to keep his sanity. Turning the small picture of his family between his fingers, he desperately tried to stay alert, wondering what he could do to help the situation. But any thought he had soon vanished as he came back to reality, realising he was only a feeble architect against big, strong soldiers. Despite the agony of not knowing what to do, there was also a nagging feeling at the back of his mind that the Defences were still unmanned, and, for all he knew, already under the new banner of the Black. He just hoped that Groga was OK and finding the Clup'ta.

"I need to get out of here," he said to himself, standing up and taking in a sharp breath of air. He turned and entered his small tent, so small that it held no furniture other than an uncomfortable bed. Stacked against the corner beam of the tent were the sword and helmet, which Captain Seer had given him. Having found a spit stone from another soldier, he worked hard on his sword each day, cleaning and sharpening it so that when he drew it there was a loud, clear ringing noise, a mark of due care. With none of his valuables in his possession, the sword and helmet were all he had, and he wanted to keep them well cared for. However, as he spent his days sharpening his sword, with each stroke he became a different man. He didn't know it, but he was starting to become a soldier, and started thinking like one as he disciplined his mind as to how he would wield his weapon.

Sighing deeply, he looked at the fort again: a symbol of tyranny, decisions made by the few to benefit themselves at the cost of so many … *No!* He couldn't cope with it any more. He knelt down by his bed, and, clasping his hands together, he closed his eyes.

My wife, my children … you're so beautiful. I miss you greatly, but now a time has come when I cannot be the man you once knew. I must now become a fighter … a warrior. Forgive me if I fail, forgive me if you don't want me to be this person, but I need to be. I need to find the Clup'ta; I need to help Groga; I need to fight for this land. I love you and hopefully soon, very soon, I will join you.

Opening his eyes, he expected to see a change in the air around him. But there was no change – everything was as it had been before – but he felt better inside. After placing his helmet on and tying his belt around his waist, he positioned his sword so he was comfortable with it by his left thigh. He had been practising drawing it, as he had recalled the memory of fighting the elf creature at the Defences, and the scabbard coming up as he pulled the blade out. Now, standing still, he braced his feet firmly; then he placed his left hand at the top of his scabbard and drew the blade, cleanly, crisply and with confidence. It was something he was now doing every time he put the belt on. He sheathed his blade again, stood by the entrance to the tent and looked out. He felt as though he was doing something wrong; he was scared and he was right to be, for if caught, who knew what torment he would be subjected to? But, looking around at the camp, he knew he had to do something. And so, he stepped out.

As soon as he took his first steps he felt different, like he was breaking the law and waiting to be caught. He wasn't really sure what to do, but thought that with his masquerade he could start with some reconnaissance of the fort.

As he walked through the camp, none of the few families seemed to regard him. They were all tucked away in their tents, hoping to stay out of sight, fearing that, if seen, that may be all that was needed to get them banished. Then again, it probably worked in Fandorazz's favour, for even though he resembled a soldier, he walked in too dignified a manner, his higher-class roots causing him to stride like an officer or even a king. There was an elegance about him, a dignity, something that someone with a huge amount of pride would hold, and it was all in his gait and the swinging of his arms. But if there were any soldiers watching, they could pick him out like a candle in a dark room.

Much of the forest had been cleared away, with the taller, chunkier trees left standing, as they would be too difficult to cut down. Large bushes were also dotted about. The ground had all the leaves swept away, leaving mud and patches of grass.

Fandorazz walked close to the trees, peering around them at the fort. As he did so, he felt that he could see through it, to its beams of support, how deep into the earth it was dug, and the thickness of the walls. He knew the design, it was a simple one. As he walked, he saw a large cluster of bushes to one side of the fort. The fort was quite small – he almost thought it to be irrelevant in its location, like an abandoned house in the middle of a wood where a witch would dwell. It was made up of three large cubes on the ground with one larger cube sitting on top joining them all together. It was made of wood, with just the one entrance at the front, and no windows; the walls looked thick and fortified. Pacing around above were archers, and his eyes narrowed as he looked at them, for he knew that they were not Camion. Wearing their own garb, they looked like commoners, but each one's face was covered by a rag. They watched everywhere carefully, and he had to pull his head back several times to make sure he wasn't seen.

He began walking again when he felt he had stayed there too long. He walked around to the front of the fort (this time a little further away), and ducked down behind a large bush. Seeing that there was room enough to crawl under it, he lay down and slid into the undergrowth. Making himself comfortable, he lay on his stomach and watched on, counting in his mind for the weaknesses of the fort, counting the time it took for the generals to conduct their patrols. Unfortunately, they conducted them at random, walking when they felt like it. But there were so many of them that there were plenty circling the fort. He started to wonder if he could burrow his way underneath over a few nights, but surveying the area around it showed that it would be impossible. The officers had erected a palisade all around the fort – he would be spotted before he could do anything. The only way in was through the front door.

"OK?" he said to himself. Now he knew how to get in, what would he do once he was in there? He could kill her, but the thought made him cringe, for he was not a murderer. Stroking the skin around his mouth, he sought to think of what to do.

Suddenly, he jumped as a voice broke his concentration.

"What the —"

Turning, he saw the glint from someone's armour. There, crouching down, was a man – slim, average height, the same as him – staring through the shrubbery at him.

"What are you doing, soldier? Get out, now!" the man bellowed, as he held down a branch to get a clear view of him.

Fandorazz started trembling as he crouched and looked up at the general.

"NOW!" he roared.

Fandorazz crawled along the bushes. Coming face to face, Fandorazz just stared at his eyes through the dark helmet. Then, two hands came forward, grabbing him by the scruff of his fine garment, and he was heaved out of the bush and made to stand in front of the general.

"Why the hell are you lying in there, soldier? Looking for something, were we?"

Fandorazz said nothing and just stared into his eyes. But the general became impatient and shook him.

"SPEAK!"

But Fandorazz could not. With his free hand, the general pulled the helmet from Fandorazz's head, revealing the architect.

"You! What are you doing here?" he said incredulously. He was caught off guard – he really didn't know why he was there, or why he was dressed like a soldier. But it was clear he knew all about Fandorazz, his life, his personality, everything.

Fandorazz looked around and saw that there was no one else in sight. In a moment of panic, as the general's guard was dropped and he was trying to figure out why a depressed architect lay in the bushes, Fandorazz grabbed his scabbard, wrapped his right hand around the hilt of his sword and forced the pommel up into the general's chin. The general released his grasp on him and staggered backwards, his helmet falling off. Worried about someone hearing, Fandorazz shot forward, pushing the general to the floor, and hit hard again with his pommel at the general's forehead, leaving a nasty round mark. The general's body jolted with the impact, but then he lay perfectly still, his eyes facing straight ahead as if caught under some spell. Then, a straw-coloured goo started to seep out from his ears and his breathing slowed right down.

Looking left and right, Fandorazz looked to see if they were alone; they were. "What have I done?" he said, bringing his clenched fists to his head and looking down at the general's motionless body. Panicking, he tried to lift him up, which proved difficult with the weight of his body doubled by his armour. Instead, Fandorazz dragged him to his tent by pulling him by his arms. He kept checking in every direction to make sure he was not seen. As soon as he got into the tent, he lay the general on the floor and yanked on the cord holding the tent flap down.

"What have I done?" he said again, looking at the general, his face stuck in a grimace after the knock. Fandorazz wasn't really sure of what to do next; he had committed a crime, and, like a criminal, he tried desperately to cover his tracks by making sure there were no gaps between the tent flaps so anyone walking by could not see in. Looking back down at the unconscious body, he threw his helmet onto the bed and ran his fingers through his hair, scratching his head, trying desperately to think of what he should do next.

"OK, tie up the body – yes, that seems to be the logical thing to do," he said out loud, trying to reassure himself.

He hauled the general onto his bed and placed a rag around his mouth, so that when he awoke he would not be able to speak. Then, with the string from his bootlaces, he tied the general's hands to the bed.

Fandorazz relaxed somewhat, but still panicked that someone would enter his tent. No one had acknowledged him since he had been there, but, because he had done this, paranoia set in and he worried that it would be just his luck that someone would enter at that moment. But something in the air changed. It was quiet, too quiet. Looking at the general, Fandorazz saw that he wasn't breathing any more. Bending down, Fandorazz wanted to touch him, but didn't. Several thoughts passed through his mind: did he have a family, kids? Shrinking down in the corner of the tent, Fandorazz wept; tensing his body, he wished so much that he had just stayed inside the tent – *Why did I go out? Why?* He started to hit himself on the head, before burying it in his arms and weeping.

The general emerged from the tent. With the armour adjusted slightly at the hips and shoulders to fit the new owner, it seemed to suit Fandorazz. With the fort in his sights he paced towards it. He came to the palisade; another general sat on a tree stump, pushing tobacco into a pipe. He noticed his presence and gave a nod, "'Ow are things, Zarim?"

Fandorazz just gave a bored shrug. The other general laughed and began to light his pipe.

So, that was his name? Zarim! The man he had killed now had a name, and that tore a deep, dark hole into his heart, for it started to become all the more real again.

But, carrying on with his masquerade, with one hand on the hilt of his sword and the other moving in time with his gait, Fandorazz pressed on towards the imposing, thick wooden, double doors of the fort, with the two guards standing outside opening them for him. He was still not sure what he was going to do, but, trying to discipline his mind, he worked on the here and now.

As Fandorazz entered the building, he came to a T junction. To his left was a wall lined with torches; to his right was darkness, as if it were the entrance to the Shadow World. Naturally, Fandorazz turned left and walked to the end. Rounding the corner, he saw a long corridor with a door at the end. Standing either side were two soldiers, dressed similarly to those pacing around on the roof. They both had a hostile aura about them, but he proceeded to walk towards them. But, as soon as he approached, the guards drew a dagger each and approached him. Fandorazz stopped fast and held the palms of his hands up.

"You know that no one is allowed in without just cause," said one of the guards.

"I have just cause," said Fandorazz hesitantly.

"I see," said the other, "and where is your paper signed by the others?"

Fandorazz realised that protocol was more stringent than he had predicted, and so withdrew, watching the men as he backed away. As he rounded the corner he went to walk back out of the door, but stopped as he looked down the dark corridor. He took in a breath. *What am I doing* here? He thought. But he knew that if he left, getting back in would not be easy. Taking his hand off of the door he stepped into the shadows, he felt his way along the walls as the light quickly faded behind him. It felt colder; the blackness was so dark he could not see his hand in front of his eyes. The walls felt damp – it was as if he were walking into another place altogether. He kept walking, until he felt something, something soft. He felt some sort of cloth and worked his hands around it, trying to figure out what it was.

"I'm going to charge you if you carry on," said a voice, making Fandorazz fall back.

There was a clink of metal and sparks flew in front of him. A torch ignited, and, sitting there on a stool, was Atken, looking very sorrowful.

"Oh, good. The company of a general – how quaint," he spat.

"What're you guarding?"

"Ha! What do you mean, what am I guarding? Surely you lot know – you stuck me here." Atken revealed a chain on his ankle, attached to the wall. "On pain of death, I must raise the alert to any issues. You're an issue – shall I shout?"

It was clear that there was no loyalty in him for the senior officers, and so Fandorazz removed his helmet.

"I have seen you, by the side of the King," said Fandorazz.

Atken looked at him incredulously. "You! You're that architect, the mad one."

"I am, I was, I —"

"Why are you wearing a general's uniform?"

"Opportunity."

"Well, what opportunity do you seek?"

"What lies behind this door?"

"More tales than we speak of now."

"Treasures?"

"No – all I have seen behind here are scrolls, thousands of them. When the King arrived, I was forced to sit here by that cut-throat ox in there, but just before they locked it, I saw the room full of scrolls."

"Can we get in?"

Atken smiled in positive response. "They may have locked it, but I have become bored in this abyss."

Atken lifted the handle, and the door swung open. He gave the torch to Fandorazz, and he entered.

"Take as long as you like, Architect, for I will turn away any unwanted ears out here."

Fandorazz gave a nod as Atken closed the door. Behind it, he could hear humming as he sang to himself.

Inside, the room was full of chests of varying sizes, some open with scrolls hanging out. They had been placed in a disorganised manner – just dumped there. As Fandorazz cleared a heavy chest off the table and it accidentally slammed onto the floor, there was a sudden thump on the door from Atken. Fandorazz knew he was making too much noise.

After lighting the candles on the table, Fandorazz started reading the scrolls, the words revealing the secrets within the chests.

Untold hours passed as Fandorazz read. Fortunately for him, there were several cases of wine stacked in the room, which he delighted himself with. He also passed a bottle through to Atken. The humming had stopped and Fandorazz was pretty sure he could hear snoring – yet learning the secrets of the scrolls proved thought-provoking. He removed his armour, and sat down comfortably with one leg slung over the other as he read the scrolls in the flickering candlelight. When he had finished, he organised them in a nomenclature system on the shelves.

Most of the scrolls appeared to be Silence Letters – favours made directly from Imara to those who needed something; in return, they pledged themselves to do whatever she required, with these declarations as her leverage. There didn't appear to be anything too horrific to read, most were small favours, such as making sure someone got a knighthood, or that their business would be promoted. But, as he made his way through the chests, the scrolls started to tell tales of woe, some which made Fandorazz gasp. In one, a Lord Y'tel pledged his family's fortune to assassinate his rival, who had taken his business. At the bottom, there was a big, red tick. There was something strange about the texture of the red mark, though, and as he sniffed it, he realised it was written in blood. It would suffice to say that this scroll created its own pile on the floor. But, as he read on, that pile started to grow bigger. As he kept reading, more and more horrors were discovered, some to people he knew, and he started to understand why he had never seen some of those people again, or why they had made strange decisions, which they had been forced to make under blackmail by Imara. She had used her influence and wealth to control the city.

It wasn't just from the rich, either. As he read on he found that people from the poorer slums were giving up their freedom in exchange for help. One woman had sold her life to Imara to do anything she was told, in order for her children to be sent to the far away trading port of Icelin for a better life. At the bottom, there was a red cross – again it smelt of blood.

The pile continued to rise as Fandorazz read on, anger building up within him. But as he went to pick up another scroll, something caught his eye. A slightly older scroll, just buried under a few others, poked out, with a name he found very familiar, slightly obscured. He pulled it out and read it:

Hembel, of the house of Parzarian

Fandorazz's lips firmed, for the last time he had seen him, Hembel had attacked him, shouting all sorts of nonsense about his family. He read through the scroll and saw several exchanges of money and favours between Hembel and Imara. Most seemed innocent – just a few favours for good fortune, or assistance with courses he wanted to go on. They were all for architecture, nineteen in total. As he read through, he found that all the courses were very highly acclaimed indeed; some would just have four or five students at a time, reaching far and wide across the known world. Fandorazz had attended a handful growing up, but he had been above all of them. He remembered, in most classes, taking the chalk from the teacher and showing them a better way of doing things, and so he was no longer allowed to attend. But he also remembered that his unpopularity had pretty much started there. But Hemble had kept going to them, as if he had failed each one.

As he put the scroll down, he thought back to how helpful Hemble had been after his family's death. He hadn't left his side, and a thought occurred to him, one he didn't want to believe.

Shaking his head clear, he continued to read. But as he read the details of the exchanges, his eyes went wide with horror and a dismay made his skin crawl He lowered the scroll and stared into space, as a new, stronger and determined man started to emerge from within him. He stared at the wall, which Imara must have been behind, wondering what she was doing; tears were running down his cheeks from his deep, frowning eyes, his hands shaking with fury. He started to breathe more heavily, his chest rising with his gasps as he tried to catch his breath, but his body was focused on something else. If it were not for his self-control, he would have screamed into the air. But, as he held the scroll, he read it again, just to be sure of what he had seen.

Placing the scroll down, he decided to be smart about the situation. He knew he was better than this, but if he had learnt anything recently, it was plotting and planning – this was what would get him his retribution. And so he turned the page over, picked up a quill, cut the top of his hand with his sword, and, dipping the tip of the quill into the wound, began writing away in his best handwriting on the parchment. As professionally as he could, he set about his retribution.

Chapter Eleven
The Mission

"Like this?" said Hilclop, holding his hand in the air with his fourth and fifth fingers bent down.

"Nearly," said Feera, sitting opposite, as he reached over and corrected him. You need to make it clear: if it's dark, you're far away, and they need to see what you're saying. Otherwise, think of what could happen if you gave the wrong message."

Hilclop's mind wondered about the possibilities.

"OK – now, let's put all that into one."

Sitting cross-legged, Hilclop frowned, took in a breath and then raised his hand. Keeping it flat and waving it horizontally from side to side twice, he then pointed it upwards, keeping his fingers together, showing the front to Feera. He turned and placed his index and middle fingers on his wrist, then clenched his fist and started hammering down with purpose, finishing by holding his hand high with his fourth and fifth fingers bent.

"Good! That was *really* good, Hilclop." Feera reached over and patted him on the shoulder. "Now, do it again and tell me what each one means."

Hilclop proceeded to do so. "Urm, flat land for one hundred yards, no cover, two sentries at the end, must be killed, use a distance weapon."

"Yep, and if I said to just knock them out, what would the fist do?"

Hilclop thought and held his fist in front of him. "Hold it horizontally out in front of myself and do not move it."

"Good," Feera beamed. "And if they were halfway between you and your destination, where would you put your fingers?"

"On my elbow."

"And if you had to sneak up on them and garrotte them, how many fingers would you show?"

"Just my thumb."

"Isn't it amazing how many words you can get into one hand gesture?"

"It would be simpler to do this than talk."

"Agreed."

They were both startled by the sound of shouting coming from inside the apothecary. There was no doubt as to who it was – Buskull's cries were so powerful that birds started flying away from all over the city. Feera jumped to his feet and ran inside as Hilclop stood watching the door, too fearful to enter. Moments later, though, the mother came running out and whispered into Hilclop's ear; he turned and ran to find General Drorkon.

The city of Minta was now back to full strength. With the walls lined with Camion soldiers and new gates made from the wood of wagons or derelict houses, the city was ready in case another attack came. Unfortunately, the count of the dead was still escalating, as it was found that over three-quarters of the populace had been killed or gone missing. Some had managed to flee in all directions outside the city, and had returned upon hearing word that the Golesh had been defeated. The city walls had also been fortified, with giant makeshift crossbows mounted along the battlements, and long spears tied to the parapet, facing diagonally downwards to fend off ladders. Any barrels were placed next to the parapet and filled with spears and arrows. The Three-Thirty-Third and the Two-Twenty-Eighth marched along the top, making it look like a stronghold within. However, Minta was big – so big that even if all the Camions were atop the battlements, there would still be large spaces between the men.

So, Drorkon came up with a cunning idea to double his force. He took the armour from the dead, filled it with straw and stuck them on a wooden cross in a sentry position, dotting them along the wall. He even ordered the Camions to stop and talk to them, which most found uncomfortable – they would laugh and joke with each other as they spoke to the distant figures. One or two, though, did take to it quite well and spoke of their sorrows to the "Strawmen".

The women and children were told to stay in the centre of the city so they could be better protected. Longhouses were cleared out, with lines of beds inside. Food stores were rationed, with sergeants outside taking stock of what was there. Work was also under way to restore any buildings that could be salvaged, but Drorkon did this mainly to try to win the favour of the civilians, as he sensed the hatred they had for them. The Golesh prisoners, now counted to be seven hundred and thirty-one, were either jailed or put to work labouring in the city they had destroyed. Surprisingly, they proved a strong workforce, but not an efficient one. Some had been shot by archers on watch as they tried to make an escape, but most behaved themselves. The Camions could not stop staring at them, though, completely perplexed by such a race of violent beasts they had never seen before – so hideous, so vile, it was almost as if they were locked in a dream with no escape. But there they were, before their eyes, as clear as day.

Drorkon had no idea what to do with them. He had thought about public executions, but this feeling was mainly based on retribution. But enough blood had been spilled as a result of them, and he didn't want the town to suffer any more.

He stood in the tallest tower at the centre of the city, staring out, his mind plagued with thoughts. The building was square, with long, open windows on each wall. He could see for leagues in the event of anything approaching. A bell below lay smashed through a house, having been cut down by the Golesh as the townspeople frantically rang for help. The main thoughts he had were of how Sarka had betrayed him, how his whole plot, that he had planned for so long, had come undone so easily. But, with no evidence, there was nothing he could have done to stop him. He wished he were tougher, though – he felt soft, letting Imara and Fennel get away with so many atrocities to the cost of the lower classes of Cam, leaving the Defences abandoned and going on the run. His plan had not succeeded, the opposite in fact, and he closed his eyes in regret.

As he looked down at the Golesh, slaving away at dismantling a house – with twice as many guards standing watch, their arrows already notched to the bows – he started to wonder where they had come from. With Ambenol in the east being attacked as well as Minta, they had to have come from the south. He gazed out in that direction, as an astonishing and frightening thought had just occurred to him. *They're going to attack from the west AND the east.* His face was aghast as the realisation came to him that there was no force that could stop them – unless the Knights of Ezazeruth would fulfil their oath, the world would surely be doomed.

But he dropped his guard as he stared south; he saw that blue glow again. This time it appeared in the distance: a blue line across the landscape, with strong rumbles of thunder echoing in the background.

"No," he said quietly to himself. But the blue glow grew bigger. "No!" he bellowed, as if saying it to the thunder. "It's too powerful!" The thunder died down and vanished and it had always done. Leaning against the window, Drorkon sighed heavily, but as he thought his options through, he realised that there were no other options – this was it.

Suddenly, there was a knock at the door.

"Yes?"

Plinth entered. "Messenger for you, Sir."

Before Drorkon could turn to accept him, Hilclop burst in, panting. "Buskull – he's, he's awake, Sir!" he huffed hurriedly.

"Awake?"

"Yes, Sir – and on his feet."

"On his feet?" Drorkon said again, not quite believing it.

"Yes, Sir – refusing to sit down."

"Very well. I had better go and speak with him, then." Drorkon collected his helmet from the table and made his way down the long tower.

He reached the physician's house quickly. As he went to enter, he saw Buskull staring distantly out of a window, his arms folded but his right arm bandaged from his wrist to his shoulder.

Feera and Hilclop stood near the entrance when Drorkon approached. Upon seeing him, Feera saluted.

"Has he said anything?"

"No, Sir. He just opened his eyes and leapt up, trying to beat his body, shouting to put out the flames. When we told him there were no flames he, well he —"

"Yes? He what?"

"He began to cry ... Sir, and now he's just staring out of the window."

Drorkon took in a deep breath before entering. The young lady who had been caring for him stood in the corner, frightened, for she did not know what to do. Drorkon kindly motioned for her to leave, and she scurried out of the door but stopped and hid in the corner, looking in, concerned. Drorkon had seen her expression before, she looked like she cared for Buskull but it wasn't as much as that. For Buskull had saved her daughter's life; she felt she owed him something.

"Buskull?" he said softly. He also felt the same fear, as though a wild animal was before him and he didn't know what it was going to do.

Buskull said nothing, but continued to stare out of the window.

"Buskull, is there something you need to tell me?" he said, recognising his distant and reflective gaze, for it matched his own in recent days. But Buskull still did not speak. Drorkon stepped closer and slowly reached out and put his hand on his arm. But Buskull did not react. Slowly, he pulled him around.

Buskull looked down upon him.

"Are you fit for duty, soldier?"

"I am, General." His voice was slightly croaky, but he maintained his dignified tone.

"Is there anything you need to tell me?"

"No General. I have had my moment, and I am the man you know me to be again."

"Good, because it has been three days and I have another assignment for you."

"Oh?"

"The creatures that attacked this city, I think they came from beyond the Rogan Defence Line. I need you to go there and find out what happened; see if the Ninsks have betrayed us."

Buskull breathed in deeply through his large nostrils. "I have been through a lot in my lifetime, General, and there is little that you can ask me that I won't do. However, if we go there and they *have* betrayed us, they will surely kill us on sight. I can't help but think, General, that there must be another reason for us to go there?"

Drorkon sighed and rubbed his face, still questioning whether he should speak his thoughts – not just speak them, he had to justify them. He turned, and closed the door and the shutters in the room, to make sure that no one else could hear their conversation. He even paced over and shut the door on the mother peering in.

"There is something I need you to get me," said Drorkon after taking in a breath, "but no one else apart from us must know of it."

"Very well."

"There is an artefact – something that will help change the tide of this war to come. We need it! But it lies beyond the Rogan Defence Line."

"What is it?"

"It's a blue crystal. It contains a power beyond reckoning, but for what I need it for, it may well unlock a power that will help us."

"Beriial?" Buskull asked.

Drorkon's face froze. "You know of it?"

"Aye, General. That stone is too powerful for any man to control. It's too dangerous."

"I know of its power, soldier, and I can handle it, but we need an edge in this war and that will give it to us. Your mission will be to seek it out and bring it to me."

Buskull shook his head. "Sir, that power is nothing but destructive. If you tried using it on an army, it would not just wipe them out, but any allies and civilians within leagues of that area."

"Buskull!" Drorkon interrupted. "Do not lecture me – just get the stone and return it to me! Those are your orders."

Buskull looked at him long and hard, torn between his morals and his duty. "Yes, Sir," he said dully. "How will I find it?"

"I'll give you a map." He turned and went to leave.

"So," said Buskull, "Beriial is beyond the Rogan Defence Line, all this time, with the very enemy that wants to destroy everything we hold dear?"

"Where better to keep something than right under their very noses?"

There was a moment's pause as Buskull took it in.

"General, there is something I need to tell you … about Havovatch."

Drorkon turned sharply. "Yes?"

"He was killed before my eyes. There was nothing I could do to save him."

Drorkon relaxed. "I believe you." He turned and went to leave again.

"No, General!" Buskull interrupted. "There is something else you need to know. When we made our escape, I looked upon his body, and he … well, he was not dead."

Drorkon's mouth opened slightly, and he frowned. Captivated by this new piece of information, he let go of the door handle and stood, arms folded.

"Explain!"

"His body was breathing ever so slightly, despite there being a huge wound to his chest that would have killed a man, and …" –Buskull put his hand on his forehead as if he was about to say something silly – "a white orb appeared above him and spoke to me in a language I know, which no one else knows upon this earth."

"What did it say?"

"'There is still hope; lead the unit and find the white rabbit.'"

Drorkon smiled, the first real smile he had in a long time.

"You know the message, Sir?"

"I'm do, Buskull, I do."

"What of Havovatch?"

"General Drakator is seeing to him."

Drorkon continued to smile, as a he remembered the name he had not been called in a long time.

"Sir?"

"Nothing, Buskull. But thank you, thank you for this piece of information."

"Yes, Sir."

"Come now!" he said clasping his hands together. "Leave everything else to me. Just concentrate on your mission. Get to the Misty Desert, retrieve the Beriial and get it back to me."

Buskull closed his eyes and inhaled.

"Buskull, not all power is for destruction. I would never do anything that could cost the lives of others."

"Yes, General."

"Very good. You don't have long Buskull, get back as soon as you can."

"Sir? It will takes days to get to the Rogan Defence Line, but I will push hard."

"Yes, I know, but we don't have long until the Knights pass from this world, don't you worry about getting there and back, just get the jewel!"

"You would still call upon the Knights? After what they did?!" he said with distaste.

"Oh yes – they are the guardians of this land, and now it has been defiled, it is their duty to protect it."

"Very well. When must we leave?"

"Now. I will get you there. Have your unit ready outside on the ridge to the south in an hour."

"Yes, Sir. Oh, Sir?"

"Yes?" said Drorkon, as he was about to leave again.

"We have picked up an acquaintance along our way."

"Good. Anyone I know?"

"I fear not. He is a creature of the Black, but claims to have forsaken them. We fought him at Haval and his army lost. Now, he wants to join forces."

"What name does he go by?" Drorkon said, frowning, as if he knew it.

"Wrisscrass."

He nodded gently. "Take him with you."

"But Sir, can he be trusted?"

"At this moment in time, yes, but if you ever have the need to kill him, do it!"

"Yes, Sir."

Drorkon left and Buskull paced around the room. Bending down, he went to pick up his axe lying on the bed, when he felt another presence staring at him. Turning, he met the young woman who had been looking after him starting through the partially open door. She stood there looking expectantly up at him. He felt she had seen enough of war, so he pulled the blanket over his axe.

"There are very few who can sneak upon me without my knowing," he said.

"Apologies."

He turned and held his hands in front of him.

"None required," he grinned. "Gratitude for your hospitality."

She walked forward and put her hands on his giant arm. If he had been any shorter she would have pressed her lips against his, but instead, she stared up into his eyes.

"Do you have to go?" she said innocently.

"I'm afraid so."

"But we need you. If they come again we will be destroyed."

"There will be people here to help, but I have to go. I'm afraid to say that there are people like me in this world, so that people like you may live, safe."

She still clung to his arm, yet her warmth and gentle touch didn't bother him – in fact it gave him a sense he vaguely remembered, and he didn't want it to end.

"I don't want you to go," she said softly.

"I saved your daughter, but that is no reason for you to feel that you owe me a life debt. Go, be at peace here, and find someone who's not dangerous, who's not broken, who cannot bring you to harm."

She squeezed her grip around him. "Please, I beg of you."

Buskull looked into her eyes and sensed truth. He wanted to lift up his giant hands and brush her hair away from her eyes, revealing her face, her thin nose, her innocent eyes. She was stunning to him. But the image of Ellisiot clouded his mind, and the image of her dead body. He brought his arms down and pushed her away. Bending down again, he pulled the blanket back and lifted his axe, then went to leave the room, as the woman sat on the bed, sobbing.

An hour had passed, and Buskull stood with a Manica covering the burn marks on his right arm, from his wrist all the way up to his shoulder. He stood thinking about the jewel, his mind deep in thought. But he was taken from this train of thought by the annoying sound of Hilclop scratching a spit stone along the edge of his new blade. Buskull sighed.

"What you thinking about?" said Hilclop.

But Buskull chose to ignore him.

Feera was pacing about; he felt stressed. Having not ridden a horse for so long, he felt frustrated always being on his feet. As for Wrisscrass, he stood proudly as he was reunited with his fangerlores, and grinned, knowing that he was getting his way – although Buskull's eyes narrowed as he watched him, wondering what his hidden agenda was. He had on him a new jerkin, it was hand made by himself and made from three smaller jerkins from the Golesh corpses within the city. Surprisingly, it looked neat and comfortable and showed a skill none would link to Wrisscrass.

As for Hilclop, he had raided the armoury in Minta, taking whatever he thought made him look good and ferocious as a warrior should (pictures of gods in his head, with his face pasted over theirs). With a pair of double-edged swords, shoulder pads and a large belt, he certainly had picked well. Then again, he still wore his green tunic, which made him look ridiculous, as he was supposed to be bare-skinned with the equipment he wore, although he didn't have the body for it. The only thing that made him look Camion was his bronze helmet.

He crouched down, chewing on a piece of grass as he sharpened his new swords with a spit stone, despite them already being sharp. He relished the new weapons and wished to maintain them, although he had dug one into the ground as he worked the other.

"He said to be here for now. So, where is he?" said Feera, getting frustrated.

"Still in the city?" Buskull said, sensing him.

"General Drorkon is not a man to be late!"

"We are where he wants us at the time he wants us to be at – that's all we need to know."

Suddenly, a light caught Buskull's eye. Looking into the city he noticed that the tallest tower in the centre had a bright light coming from within. Squinting, he looked on and noticed the light was in the shape of a cross (or a human with their arms outstretched). He flinched as the bright light passed out towards them like a sun beam through a cloud, and he raised his hand to cover his eyes, thinking he was about to be hit by the ray. His feet fell from under him, and his arms and legs flew around wildly as if he was falling. But, suddenly, the ground was under him again. When he opened his eyes, he was somewhere very different, and something was in his hand.

Chapter Twelve
The Shadow Warriors

Drorkon sat in the street, whetting his two short swords, the sound of metal ringing out. Two women walked past him and quickened their pace – clearly the screeching noise of a weapon was too painful to hear after the recent attack. Nevertheless, Drorkon carried on, oblivious to what was around him. He was grateful for the peace. His officers knew what they were doing, his men and the Three-Thirty-Third had secured the city, and there was nothing else that needed his attention – so he found the quietest street he could find and sat in peace, with just the company of his thoughts. As he rubbed the stone up the edge of the blade, his eyes followed it delicately, as he tried to rub away the dents and abrasions. His mind was lost in relaxation, so it was no surprise that he jumped as he heard someone shouting.

"General!" a young lieutenant of his bellowed, as he ran towards him. He looked exhausted as he was gasping for breath. Clearly he had run everywhere trying to find him.

"What is it?" he said, getting up and sheathing his blades.

"An army approaches..." as soon as he took in a breath he had to let it out and breathed in again. "...small, one rider with a group of dark-clad men following."

"Dark-clad men? Is there a banner?"

"No, Sir."

The corners of Drorkon's mouth curled into a smile.

"Then, let's welcome some guests."

"Sir?" said the lieutenant, puzzled.

Drorkon walked briskly towards where the scout directed him.

Standing directly behind the gates, with his hands behind his back and chin in the air, he gave a nod for them to be opened as he waited for the mysterious group to enter. The garrison looked down at him from the battlements, confused over allowing an unknown force into their haven. Yet, they did as instructed.

Soon, a tall, white steed trotted in, with a large, squarely built man atop with a thick, bushy, red beard and matted hair, looking ragged and tired. Behind him marched a dishevelled horde of men and women, stressed and fatigued. The red-haired man approached Drorkon and held the palm of his hand up to him in welcome.

"Greetings ... old friend."

Drorkon took the reins of the horse and gently started to stroke the side of its head, his ancient bond with horses meaning he could never stop himself touching one.

"It is good to see you, Thiamos."

"As it is to see you."

"How did you know we were here?"

Thiamos looked around, seeing if anyone was close enough to hear.

"We need to talk in private."

"Come, I know somewhere we can go."

Thiamos dismounted. Drorkon nodded at one of his men, who took the horse and led it away. It clearly needed a rest and something to drink.

"So ... do you believe me now?" Drorkon said sardonically.

Thiamos let out a long sigh of regret, his breathing still heavy from the long march. "I can think of nothing worse than betraying you, Dror. I should have known Sarka was up to something ... I'm sorry."

Drorkon waved a dismissive hand at him. "It's not important now. We do need to take control of this situation, though."

Thiamos removed his gauntlets and undid the top button of his tunic, allowing himself to breathe easier. "Imara has gone mad with power – she has titled herself *Queen*. She is even kicking out some of the rich folk in order to tighten her grip around her. Many soldiers have deserted, unhappy about serving under her."

"Do you know where they have gone?"

"Some have returned to Cam, but we have had no word from them in weeks, others ... well, let's just say we found a lot of evidence of them spread across the land, slayed by the Black. They're running free around this earth, and attacks are increasing."

"From the east?"

"No – we had a few skirmishes on the way here. They appear to be coming from the south-west."

Drorkon didn't tell him of his thoughts, but was glad that the mystery appeared to have been solved.

"So many men, coming to such a bitter end. They swore allegiance to our country, Thiamos. They swore allegiance to us! And we have failed them," Drorkon said, rubbing his face.

The two Camions continued to walk down the street, as it filled with people keen to get a glimpse of the newcomers.

Drorkon held his hand out, guiding Thiamos to a more secluded area, where houses were so badly burnt that it was too dangerous for anyone else to be. As they walked, though, Thiamos started removing his armour, passing it to a squire who hurried behind him, trying to hold it all.

"I have a plan, Thiamos – one I think you need to consider," Drorkon said once the squire had gone.

"Oh?"

"The Special Forces are under your control. They are the only part of the military Imara cannot touch. Small in number, they are highly effective in ability, and for that reason, I have a plan!"

"Well, I will hear your plan before I let you run free with *my* men."

As Drorkon approached a corner, he could see two Hawk helmets spying on them; he could not see their faces but knew they looked worried.

"Ermm … before I do, do you remember when you broke my chisel blade?"

"Ha!" Thiamos boomed. "How could I forget? I've never seen so much hatred in a man's eyes before." Thiamos stopped. "Wait – why would you bring this up?"

"Today, my friend, we're even."

Thiamos faced him; the smile vanished from his face, the furrows of his brow deepening.

"What have you done?!" he demanded harshly, knowing that it must be a great peril to him or someone.

Drorkon motioned for the two Hawks to come forward. As Thiamos looked up he saw a tall, broad Hawk being pushed into the street, much to the Hawk's delight. He disappeared back behind the wall and dragged a smaller Hawk with him, a set of quivers strapped to his back and thigh.

Thiamos pointed his long finger at them, sucking in a breath, his eyes wide. He knew exactly who they were, despite being unable to see their faces – he could tell by the mismatch of their armour or the weapons they held; he knew every Hawk under his command.

"Why are they not three hundred leagues east of here?" he boomed.

Drorkon put both hands up to try to calm him, knowing the fury that was about to erupt. "Undrea is fine – trust me on this! But we need every man we can get." The two Hawks stood before them with their heads bowed and hands behind their backs, as if Thiamos was their father and they were mere children who had been caught doing something very wrong indeed. "They left under my guidance – I will take the blame."

Thiamos ignored him. It didn't matter if he had put a spell upon them – there were no excuses for the Knight Hawks.

"I'll deal with you two later!" Thiamos roared like a lion.

"Yes, Sir," they said quietly, in unison.

Thiamos glared at Drorkon with enough anger to shatter a building.

"As I said, we're even," Drorkon shrugged.

Thiamos sighed and shook his head. Drorkon winked at the Hawks and ran to keep up, patting the smaller one on the shoulder as he did.

"What mission have you got for me, Dror?" said Thiamos with contempt, hoping that it would take his mind off what he had just revealed.

"Not here," he said, noticing that there were more people about than he'd hoped. The looks he received were not friendly, either; they appeared incredulous and untrusting. Camia was still a dirty word in much of the world, and despite having been saved by them, the townspeople looked on, worried that in doing so, the Camions were taking over their city. Drorkon, though, knew that this was not going to be the case. But they wouldn't believe him until they were gone.

As they came to a junction, a little girl, no older than six, stood holding a teddy rabbit and looking at the rubble of a house. A woman was behind her with her hand to her mouth, crying as her husband tried to calm her down.

Thiamos stopped and bent down, looking at the girl with sympathy. "What's your name, little dear?"

She didn't answer; she looked sad and just held her arms by her sides, with the rabbit's paw in her grasp.

Thiamos reached out and took it. Looking at the floppy creature, he smiled.

"What's his name?" he said, with a lightened tone.

"Meebo," she said softly.

"Meebo!" he repeated with a bigger smile. "What a lovely name! Did you name him yourself?"

The girl nodded and a slight smile appeared on her face.

"Well, Meebo is very lucky to have such a wonderful mummy." He handed her the rabbit back and she wrapped her arms around it tightly under her neck, feeling reassured by the strange, giant man before her. Suddenly, though, a shadow appeared over the girl, as her angry mother pulled her away.

"What do you want?" she demanded.

Thiamos stood up and towered over the woman. Although he did not want to come across as intimidating, he couldn't help it with his stature. His mouth hung open as he tried to explain that he was just comforting the sad girl.

"You know what? You've saved this city, but there is no need for you any more. Just go!" she shouted, before turning and pulling the young girl away. But the girl turned and waved, and Thiamos held up his hand to wave back, a small grin appearing behind his red beard.

Drorkon stood behind him as they watched the family disappear down the street.

"You know, Dror, we have fought in many wars, but we never let innocent people come to this," Thiamos said, maintaining his eye on where the family had gone.

"We are not dealing with normal creatures who feel, Commander. We're dealing with the scum of the Shadow World."

"What happened here?"

"The Black attacked this place in their thousands. I and the Three-Thirty-Third arrived just in time to save what was left."

Thiamos turned sharply and looked at him. "The Three-Thirty-Third?" he said, puzzled.

"Oh, yes. They were not wiped out – quite the opposite in fact. One of their scouts spread the word because Sarka was sending assassins after them."

"Well, I'm somewhat relieved to hear it – I have two nephews in the regiment," he said, looking around, trying to find them.

Drorkon put his hands on Thiamos's huge shoulders. "Come, my friend. We have much to discuss. You can find them later."

He followed, but Thiamos's gaze was still squarely fixed on the Three-Thirty-Third soldiers walking to and fro in the streets.

They stopped outside a tower in the middle of the city. "Operations is in here," Drorkon said, pointing the way in.

As they ascended the steps to the top, Thiamos noticed that every room had been turned into an operational base, with officers in each one with their own specific duties, messengers and soldiers constantly entering or leaving and giving information and intelligence. Drorkon took Thiamos up to the top floor – the highest point in the city. Entering through a door in the floor, they came into a square room. Inside were two scouts checking the landscape for any trouble.

"Gentlemen, please leave us."

They did so without question.

"Just like the Watch Tower of Pygros?" Thiamos laughed. Looking through the windows at the city below and the surrounding landscape, just in the distance he could see the faint black line of Pygros shooting into the air.

"Not as tall, though," said Drorkon, shutting the door to give them some privacy.

In the centre of the room was a large map with statues on it, although they were few. Thiamos delved into his pocket and produced a wooden crafted Hawk, and placed it next to a reared horse and a Camion warrior on the map.

"How we have fallen from our mighty pedestal in this world," Thiamos said, letting out a heavy sigh and leaning on the table.

"I know." There was not really much to say – what could he say?

"You have done well, but I guess I need to know, what is the plan?"

"First, *I need to know* of everything that has happened."

Thiamos crossed his arms and leant against the window sill, as the sun set behind, turning the land a beautiful golden colour in the summer's evening.

"Well – the King's entire armada was wiped out in one hit by some sort of … I don't know what … a giant, biblical, colossus type of … thing?"

"What are you on about?" said Drorkon, perplexed.

Thiamos held up his hands as if they were not his words. "I'm not too sure. The King is in shock and unable to talk about it. He has not spoken at all, but sits in the corner, looking into space. Atken, his personal butler, told me that the ships were approaching land after three weeks of sailing, but as they did so, a cloud emerged and thunder cascaded down, wiping out the fleet."

"Oh, no," said Drorkon, losing himself. "So many men, so many." Tears formed in his eyes at such a disaster.

"The King's ship was able to tack out at the last minute with a few others," continued Thiamos, "but they were pursued. Only the King's ship made it back, with the King and Atken."

"Did he say what colour the thunder was?"

Thiamos looked at him incredulously. "No?"

"Just curious." Drorkon clasped his hands over his face, trying to rub away the stress. "May the Grey Knight of the soul guide those brave men and women to the everlasting light."

"May it."

There was a chilling silence between the two officers after the revelation, as they mourned the tens of thousands of men and women who had perished on the voyage.

"Duchess Imara has isolated the King, with no visitors allowed, and I haven't seen Atken, either. I wanted to bring them with me before I left. She has completely taken over his affairs in Imara Forest." Thiamos said breaking the silence.

"*Imara Forest?*" Drorkon said sceptically.

"It has been renamed after her good self. Oh, and, unfortunately I have been remiss in bringing an invitation to her wedding to Lord Fennel."

"She is despicable, leaving the entire population of Cam defenceless, isolating the King—"

"Capital punishments," Thiamos interjected.

"For what?"

"For whatever she feels like – she has gone mad with power. All is under her control and those who do not accept are killed, quickly, to keep the others in line." Drorkon sighed again, rubbing his face even harder, trying desperately to understand what was in that woman's head. "She has employed mercenaries as well, to spy on the men. Anyone caught saying anything against her disappears. The Camion military will be very few soon. Unfortunately for them, they tried attacking two of my Hawks who were speaking their mind, much to their demise. After that I gathered my Hawks up and left, for we are not safe there."

"If only she were from another country, we could attack the forest and overthrow her."

Thiamos shook his head. "It would still be futile. She has more than sixty thousand men still under her command, from every section of the military. She has set up strong encampments within the forest, and getting to her would be an impossible task as she is secluded in her fort at the centre."

Drorkon turned and leant on the windowsill, looking out. As he peered down at the Golesh workers slaving in the town, an idea struck him.

"Maybe so, but we are Camions – we have infantry uniforms. Could we not try to infiltrate … *Imara Forest*, and assassinate her?"

"It would be a long shot. The outer perimeter is heavily defended, with copious bodies of men on watch. If we *did* get someone in, they would have to show papers for clearance at each level into the forest, and the closer they get to her the tighter and stricter the measures become. There are several layers you will need to penetrate, each guarded by a regiment, and they would need to change their clothing in each section."

Drorkon smiled as he saw the Hawk brothers looking up at them. They appeared anxious to get on with their punishment or be relieved. Thiamos followed his gaze, and raised his eyebrows.

"It appears your idea of letting them come with you may have paid off. Pausanias is perfect for the job."

"Want to bring him up and tell him?"

"Not yet. Let him sweat it out a little longer."

"What of his brother?"

"Andreas is young and naïve. Pausanias will be better off doing this alone."

"They seem a tight pair, though?"

"Indeed. You would have heard of their father, Herallis. A remarkable man. He was one of my Hawks – one of the best. No matter how many tasks you gave him, he always found the time to go and accomplish them. He even created his own self-defence system, which all Hawks use today, as well as designing the weapons we use. There was not one mission he did not succeed in." Thiamos smiled reflectively.

"What happened to him?" Drorkon could sense dread behind the positives of which Thiamos spoke.

"We don't know. One day he came to me in private and begged me to let him go on a personal mission. At the time, I had few Hawks available, but he twisted my arm and off he went. I saw him the day he left; he was dressed as a civilian, and took a set of broken-back Seax swords and a bow with two quivers."

"But that's what his sons have."

Thiamos nodded. "He told me he was going to the Death Marshes in the far north. I ordered him to tell me why, but at this point he was outside the city and refused. The last I saw of him, he was walking away. Four seasons passed and he hadn't returned. Now, this man has saved my life more times that I can remember. So, I personally led a mission with sixty Hawks and thirty support troops to the Death Marshes. When we got there, on the edge of the marshes, piled up neatly, were his weapons, with no sign of him."

"What do you think happened?"

"I honestly have no idea. The quivers were empty, the swords were battered and used: it was definitely a warning, but from whom, I do not know. We marched in for two miles but found nothing."

"Who dwells in the Death Marshes?"

"That is just as mysterious. All we know is that whoever enters never comes out. That's why we only went in for two miles – I couldn't risk all their lives."

"Why would he go there?" said Drorkon with his finger to his lips, thinking hard.

"I don't know, but his sons together are as good as him. For this mission, though, Pausanias is all we need."

"Fine. We need to take control of the Camion military, and taking Imara out is now our main objective. We still have friends within all those regiments."

"I am with you, but just so we are clear, we are talking about treason?"

"No! Treason is betraying this state. She did that as soon as she took hold of it. We are merely saving this country from her."

"Very well. What is your plan?"

"We get the remaining Golesh to attack *Imara Forest*," he said, rolling his eyes at the name. "Pausanias will be amongst them in disguise.

They will naturally be beaten, but it will give Pausanias a chance to undress during the battle and join the ranks. From there, his mission is to penetrate the levels and kill Imara."

Thiamos stroked his chin – it was simple. "Agreed. I will speak with him."

"Think it will work?"

"I don't like to think like that, Dror – let's just hope for the best. What of the rest of the Hawks?"

"How many do you have?"

"With me, four hundred and sixteen. But some are still spread out across Ezazeruth. A call has gone out. I sent hawk birds to find and warn them; they will now go to a neutral location and await further instructions. But the main body of my army is here."

"Good – they will be useful."

"In what?"

Drorkon held up a finger as if to stop him, so he could explain something else first.

"OK: before I tell you of my plan for them, I need to tell you about something else. Do you know who these Black are?"

"Well, all that has been found is that they are part of an ancient empire."

"More or less. They are ruled by a demon called Agorath. And I don't think he is coming here. I think – I hope – that will be his biggest blunder."

"Right ..." Thiamos looked at him incredulously. "How do you know this?"

"It's best you don't know, but the reason I know is in our favour."

Thiamos looked on, confused and slightly fearful.

"Do you remember Captain Havovatch?" said Drorkon, wanting to break the silence.

"Remember? How I could I forget? The young boy promoted to captain."

"Aye, he was sent on a secret mission by King Colomune to find three armies whose purpose was to protect the world from evil."

Thiamos's look of confusion doubled.

"Who? What army? I've never heard of them!"

"Few have. They're called the Knights of Ezazeruth, and are part of an ancient legend. Now, something happened to Havovatch, but

Buskull is now leading his unit to the Rogan Defence Line. I feel that we may have been betrayed by the Ninsks. I am certain that the creatures behind the mist have swept across our lands from the south."

"What makes you think this?"

"Where else could they have come from? No one knows what is beyond the mist – it *must* be these creatures. Now, this is my idea. I will persuade the Knights to sweep across Ezazeruth and fight the Black – they are more than a match for them, but we need to take out Agorath."

"How?"

"The Knight Hawks! They're strong and effective as a small force. We send them to the Black Lands, they find a way in and they take out Agorath. If they do that, this all ends."

Thiamos puffed his cheeks and breathed out. "Well, it could work, but what if they get destroyed by the same thing that destroyed the fleet?"

"One thing at a time, but this is our best shot. I'll send Drakator with them though, he may be able to help."

"OK, but how will killing him end all this? If what you say is true and he is not coming with them, then how will his death stop the army?"

"As I said, one thing at a time."

Thiamos rubbed his head. "There are a lot of 'what-if's, Dror! You mentioned this army, and the young Captain Havovatch going on some … mission? I don't recall that?"

"You won't – only a few were privy."

Thiamos grunted, unhappy that the commander of the Camion military had secrets hidden from him.

Drorkon leant against the window on the opposite side of the room, as the sun cast long shadows over them, and explained from the beginning to the present about Havovatch's mission.

***

Ferith sat on a wall, looking thoughtfully at the Knight Hawks before him. Some sat quietly by themselves, some slept and some talked quietly in groups, with the odd few playing juvenile pranks on each other, with everyone turning to join in a chorus of laughter. One of them, a tall, broad man, broke away with a bowl of soup and sat next to him. He was quiet and distant, with thoughts clearly plaguing his mind.

"Greetings," Ferith offered.

The soldier grunted.

"Impressive weaponry you have," he said, marvelling at the assortment of armaments on his person. But Ferith could tell the soldier did not want to talk, as he continued to ignore him. "Fine – I was just trying to be friendly." He went to leave.

"Sit!" said the soldier hoarsely.

"So, now you want to talk to me?" Ferith said, throwing up his arms.

"I don't mind strangers around me, but some things I hear all too often to keep answering."

Ferith conceded. "Ferith," he said, lending out a hand.

"Pausanias, of His Majesty's Shadow Ops." He said taking it in a firm grasp.

"Enjoy it?"

"Ha! Now, there is a question I haven't been asked."

Pausanias sat motionless for a moment, as if dissecting the question and trying to work out the answer.

"Yes, I suppose I do," he said eventually.

"So, what do you do?"

"Me personally? I am a rather unique soldier: I choose my own missions, go where I please, do as I want."

Ferith beamed with a smile, liking the idea of being part of a specialist unit and doing as he pleased. "I'd love to do that. Do you think I have a shot?"

"I doubt it," said Pausanias. "I've proven myself, to be allowed special dispensation."

The large Hawk kept looking up at someone; Ferith followed his gaze. He was staring at a younger Hawk as if he was making sure he was OK. The younger Hawk had a broad smile on his face as he chatted to the others, completely unaware of the larger Hawk's focus.

"A friend?"

"My brother."

"Oh, yes – he looks like you, but he has a bow, not as good with a sword, I guess," he said with a nudge and a smile.

"Yes, but look around – every one of us has different weapons."

Ferith took another look at the Hawks – he spoke true. Every one of them was different in some way.

"Each soldier has their own way of dressing and fighting. When we officially become a Hawk, we are all given the same uniform, and it is up to us to decide which parts of it we wish to wear."

"I see. So he has shoulder pads on, and he doesn't," he said, pointing a bit too obviously at the Hawks, who looked on disgruntled, wondering why they were being talked about.

"Yes – some prefer to wear leg guards, others don't; some wear guards down one arm, some wear guards on the top of one arm, some wear no armour altogether. It depends on how they feel comfortable in their role, but they all have to wear their helmets."

"OK – well, that's strange. I would have thought you would all wear the same."

"It is about making us feel comfortable. Did you ever hear the saying that *a comfortable soldier is a better soldier*? Now, take a look at their weapons."

Ferith saw that they also all had different weapons – not just swords, but different types of swords, staffs, spears, wooden spears, metal spears, spears with tooth spikes, maces on chains, maces on staffs, knives, axes, hammers, a whole multitude of weapons, some he had not even seen before.

"So, again it is what they feel comfortable fighting with?" he asked.

"Sort of, it's for that reason, but also because if you had a thousand men all fighting with swords, then you would have a thousand men fighting with the same weapon. Now, tell them that they can fight with whatever they want – then you have a diverse force, fighting against an enemy that has to keep changing its defence style to suit us."

"That's impressive."

"That's reflection after constant battles, and being able to better ourselves." Pausanias looked off into space for a moment, troubled by the person who'd made the Hawks what they are today.

"OK, but you have several weapons on you. So why don't you fight with one?"

"It depends on who I am fighting, the place I am fighting, what needs to be done, as, like I said, I'm unique."

"May I have a look?"

"No! A warrior never gives a weapon to someone he does not know."

"Apologies – I did not mean any offence."

"No need for apologies, for I have done far worse in my lifetime, for which I should be more apologetic than you should be for insulting me."

They continued to sit in silence, taking in the evening's events and the high-spirited camaraderie of the Knight Hawks before them.

"So, what exactly are the Knight Hawks? I know you said that you're a Shadow Ops, so does that mean you just go around in your regiment winning battles?"

"HA-HA!" Pausanias burst out. Some of the other Hawks had overheard what he said and joined in. Ferith looked around, uncomfortable with their mockery.

"No," he said, wiping away a tear of laughter. "This is the first time we have all been together outside of the city in years. We operate in groups of five, six or eight and go on specific missions. Some of us go out on our own or in twos. We infiltrate cities to sabotage events or foil plots, and gain reconnaissance on our enemies. We very rarely fight in battles – that is for the regiments, we are more proactive than that."

Hearing the special ways of the Knight Hawks put a warm feeling in Ferith's stomach. "Wow – that sounds brilliant. I'd love to become a Hawk!" he said; to him, they were the mighty warriors, the best in the world, like the heroes in tales he had heard when growing up.

Pausanias shook his head. "Sorry, chap. It's not for the faint-hearted. You have to undergo a gruelling test that will change you as a man. I can spot who will make a clear Hawk a mile away and I'm sorry … but it's not you."

Ferith withdrew feeling slightly insulted. He had explored a lot of the world alone and had already been through a lot. Now he was told he could not become something as interesting as a Knight Hawk!

"Don't take my insult to heart, stranger. You will rise up in whatever you want to do. But it won't be in the Knight Hawks."

"How do you know?" Ferith spat. "I lasted here during the battle!"

"Really?" said Pausanias as if he knew it was not true.

"Yes…?" Said Ferith cocking an eyebrow, wondering what he knew.

"I don't believe you."

Ferith laughed. "What, were you here? I cut down many before you lot came."

"I doubt that."

Ferith looked at him incredulously. "Do you know something I don't?"

"Firstly your voice is the biggest giveaway. Your tone is all over the place so I know you're lying. Also, the soil on your arms, legs and clothes is dark, like clay, that suggests you've been underground or hiding in the dirt. You have no cuts or abrasions on you at all, nor the blood of the creatures you've fought," as Pausanias spoke he pointed out the bits of Ferith he spoke of with his spoon, "if you were in battle you would be covered in it." Pausanias leant back revealing his blood stained uniform. "Also, your sword looks too clean to have been used recently. So, I'm guessing you sought shelter here. The town was then attacked, and you hid whilst it all went on?"

Ferith partly drew his sword and saw the gleaming silver. "Maybe I cleaned it?"

Pausanias shook his head. "Hardly. These beasts bleed black blood, it's so thick that it tinges the steel slightly. You'd have had to polish it for hours before you'd get it that shiny again." Ferith went to speak but Pausanias cut in before he could. "And don't tell me you had done because you would have said so by now!"

Ferith sat there feeling foolish, some of the hawks had turned and were standing there looking down at him with their arms folded. He felt like a man on stage being judged by everyone in the audience.

"Yeah! Well, I've done a lot in my life, more than you know! I have travelled the world, I have been in fights, I have been hunted and had to survive. I've even —" He stopped at realising a truth he was trying to ignore. He didn't realise it, but he was standing up and gripping his fist. Pausanias looked at him incredulously – he could sense that there was something more to what he was saying about his past, something he was trying to run from.

"Sit down," he said plainly, again gesturing with his spoon. Ferith did so. "That's all good – now go and join the infantry, but you're missing one important thing necessary to becoming a Hawk."

"What's that?" he said quietly, trying to calm himself after his outburst.

"Hate, for it's the only thing that will feed you!"

Ferith didn't like being told what he could and couldn't do, so he stood up straight and stormed off.

Pausanias watched him go, then leant back and relaxed. Closing his eyes he felt pressure relieve his spine as he enjoyed no interruptions. That was until a shadow passed over him as someone stood in front, blocking the light.

"Yes?" said Pausanias abruptly, not recognising the silhouette before him.

"Commander Thiamos and General Drorkon request your presence."

"About time," said Andreas, breaking away from his conversation.

"No, not you. Just Pausanias!" said Plinth.

Pausanias looked cautiously at Andreas, gave a nod, and followed Plinth through the city.

Pausanias joined General Drorkon and Commander Thiamos at the top of the tower. As he came through the door in the floor, Thiamos pulled a lever, closing it. Pausanias stood straight, putting on his best official posture, hoping to gain back the respect from his commander, although he couldn't remember a time when he had been more nervous.

"Pausanias, how are you?" Thiamos said, his manner friendly. But that just made things worse for him.

"Fine, Commander."

"Good. You know, I'm not happy with you," Thiamos said, as he started to pace around him with his arms folded. "Against my orders, MY orders," he barked, "you left a member of the royal family unguarded."

"Yes, Sir."

"This doesn't reflect well upon the Knight Hawks, nor yourself!" He continued to walk circles around him. Every time he spoke, he leant close to Pausanias's ears as he passed. "Now, what do you have to say for yourself?"

"Sir, I have, and will always hold my position as a Camion, a soldier and a Knight Hawk in the highest regard, but I do have my reasons – for the life of me I cannot explain what they are."

Thiamos pressed his face up against Pausanias's, pushing hard, and bellowed into his face. "Do not patronise me, Hawk! You broke your orders; you have put your brother's life on the line. And your excuse is that you cannot explain it? You're lucky that it is me standing before you and not the interrogators. You will be five hundred yards underground in the dark, as slippery, slimy scum question you by any means they see fit. Now, I will not ask you again. Explain yourself!"

Thiamos looked deep into his eyes, but, through the chastising, Pausanias had not flinched. He was too well trained, by Thiamos himself as well as his father.

"Sir, an apparition appeared, twice. It said to us that we must follow General Drorkon. The man said that Undrea would be OK, and he spoke a word about my father that only I, Andreas and my father know."

Thiamos's eyes went very wide, his mouth hanging open. "Oh, my gosh – he's gone mad."

"Hang on," said Drorkon, holding his index finger up to Thiamos and turning towards Pausanias. "This man, was he tall? Dressed in white? Thunderbolts echoing, hazy purple?"

Pausanias looked at Thiamos for permission to speak. He gave a nod.

"Yes, exactly like that."

Drorkon smiled. "OK," he said with a grin.

"What do you mean – *OK*?" Thiamos shouted despairingly at the two of them. "Can someone tell me what the hell is going on?!"

Drorkon kept smiling. "Again, I'll explain later. Right now we are short on time and we need to get moving."

Thiamos stood with his hands on his hips, then looked at Pausanias. "Fine, but when this is all over you have a lot to explain to me."

"That's a good sign," said Drorkon.

"What is?" Thiamos replied.

"You think this will all be over?"

Thiamos grunted and tucked in his tunic, which had come unstuffed. Turning back to Pausanias, he assumed the position of seniority he always had when giving out orders.

"We have a mission for you."

"Yes, Sir."

"You know what's going on – we need to take control of the Camion military. But as long as Imara is in charge, they will not disobey her. So, we need you to infiltrate Bysing Wood and assassinate her."

Pausanias knew it was treason – he knew King Colomune had appointed her in charge, but he looked on seriously. "When do you want me to leave?"

"Tomorrow. This is what we propose. You disguise yourself as one of the Golesh. We will lead them towards the forest, where they will be attacked. During the battle, take off your disguise and fight as an infantryman; then, when they return to the forest, you do so as well. Penetrate each level, find Imara and kill her! When you succeed, take command of the Camion military."

"With delight, Commander."

"Will you need any help?" said Drorkon.

"No – it's better for Hawks to work on their own on a mission such as this," assured Thiamos.

"All due respect, Commander, but my brother would be useful." Actually, Pausanias thought he would be more of a hindrance. But he wanted him nearby.

Thiamos sighed and rested his hand on his chin as he thought about it.

"He's a good Hawk in battle, but not infiltration."

"No, but I have my reasons. Please trust them."

Thiamos looked at him hard. "A lot is riding on this, Pausanias. He would be better placed elsewhere."

"Sir, I beg of you."

Thiamos looked at Drorkon, who shrugged. "You can never break the bond of love between two brothers."

Thiamos nodded.

"You must succeed in this mission, Pausanias. I cannot stress the importance enough."

"If I die, Sir, you may punish me by any means you see fit."

Thiamos eyeballed him. "Any questions?"

"I know my orders. Let me know when we are to leave."

"Thank you. Dismissed."

Pausanias did not salute; it was not their way. Being a small, specialist contingent, they were more of a family than a regiment. What Camion would salute their parent?

Once Pausanias had gone, Thiamos closed the door and assumed the same position as General Drorkon faced him.

"Dror, I have been thinking about your proposal for the Knight Hawks. How will we get to these Black Lands?"

"*You* won't."

"What?"

"Commander, you have much experience and invaluable skills in warfare. For that reason, you must stay put."

"But I am their commander."

"Then we create a position for your replacement."

"No!" he said, aghast, "I cannot. They're my sons and daughters – I cannot let them go to a distant land and fight and die!"

"You're an old man, but a great commander, Thiamos. We need to get rid of Imara and reinstate the Defences of Cam. When the Black arrive, that will be the first city they will attack. Your skills will be better suited to this purpose than fighting the Black on their home land."

Thiamos knew he was right. "But who will command them – Buskull?"

"No, I have someone else in mind ..."

Later, Drorkon left the tower with Havovatch's bronze helmet. It took some time, and a lot of asking the locals about what he was looking for, but soon he found it. After entering the building, with a hammer and anvil swaying on the sign above, he spoke to the owner.

Chapter Thirteen
The Mist

A strong wind blew past him and it was cold, bitterly cold and the air was thin. Buskull could sense they were high up, but he couldn't understand where. Dropping his hand after shielding his eyes from the flash, he realised that they were somewhere very different indeed, but where? He also looked at the object in his hand, and saw a thin leather pouch which looked worn and used, not to mention centuries old. He looked down at Feera, Hilclop and Wrisscrass, who were lying on the ground, exactly where they had been moments earlier. When they had landed, they obviously hadn't got their footing.

Buskull quickly pushed the leather pouch into his satchel, bent down to help them to their feet, and turned to survey his surroundings. After a moment, he came to the conclusion that they were at the top of what appeared to be a watch tower. They were on a circular platform with a small, hut-shaped building in the middle; there was very little else. But as he looked straight ahead, his heart suddenly jumped into his mouth, for he had not expected the staggering view that stretched out beyond the world before him. He could see snow-topped mountains at eye level, hills on the terrain appeared flat, he could see no roads or paths for he was so high up they would be indistinguishable.

Next to him, Feera, Hilclop and Wrisscrass stood, equally surprised. Under the extreme cold and battering winds, they hugged their cloaks about themselves.

The unit were not alone at the top of the strange tower either. Emerging from the hut came three strange creatures, which just walked straight out and stood at the edge of the balcony, playing with some contraption fixed to it. Buskull wasn't entirely sure what they were at first, for he could not recognise their armour. Standing seven feet tall, with black, shell-like armour and furry legs and arms, they were a strange sight. But as Buskull looked above the hut in the centre, he suddenly realised where they were. There was a flag, showing a brown desert spider on a beige background with a thick yellow line running across it. He then knew that the guards were Ninsks, the Human Spiders.

He went to speak to ask what they should do, but held back, for he did not want to startle them by just appearing mysteriously. Buskull knew that Ninsks weren't to be trusted, and certainly not to be sneaked up on; they could devour a creature with their bare talons in seconds should they wish to.

"Greetings," he said loudly over the noise of the deafening wind, bracing himself in case they reacted.

To his surprise, one of them turned, regarded them for a moment – but took a long look at Wrisscrass – then turned back again, not caring that they were there.

"Can I please speak to someone who is in charge?" Buskull inquired, although he didn't know why he was being so polite.

"He will be upss in a minutess," said another without turning. The Ninsks seemed to speak as if they knew the unit were there but were not at all concerned about it. The unit were taken aback by the strange meeting, and exchanged confused glances.

"Where are we," bellowed Feera, "and how did we get here? One minute we were in the green hills and now we are here. I don't like it!"

"If I am not mistaken," said Buskull, "this is the Watch Tower of Pygros. I know this is confusing, chaps, and I have as many questions as you do, but we are here now and there is nothing we can do at the moment."

Buskull then noticed that Hilclop had his back flat against the wall of the hut, as if he feared he was going to fall. "You OK, laddie?"

"I ... I ... I am, I just, I want to get down!"

"Find your feet, laddie. You will be fine."

Hilclop was hyperventilating, clearly shocked by the height they were at.

Soon, the door flung open from the hut in the centre, and a jittery, robed man stepped out.

"Buskull, I presume?" he said, with a very cheerful expression.

"Yes, I know our presence may come as a shock —"

"No, Buskull. General Drorkon informed me you were coming," he said, seeming rather relaxed. Again, the unit exchanged a look as to how that was possible. "If you have not already worked it out, you are at the top of Pygros, the watch tower keeping an eye on the south. And I am the commander of the Tall Tower, Commander Xat."

He shook each of their hands enthusiastically, although Hilclop did not take his eyes off the ground.

"I would have been up here sooner, but there are rather a lot of steps to climb, as you will soon find out. I let my Grones here know you were coming via our new talking system," he said, proudly showing them a funnel protruding from the wall with a smile, as if they should be astounded. They weren't, and stood waiting for him to explain what was going on. "Still, you are here now, so let's make our way down and I will brief you on the next stage of your mission."

Buskull looked at the others wondering why Xat was not shocked that they appeared at the top of the tower.

"You know of our mission?" Buskull said incredulously, keen to know how much and why.

"General Drorkon only told me to tell your good selves to head for the wall, where you'll meet my brother. Other than that, the rest of your mission is yours to know. To be honest, I have rather a lot on my mind anyway."

"Oh, such as?"

"Have you not heard?"

Buskull and the others exchanged glances and shook their heads.

"I think a drink is in order. Please follow me and I will explain all."

Xat walked back through the door into the small hut, which led to steps descending down a narrow, spiralling staircase. There were no bars to lean on, and just solid stone steps glimmering in the dim light cast on the walls by the torches.

"Fifteen hundred years this tower has kept watch of the murky south. I am the fourth generation of my kind to command it, ever since my ancestors carried out a coup against the dictatorial leader *Meza*."

Xat continued to give a long and detailed history of the tower as they descended, he spoke like a historian putting in some fun facts or quirky anecdotes. He kept laughing to himself but the unit weren't the least bit interested – they were more confused about how long they seemed to have been walking for. The further they went, the wider the stairs became. The passage they walked down started to straighten slightly as the tower became wider nearer the bottom.

Eventually, after what seemed a life time of walking and painful aches in their knees, they finally came to a large, rectangular hall, with large metal doors on both sides and a large table in the centre; it was like a feasting room but lacked … presence. For it was quiet, too quiet.

The room was dimly lit, with a huge chandelier hanging from the ceiling, with hundreds of candles all flickering dimly as they had nearly burnt through their wicks. Hilclop looked on incredulously, wondering how they had lit them all.

"This is the centre of the tower," Xat said cheerfully, Feera and Hilclop gasped and looked at each other, *the centre?* mouthed Hilclop, "big enough to put a few rooms in. We spend all of our time here, only ever going lower when we have to, for supplies, transfer and such. It has been eight months since I last left, though," Xat continued to explain, as if the unit were interested.

He walked towards a door at the far end of the hall, and went through it, with the unit following. They entered a room that spanned the width of the hall, but was only about fifteen feet long. It had a balcony with a view of the south. To one side of the room was Xat's bed, but it did not look as though it had been slept in for some time. To the other side was a desk, covered in scrolls and maps. As if there was something there he didn't want to see, he rushed forward, covering it with a blanket. He turned and smiled at the unit, but said nothing. Again acting as if he was hiding something, he threw his arms out in front of Wrisscrass, making him jump. Quickly picking up a random and very old bottle of wine, he gestured for the unit to leave.

"Arr, here we are – I have been saving this for such an occasion," he said, raising the dusty and cobweb-covered bottle.

He led the unit back into the hall, put five wooden goblets on the table, popped a cork and poured the fine red liquid into each one.

Each member of the unit took a goblet and stood waiting for him to toast.

"I got this when I was eighteen years old. It is a vintage that was itself eighteen years old when I was given it, corked on the day I came into this world. I felt that I would wait until I was thirty-six until I opened it. But there just never seemed to be the right time."

He had a slightly solemn look on his face; bringing up the past clearly disgruntled him.

"I am now sixty-three, and the one thing I have learnt is to not waste the good things, but use them when you've got them, and I wish I had drunk this a long time ago," he said, surveying the bottle as if it held the stories of his past. "To your mission, gentlemen."

He raised his goblet and toasted, as did the others.

"Please, gentlemen – sit!"

Pulling up a chair, they each made themselves comfortable, as Xat strolled around the hall, goblet in hand.

"There has been some frightful news from the east. As you may know, the entire armies of Ezazeruth have gone to fight another war, but at a cost. Unfortunately, *all* have perished. Some of them were my men."

"Sorry, but did you say that *all* the armies in Ezazeruth have … perished?" Buskull said, not truly believing it.

"That is correct, giant warrior." Buskull was so taken aback by the news, he didn't even realise the insult.

The unit could drink no more, for all they could taste was blood.

"I regret, gentlemen, that there are more pressing matters I have yet to inform you of. When the call came out, my Ninsks manning the Rogan Defence Line were cut down to a third, and we have been monitoring a lot of movement upon the horizon. If whatever is out there attacks, we do not have the force to stop them, and I fear that even more will meet their demise."

"What's out there?" asked Feera, now engrossed in his tale.

"We do not know, but a few weeks ago, a large force did attack and broke through. All we have been able to establish is the remains of two hundred of my Grones. Whatever got past us must be causing acts of devastation."

"I think I know," said Hilclop.

Buskull cut in, clearly wishing to tell the commander what happened rather than letting Hilclop do it in his sloppy way.

"Commander, a city to the north has been attacked, by at least ten thousand creatures we know to be called Golesh. They have been decimated, but at a cost. We thought they may have come from the south."

"My lords! Did many suffer?" said Xat, sitting himself down with his hand on his heart, though there was something about the way he did it which seemed rather theatrical.

"Yes, but the Golesh paid for it with their lives."

"Well, ten thousand is beyond what I thought would be possible, but there are far more down there. We have been seeing increased movement beyond the mist. Whatever is coming, will be coming very soon!"

The unit sat in silence at the news, knowing that something was coming and that nearly every soldier in Ezazeruth was dead. Talking and drinking was just not for them, apart from Wrisscrass, who had his head tilted back and the mug above it as he tried to get every drop out of it.

"So, how long have each of you been in the military?"

Buskull shook his head. "Sorry, Commander, but we are on a tight deadline – I must say that we need to move."

"As you wish," Xat said with a sigh. "Apologies, but walking up and down these wretched stairs wreaks havoc on my knees. I will wake my second up; he will lead you down."

"Thank you."

After finishing the bottle by himself, Xat sluggishly made his way to a door and knocked hard, the sound echoing around the room. He spoke harshly to someone inside, then the door closed.

"He will be out presently. When you get to the ground, head south towards the wall; there you will find my brother. Apologies – you must excuse me, gentlemen. I will take my leave. I need to write my notes for the day."

Xat staggered back drunkenly to his chambers and closed the door behind him, leaving the unit in the eerily silent room. Hilclop became curious and looked around, noticing the crude weapons and strange paintings on the wall. One showed a giant battle erupting as man and beast fought between two peaks; atop one was a large demon holding a staff with a red jewel, on the other was a man holding his sword in the air, thunder cascading down onto it. Despite it being a still picture, Hilclop thought he could see what happened, almost as if the picture came alive and the characters started moving. The dark creature with the red jewel shot bursts of magic at the army below, taking out the men and the beasts in one fell swoop as the battle erupted. Men were crying in the background as they fought, and the sky above started to circle around the battle, with lightning strikes flashing in the sky. Then, the man with the sword threw his weapon high into the air and all the lightning shot towards the sword. As if holding the lightning, the man threw his arm back and went to shoot it across the valley.

"Hilclop!" shouted Buskull again.

Hilclop steadied himself. He was sweating and trembling, as if he were there in the battle himself. Glancing back at the picture, everything was as it was, just a painting of one's imagination.

"Hilclop! You're either coming or staying!" Buskull boomed.

Steadily, Hilclop turned and saw the second. A tall and shady looking character, its face was hidden behind its helmet, yet Hilclop saw the glint of several eyes through the face guard. He couldn't see much of its body; it stood like a human, its armour attached to its chest and shoulders, and almost like a strongman with muscle definition, though instead it had black shells. It stood aloof, waiting for Hilclop's full attention.

"Rightss," it hissed, "shall wess? It'ss a long tripss down."

The creature turned, took a torch from the wall and headed through a large arch at the other end of the room leading down. With little light, it was just a black abyss illuminated by the second's torch. Wrisscrass, Feera and Buskull followed casually, although Hilclop took another quick glance back at the painting.

The descent certainly did seem endless, the constant stomping down on the steps started to affect their knees as well as they kept pressing down on the stone steps, which caused Feera and Hilclop to slow down. But as the unit got nearer to the bottom, the staircase grew wider – so wide, with the base of the watch tower being so big in diameter, they were almost walking straight.

"We're heress," groaned the second.

They walked into a large room shrouded in darkness, as the second followed the wall around until he got back to the staircase, lighting torches as he went. The light revealed a room with a pulley system hanging from the ceiling. Embedded in the wall to their right was a huge metal door, with studs covering its face and giant bolts holding its metal frame to the wall. It looked strong enough to hold demons from beyond the Shadow World.

"Give mess a hands, Giantss!" said the second.

Buskull showed his disgust, but in mind of the second not knowing of his insult, he said nothing. The second pulled a large bar away from the door. Then, with the second and Buskull grabbing its large handles, they braced themselves; pushing their feet into small grooves in the floor, they pulled. The door creaked – it needed oiling. But as it opened, a slit of light appeared around its edges and the room became brighter.

Hilclop sighed with relief. "Finally," he said, pacing forward. Looking out at the landscape before him, he went to step out. There was a shout as the second rushed forward, but it was too late – Hilclop fell.

Just grabbing him by his wrist, the second lay on his stomach with both arms out, Hilclop hanging on the other side of the door. Glancing down, eyes wide, Hilclop saw that he was still a hundred yards from the ground. Holding on desperately to the second's arms, Hilclop was still, for panic gripped him. They were both pulled up, though, as Buskull grabbed the second's foot and yanked them both back into the room.

"Stupid boyss!" it shouted between shaky puffs of air. "Did youss not knowss that there isss no staircase to da' groundss?"

Hilclop said nothing, just feeling inadequate that he had made a mistake … again, although, he couldn't remember the last time.

The second straightened himself up, and showed them how to get down. "We could either put youss in basketsss, or if you wishss, we canss loop thisss rope under your armsss and lower youss down, much easierss and quicker we foundss."

Buskull went first. The noose went under his armpits and he sat on the edge of the step looking outside, unfazed by the height.

"How heavy are youss?" the second shouted over his shoulder, as he stood next to a platform where the pulley system ended, hundreds of bricks loaded into the wall next to it.

"Seventy-two meras."

The second selected several large blocks from the wall and put them onto the platform. "OKss, ready when you aress, but when you get to da' groundss, don't take itss off straight awayss, give me momentss to take da' bricksss off. When itss slackensss, then let goss."

"Very well." Buskull then pushed himself off and immediately descended at a slow pace to the ground. When he got to the bottom he waited, and the strain from the rope loosened, so he took it off and it quickly went back up.

Sand was everywhere down below, with the tower next to him making him feel tiny, for it certainly asserted its dominance in the area. He couldn't even see the ends, for it curved around. As Buskull stood assessing it, he wondered how something so tall, that it took nearly a day to descend, could be built. Yet, there it was, before his eyes.

Soon Feera and Wrisscrass emerged and they stood looking up, waiting for Hilclop.

"He's taking a while," said Feera, squinting.

"Probably because of pulling himself off the step," said Wrisscrass, but, as hard as they looked, they still could not see him.

Suddenly appearing, Hilclop came down quite quickly, a lot quicker than the rest of them.

"Took your time?" Feera jeered.

"I ... I, was waiting until I felt OK to step off. I don't like that second!"

"Why?"

"He pushed me."

The rope went back up and they heard the clang of the metal door shutting above. The unit then looked around at the bleak desert. They were alone in a part of the world they did not know. There was just a constant abyss of sand and air, the three moons appearing as the light started to leave. The wind picked up, and, wrapping their cloaks around themselves, they made their way south towards the Rogan Defence Line.

The unit walked all night. It was cold; Feera and Hilclop had never been in the desert before and did not know that the temperature dropped so low at night. They walked staggered with their arms hugging their bodies, shivering as the wind cut into them. If they were attacked, their fate was decided, with their hands too numb to grip and their bodies too exhausted to run.

Buskull received scornful stares from them as he led the unit in just his vest, unaffected by the weather. Wrisscrass walked at the back of the unit; with his fur jerkin covering him he didn't seem bothered, but he was rarely bothered by anything – especially the weather

The others didn't realise it, but Buskull knew of their upset. He kept an eye on them, but he knew that he had to keep them moving, otherwise the cold would kill them – not the death they deserved.

Walking at his usual pace, Buskull relaxed. His senses told him there was no threat around them. He could sense a burden of what he would call suffering before them – a heavy burden, like being punched. But it was far enough away that he could lower his guard somewhat. Picking out the small object from his satchel, he undid the small string, which broke away in his hand, it was so delicate. He then pulled the fabric away, revealing a very thin piece of parchment with faint drawings on. From what he could see, it was a map, with a line of triangles at the bottom, then tributaries of rivers leading to a lake, with a glint at the end. Etched at the bottom was a small line, burnt into the paper. It looked fresh, and Buskull frowned as he felt warmth from the burning mark.

"What's that?" came Feera's voice from behind him. Buskull jumped, for he was so engrossed in the map he hadn't even sensed him coming.

"Nothing," he said, walking on towards a thin line of flickering lights in the distance.

Eventually they came to the Rogan Defence Line. The land sloped up to the tops of the battlements. At the bottom of the slopes were store houses and barracks dotted along the landscape. It was quite sparse and barren otherwise, with a building every league or so, but nothing between. It was a bleak, desolate place, far from the beauty they were used to in Camia. They wouldn't notice it yet, but the sand was not actually yellow – it was grey, as if made from ash.

Seeing a cluster of Ninsks on the wall, Buskull and Wrisscrass made their way towards them, whereas Hilclop and Feera saw a roaring fire – in what appeared to be a well, but made for burning instead of collecting water – at the bottom of the slopes. Showing the palms of their hands to the flames as close as they dared, they welcomed the warmth.

As Buskull walked up the steep slope leading to the battlements, he was amazed by the design of the wall, for it was not made of wood or stone, but looked as though it had once been an ocean that had frozen in place, leaving spiked waves shooting high up into the air, creating the wall with natural parapets. The other side was a sheer drop about fifty feet down, as the frozen wave surged up, creating the wall. The Ninsks turned to see Buskull coming and made ready with long spears.

From behind their helmets was a strange noise as their fangs twitched together frantically, as if warning him not to come closer.

"I am Buskull of the Camion military," he reassured, with his hands up to show no hostility.

They relaxed upon hearing his word. "Our commander isss further downss to the westss," one said plainly as they returned back to their huddle.

"Appreciation, brothers." But he barely received a grunt from them.

He turned and saw Feera and Hilclop warming themselves by the fire. Pinching his thumb and forefinger together and placing them in his mouth, he whistled them over, and, again cradling their bodies for warmth, they ran to him.

"It will be dawn soon, and this night will be behind us. Keep a strong mind and the cold will not affect you," Buskull tried to reassure them.

"That's easy for him to say!" Hilclop said sulkily as he followed.

They walked along the wall. The Ninsks had not expected to see them and kept going to guard, with Buskull having to explain himself every time. Because of the slow progress, Buskull became impatient and demanded that a young Ninsk – easily manipulated – should escort them the rest of the way, to its reluctance.

Following the Ninsk, the unit ended up walking for over an hour until they came to a rise in the fortification, with steps leading steeply to the top. At the top were two spiralling towers, but again they were definitely not man-made. The waves naturally shot higher into the air and spiralled around themselves, creating the towers. They had since been modified with wooden structures to make them more suitable for use in the modern era. As they approached, Buskull was astonished to see that there was a slope leading down into the mist on the other side, with no gate to defend it, and in the middle of the floor were what appeared to be faded footprints, like one would see in cement before it dried. But they were actually *foot* prints, not the soles of shoes or boots; whoever they belonged to had long big toes with narrow feet.

The escorting Ninsk spoke to another and left, giving Buskull a long stare as it passed, not happy that it had had to walk so far from its post.

"Wait heress. The commander hasss been expecting youss. I will summon himss," said the new Ninsk.

Soon a man came down. He looked almost exactly like Commander Xat, and had the same jittery pleasantness to him as well.

"Greetings, friends, greetings. How are we on this fine night? I am Commander Xot," he said cheerfully, grabbing each of their hands as if they were old and trusted friends – that was until he realised Wrisscrass was there and looked at him incredulously as if trying to work out why he was there. "Greetings," he said again, not taking his eye off him.

"How's it going, chum?" Wrisscrass responded by giving Xot a thump to the chest.

Xot stumbled back somewhat, with Hilclop unable to hold in his snigger.

"Xat has informed me all I need to know," he said, rubbing his chest. "Well, here we are, the slope into the mist. You can go now … or if you wish to stay around, we could maybe have a quick drink?"

"No!" Buskull said, more as a reaction than out of kindness, keen not to hear any more depressing stories, more for Feera's and Hilclop's sake than his own; their morale was already low due to the cold. "We have a strict deadline, but please tell me, we all know of the wall, but what exactly are you defending it against?"

"Well, that is something I wish I could tell you, for even I do not know. Long has this wall been here – we just serve to guard it."

"Have you fought anything on it?" stuttered Feera as his teeth chattered.

"Myself? No, but history has documented some incidents; unfortunately all the documents were burned during my ancestors' coup. We have not really seen who we are defending against, but we do hear them, though. Nothing has ever passed the wall from the land beyond!"

"We heard that an army did cross recently?"

"Oh, you did? Well my brother is one to gossip. Yes, that is the case. I just do not wish to tarnish the reputation of my garrison after all its hard work. Recently, in Sector Westman, further down, the line was overrun. All two hundred of my Ninsks were found dead – no bodies of the enemy, though."

"At least they died as soldiers. Few have had that chance recently," Buskull tried to reassure him.

"Yes, yes," Xot said, looking down; but then his face brightened up and he walked over to the top of the slope leading into the mist. "So, here you are. If you're leaving now, here it is," he said, gesturing down the slope with his hands.

"Just go into the mist?" questioned Hilclop. "Is there no other way?"

"Well … no. If you want to go into the mist then that is the only way."

"Could we sail around the wall?" asked Feera despondently.

"Noooo!" Xot shouted, as if he had just mentioned the forbidden. "The waters are poisonous. Nothing lives there. It will corrode the very vessel you are on before you can get to land. The sea around the entire coastline is cursed!"

"So, the mist is the only way?" asked Feera.

"Yes, although I fear it will be your demise."

"Really? Why is that?" enquired Buskull.

"Do you not know of the history of the wall?"

"We do not really learn history in our nation."

"Well, I shall tell you then." Xot put his hands into the sleeves of his robes to keep them warm, and leant against the wall. "Eleven men have gone into the mist." He cast his hand over eleven ropes hanging from the tower, all showing different signs of age – worn and tattered, but all of equal length.

"Each man walked down the slope with one of these ropes attached. As soon as they went into the mist, the rope went slack instantly. No noise was heard, nothing was seen – there was just the rope left."

Buskull examined the rope ends. "It looks as if they have been gnawed at?"

"Yes, that was our assumption too, but no one will venture down to find out. Some men have fallen in when they were drunk, or in the odd scrape or two, but, as I said, they were never heard of again."

Feera and Hilclop shared the same frightened expression, and suddenly wished to make friends with the cold, keen not to go into the mist.

"This wall is unusual," Hilclop said, trying to delay their fate.

"Is it? What walls are you used to?"

"Well, brick blocks put together."

"HA! They can fall apart. This wall is impenetrable," he said, thumping its side. "No rock, nor boulder, nor any substance known to man can break it."

"So, how did it get made, then?" said Hilclop, still hoping to prolong their time before entering the mist.

"Now that is a very interesting story," he said pointing at him, "it is not known how it came to be. Legend has it that a sorcerer stood on this spot" he said pointing to the faint footprints, "and cast a shadow to the south, forbidding a foul civilisation never to return, but a volcano erupted to stop him. The lava flowed quickly and furiously to fight him. But as the surge approached, he froze it in this state, leaving a perfect defence against the vermin behind it. With the heat of the lava extinguished, all that was left was a lot of steam which is present to this day."

Hilclop and Feera were engrossed in the story, so much so that they jumped when Xot suddenly burst into an uproar of laughter. "Ha ha! But that is only a folk tale – there are no such things as beasts and monsters in this world."

"So, what's a Ninsk, then?" said Hilclop.

Xot just stared at him with a sneer as if he were an uneducated idiot who didn't know how to count.

"So, let me get this straight," said Buskull, trying to get things back on track. "If we go into *that* mist, we will surely die?"

"Well, yes, but I do not question your objectives, I just do my duty and show you."

"Can I have a moment with my unit, please?"

"Of course. If you don't mind, I can see my brother signalling to me. If you require anything more, just ask – otherwise, there's the mist." Xot ran back up the stairs and the unit were left alone, huddled together out of the wind.

"What exactly are we supposed to find?" Wrisscrass asked, wondering whether it was worth it.

"General Drorkon wants us to see if there is proof that the creatures that attacked Minta crossed the Rogan Defence Line."

"We know they have – he's just confirmed it," said Hilclop.

"Yes, and no. We need to go into the mist and find out if the lands have been cleared."

"If we go into the mist, we will die. Even if we get past the mist, whatever is beyond that wall will kill us," put Feera, a bit more abruptly than he had meant to, but the cold had certainly put a dampener on his temper.

"There must be a way," Buskull said, stroking the corners of his mouth.

"Well, you must know something?" said Hilclop, rather sarcastically.

"Why must I be the one with all the answers?"

"No, I mean your axe – look at the patterns."

Buskull turned the axe onto its side and, to his surprise, the patterns showed the gap between the towers, and the slope with the mist. He stared, astonished. Holding it at an angle, he stood back and matched it to the scene before them.

"In all my years, I thought the pattern might mean something, but there is no mistake – it is what we see."

"Does it say anything?" Feera said as he squinted, trying to examine it.

"No – just pictures, and now I see it in a different light, there are others as well, familiar designs I cannot point out." Buskull showed a true expression of surprise, much to the astonishment of the unit.

"Right – so we know your axe may be a map of destiny, or are we are in one big coincidence? What do we do now?" said Wrisscrass with his hands behind his head as he stretched.

"What we were ordered to do. We go into the mist."

Buskull went to the edge of the slope and started descending. He stopped mere inches from the mist, staring at it intently, as if trying to work it out. It was a disturbing sight to him, to any man for that matter. The mist flowed deep and heavy like an ocean, as if dead souls mourning at the base were trying to climb up the slope. As he stood trying to examine it, it towered above him as if there were a shield stopping it from getting any closer. Staring at it instantly filled them with feelings of despair and fear.

"We must stick together," he said, not looking away. "Hold the back of my belt, and do not let go, whatever happens!"

Hilclop and Feera looked at each other, and with shaky hands they gripped onto the back of Buskull's belt, and were pulled into the mist, Buskull's body disappearing immediately.

Wrisscrass stood before it, laughing to himself. Putting his hand in, he touched the vapour. He knew what was in there – he felt them, and, smiling even more, he entered.

Above, Xot stood at the top of the tower, looking down grim-faced. Then he cast his eyes up to the mountains towering on the other side of the mist, and smiled.

Chapter Fourteen
The Long-Awaited Meet

Drorkon strolled into the tent with purpose, pushing the flaps apart, and looked upon Duruck for the first time in two thousand years.

Duruck was leaning on the balls of his fists on his desk, looking down. He was trying to control his heavy breathing as he snorted through his nostrils with contempt. Wrapped around his right arm, and just beneath his tunic at his neck, were bandages, as if he had been hurt. Drakator stood with his arms folded quietly on the other side of the tent.

"Hello, Father!" he spat, not looking up at him.

"You killed an innocent young man, Duruck!" Drorkon said plainly.

"You think so?"

"Did you?"

"I knew his death would bring you to me. You have been distant of late – some two thousand years!"

"And here I am!" Drorkon offered, with his arms open so Duruck could let out his grievances.

Duruck's knuckles cracked as he looked up at him. Two thousand years he had thought about their meeting, two thousand years of planning his retribution, and in that moment he saw him – his face, his height, his hair, the colour of his eyes, and the look of contempt as he stared at him, the latter being the only thing he could remember correctly about his father. Any strength he had to follow through with his plans quickly vanished.

"I knew you were alive – my sources told me – and it has taken so much not to come and find you, to kill you!" he said slowly, with more scorn in his eyes than Drorkon had ever seen.

Slowly, Duruck looked towards Drakator, who was standing on the other side of the tent his face obscured behind his helmet. He knew that all the time he was there he could not touch his father.

Drorkon took advantage of Duruck's fear of Drakator and walked around the desk confidently towards him. But Duruck, wanting to be nowhere near him, walked away around the other side of the table as if playing a pathetic childish game, and stood staring outside with his hands behind his back, rocking back and forth on the balls of his feet, trying to get back into his comfort zone – being a commander.

Drorkon casually sat down in his chair, crossed one leg over the other and stared up at him intently, trying his hardest to dominate the situation.

"So, a tent? When you have a city of bricks and mortar behind you?"

"It was the first thing we created for this city. I won't give it up!"

"You can hate me all you want, Duruck, but it will not change the past." Duruck let out a slight laugh. "What would you have done in my place? Afthadus threatened to kill your mother!"

Duruck turned sharply. "She would have rather *died* than put my men through what you did."

Drorkon jumped up, kicking the chair back, "YOU DID NOT KNOW WHAT SHE WANTED!"

Duruck went silent, his eyes wide. Bringing up the real memories of his mother that he had managed to suppress brought tears to his eyes. This is not how he had wanted to meet his father – he had wanted to meet him the same way he had met Havovatch.

"You were too busy in your career to notice, Duruck. She loved you, and she let you go off to become the soldier you are! The commander you are! And now look what you have turned into. Do you think she would have wanted to see this?"

"I have lived for over two thousand years!" he shouted sternly with conviction, with a wrapped fist of hatred and tears welling up in his eyes.

"As have I! I did not walk away from this. I have regenerated over and over again – had to re-learn skills I already knew, fit in with new generations, watch the world grow out of my control. I have had equal suffering to make sure that *your* legend is fulfilled!"

"I know you have been alive: I have been watching you!"

"Then why did you not seek me out?"

"And why did you not seek me out?"

"Because it wasn't time."

"Well … it cannot change what happened. You and your … mute minion," Duruck said, waving a mocking hand at Drakator, "have tried to create the course of the future in the present, and what have you achieved? Agorath is still coming, the ancient Golesh are rising up from the south, the armies of this world have been obliterated – this leaves us with a problem?"

"No!" Drorkon shouted. "This leaves us with the Knights of Ezazeruth!"

Drorkon paced over to a wrapped object hanging from the beams of the tent, picked it up and handed it to Duruck. "You have a destiny to fulfil", he said, "as do your men, and if you do not, in a couple of days your brethren, who swore an oath alongside you, will perish. If not for me, then do it for them, fulfil your oath, Duruck!"

Duruck just stared at the weapon, his jaw quivering with emotion. "I cannot change the past, but you can save the future."

Duruck's face did not change, but a slight tear ran down his cheek. For so long he had thought of seeing his father, and it had not gone the way he had wished.

"Do you know who called you Duruck?" Drorkon said calmly. "It was your mother. It is one of the oldest names in the world, and in all my time I have *never* come across anyone who shares it. You are unique – you are special, as are your abilities and your life."

"It means nothing," Duruck said, turning away to look at his city through the flaps of the tent.

"It means strength and honour, Commander."

Duruck turned to face him. "Yes, and where has your honour gone?" Duruck unfolded his arms and stood still for a moment, then stormed out of the tent, walking purposefully across the plaza.

He stood looking up at the statue of him – leaning on his sword as he looked up at the sky, his followers kneeling around him.

Drorkon followed him outside, his anger getting the better of him, his confidence still high with the presence of Drakator who trailed behind.

"You killed an innocent young man, Duruck! He did not deserve that! *He was a messenger!*"

"Do you really think he's dead?" Duruck turned and shouted.

By now, some of Duruck's knights had gathered to see what was going on and to support Duruck; but they all grew wary with Drakator's presence. It was as if they had heard rumours of him – they were visibly shaken by him.

"I did not kill him; he yet lives."

"How?" said Drorkon, still mindful of what Buskull had said but not understanding it.

Duruck nodded at his sword in his father's grasp.

"It's a Castion Sword, remember?"

Drorkon looked down with a face of dread. "This does not have the power to sustain a life, Duruck," he said in a way that suggested Duruck had overlooked something terrible.

Duruck's expression changed and he faced his father, concerned, as reality dawned on him about what he had actually done to Captain Havovatch.

"What do you mean?"

Duruck strode off to the tent Havovatch was kept in, with Drorkon keeping pace.

"What are you on about, Father?" Duruck demanded.

"The Castion Sword has many powers, yes! But it does not have the power to keep a soul!"

Duruck showed his concern and they both ran, keen to get to Havovatch.

They stepped into the tent and looked at Havovatch's lifeless body. They got closer, and Buskull had been right – his chest was rising ever so slightly as if he was breathing, but only just; his skin was pale, and they both felt a presence in the tent.

Drorkon looked down upon him as if he were a child, and stroked his hair. "I have met many soldiers in my time – old, brave, cowardly, stupid, all qualities of a soldier at some point in their career. But he was unique, to take on such challenges, such responsibility to do good, when at any moment he could have turned away … and he nearly succeeded."

Duruck looked up at his father in expectation and hoped that he could somehow put things right.

Drorkon eventually took his hand away and let out a sigh of relief. "You were wrong, Duruck. Your sword kept his body alive but not his soul. He would have been like Drakator!"

"What! What are you talking about?"

"The Castion Swords have many powers, some of greatness and others of devastation. However, the powers are not strong enough to sustain a soul – an oversight on your part. But today we have been blessed. There are forces beyond our understanding working for us … with us. And they have prevented Havovatch's soul from passing into the Shadow World."

Duruck looked up at him incredulously. "You expect me to believe that drivel?"

"And yet you're a two-thousand-year-old warrior."

That trumped Duruck.

"So, what now?"

"You killed him, you bring him back … now!" Drorkon said, pushing the sapphire-blue hilted sword into his chest.

Duruck looked down at it and swallowed hard, as if he had to admit he was wrong. He took it in his left hand, and, placing his other hand over Havovatch's chest, he closed his eyes and concentrated; and his sword began to vibrate and glow.

Formida âpron decil.

For a moment there was silence, but the atmosphere changed in the room. Duruck's eyes turned white and vacant, his head paled, with blue veins protruding. There was a physical presence in the room as everything around seemed to dissipate, white noise echoing loudly in the background, pulsating around them.

From outside the knights looked on as the tent became a beam of light piercing through the flaps, an echo roaring out that stopped them from venturing near.

Then, as if a shadow had appeared, a figure emerged and stood between Duruck and Drorkon. Only the outline of its being could be seen, burdened in heavy armour from head to toe, holding a large oval shield and a long spear that seemed to be on fire. But every part of it was grey, including the flames.

Duruck was in a trance and did not move. Drorkon was forced to the ground as he looked up, terrified.

"Grey Knight, please allow this power to proceed. Don't fight it," he begged.

But the Grey Knight's sword flared violently as if his anger had boiled over.

"Please, I beg of you!" shouted Drorkon, but the Grey Knight showed no remorse.

Drorkon could tell that the knight would not relent, but he heard the noise in the background, the noise of thunder. Grasping his sword, he pulled it from his scabbard and pointed it towards the other end of the tent.

"SATIE!" he hollered over the noise.

Then, a calm noise started to flood into the tent and the Grey Knight went into battle stance, bracing his feet and throwing his flaming spear over his shield towards the end of the tent where the noise was coming from. An apparition appeared on the other side, as if human: a man stood there, tall with a stubbly head, dressed in white but shrouded in a purple haze. And around him, as if joining him, came purple skeletons – but not human, far from human; their frames matched no known creature ever seen or heard of.

One by one, half a dozen or so of them stood around the white man, all looking at the Grey Knight.

"This will happen!" yelled the white man to the knight.

The Grey Knight's sword grew in its intensity, but as it did so the purple skeletons joined what could have been their hands, and their colour intensified.

"You cannot have him!" shouted the white man.

The Grey Knight shouted something, but it was not in a language anyone on earth would know, yet the intensity of his words showed his anger, and his power.

"YOU-WILL-NOT-HAVE-HIM!!!" shouted the white man again with clear conviction, as if he had no fear of the Grey Knight.

The Grey Knight seemed to shout as if he had no other options, yet his spear, now a blaze of grey fury, exploded.

"YOU-WILL-NOT-HAVE-HIM!!!!" shouted the white man again, his tone thundering authority at the Grey Knight.

All the while, Duruck was oblivious to what was happening and stood on the spot with his eyes closed, whilst Drorkon cowered in the corner, shielding his eyes from the wind roaring around him as the battle of spirits unfolded before his eyes.

The Grey Knight crouched lower as if to parry forward, but every movement he made was matched by the spirits. The light from the purple skeletons grew so bright that at that moment ... it stopped.

Drorkon blinked and looked around him at the still tent. Duruck was on the floor, unconscious; the spirits had gone.

Drorkon pulled himself over to Duruck as if wounded, but he wasn't – he was merely exhausted.

Assessing his son, he reached out and touched him. Although he was smiling, he burst into tears, having finally touched his son for the first time in so long – too long. Sobbing uncontrollably, he nuzzled his head next to Duruck's and took advantage of his son being unconscious so he could finally show his love, and only wished he would love him back.

A while had passed and Drorkon wiped the tears away. He knew Duruck would be fine, but his mind needed to rest after the spell he had performed.

He stood up and went over to Havovatch. His chest was moving normally now, his eyes were flickering and his body was working again. The wounds that Duruck had inflicted upon him had healed over, but his body still bore the scars from the duel.

Drorkon placed his hand on Havovatch's chest to feel it rising steadily, but then, to his amazement, Havovatch opened his eyes.

Drorkon stood back slightly.

"Havovatch … Captain?"

"We have work to do!"

Part Four

Chapter Fifteen
The Born General

Havovatch sat upright on the table, cradling his torso with one arm and looking at his hand as if it were a strange object. Drorkon stepped in with a cup of water.

"Drink this – it helps," he said, with a hint of experience.

Havovatch took the cup, but it fell from his grasp. Closing his eyes, he began to whimper.

Drorkon bent down and picked it up. As he cast his hand over it, it was refilled again, and he held it up to Havovatch's lips. "Death is a strange thing to recover from."

"Yes, it is," Havovatch said slowly, his voice croaky.

"Do you remember much?"

Havovatch frowned and looked at the floor, trying to summon the memories. "A little."

"That doesn't surprise me. Your memories stay in your mind, which is in your body, but your spirit will pick up some things."

Havovatch continued to sip from the cup.

"I keep thinking about … about…"

Drorkon closed his eyes and placed his hand on Havovatch's shoulder as he tried to gather his thoughts.

"A purple haze," Drorkon said.

"Yes. Is that what life is like beyond the living?"

"No – your body dies, but not your soul. As time goes on, you will remember more. But, at the moment, your soul is readjusting itself to the body, just like a broken sponge at the bottom of the ocean."

"This is not natural."

"No, it isn't."

Havovatch just continued to look into space.

"This is what happened," Drorkon continued. "There is a being in the afterlife, one you will come to know. He has been watching over you all your life for one reason … you're part of a prophecy, Havovatch – your destiny is already mapped out and he is there to make sure you fulfil it. We all are: myself, Undrea, Drakator. It was he who stopped the Grey Knight from taking your soul, and when Duruck tried to bring you back, the Grey Knight tried to stop him before your soul attached itself to your body; if he had done, you would have been lost forever."

"Who is this man?"

"Take another sip. I know you have many questions, Havovatch, and they will be answered in time, I promise, but for now you need to revive yourself. I need to know what happened after we last met."

Havovatch took another sip. His memory started to flood back with each gulp, along with emotions and every sense he had. Drorkon kept taking the mug and refilling it.

"How does water help?"

"Your mind is mostly water – hydrating you helps the body get what it needs."

They sat in silence for a moment as Havovatch sipped on his own.

"What happened after you left my camp, Havovatch?"

Havovatch, recalling the memories, explained in detail what they had been through – the battle at High Rocks, Hilclop's injuries, finding the Oistos, Mercury's death, on to Haval, the Busy City, the Ippikós and then their journey to the Xiphos. But when he came to his duel and subsequent death he froze, as lifeless as he had been minutes earlier.

Drorkon listened with keen interest, but did not interrupt.

"That, my boy, is one heck of an adventure."

"One I'd rather forget."

"The Camion way?"

Havovatch shot him a look.

"Do you recall what I said the night you dined with me? *Remember our past, so we don't make the same mistakes in our future.*"

Havovatch nodded and sipped again.

"It appears, General, you also have a lot to tell me?"

"Oh?"

"I spoke with Undrea. She explained a great deal, and you also left me in much doubt that you know the Knights of Ezazeruth, *personally!*"

Drorkon sighed and leant back in his chair to make himself comfortable.

"Very well. You want to know the truth? I shall tell you. I am a warlock. My real name is Tremgal. I was one of the most powerful in the world, and head of my order. But I was also a diplomat, warrior, healer; I had many qualities and only used my spells where needed. My speciality was in rare gemstones, but over time I have had to advance into new areas of expertise."

"Are there any more of you?"

"Few. There was a mighty war many moons ago, Havovatch, the second war we had to fight against Agorath. Most of my kin died trying to repel his magic, but … I was weak, I was one of the many fathers fighting in those wretched days. You see, warlocks do not pursue family life, but devote all their abilities to magic and the good of humanity – under strict rules, you understand."

"And what happened to you?"

"I was young," he said with a reflective smile, "and I was invigorated by the presence of a young woman – she was beautiful, funny and intelligent; she had long, brown hair that twisted down behind her back; she walked with such elegance and grace, with a charm no other woman could possess."

Havovatch instantly thought back to the first time he had met Undrea.

"Soon we were married, and then Duruck came along. One thing I noticed that everyone dismissed: he was born holding onto a blood clot in his fist … the sign of a true and ultimate warrior. I was proud. I did not care what anyone said, but looked forward to the fact that my son was going to be magnificent.

"I could not have asked for a better mother or son. But as he got older, we noticed he was vastly different to others his age. He commanded great respect from his peers, he won any fight he got tangled up in, and was a true leader to his friends. And as soon as he became of age, he enlisted into the military."

Drorkon, coming back to reality, had to stop for a moment to compose himself before carrying on. He looked down at Duruck who still lay motionless on the floor.

"Soon he was a soldier, then an officer. We seldom saw him, as he was always away fighting mighty battles and gaining valiant victories to his title. His name spread far and wide. Before you knew it, he had climbed the ranks quicker than anyone could have if they had paid the officers above them. But when that fateful day came where darkness marched upon this world, the last of the kings met and we marched on the Black. Duruck led part of the infantry – five thousand men under his command. You should have seen him, Havovatch: he was a marvel, so courageous and inspiring. Men, young and old, followed him wherever he went. But I was told to go with the other warlocks to fight Agorath ... but I could not – I promised my wife I would look after him, and many men unknown to me paid the ultimate price for that decision."

Havovatch sat staring intently at him, and could not help but think that Duruck was the soldier he wanted to become.

"I disguised myself as an infantryman and followed in the first rank behind Duruck. It wasn't difficult – so many men from all across the infantry sneaked into his regiment and it swelled to at least eight thousand, just so that they could say they fought alongside Ezazeruth's greatest warrior.

"As soon as we saw the Black march over the hill, their Black ranks like a poisoned tide upon the landscape, the gasps from our side were audible – they had a right to be shocked. Agorath had a huge army under his control, filled with beasts, monsters, creatures of indescribable vileness, and it struck every human that day to their core. But Duruck did not yield to their intimidation, and, seeing the moment when they dipped below a hill, he charged.

"Sprinting straight for the horde head-on, he ran as fast as he could, so that they would meet him as they marched up the hill, expecting to meet a stationary army that had been watching them from further away. It took a moment, a moment that seemed to take forever, but then the regiment charged after him. When he collided with the stunned Golesh, not expecting to meet him as they marched over the brow of the hill, he cut down many, as if he were an army by himself. I was always behind him, protecting him. Never had I spoken so many spells so quickly. Every arrow, spear, blade, everything that came his way, was deflected, and so many times he came near to injury or death, but I prevented it – I kept him alive and killed anything that tried to hurt my son!

"He was in his element, though, and, unfazed, he fought for the freedom of Ezazeruth. But my actions cost those on the east side of the battle, where I was supposed to be. The left flank fell and eventually the vanguard, where Duruck and I were, we became the left flank and we maintained it.

"We fought for well over a day. I had to keep conjuring charms to keep the men energised. The Black were constantly on the back foot and having to withdraw and regroup, but Duruck rarely rested and kept chasing them, barking orders, asking for reinforcements – oh, he really was in his element. Sometimes he was fighting the battle on his own, but I stayed close.

"Soon the creatures gave up and retreated as one across the Merton Plains, leaving no defences, no rearguard. Duruck seized the moment and charged the last of his exhausted army. We hunted them day and night, killing many in our wake, all the way to the shore you know as the Defences. I was experiencing an exhaustion I never learnt to know again, fatigue preying on my very survival. But I kept having to spell myself, Duruck and others around me with energy bursts in order to keep us alive and alert.

"And then we met him. Agorath! The cause of so much death and destruction. I did not know what to expect. He was … an abomination, twice as tall as a man, his legs thin as bone, his torso wide as a tree trunk. His arms were bare with silvery scales, and on his head he wore a large, dark helmet with two red dots deep inside the eyeholes – he was terrifying, but not to Duruck.

"Duruck scratched a spit stone across his blade to get one last use out of it, then he charged.

"Agorath used his staff with a red jewel-crested top, and shot a beam out, taking hold of Duruck, elevating him into the air paralysed, and trying to part his sword from his grip; but Duruck did not let go. I shot a beam back, and used every gem and spell I knew.

"Agorath could not use his magic and resorted to a blade at the bottom of his staff.

"Powerfully, he struck at my son, but I was using all my power to stop him from using his.

"Duruck's skill, however, showed through: ducking, diving and almost dancing, he played away from Agorath's weapon and cut him, again and again."

The description made Havovatch uncomfortable, as he thought back to his own death at the hands of Duruck. But Drorkon carried on, unaware of his discomfort.

"Eventually, Agorath conceded – he just could not muster the strength to fight Duruck, and with the hills lining with reinforcements, he was pulled away by his minions.

"Duruck did not fall to his knees; he did not sigh in relief. Instead, he lifted his chin, looked at the man nearest to him, and shouted at him to clear the mess up."

Drorkon smiled reflectively.

"Did he know it was you who was there?" asked Havovatch, engrossed in the story.

"He said little about the battle afterwards, but I don't think he knew I was there. But it was necessary, for he would not have done what he did without me."

"And then he joined the Knights of Ezazeruth?"

"Yes. His army was the most disciplined I had never seen: strong, mighty. They would never run, they would never surrender, and he trained them every day to be as good as he was – training with them, teaching them all he knew. He commanded more respect from them than any leader I have known. Then one day, a ruthless and brainless king came to me and told me to curse them never to die. I said no, of course. So he had a guard point a crossbow bolt at my wife; I had to accept.

"He then took her away, saying that if I lifted the curse she would be killed. I begged for him to keep her alive and he said that she would be … but I never found out what happened to her."

"So you cursed them?"

"It took but a moment. I had three gems left for the job, green and sparkly. I rammed each one into the end of my staff, went to each of the barracks, and cursed them. The worst thing was they did not even know what had happened until, one day, a young boy named Fredra had just joined the Xiphos; he forgot to duck, and his trainer hit him around the head with his sword, but he did not die, and I sat there watching the chaos unfold, as men realised their own mortality and that nothing could stop them from being killed.

"Afthadus told them what he had done. Duruck went through the motions: shock, horror, anger, disbelief. Then he found out it was I who had done it." The corners of Drorkon's lips dipped; he closed his eyes and sighed as he brought back the memory. "He came to me to ask me if it was true, to look me in the eye, but I did not answer. That was the last day I saw him."

"Why did you not lift the curse when Afthadus died?"

"I would have, but the curse was irreversible without another of the green, sparkly stones – they are rare, very rare indeed."

"If you find them, though, could you remove the curse?"

Drorkon said nothing.

"Sir?"

Drorkon still refused to speak.

"Because, if you remove it, there will be no army to protect this world," said Havovatch, figuring it out.

"I have seen this world. It hasn't grown. Sure, technology has helped us, but man is still the same! Look around, Havovatch – Agorath is now coming, you have seen what he can do. The Knights of Ezazeruth are the world's only salvation!"

Havovatch chewed his lip. "It is not for me to decide if what you have done is wrong or right – I just needed to know."

"Very well."

There was a tense silence between them after that.

"Hang on … how have you lived this long if there are no more of these … green gems?"

Drorkon sighed, stroked his face and spoke very quickly and matter-of-factly. "I have done a regeneration charm. Simple enough – my mind stays as it is, but my body becomes young again. I go to a cave in the Hadicul Mountains, locked in and surrounded by jugs of water. I'm trapped until I remember how to get out and begin my life again as a young, strong man. Now! We have more pressing matters we need to attend to," he said, clasping his hands together.

"And you have been with the Camion military all this time?" Havovatch said, sceptically.

"Yes, regrettably. I have had to, to make sure that when the prophecy comes about, we're ready."

"You keep talking about this prophecy – what is it?"

"It's a little complicated, Havovatch. Maybe that's a story for another time. As I keep saying, we need to move."

"Fine. I need to get back to my regiment. We need to prepare for the Black," he said, getting up, but wincing as his body ached.

Drorkon was about to walk out, but instead sucked in a breath. "I'm afraid to say that your regiment of the Three-Thirty-Third is no long under your command."

Havovatch looked aghast. "What?" he pleaded.

"You died, Havovatch, therefore the next in command automatically takes charge."

"So, what am I now? Just a mere soldier again?" he said despairingly.

"Oh, no, dear boy – you're far more than that."

"What do you mean?"

Drorkon beamed with a smile. "It's time for your next mission, Havovatch. You must now leave the soldier you were behind, and become someone very different." Havovatch looked at him dubiously. "Come, I will explain. There's someone I think you would like to meet."

Havovatch slumped down off the table. Drorkon held the tent flap open for him to step through, although he did so slightly sluggishly, his body still reviving.

Still on the floor, Duruck lay as he did, his eyes open. He heard every word.

"Oh, and Undrea sends her regards." Said Drorkon as they went to leave the tent.

Havovatch stopped and looked at him.

"Is she OK?"

"She said she lost contact with you? She spoke with a creature and then, well, that was it."

Havovatch shook his head. "I lost her handkerchief. She said it was her mother's."

"She's fine. She was more concerned about you."

Havovatch nodded. All he could remember before he had died was her, and he smiled – he liked the fact that she was thinking of him. And he couldn't wait to get back to her.

As they stepped outside into the dim light, Havovatch almost walked into the back of Drakator, who stood facing out with his arms folded and wearing just his helmet, a black rag around his waist and a large belt. No one dared come near. But as Havovatch looked around, he saw that the world around him was quiet, very quiet. There were no guards in sight; some women and children were walking about, but they looked sorrowful.

"What's happened?" said Havovatch.

"The Xiphos have gone to Shila," said Drorkon, following his gaze. "They have but a few days to get there, or they will have forsaken their kin."

"Will they make it?"

Drorkon shrugged. "I'm sure they will." But his face showed his concern.

Havovatch stood staring at the swaying blues before him as the portal made a strange, atmospheric noise, a noise he couldn't describe. The experience froze him with fear.

Drorkon rubbed his face. "For the seventh time, it will not hurt you. Just step through!"

"How do you know?" Havovatch said sharply, not taking his eyes off it.

"I just do. Now walk through it!"

Havovatch continued to stare.

"Imagine looking at a lake. If you jump into the water, you're still fine. This is the same thing."

"Not if you drown!"

"Look – sometimes you have to do things that you don't want to do. Just trust me!"

Swallowing, Havovatch took a step forward into the swirling mass. He closed his eyes, then felt a sudden shunt from behind as he was pushed through the vortex.

He suddenly felt very cold, with strong winds battering him from every angle. He opened his eyes and had to steady himself as he saw the world before him, as he stood at the summit of the Northern Mountains.

"Wonderful, isn't it?" Drorkon shouted over the blustery weather.

"Huh?"

"It amazes me, when you see the world like this, how can there be suffering and war?" he smiled as he gazed out at the vast landscape before them.

"Yeah!" Havovatch shouted back, although he could not really hear what he was saying.

Drorkon held out an open hand, inviting Havovatch to follow a path downwards by the side of the cliff. As he descended, Havovatch started to recollect the trail.

"There's a cave just to your right," Drorkon shouted behind him.

Havovatch jumped down and saw it – a large crack in the mountainside. Quickly, he entered, keen to get into cover as he shivered uncontrollably. He stood there, trying to get the feeling back in his hands by blowing on them and frantically rubbing them together. Turning, he realised that he must have sped up, because General Drorkon had not caught up with him. But he sensed another presence that made him realise he was not alone. Turning again, he saw a stranger emerge from the shadows. Whoever it was, they were tall and dark, and approached slowly.

Havovatch went to draw his sword but realised he didn't have one. So he stood defensively.

The shadow continued to approach, they made no noise. There was the gruff sound of their breathing which was heavy. Light caught vapour being blown from the shadow but Havovatch could still not make out any features.

"Stay back!" he shouted.

"I would stop that now,, young man!" boomed the voice which echoed in the cave.

But Havovatch, didn't – he stood defensively.

"Step down, now!" came Drorkon's voice from behind. As the tall, dark figure came closer, Havovatch lost his breath as he stared at such a rare sight.

"Commander," he said with disbelief.

"Come now," he boomed. "I am no celebrity. This way – I have made a fire, and it's far less noisy there," he smiled, and invited them to follow him deeper into the cave.

Havovatch turned to Drorkon, who winked, and allowed him to go first

Havovatch was shocked to see the commander. For any Camion soldier, Commander Thiamos was like a second father. He looked after them, and although he was rarely seen, he always had gifts of beer and extra coin dished out (especially if their unit did well). He was a marvel to see, which was usually only at formal functions where a speech had to be given. Rarely, very rarely, would a mere soldier (or even an officer) meet him in person. There were so many stories about Commander Thiamos's conquests, yet Havovatch did not know which were true and which were false, as they seemed so exaggerated – the strangest being that he had fought a lion and cut its mane off as a trophy, and that was why he had such a big, red, bushy beard.

Havovatch followed him deeper into the cave. It was narrow, and curved around to his right; the noise of the wind died away behind him, and he felt warmth coming from in front. Then he emerged into a small room cut into the stone. The only source of light was a small fire with three large rocks circling it. Thiamos bent down and made himself comfortable on one, as Havovatch stood gawping at him.

"You can stop looking at me like that, Captain. We have much to discuss," said Thiamos abruptly, but Havovatch could not help himself. He felt foolish, though – he wasn't sure how to act or what to say in the company of those higher than him, and instead beamed with a goofy grin.

Drorkon sat down and showed the palms of his hands to the flames, as did Thiamos.

"I've heard of your quest, young man," said Thiamos. "I must say that I am very impressed!"

"Thank you, Sir," Havovatch said weakly.

"Alas, though, we are short on time, and I must impress upon you the urgency of your next mission," Thiamos continued.

"Oh?"

"A position has opened up … mine." He bowed his head as if he were being forced to say it.

"What? You want me to take over the Camion military?" Havovatch said, aghast.

Drorkon laughed.

"No," Thiamos said plainly. Clearly, what he was about to say bugged him. "I want you to take command of the Knight Hawks."

Havovatch looked at Drorkon to see if it were true, then let out a laugh. "This must be a dream?"

"I can assure you it is not!" Thiamos said, his expression very serious indeed.

"Sir, I have heard of the tests soldiers undergo to become a Hawk. How can you expect me to lead them, let alone be one?"

Drorkon cut in.

"Havovatch, there is much to tell you, but we simply do not have the time. To cut it short, we are sending a small force, the Knight Hawks, to the Black Lands to kill Agorath. He would empty his lands to send his forces here. We will hold out as long as we can, but we need the Knight Hawks to execute him. And all this will be over."

"Right, and you want me to command them?"

"Yes. The young general here has made it clear that I should remain here; with my knowledge and experience of battle tactics, it would be prudent for me to stay put. But I need someone I can trust to lead my Hawks. The general has implored me that you're the right man for the job?" he looked at him intently, as if waiting for confirmation.

Havovatch sat with his mouth hanging open.

"Sir, I am not yet twenty-one; I have barely been in the military a year. I don't think I can lead the Knight Hawks."

Thiamos looked to Drorkon for an explanation.

"Havovatch, in the last couple of months you have commanded a regiment of over eight thousand men, you have led a small unit against impossible odds, you have taken on responsibilities, you have killed, you have sacrificed, you have fought in battle. You also were captured and withstood interrogation, several times I might add. And you have also shown great fortitude, strength, skill, determination, courage and above all, leadership. I am more than confident that you're ready for this position."

Havovatch stared at the fire as he spoke, and thought he was seeing the experiences of his life as they were spoken out.

"I just wished to become a solider," he said quietly.

"Our paths are not always laid out for us young man. We become who we are through our experiences, and right now, you have this path before you," said Drorkon.

Havovatch took in a deep breath through his nostrils and rubbed his face, then looked at the two officers.

"Very well. What do you wish for me to do?"

"Kneel," said Thiamos, who stood up and drew his broadsword.

Havovatch crouched down onto one knee and bowed his head. Thiamos stood over him for a minute and closed his eyes, as if questioning what he was about to do. Drorkon could tell that giving up the Hawks was proving more difficult than the commander had expected. Thiamos picked up his sword and rested it on Havovatch's head.

I officially award you the rank of General Havovatch of the Camion Knight Hawks. May you lead with honour and justice, and fulfil your oath to me, the King and the Kingdom. Now rise a general and leave the man you were behind: go forth and fulfil your oath!

"I will fulfil my oath." Havovatch stood up.

Thiamos turned and picked up a sack sitting in the corner of the cave. It looked like a present, with bulges, and made a metallic sound as its parts clinked together.

"This is your new uniform. You can get rid of your current garb, for this Hawk steel is far better."

"How so?" he said, taking the sack; it was heavy.

"Hawks usually wear what they want so that they can feel comfortable. I would say you're a Front, so I took the liberty of making the choice for you – I hope that it's to your liking?"

"A Front?"

"Yes. Hawks all have a specific position in an Infiltration Line: you have Fronts, Backs, Centres and Leaders. Your size, skill and rank determine what you should wear to be effective at your job."

"And what's an Infiltration Line?" Havovatch said, shaking his head as he tried to take it all in.

"That's another story."

Drorkon then picked up a dark object. "This is for you, dear boy. Buskull brought it back. We have modified it a bit but I think you'll like what we have done?" he said in earnest.

Havovatch dropped the sack and smiled as he looked at his helmet – the very thing he had grown up wanting, the very thing that had kept him going during his training when times had been bad, through the mud, the blood, the pain, everything. However, he frowned as the light from the flames revealed it to be very different from what he remembered.

It was black with purple streaks like the current of water in a stream brushed across the steel, creating a strange pattern. The cheek guards were longer and frayed out at the ends; the eye slits were thinner and longer too, with pieces of metal added just above, like long, pointed eyebrows. If he headbutted anyone he knew that they'd certainly cause some damage. His vertical blue crest had been removed, and three smaller crests of rust-coloured feathers were fixed to the back of the helmet, like fins on the back of a fish (the insignia for a general in the Knight Hawks). And, strangest of all, was the black fabric – which looked too dense to see through – covering the eyeholes and mouthpiece.

As he stood in newly acquired admiration for his new helmet, Drorkon handed Thiamos a long, wrapped object. Thiamos held it horizontally in both hands and approached Havovatch, as if giving the final part of a gift which was best left until last.

"When one becomes a Hawk, it is not their helmet which identifies them, but their sword, a very special sword indeed. This is your new weapon, Havovatch."

Havovatch took it, and, after unfastening the binding and unravelling the blanket, he stared upon a strange-looking blade. It was no longer than his Kopis, with a solid handle and double-edged blade, which wasn't shiny but tinted black so it could not reflect any light. The blade narrowed slightly near the middle and widened near the end like a diamond – it was a fearsome weapon. The hilt was in the shape of a hawk, with outstretched wings and two ruby-red eyes nestled into the metal.

"Get dressed, Hawk, for we need to get moving," said Thiamos, before leaving quickly, as if he couldn't bear to look at him any more. Not because he didn't like Havovatch, but because he was upset about losing his Knight Hawks.

Havovatch emerged from the cave entrance a short while later, a very different person from the one who had entered. If anyone who knew Havovatch stared upon him in that moment, they would not recognise him as the former captain of the Three-Thirty-Third. He walked out onto the ledge where Thiamos and Drorkon stood talking. The wind had calmed, with breaks in the cloud highlighting the landscape, making it all the more breathtaking.

Havovatch stood confidently, holding a large crossbow. Down his right-hand side, he wore armguards of the same colour as his helmet. His left arm was bare, and a guard with a shield was fixed to his right shoulder to protect the right side of his face. The cuirass fitted tightly against his torso, with an outstretched winged hawk embossed on its breastplate. He had a thick black belt on, with dark trousers and shin guards. He looked elite by any measure. As well as his new blade, fixed comfortably to his back and reachable over his left shoulder, he also had his Kopis fixed to his left hip, although it looked out of place with its bronze handle. Just as with his old armour, he had a much larger dagger fixed upside down to the left of his chest and another, the same, strapped around his right leg. Around his right arm he had a belt of crossbow bolts, and a strangely small quiver was fitted to his right hip, filled with more bolts. He was also surprised at how well he could see through the fabric of his helmet, for he was sure no one could see his face, and yet he could see as clearly as if nothing were there.

"Ready?" Drorkon asked, as if he was about to do something that he should prepare himself for.

Havovatch just nodded.

Thiamos approached him. He seemed grumpy as he breathed heavily through his nostrils. He stood before Havovatch, who looked up at him dubiously, wondering what he was going to do, as if he couldn't bear it and was about to take back his command. But instead, he reached down and took the crossbow from his grasp.

"This is a Malorga – it's deadly!" Taking a bolt from the belt around his arm, Thiamos fed it into the top of the crossbow, pushing his thumb in behind it; there was a loud click. Thiamos then took another two bolts and fed them in the same way. Then he pulled the crank – a large lever on the top of the crossbow – back three times. As he did so, Havovatch saw the string pull taut against the tension of the bow.

"It's easy to load and fire: just copy what I did – hold it straight and aim along the top." He demonstrated how.

Havovatch took it back and held it delicately, worried about the devastation it could cause, making sure he pointed the end away from himself and his commander.

"There's a safety – just push it down with your closest finger," Thiamos said as Havovatch held it.

The bow was carved out of one piece of wood, with a hole in the top to load the bolts. The handle was underneath, near the front, just before the handgrip. It was shaped like a thick ring, with a long piece of metal curving around it for the trigger. Placed just behind it at the bottom was a small lever, blocking it from being fired. Havovatch used his little finger to push it down. Placing his thumb through the ring hole and squeezing lightly with all four fingers against the trigger, he felt its strength, but did not fire it.

"Squeeze, don't pull," Thiamos said softly, as if these were the last words of advice he had for him.

Standing back, Thiamos gave a nod of good luck; Havovatch returned the gesture. Drorkon smiled.

"Ready?"

Havovatch nodded.

Drorkon drew his purple-hilted sword, looked up and closed his eyes. When he opened them again, they were glazed over white; there was a sudden thunderclap that echoed all around. Another ray of sunlight broke through the clouds, and a tall, thin, black, vertical line could just be seen off in the distance.

"Find your unit, General. Make sure they get back here as soon as possible," cried Thiamos above the sudden wind and thunderstorm erupting around them.

Havovatch then heard a word spoken by General Drorkon – not one he could repeat, for it was spoken too quickly and in a voice that seemed unreal. Suddenly, he felt as if he were falling – it was for just a second, so quick that he found his feet before he realised the shock. When he came to his senses, he realised that he was in a warmer climate, but still slightly cold. Opening his eyes, he saw a gathering of three creatures standing on a platform. He didn't know what they were; he could only explain that they looked like knights, with thick, black armour covering their torsos, and thin, wiry pieces of fur down their arms and legs. It sent a shudder down his spine.

"Excuse me," he said politely.

"Wait theress, the commander willss be heress shortly," said one of the creatures stubbornly.

Chapter Sixteen
The Murky Depths

Still clutching Buskull's belt, Feera was shaking frantically. He closed his eyes tightly, not wanting to look at anything, and proceeded to walk blindly. Now and again he went to open his heavy eyelids, but with the fatigue dawning upon him, it was easier just to shut them and follow where Buskull pulled him, his mind almost drifting into a hypnotic state. All he could feel as he walked was the vapour upon his face and the trudge of soft, wet sand beneath his feet. Hilclop was pretty much in the same state, allowing his legs to walk as he drifted into and out of his slumber.

Wrisscrass walked nearby, looking aloof. He wasn't too bothered by what was going on, and yawned, showing his boredom, kicking pieces of dirt into the mist, just hearing them rolling away but not seeing them.

Buskull, though, walked cautiously. With the dawn's light appearing, all he could see before him was grey. Holding his axe in both hands in front of himself, like a torch leading them through the darkness, he looked inquisitively around, his nostrils flaring as he sensed the creatures around them.

An hour had passed by and the terrain had not changed – just the continual abyss of soft ground and dead trees. Feera started to relax somewhat, though. The human body can only take so much stress, and he looked around feeling tired, but was no longer shaking. Soon, the land started to slope upwards; Buskull stopped. He shoved the axe handle into the ground and motioned for the unit to huddle around it.

"We're nearly out," he said quietly.

"Good – I can finally relax," said Hilclop, stretching in an attempt to unkink his neck.

"Relax now, laddie. I sense a darker threat above the fog than what is around us."

"What *is* around us?" said Feera.

It was then that he noticed Wrisscrass smiling devilishly, as if he was pleased with what they were going to meet above the mist.

"Nothing I have heard of, but they are scared of the axe. They have followed us ever since we left the Rogan Defence Line, but they have not attacked."

Feera looked around, but could not see anything, just mist.

"Why are they scared of the axe?"

"They seem primitive – scared by magic, I'd imagine."

"Your axe is magical?" sneered Hilclop, not quite believing it.

"So, what do we do?" said Feera, rolling his eyes at him.

"Wait for nightfall, then we'll emerge under the cover of darkness."

Wrisscrass groaned. He had his fists gripped and fangerlores ready. Hilclop sighed – he could not take any more of the unknown torment. Neither could Feera – training for war and fighting had its own challenges that he had learnt to overcome. But fighting beasts and learning of the unknown was putting too much strain on his mind, and he wished to be back in the ranks, and to hand his role over to someone who could cope with it.

Buskull noticed their discomfort, and, producing his waterskin, he delved into his satchel and produced a brown cube, then put it into the bottle, shook it well, and offered it to his unit.

"What is it?" said Hilclop, a little warily.

"It will help calm you."

"Cool – so it's a remedy that will make me relax?"

"No, it's a block of brandy that I solidified and mixed with water and now it's brandy in a flask. Don't drink too much!"

Hilclop sniffed it and pulled it away.

Feera laughed. "A man's drink!"

Hilclop picked the bottle up to his lips and slowly poured a trickle into his mouth. Holding it in his mouth, he tried to swallow and puffed out his cheeks. Wrisscrass grinned, shot out an arm and grabbed his nose. The shock made Hilclop swallow. Instantly pushing his tongue out and rubbing his sternum, he pushed the bottle into Wrisscrass's chest. Wrisscrass laughed even more at his torment, and, showing him how it's done, downed half the bottle without so much as a cough.

With Hilclop hunched over, his knuckles white as he gripped the top of Buskull's axe, Feera took the waterskin and wiped Wrisscrass's spit off the top of the flask. He poured in a human-sized amount, not more than a couple of teaspoonfuls. Cocking an eyebrow and with a grin, he tried to keep control, but the drink was strong.

"Smooth!" he said, his voice slightly deeper than usual.

Buskull finished the rest off, showing delight with his own creation. Looking at the waterskin, he raised his eyebrows and gave an impressed nod.

"Could do with being a bit stronger?" he suggested.

The drink had certainly done the trick. Hilclop was thinking so hard about the feeling flowing through him, he had all but forgotten where they were. In fact, he was struggling to stand up straight. Wrisscrass stood with his arms folded, watching him with delight, as was Feera. Hilclop was putting on quite a show!

"Right, it's nearly time to go. We'll move quickly but quietly. Hold onto my belt until we're clear of the mist, and then run! I can sense the terrain ahead – it is about thirty yards of open ground until we can find cover. OK?" Buskull said, looking at the others.

Feera and Hilclop drew their swords and stood with their legs bent slightly; with their free hands they held onto Buskull's belt, although Hilclop was holding it more for support than anything else.

The light was dim, and Feera could only just make out Buskull's silhouette before him. Knowing that they were about to either run through a hail of arrows or meet an army, Feera closed his eyes, murmuring prayers to Grash, praying for either a quick death or a heroic victory. But his prayers were interrupted by a trudging noise. Next to them, they heard a stomping on the ground, as Wrisscrass jumped and stretched on the spot as if making himself ready.

"You take this seriously, don't you?" slurred Hilclop.

"I do with this lot, back where I come from. We're thrown into the jungle and have to survive against 'em."

Feera looked incredulously at the mist, wondering what could be beyond.

"Do they have a weakness?"

"Yeah, only when they're dead!" he grinned.

"Now!" shouted Buskull, and started running, as the others were dragged on and tried to keep pace with his massive strides. Wrisscrass was level with him.

As if a curtain had been pulled away, they came out of the mist and looked upon the shards of a mountain jutting high into the air as if it were a natural castle, with jagged rocks everywhere. Battlements had been carved into the rock at different levels, but it looked terribly worn and run-down. But their attention was drawn to a group of creatures milling around the firelight at the base of the wall. One turned casually towards them.

"Noshka!" it shouted, as if seeing a creature that it hated as much as the creature hated it.

The startled creatures turned to see the charging unit. Before the first could collect its spear – which stood upright in a pile with the others – Wrisscrass had cut clean through its neck and barged into the others.

Buskull just ploughed into the last, crushing it against the base of the wall. As Feera and Hilclop arrived there was nothing left to do, with Wrisscrass taking all the glory for himself. He finished the last one off, holding it up against the wall with his left arm as he repeatedly punched his fangerlores into its gut. He then threw it to the ground and spat with disdain upon its lifeless corpse.

Afterwards, he was breathing heavily, his shoulders visibly rising with each breath, yet he seemed pleased with his performance. "That was satisfying – let's find some more," he said excitedly, and ran further down the base of the wall, disappearing into the darkness. The unit paused and looked down at the creatures they had slain. They were different from those they had met in Minta – their skin was scaled and glittered turquoise in the firelight; with long tails like talons, they appeared strong, with visible muscle definition.

"These are Golesh?" asked Hilclop.

"I don't know what these are," Feera replied.

Feera too was intrigued with them, for they looked far less fearsome than the Golesh, but still nothing like anything he had ever seen in his life.

"But why are these not defiling the land?"

"I don't know, but let's just get what we need and go," said Buskull as he chased after Wrisscrass.

They couldn't see him, but they heard the clash of metal and followed it into the darkness.

***

"Sir?" Plinth said cautiously as he bent down and looked at his general.

Drorkon appeared uncertain. Kneeling before the chest with his hands by its sides, he was ready to lift the lid but was filled with trepidation. "Plinth, my friend, I cannot do this alone; yet I also cannot let you be here. I need at least one other to communicate with them, and you don't know how to fight against the curses."

Plinth knelt down on the other side of the chest. "I will do whatever is required of me, General," he said softly.

Drorkon was panting and sweating, not because of anything that had been done, but because of what he was about to do. Sitting in his tent in the middle of the camp, Plinth had ordered a ring of soldiers to surround the tent, facing outwards, all holding spears. Their orders were to let no one in, no matter the circumstances. He couldn't risk his own men coming in and affecting what was about to occur.

"I shouldn't do this alone," said Drorkon. "Their power is too great."

"What could happen?"

Drorkon looked up "... I could lose my soul."

Plinth swallowed hard.

"General, I have always remained ignorant to your mysteries, but, I ask: what is happening?"

Drorkon signed and rubbed his face. "There are ... spirits, helping us, my dear friend. They are trapped, and we can only communicate with them this way, or summon their help with this" he said patting his purple tinted blade, "but to do so alone is dangerous. I did it once," he paused, remembering and wishing he could forget. "I never want to do it again."

"I've seen you use this box alone before, though?"

"Yes, you have. To speak with my fellow kin spread around the world, that's fine, but to talk to the undead ... well, there are certain powers, my friend, that you ordinary humans cannot contend with."

"And Undrea can?"

Drorkon smiled reflectively. "Undrea? She is very special." He gazed into the distance, as if thinking about her. In fact, he was – the first time he had met her growing up they had touched hands, as he bent down to kiss her hand, and he received a static shock; he realised from that moment that she was special.

Plinth placed his hands on Drorkon's reassuringly, taking him out of his trance. "I may be more confused now, but I am no less loyal."

Drorkon looked at him long and hard. "Thank you, my friend. This is what I want you to do: no matter what you hear, no matter what you feel or smell or imagine, you do not open your eyes. You will be fine if you keep your eyes closed, but I cannot deny, I do need you here to help me."

"Yes, Sir – there is no question."

"You do *not* open your eyes, Plinth!" he repeated firmly, pointing at him, the furrows of his eyebrows frowning deeply, his lips pursed.

"I will not, Sir."

"This is difficult on my own, and when I awake, I will need you to do whatever I say; but I will be weak, feed me water, then let me sleep."

Plinth bowed his head into his chest and closed his eyes, his chin hidden behind his huge, bushy beard, his hands together on his lap. He heard the chest creak open; instantly there were swirling noises, as if a sudden wind had appeared in the tent and pulled everything towards the chest. He felt his beard pull away from him, but did not open his eyes.

"ARGHHH!" screamed Drorkon. "No, nooo!" he begged.

But Plinth remained calm, purposefully controlling his breathing and forcing his hands to sit on his lap. He did not open his eyes. Despite the continual screams and endless babble, he remained calm and ignored him.

"Yubba! Af-f-faaaa! No! No! Nooooo! I will not!"

Plinth jolted slightly, as if his body were fighting against his reactions, but he took control, although it was the most difficult thing he had ever done. Around him, he was sure that there were several other beings in the tent, but he still did not open his eyes.

After several moments, there was the sound of the box lid slamming shut, and Drorkon fell back trembling as if he were having a fit, murmuring as he convulsed like a madman.

"P-P-Plllinth," Drorkon begged as he lay on the floor, his hands clasped together at his chest and shaking uncontrollably.

Plinth opened his eyes and everything appeared to be as it was before he shut them. But he looked startled at his general who lay withering on the floor. He was right by his side, and took his hand and cradled his head as if he were his little boy.

Drorkon looked deep into his eyes with horror as he tried to speak, speak one word, a word which he needed to know.

175

"What is it, General? Tell me."

Plinth grabbed a jug and gently tipped it, allowing water to pour into Drorkon's mouth.

The convulsions slowed somewhat, but most of the water was spat out.

Drorkon tried desperately to say something.

"D-D-D-D-D."

"Shhh," Plinth said, putting his hand on his forehead to calm him. He placed his ear against his mouth.

"D-D-D-Defences."

"Lieutenant!" he cried at the tent flap behind him.

The lieutenant instantly burst in, and started at the sight of his general lying on the floor, shaking uncontrollably.

"Send word to Pausanias – he must get everyone to the Defences."

But the lieutenant just stared at Drorkon, his face filled with concern.

"Now!" Plinth roared.

Chapter Seventeen
Infiltration

"They stink!"

"SHHH!" Pausanias said, more harshly than he had intended. Even on a covert mission, Andreas seemed unable to keep his mouth shut.

"This is exactly why I don't invite you on Shadow Ops," Pausanias said a little more quietly, as if it were something he had been longing to say for some time.

"Your loss."

Pausanias shook his head, and, hunched over, they staggered along with the rest of the Golesh. They were positioned near the rear of the group, with just a large helmet and poncho of Golesh cloth around them. Pausanias knew what it actually was, but thought that telling his little brother that they were wearing human skin may upset him somewhat. The poncho was large and heavy, but it had to be, to cover their armour underneath. In battle, rather than having to take each bit of kit off, they wanted to throw the two items off and instantly look Camion. Underneath, they both had standard-issue armour, with a double-edged sword and varying-coloured tunics which some of the new recruits had to relinquish, much to their dismay considering they hadn't long had them. Andreas had a standard-issue bow and set of arrows with him. Reluctantly, he had left his own with General Drorkon, who almost had to prise them away from him. The only other item Pausanias had was a satchel carrying the one thing he could go nowhere without, and kept placing his hand on it to make sure it was still there.

Pausanias looked behind him; he just saw the Two-Twenty-Eighth riding away, seemingly leaving the Golesh to walk on their own. They appeared confused, for moments earlier they had been given their weapons back and told to leave. But to Pausanias they did not appear intelligent, and just did as instructed.

As they marched on, though, a figure ducked down behind a hillock, watching surreptitiously and making sure the cavalry unit would not see him.

It was difficult for the two Hawks to match the way the Golesh marched – the latter walked with long paces, not in a straight line but zigzagging forward, as if they were severely intoxicated.

"The forest is near. Remember what I told you!" he whispered, just seeing the edge of the forest coming into view.

Andreas let out a grunt. He started to walk quite quickly, but Pausanias threw his arm out to pull him back.

"No! The archers will rain arrows down on them and then the infantry will attack the vanguard. We want to stay near the rear."

But, as ever, Andreas was keen to get into the action, and too built-up on adrenalin to hear his words.

They did not have long to wait. It happened so quickly, as if the trees themselves were spitting out splinters; long, thin lines could be seen against the blue sky, as if a swarm of birds had come hurtling towards them. The front ranks of the Golesh perished, as the white-feathered arrows fell upon them. But the creatures behind them remained unfazed about the state of their brethren, and charged at the edge of the forest, their demeanour changing from idle curiosity to savage rage. Some of the arrows reached the brothers, but only a very few, and, crouching low, Pausanias gripped his sword hilt under his poncho, his other arm outstretched to grab his brother.

Howling, the Golesh charged at their unseen enemy. Then, out of the forest, almost as if the bushes on the ground had vanished, bronze-clad soldiers charged at the melee, and the heavy sound of metal upon metal and screams of pain filled the air. Behind his helmet, Pausanias closed his eyes for a moment as he steadied himself, then drew his sword from under his poncho, and, in one swift move, threw it off with the helmet and attacked at the rearguard, hewing down his weapon in a thunderous rage. Andreas felt his brother let go of his arm, and, pulling the bowstring back, he too emerged from the masquerade and aimed his arrow. Yet, as he went to fire, the creature next to him turned in surprise and howled with its vicious fangs, noticing who they really were. Suddenly, every creature around them, as if hearing the call, turned and faced Andreas.

"Oh Sh—," cursed Andreas; he turned, and ran as the creatures chased after him. Leaving the battle, he ran out onto the open plains with half a dozen creatures chasing him. Pausanias was so busy fighting he did not even notice his brother had gone.

Yet, from another direction, a small group of cavalry soldiers came charging out of the trees and headed for the small group chasing Andreas.

Pausanias quickly dropped an impressive amount of bodies. Although, he was mostly attacking the backs of the beast, by repeatedly shoving his sword into them and pulling at their armour to run them through. But, turning, he saw that something was amiss. Standing there with a thin blade was Ferith, trying desperately to match his fighting style.

"What the hell are you doing here?" he demanded.

"I'll show you – I can fight as well as you. I can become a Hawk!" he said, continuing to stab and slash at the creatures.

Pausanias too was fighting and trying to get closer to him.

"You have no idea what you've done?"

Ferith suddenly looked at him, and the expression across his face changed as he realised something was wrong.

"You're not just fighting these creatures, are you?"

"No! We're not."

The battle started to draw to an end as blue cloaks started to flood the area.

Pausanias drew closer to him. "Get out now … now! GO!"

Ferith looked at the scene around him – it was just carnage as the Camions pummelled into the Golesh. He turned and ran back out as two creatures chased him. Pausanias brought them down and watched him disappear behind a hill.

"What was he thinking?" Pausanias said out loud.

Turning, he saw the battle was drawing to an end, and the clean-up began as those left standing started to thrust their swords into any injured creatures. As he walked amongst the bodies, he randomly stuck his blade into their torsos whether they were dead or not, just to act the part. Standing there doing nothing would draw attention to him, although he kept looking back to see if Ferith was still there, but he had disappeared. But then another thought struck him: there was an emptiness, something that should have been there wasn't. As he looked around he saw that Andreas was nowhere in sight.

Pausanias looked around hurriedly, as if he were a parent who'd lost their child. He'd suddenly forgotten his position and started pacing between the soldiers, trying to look between the eyeholes of their helmets. But none of them was Andreas.

"Oi, you! You're not from this section!" a captain bellowed at him.

Pausanias paused on the spot, torn between trying to find his brother and his duty.

"No, Captain – apologies." He approached him as he kept looking around, hoping to find some glimpse of him. "I'm from the North Watch. I was so desperate to see what was going on, I, well, I got tangled up in it. Forgive me," he said, bowing his head.

The captain took some sympathy upon him, and let out an understanding sigh – he knew as well as everyone how difficult it had been for the men, and knew most wanted to vent their anger.

"It's OK, but I suggest you get back there, now! Before your commander realises you're gone."

"Yes, we will … I will," he quickly added. The captain looked at him incredulously. "Sorry, Captain – I thought my friend was with me. I bet he has already run back to our post," Pausanias quickly added in an unschooled tone, helping his masquerade.

"Very well. Go!"

Pausanias jogged off along the treeline. As he looked into the forest he could see all sorts of movement from within. But, as much as he looked around, Andreas was surely not to be found. He hated it, but he was a soldier, he was a Hawk, and he needed to fulfil his mission. Before he entered, he took one more look across the battlefield, but saw no Camion lying on the floor. *He must be alive, but where?* he thought.

Stepping into the forest and wiping his blade on a large leaf, he gave a nod at the stationary soldiers who had eagerly been looking on. They shook their heads at him, knowing that he had got away with leaving his post to join in with the fun. He gave a cheesy grin back and then assessed his surroundings. Taking a breath, he knew the easy bit was over, but the situation was made complicated by the disappearance of his brother.

Now he had to infiltrate as many defences as there were, and work out where the fort in the centre of the forest was, all the while making sure he did not get caught. He stayed on his toes. However, now Andreas could be anywhere, and the captain at the battle certainly knew his men well; this made him realise that if captured he would be taken straight to Imara and interrogated – he needed to get there first. Wasting no time, he merged further into the forest.

At first, it just appeared to be a large camp in the woods, with tents erected between trees. Some lookout huts had been built up in the canopy, but they were very run-down. After about ten minutes of walking and giving friendly nods to his comrades, he came to the first defence. A shabby palisade of pikes had been dug into the ground. He knew he could easily wait until nightfall and get through without being detected, but with Andreas missing he had to get in now.

Drawing his knife, he looked around to see if anyone was looking, but few were about, and most were asleep. He leant against a tree for support, then cut himself across the top of his arm. He squeezed the wound to let as much blood out as possible and make it look worse than it really was, then limped towards the guards standing at the entrance, holding his wound with blood oozing between his fingers.

"What happened?" said a cavalry colonel, who quickly approached whilst fastening a belt around his waist.

"There was an attack, Sir, we won, Sir, but me captain told me to get this seen to, Sir."

The colonel looked at the blood between his fingers as he held his wound, but appeared more eager to know what had happened.

"OK, so why don't you go and see your own surgeon?" he said, looking off into the distance at the commotion.

"He's got too many to heal, Sir. So me captain told me to get this stitched up by one of your surgeons, Sir. Please, Sir, he's not a patient man."

The colonel took another look at him and nodded. "Very well – go and get yourself stitched up." He then looked to his guards. "I'll be back in a minute," he said quickly, and paced off to the forest's edge.

Pausanias went through and bowed his head, making the guards think he was a young recruit and intimidated by their presence; one sniggered as he passed.

Finding another tree he could hide against, he began cleaning the blood from his hand and arm with a cloth. He tucked the stained fabric into the trunk, then wrapped a bandage around his wound.

All the while, he was using his senses to work out who was around him; most had heard the noise of battle and were lining the fences to see. Some, though, were milling about.

He set off again along a line of tents. They had dug small craters into the earth and placed tents over them. He saw that they were all vacant and quickly stepped inside one, eager to ditch his blue uniform. He hooked his fingers into his blue tunic; there were already cuts there to make it easier to pull off. Pulling hard, he ripped the blue tunic out through his armour. He moved nearer to a camp bed and, lifting the mattress, placed the tunic underneath; then he stopped, and straightened up; he could hear talking, the sound coming towards the tent. Looking at the entrance, he saw two pairs of boots.

"So, what you gonna do?" the soldier whispered to the other as they entered the tent.

"I don't know. I miss her. I just hope she's OK. Growing up, she was never any good at looking after herself."

They both sat on their beds and looked at each other, keeping their voices low and keeping an eye on the entrance to make sure they were alone.

"Things are getting worse here. I heard that Imara chucked another twenty people out – they were from the upper class as well, and she just chucked them out once they had run out of money. Women, children! This isn't what I'm fighting for."

"More and more soldiers are deserting by the day as well," said the other.

"But if we do run, we could be killed. I heard reports that any who have deserted were found dead."

"Shup! That's just scaremongering from Imara, to keep us in place."

"So you don't believe it?"

"Listen," he said, leaning closer, "we will get out of this and we will find your sister!"

"OK – I'm with you."

The cavalry officers stood up and left the tent.

Pausanias pulled himself out from the tiny space underneath one of the beds. He winced and gritted his teeth as he pulled his torso out, dragging on the frame. The space was far from large, had been even less so with the guard sitting on top.

He stood up, then doubled over and took in a long gasp. He had to hold his breath because it was such a tight space, and it showed in his face, red from the strain.

He approached the entrance and peered out, but pulled back as another two guards walked past. To help with his disguise, he swiped one of the officers' helmets – which fortunately for Pausanias had been left behind – and put it on, then briskly stepped out and wandered further into the forest.

The area the cavalry had set up camp in was far larger than the one used by the infantry. Not only men had to camp but horses too, although he came across a distressing sight, with three piles of dead horses with flies buzzing around them. He knew what had happened – being cooped up and unable to graze and run around had made them restless, and Imara had probably had them killed, for their wounds suggested slaughter.

Pausanias tried to channel his energies. He liked horses and hated to see them like this, but the sight helped fuel his anger, the one emotion he relied on in his career.

Pausanias soon came to the next defence – a line of scouts (which were now plenty since the rules of war had added to their number), standing along the picketed line. But he knew one thing was on his side – they were far from experienced soldiers. He relaxed somewhat at the easy challenge, and walked purposefully towards the opening between the pickets.

They saw him coming. One scout nudged another to intercept him; he stood up but did not pick up his spear. He had his arms folded, and yawned.

"Yes, Sir?"

"I'm going to see Queen Imara. I have a message."

The scout nodded. "Very well," he said tiredly and went to resume his seating position, probably so he could get back to sleep.

For a very brief moment, Pausanias felt more ashamed of his comrades than his so-called Queen for allowing a man to enter what was supposed to be a secured location. But he shrugged it off, knowing it was fully in his favour.

"Stop!" shouted a voice behind him, a voice of such fierce authority that, at that moment, every scout jumped to attention.

Pausanias's heart skipped a beat – not something that happened often.

He stood where he was, looking ahead, waiting for the officer to speak with him. As he stepped in front of him – a tall man with the insignia of a colonel – he knew he was outranked, and saluted.

The colonel looked at him long and hard through the gaps of his helmet. "We need to talk. Come with me!" he said at last.

Pausanias was confused – it was as if he knew him. However, he followed.

Nodding to his escorts to stay put, the colonel walked to a secluded area where a large tree had been uprooted.

"It's good to see you, young man," the colonel said, removing his helmet and looking around to make sure that they were alone.

Pausanias removed his as well, and looked at the familiar face of an old friend.

"How did you know it was me?"

"Ha! I recognised your gait, and the scar along your arm."

"It's good to see you, Sir."

They shook hands firmly.

"What are you doing here? I heard the Hawks had deserted?" he asked quietly.

"You're not wrong. The Hawks have gone on a mission, far from here. They have sent me here to …" Pausanias trailed off slightly, but there was no need to. Their friendship was strong. "… to kill that filthy rekon keeping you here."

The colonel's eyes narrowed for a moment, then he leant closer and whispered, "I'll help you as best I can. The defences are thorough here, and we think she has paid senior officers to make sure everything goes her way. There have also been disappearances. Something is not right, and right now every soldier here wants to get back home. There is talk that Cam has been taken over."

"Do you know who by?"

"No, but as you can imagine, it has made our boys restless."

"Get me to her – I'll do the rest."

"I can only get you so far, but it should be enough. Come – now is a good time, as most units will be near the end of their shifts and tired."

Pausanias followed him through the woods. The colonel took him through a particularly dense part, helping to shield them from prying eyes, and Pausanias saw several people along the way whom he suspected of being spies; standing surreptitiously by trees, they monitored what was going on with those around them.

Pausanias also tried to tell him about his brother, yet the colonel walked so quickly, keen to help him with his mission, he did not want to interrupt.

As they came to each defence, and because the colonel held a lot of authority, they were both able to walk past unchallenged; Pausanias tried to act like an aide, keeping his pace right by the colonel's side but slightly behind, as if he was trying to keep up with him. The colonel walked with clear purpose, so much so that stopping him would appear to be a crime.

Eventually, Pausanias and the colonel came within view of another defensive line, but this time it was a wooden wall just off in the distance. Crouching low behind a mound, they lowered their voices.

"I can't go any further," said the colonel. "To be honest, I'm surprised we got this far."

"Thank you. I'll be fine from here. You have helped greatly."

They again shook hands.

"Best of luck, friend. We all need to get out of here. My family are at Ambenol, and I need to get to them."

"Stand still," Pausanias said abruptly, with his hand out.

Just then, appearing around them as if they were being hunted, were five Camion soldiers all wearing different garb, but it did not matter what they wore for they had not earned it – they were foreign assassins, and, drawing an assortment of blades which were not Camion standard issue, they approached slowly with large grins on their faces, thinking that they had uncovered a plot.

"Kill her!" said the colonel, drawing his blade. "Kill her and free these men!"

Before Pausanias could draw his, the colonel engaged with one of them, the other three converging on Pausanias, but they had no idea who they were fighting against, and approached the young-looking cavalryman as if they were bullies picking on a small child. Two were dead before the first hit the ground, the blade in Pausanias's hands a blur as he made quick work of them. He tried not to engage his blade with theirs, in fear of the racket it would cause, but either ducked or parried out of the way and stuck his into them with dedicated precision. He aimed for their throats, mainly so they could not cry out, each stab and slash expertly done.

Once the deed was done, he crouched low to make himself a smaller target and surveyed his surroundings. With six lying dead before his feet, he was panting slightly, so he held his breath and checked around to see if anyone had heard; maybe they had, but no one came towards them. But a thought struck him: there were five assassins but six bodies. Turning, he saw his friend lying upright against a tree stump, holding a nasty wound to his side, his fingers covered in blood.

"Pausanias." He winced in pain.

Pausanias removed the colonel's helmet and his own and bent down. Moving his hand, he assessed the wound, but knew that even if they had a field surgeon there, there was little that could be done.

"You won't have much time. If anyone comes, I will direct them away," he coughed.

Pausanias held his hand as tears appeared in his eyes – amongst everything, why did he have to die like this? Yet, he could not leave him alone.

"Kill her, kill that wicked, horrible peace of filth," the colonel groaned as he tried to grip Pausanias's hand. Then his grip went limp as his eyes looked up and his body relaxed.

That was it now! Imara had crossed a personal line with Pausanias. He was angry, well, he was always angry, but now she had lit a fire in his belly that the ocean could not extinguish.

He took the colonel's sword and placed his hand on his shoulder.

"Goodbye, old friend."

Then he stood up and wiped away the blood from his sword and the colonel's, using the jerkin of one of the assassins. Looking around, he saw no one approaching – no one had heard the duel. And, looking at the fort in the distance, with a tall tower overlooking the canopy, he knew he was now close – he knew his target was in there, and with a throw of a knife, the slash of a sword or the breaking of a neck, this would all be over.

His hands were still shaking from the adrenalin of the fight, or maybe it was from his anger over his friend's death, he was not sure which, but he used it to his advantage, nevertheless.

Staying as low as he could, he sprinted towards the fort, hiding behind bushes and trees. Soon, he was less than an arrow's shot away, and he pulled a branch down to see who was guarding the fort. And a picture of horror spread across his face. For they were not guards; the fort was not manned by infantry, scouts or cavalry, or even by the assassins – it was manned by senior officers, and not just captains but colonels and generals. It made him sick to realise that some of them were people he knew. He was starting to think that they had been bought and were personally protecting their asset: Imara. Their defence was tight as they paced around.

Anyone who came near had to fully justify why they were there, and the officers jumped on them boisterously, all surrounding the messenger and asking lots of questions.

As Pausanias looked on, trying to work out how to get in. He knew that even at night, and in the rain, he would have difficulty infiltrating the fort, but the night held shadows for him to dwell in and rain hid any sound he would make. *It would be quicker and easier to dig a hole underneath,* he thought.

Crouching in the shrubbery, he stroked his chin and searched for a weakness. But he was distracted as he heard marching, and looking to his left he saw two lines of soldiers approaching the fort – with Andreas marching unarmed between them.

Chapter Eighteen
The Silent Rock

The dawn light appeared, giving the unit their first glimpse of the bleak and barren land beyond the Rogan Defence Line. Known only as the Misty Desert, there was nothing anyone knew about it; in fact, the only humans to have seen it were sitting in a gulley, resting after the night's events. They had found a path over the mountain line, bringing them to the south side.

"This isn't right," said Feera as he looked at the mountains lining the landscape, stretching off beyond the horizon in both directions. "I've seen mountains before – I've climbed them back home – but I have never seen mountains like these."

Wrisscrass snorted as he slept, sitting upright with his legs and arms crossed; the night's events of killing had made him very tired. And yet, the unit had done little apart from try to keep up with him.

"That's because these are not mountains," said Buskull from behind, following his gaze at the giant peaks reaching high up into the sky. "They're volcanos … or at least I think they are."

"What? No! Volcanos don't look like that. You certainly don't get a line of them – they're just one peak."

"Well, I'm telling you that's what they are. I mean, it makes sense." Buskull bent down and picked up the earth. As he crumbled it in his hand, dust fell with the wind. "It's ash. How do you explain these strange surroundings? How do you explain the terrain? You can feel it when you breathe – you can sense it in the air."

"But they appear dormant. There's no smoke, no ash clouds, no noise, no steam, nothing – just silent rock sitting idle."

"Maybe it's because that's what they are: dormant?"

"Well, I don't like this – I want to go back."

Buskull placed a hand on Feera's shoulder. "Me too, so let's get this mission over with."

"And what exactly is our mission?"

But Buskull ignored the question. Stepping back down into the gulley, he went to the other side and faced south. He risked being seen, but he needed the view. Producing the map that Drorkon had given him, he held it up to see if the symbols matched the terrain. The map showed that behind the mountain line (which he now knew was made up of volcanos) there was a tributary of rivers, or possibly paths branching out across the land. And as he looked at the land he saw the exact same patterns on the map. It showed that just beyond there would be a lake, and again, as he looked off to the distance, there was a glint of light reflecting off water.

"Rest's over – let's go," he said, keen to get on and get back.

Wrisscrass remained sitting where he was, with his eyes closed. As Hilclop passed, he gave him a kick to the side of his leg, but a giant fist shot up and punched him in the groin.

Feera went to chuckle, but remembered his resentment for Wrisscrass; looking at him intently, he passed close by, shunting into him as he did so.

Wrisscrass could do nothing but grin.

Buskull walked quietly at the front, sensing nothing as they wandered the strange land. Usually, anywhere he went he always felt something – a trail laid by someone who had walked by a few hours earlier, or animals skulking about – but here he felt nothing, just emptiness. If his senses were sight, there would just be blackness.

The gulley they walked along was deep and long, and was one of the tributaries leading to the lake. Despite their legs feeling heavy with the sticky ash clumping around their boots, the unit seemed more relaxed – even Wrisscrass appeared calm. He wasn't bloodthirsty and eager to kill like before, but had holstered his fangerlores and was picking bits of meat out from between his teeth.

"Why are there no Golesh here?" said Feera, joining Buskull.

"I think the lands have been cleaned out – they have all gone north." He said looking at another burned out camp.

"I suppose that makes our life a bit easier." Feera was glad for the confirmation, for he could relax that bit more.

"Indeed," said Buskull distantly.

"So …" said Feera, lowering his voice and joining Buskull.

"So?"

"Are you going to talk to me?"

"Regarding?"

"Come on, Buskull!" said Feera sternly, yet keeping his voice low, looking to make sure that they were alone. He saw Wrisscrass making faces at Hilclop, who didn't know whether to laugh or run. "Every time

I bring up the question of what our mission is, you either ignore me or change the subject!"

"You trust me, don't you?"

"Of course – it goes without saying."

"Then trust me. I cannot and will not tell you of this mission, it's too—" Buskull was cut short as he felt something, something very distinctive. Suddenly, in the blackness, there was a glimmer of colour.

Feera saw his distraction.

"What is it?"

"… life," he said softly. "Pain … suffering."

They looked at each other incredulously, before venturing up the side of the gulley. Buskull buried his hands into the crusted ash to pull himself up, and rose to the top. One by one, the rest of the unit appeared. They couldn't see anything on the other side but the bleak landscape. Buskull, though, pulled himself up and followed the scent, heading straight on. As they drew nearer, they soon approached a crater, and as they came to the top, they looked upon a very strange sight indeed.

The crater wasn't very large: it spanned about the same size as a Rowlg pitch, but it was deep. The entire ground was covered in verdant green moss and fungi, with a giant, creepy-looking tree in the middle, about the same size as a large oak tree, but looking sick. Despite there being no water, the area appeared as fresh and verdant as the Oistos forest, but not in good health. And, spaced around them, almost covering the ground, were various-sized statues, or what they thought were statues, again covered in green moss.

They stepped down cautiously into the crater, and felt that the land was very different from the terrain they had been walking on. Their feet did not sink into the crusty soil, the air suddenly felt fresh and their eyes were not blurred by grey. Hilclop stopped upon seeing a butterfly flutter in front of him. The sunlight shone down upon them as it found a gap in the clouds; highlighting the crater.

"What are these?" said Hilclop, as he looked at one of the statues. It was smaller than him, and seemed to form a creature he didn't know of. With its eyes shut as if sleeping, it had two small fangs over its bottom lip, its arms holding each shoulder as if it were cold. He poked it.

"NO!" barked Buskull.

Hilclop had already withdrawn his hand, for he didn't feel stone – he felt something soft, as if it were skin or a body, and it was warm.

"What is this, Buskull?" he said, drawing back warily.

"I'm not too sure. It's some kind of graveyard, and yet the creatures live on."

"You mean to tell me these are alive?" said Feera.

"Yes, and no. Their souls appear to have left them – they are but empty vessels breathing in their silent slumber."

"Why?"

"I don't know."

Feera stopped as he looked up at a tall, very rotund, human male. "Buskull!" he called. For the man was not fully grey – he had very dark skin that seemed to be turning grey.

Buskull grimaced as he assessed him.

"Is he alive?" said Feera.

"He is becoming like them, but again, there is nothing we can do."

Buskull continued his stare.

"You know him?" said Feera, noticing his attention.

"I know of him. If I am not mistaken, this is Chieftain Framlar, from the Santamaz Islands."

"And he is becoming like the others?"

"Yes."

"It's a collection," said Wrisscrass, edging back up the embankment.

"What?"

"Can't you see? There are no two of any creature."

"Why are you becoming so nervous?" said Feera.

"Because … there is nothing like me here."

"Aww, bless 'im," jibed Feera. He wouldn't act like this to anyone else, but Wrisscrass's recent presence had caused him to sink to below his usual professional standards.

"Feera, that's enough!" ordered Buskull.

Feera withdrew as he came to his senses; he felt rather foolish.

"Come, we'd better move out," said Buskull, walking back up the hill.

The unit turned and made their way back to the gulley. They climbed to the top of the crater and then turned back, one by one, to take a final glance at the strange scene. None of them, though, saw the largest statue staring up at them, with two piercing, yellow eyes like those of an eagle, and a wicked grin upon its face.

"What are we looking for?" whispered Hilclop, as he lay flat on his stomach at the top of a rise overlooking a dark and misty lake. It lay still without a ripple, not even the slightest wrinkle from the wind; as if in the calm before the storm, the water was dormant.

"That," said Buskull as they gazed out.

Looking back at the map, Buskull saw the lone island in the middle. "We need to get to there," he said, pointing his long arm at it.

"And how do you propose we do that?" whispered Wrisscrass.

"Swim, I guess."

He shook his head. "Not in these waters, chum – not if you want to live afterwards."

"What do you mean?"

"Only death awaits anyone who steps in. Drink or touch that water, and you won't have long to hate it."

"There!" said Feera, pointing to what appeared to be an abandoned building to the side of the lake.

Cautiously, they made their way towards it, but there was little about – if anything. Buskull could not sense a single creature, and so they walked along the flat shoreline, four strangers in a barren wasteland, hunted and scared, yet, at that moment, alone.

"Hilclop, you stay here. If you see anything, let us know and take cover."

"How?"

"What do you mean, how?"

"Well, how will I let you know?"

"I don't know. Make a sound of an owl or something," Buskull shrugged, wanting to just get on with the mission.

"Ha! You won't have many of them around 'ere. Try a Grox," said Wrisscrass.

"What the heck is a Grox?"

"Bit like your giant, just more hair and walks on all fours." Wrisscrass laughed to himself and strutted towards the warehouse, as Hilclop tried to hide a grin.

"Just come and find us," sighed Feera.

Feera and Buskull went inside as Hilclop stretched out and sat on a rock, looking around. He thought to himself how strange it was that he was in the middle of a foreign land with creatures trying to kill him, yet he felt calm. But he had panicked for too long to feel worried now. All he wanted to do was curl up into a ball and go to sleep, which he did.

Inside, Buskull and the others looked for something they could use as a raft, but it was just an abandoned warehouse.

"Have you been here before, Wrisscrass?" asked Buskull.

"Not for a long, long time."

"Would anything ever go across the water?"

"No – that water is death, that's probably why nothing comes near it."

"Why do we need to go there? What is on that island that is so important?" put Feera, a little more abruptly than he had intended.

"You cannot know, neither of you, but I need to get there."

Wrisscrass sighed. "Well – short of turning this building upside down and using it as a raft, you're not going anywhere."

It was then that Buskull appeared to have an idea, and started pacing around outside and looking at the roof. Hilclop jumped to his feet, yet he didn't see the strange footsteps in the soil that had passed him.

"What are you doing?" said Feera.

"Look, the roof is solid," Buskull replied. "We can use it as a boat – it won't sink. It's the walls that have corroded."

Buskull then went to the foundations, and, with one swift hit, cut through them with his axe. The building gave way, and with an almighty crash it came tumbling down, with the roof rolling over onto its top. Wrisscrass had to dash out of the way, and gave a stern look at Buskull.

"You could've killed me!"

Buskull ignored him, and picked up a long plank. Standing behind the building, he pushed the makeshift boat into the water, then got in and looked at the confused unit.

"Don't hang around. Something would have heard that. Go back to that rise where we came from – I'll meet you there."

He then pushed the wood into the ground to push the boat into the water. And, gently rowing with the beam, he approached the small plot of land off in the distance.

The water was thick like blood. As he rowed, he seemed to disturb small silver particles that swished around the oar, like a layer of dust upon the waterline. But it helped, for the water was thick enough to make the rowing easy, and he gained distance quickly. But the closer he came, the stronger a presence he felt from something.

It didn't take long to reach the island, sitting eerie and idle. It was but a mound, and as the boat hit the surface with a bump, he jumped onto the island, with axe in hand, and walked around it. It wasn't very large – only about four times the size of the roof he had just rowed in. The strangest thing was the feeling he had, for he felt great power, a power so strong that it was pure. It felt like the strongest feeling he had ever known, drawing him in.

He walked around the little island several times, trying to work out what was so special about it, but it was just a mound of earth in the middle of the water. Whatever or wherever this power was coming from, it was from inside. Leaning on all fours, he brought his mighty arm back and in one punch he hit the ground, his arm disappearing into the earth all the way up to his shoulder. When he pulled it back, his arm was only half covered in dirt. Looking into the small hole he had created, he saw a blue glow inside, and almost fainted with the raw power that flowed out.

"I can't believe I'm doing this," he said aloud to himself. Bracing his arms before the hole, he thought hard. He knew of the power the jewel contained, and, staring at the blue glow, he didn't know what to do.

Taking in a deep breath, he then threw his arm back in and felt for the edge, then pulled it back, bringing the earth with it. The hole grew wider, as did the feeling of the power coming out. He did it again and again until the hole became big enough for him to climb through. And so he did. Sticking his head and torso into it, he looked upon the dazzling light emanating from the blue jewel, and sitting encased on what appeared to be a very small altar was the jagged shard.

"Beriial," he said softly as he assessed it.

It wasn't very big – it was but the size of a child's thumb, but it was spiky and sharp as flint.

Reaching out, he held his forefinger and thumb around it and the jewel grew brighter, light pulsating around him as if feeling his presence. He closed his eyes and touched it slowly; suddenly his body jolted. He felt a terrible paralysis come over him; it was as if he was being electrocuted; his eyes suddenly grew wide and his veins started to protrude through his skin – he felt pain everywhere. Without him even thinking about it, moments of his life were replayed before him, as if the jewel was seeing who he was. Pictures of a small boy and girl appeared, laughing and running around a farm; tears formed in his eyes at the images, yet he couldn't control them. There was a moment where he picked up his battle-axe, taking it from the grasp of his dead father, as men fell to their knees around him in sorrow. The crown on his father's head fell away into the mud. The images went on to his first kill, of a man who was about to strangle him – there was a knife sticking out of his chest, and his own hands were bloody. The images kept coming – faster and faster, some so fast he could barely make out what they were. Some showed ancient battles from far away being fought; many showed tankards being thrown into the air with beer spilling upon the floor and cheers ringing out.

But the scenes stopped for a moment, just a moment, as an image appeared that Buskull never wanted to be reminded of: the image of two yellow eyes looking at him. He felt the anger from that day as if he were there. But he was relieved when the jewel's deadly influence moved on. More images came, and as each image came and went, so did the emotions he had felt at the time: seeing war, happiness, love, peace, sorrow – so many of sorrow, as if most of his life had been plagued by it. But then it stopped – it stopped upon a familiar face; Buskull felt calmness and trust from the jewel as the image of General Drorkon stood there in the apothecary, standing still as he told Buskull to find the jewel.

As suddenly as it had started it all just stopped, and Buskull collapsed, exhausted, in a heap in the tunnel, breathing heavily, as if he had been struck by a thunderbolt and lived to tell the tale. Looking at the jewel, now in the palm of his hand, he knew one thing. The jewel had accepted him, and asked him to take it to General Drorkon. But he got a strange emotion from it: doubt, as if it didn't trust anyone. As if it were alive, Buskull was about to answer, but instead he felt intense pressure on his leg and before he knew what was happening he was flung out of the hole, and landed flat on his back on the shore. The back of his head touched the deadly water and he felt a searing pang of pain as it burned. Wincing, he looked up only to see a dark, veiled creature bearing down on him. As he kicked his mighty leg up into its face, it fell back.

Buskull retrieved his axe, which had been lying nearby, jumped into the vessel and started rowing as quickly as he could. Turning back, he looked at the creature.

As if it had been standing there all along, the creature just stood looking at him with its arms by its sides.

Buskull stared long and hard, and couldn't help but feel he had seen that creature before – but, with the Beriial in his grasp, his senses were scrambled, so he just made his way back to the unit.

"You took your sweet old time!" said Wrisscrass, walking towards him. They all saw it, the blue glow from his clenched fist.

"What's that?" said Hilclop.

"Nothing."

But before any of them could press ahead further, there was a sudden screech in the air, enough to make one shudder as if listening to fingernails scratching down a chalkboard, and it was coming from the island. All turned and looked. It came again; it almost sounded like a woman screaming beyond what she would be capable of.

Then quiet, just quiet – not even the sound of the wind. The unit looked around; there was something eerie about the area this time, something was coming, but what?

"There," said Hilclop, pointing to the line of volcanos.

There were clouds billowing out from the summits.

"Are they erupting?" said Feera.

Each one of them looked on, squinting, trying to find out what the clouds were. Each one of them, that is, except Wrisscrass, who had his back to them and was staring at the ground, his face long and drawn, for he knew what they really were.

"We need to get out of here," he said calmly. "Yet, there is no way out."

"What do you mean?" said Buskull.

"That's no cloud, that's a swarm of Gar'lesh heading our way."

The unit looked back at the cloud, and sure enough, it was heading towards them.

"What are Gar'lesh?"

Wrisscrass turned to face them, and, stepping through the unit, he walked towards the approaching cloud. As he did, he reached down and hooked his arms into his fangerlores, holstered around his legs, and pulled them up. "Imagine death, on wings." He hissed.

Hilclop and Feera cautiously drew their swords as Buskull picked up his axe, and they followed Wrisscrass.

"Stay low. Their eyesight is poor, but they will hear you."

Buskull still clutched the Beriial but wasn't sure what to do with it, for it was still confusing his senses. He lifted up his axe and pulled the bottom off, opening up a hollow tube into which he placed the Beriial. The edge of his blade glowed with a blue light, filling the patterns of his handle and axe head. As if his axe could hold the raw power inside, his senses returned and he felt whole again. But he looked back from where they had come and felt a strong yet familiar presence approaching.

"Stay in the gullies. Hopefully they'll pass over us," shouted Wrisscrass.

"Hopefully?" questioned Hilclop.

Yet he ran and the others followed.

The unit barely got half a mile before the creatures were upon them. Wrisscrass ran into a small tunnel in the earth as they passed overhead. The most unsettling thing about them was their high-pitched wails; they sounded just like the sounds they had heard from the lake – they seemed to be calling out. As they flew past, the Gar'lesh appeared to vary in size, with some tiny, and flying around in a shoal like fish in the ocean, and others large, spanning twenty feet from head to tail. Yet they all looked similar in design: with black wings like those of a bat, and a long tail, they had talons and spikes covering their body; they had a long neck that stretched a third of their length, with a tail just as long, and horns lining from the head, along the spine to the tail. It was as if they were designed so that every bit of them was a weapon. When the light caught their bodies, there was a hint of turquoise blue, making them glitter in the sky.

The unit stood dumbfounded, for they had never seen anything like them. That is all except Wrisscrass, who sneered on as if he held a personal vendetta against them. The creatures flew overhead, some stopping to look their way, but their eyesight was so poor that they turned and carried on flying towards the lake. Soon, the creatures passed over as they continued their search.

"Let's go!" said Wrisscrass.

They emerged on the other side and kept running. The gullies proved difficult, with the unit having to run up and down mounds. There was, though, a constant reminder of the distance they still had to travel, from the imposing and ever-present volcanos they could see on the horizon.

"Keep going!" shouted Buskull, constantly checking behind him to see if anything was chasing them.

Feera led the way, with one sword drawn, his free hand out for balance, as they ran over the mounds of rock and through the gullies. The constant running over the terrain started to exhaust them, and anything lurking nearby would have heard their heavy breathing. Even Wrisscrass, who showed superb strength and endurance, was huffing, and in the dank atmosphere their breath came out like thick smoke, as if they were blowing on a pipe.

But they stopped, as shadows were cast over them. Looking up, they saw silhouettes behind the clouds, so quick that they almost missed them. Feera stopped, his shoulders rising and falling with each breath. Standing still, they all looked at each other, wondering what was going to happen. Suddenly, there was the sound of something heavy landing on the ground on the other side of a rock. Just out of the corner of their eye, something else landed on another side. They huddled together, facing outwards and pointing their weapons. Then, there was another noise, and another. Wherever they looked, they just caught a glimpse of something landing. Then, footsteps, or at least something akin to footsteps, could be heard as something approached. The noise grew louder from all around them, but they could not see who or what was creating it. One by one, their wings curled up, they could just be seen foregathering behind the rock. Then they emerged, seven of them walking slowly towards the unit with menacing looks.

Feera sneered, for they were vile. Standing on their hind legs and with long necks, they appeared to be smiling. They walked towards them, snapping their talons, clustering together as they bore down on their prey.

"ARGHH!" screamed Wrisscrass causing Feera and Hilclop to jump, as he hurled himself into the air. Raising his fangerlore in his right arm, he sliced down into one of the creatures, cutting through its neck. The head came clean off, and he pulled his arm back and thrust the fangerlore hard into another creature's torso. The beast screamed, pressing its face right up to Wrisscrass's, but he defiantly sneered his evil sneer.

The rest of the unit rushed forward. As Buskull pulled his axe back he struck the closest beast to him, but his axe head glowed blue and a big circle of energy appeared, turning the creature to ash. It grew wider, and obliterated two more creatures before dissipating into nothing. The last of the creatures scrambled, jumped back into the air as quickly as they had landed, and circled above, making sad howls as if mourning the loss of their kin.

"We need to go, now!" shouted Wrisscrass. "They cannot fight on the ground, but they are deadly in the air, and the others will now know where we are."

He sprinted off, with the unit following, running as fast as their bodies would let them over the rough terrain.

The unit started to become exhausted, and their bodies were numb, with their lungs burning. Hilclop vomited by a rock, placing his hand against it for balance as the others crowded around each other, trying to get their breath back. The creatures were mainly circling the air above; now and again, when a group splintered off and came near, Buskull would sense them and shout out, with the unit running for cover until they passed. The volcano line was now in full view, yet there was still much land to cross, and with squawks from the winged beasts above, they knew that their time was running out.

"Let's go!" said Feera, who had his helmet off and was wiping away thick beads of sweat that covered his face. He stepped out of the ravine and started running again. Buskull motioned for Hilclop to follow him, along with Wrisscrass and himself. But Feera came to a sudden stop, holding his breath, with his chest aching for oxygen. He threw a clenched fist into the air for the others to stop. Hilclop, though, was not paying attention as he kept gazing back, and ran straight into the back of him. Feera stumbled forward and lay on his front. Pulling back slowly as if he were looking into the eyes of a preying cat, he withdrew. When he was safely with them, they pulled back a few paces, but a sudden yelp from the other direction made them stop. They looked at where the noise had come from, but there was nothing, just an eerie silence in a place where no one should belong.

"Rec!" said Feera to himself.

"What are *they* doing here?" said Wrisscrass incredulously, his usual jovial attitude replaced by pure confusion.

"Who're they?" whispered Buskull, just peeking above the rise to glimpse at them. The creatures they were looking at were as big as Buskull and wrapped in armour from head to toe. It was good armour as well, strong and fixed tightly to their bodies; they were bred for war. At their shoulders the armour hooked up like waves in an ocean hitting rocks. Their faces were covered with large helmets, with more spikes and horned like metal sprouting from the tops. Their weapons were large broadswords or axes, too heavy for a human to wield; yet they were shaped like their armour, with more spikes protruding from the long blade.

"We call them the Imari," said Wrisscrass. "They're from my land and guard the Black Lord himself."

"Why are they here, then?" whispered Feera. "Does that mean … does-that-mean" he swallowed "the Black Lord is here too?"

"No – I would sense him. Anyone could, even you humans, for he radiates evil."

"How does that work?" said Hilclop, not understanding it.

Wrisscrass turned to him directly. "Just pray you don't meet him, boy!"

"So, what are they doing here?" asked Buskull, trying to get things back on track.

"I can only assume that they're … messengers."

"For who?"

He looked at him, his face very serious. "I don't know."

But Hilclop held his breath, trying desperately to pull at Buskull's vest, whilst Buskull carried his gaze into the camp and just threw a dismissive hand back at him. But Hilclop continued his tugging, and as Buskull turned to chastise him, the rest of the unit followed his gaze to find one of the Imari was standing there, looking down at them. Wrisscrass quickly grabbed a knife from his belt and threw it at its heart, the strength of his throw enough to pierce its armour. Then, running forward, he let the body fall into his arms and carefully lowered it to the ground. He pulled the knife out from its chest and cut its throat to make sure it was dead, its neck being the only bit of its body that was exposed.

Hilclop grew light-headed at the sight and started swaying, holding his hand out for balance on the rock. Feera arrived just in time to catch him before his helmet banged on the ground.

"Damn!" said Wrisscrass.

"What? Do you regret killing him?" said Feera cynically.

"No." Wrisscrass stood up and faced him.

"Then what?" said Buskull, as he crouched down, assessing the body, trying to see what Wrisscrass had seen.

"Prepare to fight." He held up his fangerlores and went to the edge of the rocks.

"What are you on about?"

"These," he said, pointing his hand down at them. "They're me, well, like me, whatever, alright, they have the link I no longer possess."

"Right? So what?"

Wrisscrass looked at the approaching creatures.

"They know he's dead."

Hilclop sat up, looking yellow, but Feera slapped his face gently and drew his blade. Reacting, Hilclop drew his, swallowed and tried to regain himself, although he looked very pale from seeing the creature's throat slit.

Wrisscrass turned to the others. "Hit hard. These are tough ones!" Then, using one hand, he jumped over the mound and clashed with the first one, using brute strength that they couldn't equal. Buskull followed, Feera next. Hilclop stepped forward, but could not help but look down at the corpse by his feet. Despite the sharpness of the blade, it wasn't a clean cut – the flaps of skin looked stretched and jagged, the nectar-like thick blood seeping out. The clashing of metal in the clearing woke him from his trance. He didn't want to go forward, yet the fear of staying there alone was too much, and, pushing himself, he stepped over the mound and saw three battles raging on.

Buskull punched one of the creatures hard, with the smack echoing out into the small clearing, but it barely fell backwards – it was as big as him and he locked into a duel. Feera drew his other sword and parried at another creature, as Hilclop stepped behind him to protect his rear. Wrisscrass was the only one who seemed to know how to fight them; using brutal tactics, he headbutted, slashed, kicked and punched with every limb he had. Hilclop's defence, though, was sloppy. He fell away from Feera as he clashed with a creature. Yet, the reality quickly hit him. He looked up at the tall beast and any confidence he had evaporated and everything Buskull had taught him disappeared; he was alone. Lowering his guard he was at the creature's mercy, yet if the creature had wanted to kill him it could have done, but it decided to play. Another creature appeared and stood behind him and kicked him in the backside towards the other, which then slapped him across the face with the back of its hand. Hilclop fell to the ground and dropped his sword with his helmet rolling away from him, blood filling his mouth. He reached forward to grab his sword, but one of the creatures trod on his hand, pinning it under the handle. He screamed in pain. The others could not go to his aid, tangled in their own duels. He was alone, and he knew it. He had to fight or he was going to die.

Feera had killed one and was wrenching his swords from its chest as two more delighted themselves on charging at him, but again, they treated it like a game. All the creatures seemed to be laughing. Buskull and Wrisscrass were the only ones making any advance, albeit slowly.

Hilclop looked up and saw that the two standing over him were watching the others fight. One held a crude blade in its hand, and he felt a chill from the very sight of it, sensing it could mean his demise. He knew that if he was quick, if he could let go of his sword and make a run for it – he may just get away. But he didn't, despite being scared; he lay on the floor and looked around, trying to think of what he could use. Then, he saw a loose rock, large enough to hold and looking heavy enough to inflict damage. He reached over, but it was too far. He looked back up at the creatures who were still watching the other skirmishes. He couldn't see their expressions, for their helmets covered their faces, but there was something about their body language that made him think they were laughing, watching the fights like spectators watching a sport. One started jeering as the other laughed, despite some of their own brethren being cut down before them. Hilclop looked anxiously back at the rock, and reached further, his fingertips brushing against its side. But he heard a grunt, and as he looked up, the bigger creature knelt down and smacked him in the face with its giant fist.

Hilclop became dazed, as the world spun around him. He could just make out the reflection of the sun upon the curved blade before his eyes. He got the strong feeling that came into his head when he felt tired, and, closing his eyes, he let the sleep come.

But just then, out of nowhere, there was a *whoosh* noise and he was sprayed with water; then he heard the sound like a sack of potatoes falling to the ground. He wondered if the creature had urinated over him, but the water tasted rotten in his mouth, and the texture was thick. Moments later, another *whoosh* noise came, and then something else fell. The pressure of the boot crushing his hands went away, and Hilclop opened one eye. Everything was still blurred, but he sensed a shadow passing him. As he lifted his head, he wiped away the spray from his face and saw his hand was smeared with black blood. He tried to look around, but nothing was there, so he just sat on the ground, shell-shocked. He looked across and saw the two dead creatures, lying on the floor with giant holes in their chests. He was sure his hand was broken, feeling a sharp, crushing pain, yet he held it close and stood up, holding his sword in his other hand.

Seeing Feera pinned against a wall, Hilclop lurched forward to help him, but before he got there, the two creatures suddenly fell – much to the surprise of Feera, who also was covered in the spray of their black blood. Wrisscrass had a creature in a headlock, with another lying on the floor, punching one and kicking the other at the same time – he was having fun. But he stopped, and his eyes went very wide, when he saw something. He looked around the camp at the strange happenings. Feera wasn't sure, but he thought he could see panic in his eyes.

"Krishta!" he shouted, and ran out of the camp, letting go of the creature, as it landed on all fours and tried to get its breath back, rubbing at its neck.

Three more beasts fell in the same state, black blood spraying out and huge holes appearing in their chests as if exploding outwards.

But, on hearing "Krishta", the remaining creatures ran for their lives in all directions, some still falling in the same way.

Feera and Hilclop ran through the camp after Wrisscrass, with Buskull following but trying to work out what was going on, for he sensed something but wasn't too sure what.

They ran into a small gulley with high rises and two entrances.

"What's going on?" demanded Buskull.

Wrisscrass was panting, his eyes wide, showing his black, bloodshot, yellow eyeballs. "You!" he said to Hilclop. "Stand there – don't take your eyes off that exit!"

"Wrisscrass! What is going on?" Buskull pressed again.

"Feera." It was the first time Wrisscrass had called him by his name, and panic showed in his voice. "You face the other way. All of you, be alert!" he said, not listening to Buskull, but bringing his blades up as if readying himself to fight till the death.

Buskull grew impatient, and grabbed him by his jerkin, bringing him up to his face.

"What is the matter with you?"

Wrisscrass just kept looking every which way.

"Krishta – she is out there!"

"Who or what is Krishta?" said Feera.

"Something terrible, something … evil, no one can see her, but she kills without your knowing, and she is coming for us." He was breathing heavily and sweating nervously, looking left and right as Buskull held him.

Feera and Hilclop looked at each other. Buskull let him go. "I did not think you believed in myths."

"She is not a myth!" he bellowed.

The other two laughed at his humiliation.

Then Buskull brought up his axe, sensing a presence. "Wait – something is coming!"

They turned, and steadied themselves as they peered over the hill. Then they saw the flash of something dark as it passed a rock. Unknowingly, they grouped closer together, bringing their weapons up.

"What's out there?" said Hilclop, breaking the tense silence.

There were no sounds, not even the wind – just an eerie silence.

"BOO!"

They all jumped and looked up, and standing there was a Knight Hawk looking down at them, holding a large crossbow.

"A Hawk! What are you doing here?" said Buskull, feeling rather foolish.

The Hawk jumped down and removed his helmet. "Helping my friends."

They all looked at Havovatch in absolute shock.

"Captain?" said Feera with awe.

Havovatch said nothing, but placed a hand on his shoulder and smiled. He then looked at Hilclop, who, to everybody's surprise, dashed forward and hugged him.

Havovatch laughed.

"I saw you die!" said Feera.

"There's a lot to tell you."

As he looked at the unit, he then noticed Wrisscrass. "What … is that?"

Buskull rested on his axe. "He gave himself up to our cause. He has been … helping us."

"Right?" said Havovatch, not taking his eyes off him.

"Why are you dressed different?" asked Hilclop, looking at his new, dark and fearsome attire.

"A lot has changed," he said, not taking his eyes off Wrisscrass.

"You're a Knight Hawk?" said Buskull.

"Yes – Commander Thiamos promoted me to general. I am now in charge of the Knight Hawks."

"Wow, now that is an honour," said Feera.

"So, you're not our captain any more?" said Hilclop.

"No. Jadge is the captain of the Three-Thirty-Third, but Buskull is in charge of this unit. General Drorkon sent me to check up on you. He wants to know if you have found what you're looking for?"

"Yes, we have."

"Then we return to him. We all have our next mission."

"It won't be easy getting out. They know we are here – they will be searching this area very soon," said Wrisscrass, looking at the flying beasts drawing closer as they scavenged the skies like a flock of gulls looking for food.

Havovatch turned to him and stepped closer, staring directly into his eyes.

"And how might you know that? Are you in league with them?"

"No!" Wrisscrass spat. "I have forsaken them, for they have nothing to offer me."

"I don't care. As far as I'm concerned, your lot are trying to kill everyone I know for the past few months … including those close to me!"

"You humans make no sense. How many of my own kin do I have to kill for you lot to believe me?"

"I've seen your lot – you kill your own anyway, regardless of reason."

Wrisscrass stared down at him, sneering, showing his fangs, angry that Havovatch hadn't accepted his loyalty. "We may be vile by your standards, but we don't lie!"

Havovatch stared long and hard at him, bringing the end of his Malorga up to Wrisscrass's chin, but his attention was cut short as they all pricked up their ears in the direction of something coming.

"General!" said Hilclop, looking south. They all joined him and stood still, watching the landscape in the distance turn dark as if a cloud had passed over it. But it was no cloud – it was the vile creatures flying straight towards them, as if they had all been told where they were.

"You cannot fight them," said Wrisscrass. "There are too many. Follow me and we might just get out of this alive!"

Havovatch turned to Wrisscrass.

"Why? What makes you so special?"

"Because I know how they think, and right now you don't have much of a choice. When they get to us, they will swoop down and take us chunk by chunk."

Havovatch pursed his lips and shook his head.

"General," said Buskull, "I don't trust him either, but he has shown his virtue many times."

The creatures' howls became audible around them as they drew nearer.

"This way," said Wrisscrass, breaking his gaze from Havovatch, and setting off at a run over the mounds towards the volcanos. The rest of the unit followed, as Buskull and Havovatch exchanged cautious glances.

The creatures soon came flying overhead, flapping their giant wings as they circled the unit, screeching the other way as if calling someone. One very large monster, larger than they had yet seen, flew past the unit and moved in front of them. It turned and faced them, flapping its outstretched wings to hold its position in front of them. Buskull held his axe in both hands behind his head and threw it into the air, striking the creature in the chest. The creature curled up in the air and fell to the ground, ash puffing out from under it as it landed. As the unit passed, Buskull pulled his axe out and kept running. Feera heard a tiny screech next to him, and, turning, he saw a whelp of the larger creatures. It did not attack, but kept screaming to tell the others where they were. Throwing his sword at the creature, he cut it in two, leaving it withering like a fish out of water.

Wrisscrass turned and looked behind him, his eyes widening.

"DUCK!"

The unit fell to the floor. As they looked behind, nine large winged beasts came swooping towards them in a single-lined formation, their legs down and their talons outstretched, ready to catch them. They were poised to take the unit, or at least chunks of them. Holding their weapons in the air, they lay on their backs, and hit out at the creatures as they flew past, blood dripping over them from lacerations to their guts and legs. As the last one flew by, Wrisscrass launched himself into the air, grabbing hold of it by its neck, and continued to punch at it with his fangerlore. The creature convulsed and tried to shake him off, heading vertically upwards, but it did not fly high enough and was brought to the ground, with Wrisscrass letting go so he could land perfectly on a steep rock as the beast continued to fall below him.

The unit continued to run past as Wrisscrass jumped down to them, still slicing at the smaller creatures flying past; but more started gaining.

Running through tunnels carved into the ground, they made their way, single-file, through the desolate land. Havovatch kept turning to fire his Malorga at the creatures, but a swarm of them came flying towards them like bats. Frantically, they circled the unit, scratching them with their small talons. Using their tails, they wrapped themselves around the unit's arms as they tried to hold them in place for the bigger creatures to catch up. Slashing violently, the unit were barely able to fend them off. One grabbed Havovatch's Malorga, prised it from his grasp and dropped it out of reach. Hilclop screamed in pain and curled up into a ball, seeing his blood smear the ground. The Gar'lesh really struggled with Buskull, however, his strength was more than enough to fight against them. Swinging his axe in one long swoop, he cut several to bits, the blue energy from his axe shooting out and turning several more into ash. He couldn't see Feera, just the flapping mess around him, with his voice shouting in pain somewhere midst the fray. He pressed on towards him, grabbing them off him, leaving Feera bloody. Buskull crushed them in his grasp. But there were hundreds, all flying around, wildly screeching with delight as they hewed away at the unit. Buskull filled his lungs with air, straightened his arms and roared at the winged devils. The screeches turned to squeals as the now terrified creatures fought to get away; their ears appeared to be extra sensitive and they left the unit frantically.

The unit dragged themselves up, all covered in red blood from the attack, some with small scratches as if they had fallen into a nettle bush, others with nasty lacerations, as if they had had a fight with a nettle bush and lost.

"I thought we were done for. Good thinking, giant," said Wrisscrass, who looked the bloodiest, for he didn't have any armour on.

"Let's go," said Buskull, just wanting to get out of there.

They started to approach the base of the volcanos as they sought the path they had taken to get over. Their hearts were constantly in their mouths as they made their way across the bleakness. The creatures were still flying overhead, but keeping their distance, as if they feared them but didn't want to run from them. With uneven ground, and towers of rocks around them, it was tough going, with Feera leading and Hilclop dragging himself behind.

"Run! Just keep going!" shouted Havovatch, as he and Buskull protected the rear flank. He continued to use his Malorga, but whilst one or two were brought down, there were still hundreds around them. The weapon was surprisingly easy to use and he hadn't missed a shot yet, but he was running low on bolts. There was a loud cranking noise each time he loaded, pulling the ratchet back on his Malorga and shooting at the creatures. The bolt wasn't seen leaving the crossbow, but when it hit the creatures it flung them back or obliterated them altogether.

The unit started to ascend the volcano, as the creatures clumped together, circling them, casting shadows over the unit as they covered the sky. But in the midst of the carnage, on a high rise to the right, there appeared a sinister figure, standing there with its arms tense by its sides. Tall, with its rags flapping against its scaly body, it stared on at the unit as they fought for their lives. But its gaze was just fixed upon one of them.

"*Algermatum!*" it whispered, as if Buskull could hear it from all that way away.

But Buskull did hear it. Leaving his axe in a downed creature's chest, he turned slowly, hearing its whisper as if it were right next to him. Staring off into the distance, he saw the creature looking at him as it pulled back its veil. His eyes went wide with horror, as if he had seen a ghost.

"It cannot be," he said, aghast.

The unit didn't notice his distraction as they fought their way up the path, meeting clusters of the creatures that Wrisscrass had enjoyed fighting when the unit had come out of the mist.

"*It can be. Did you know that you're the last of your kind?*" said the creature, again whispering, then cackling with a cruel and deep laughter. "*I need you, to complete my collection, for each one of your kin did not go down without a struggle.*" Its voice showed no sign of annoyance – it seemed to relish its experiences with his race.

Anger gripped Buskull. A reality he did not want to believe was confirmed in that instant. He pursed his lips, gnarled his teeth, pulled his axe away and ripped open the chest cavity of the winged demon, spraying the ground with thick black blood. He then lurched off over the hill, taking down another beast as it flew low enough to get him. Like a charging boar, he ran after the surreptitious figure, just swinging his axe at anything that got in his way.

The unit carried on, unaware of their comrade. They had killed many, with the landscape littered with corpses as the elite unit kept going.

Feera repeatedly hit a creature in the face, before letting it fall. He had reached the summit, and looked down over the mist, with the Rogan Defence Line off in the distance. Below him, he saw the side of the volcano and surrounding landscape highlighted by the sun; the rock face had been carved out into battlements and parapets, as if defending against what could come from beyond the other side of the mist.

"We're getting close," he said, turning to the unit, creatures still flying about them, although cautiously. But as he looked, he noticed that something wasn't right.

"Hang on – where's Buskull?"

They all stopped and looked around, but he was nowhere to be seen.

Chapter Nineteen
The Cloth Demons

"I've heard of these people. They're sick!"

"Yes, they are." Malffay grinned at Sarka, as if he admired their style.

"I've never met them face to face. They say even the Knight Hawks cannot contend with them."

Malffay spat on the floor. "Knight Hawks? They have nothing on this lot. These're something very special, al'right."

"Well, they better be for the price I'm paying for them, I don't want to be disappointed."

"You won't." Malffay stared at him sternly.

Trotting gently, they approached Limni Forest, a dark and sinister place which held many secrets. No one ventured near, not even armies, for death awaited them; well, they say death, anyone who did approach was never seen again. Just several months previously an army marching from the far west was exploring the world. They ventured inside, their trail disappearing into the forest, but they never came out. And now, this evening, two lone men approached: one of them not knowing what he was about to meet, the other meeting them again.

As the treeline loomed over them, Sarka saw hundreds of human skeletons hanging from the canopy, as if they were a warning to anyone who had wandered that far to turn back. Some still had shreds of flesh on their bones. Sarka grimaced. "They must have been there since they died?" he said sneering up at them.

"Or since they were alive?" said Malffay.

Sarka's heart started to beat faster and his hands visibly trembled, whereas Malffay – although he looked on with a more serious expression than he usually had – was rather calm under the circumstances.

They proceeded towards a path that led straight, the tree branches forming a dense, natural arc all the way along, as if it were a tunnel through the forest.

"Are you sure this is the right place?" Sarka said hesitantly, as he stopped for a moment.

"Without a doubt," said Malffay, looking around as he remembered the last time he was there.

"The trees are ... strange here." He said touching a branch but withdrawing his hand because of the strange texture.

The trees and their branches looked different from those in a normal forest – they looked thicker and worn, as if they got the wrong nutrients from the earth and didn't grow properly.

"They use the blood of their victims to fertilise the ground. It's said that if you cut a branch, it will bleed."

Sarka grimaced again, he wasn't used to this, he had never wanted his bed, servants and the comforts of his tower so much. But with the Black Lord's threat, he knew he needed help; if not to help the Black Lord, then to protect himself.

"If it were not for the fact that these vile demons were costing me so much money, I'd have sent you in alone," he spat.

As they rode deeper into the forest, the trees held shadows, shadows so dark that light could barely pierce the blackness. And within these shadows were men and women, still and soundless, watching the two riders entering their domain. Only a hound could tell they were there by their scent, but otherwise, they made no sound, no movement; uncomfortable or not, they just sat amongst the foliage, waiting for their orders.

Moments passed, and Sarka trotted into the clearing illuminated by the moonlight, which covered the area in a shady blue, with long shadows from the trees making the clearing seem smaller. Malffay sat next to him, feeling relaxed, yet the shadows made Sarka feel uneasy.

"There's no one here," he said abruptly, but mainly because he wanted to leave.

"Oh, they're here alright," said Malffay, as if looking directly at them and knowing exactly where they were.

Sarka looked closer at the trees, but saw nothing. Then, out of the darkness, a figure appeared, tall and covered in navy cloth, which was tight against his body and head, with just the one sword reachable over his right shoulder. There was a thin slit in the hood where his eyes were. He didn't even have shoes on, but cloth wrapped around his feet, with strips of ribbon to tie the cloth tightly against him. He wasn't big, but the tight cloth wrapped around him showed that he was strong.

"I'm told you can help me?" Sarka said nervously, but trying to remain dignified, for he did not feel in control of the situation. But the stranger said nothing. He just stood there with his arms by his sides, as if waiting for something, something more than the words Sarka spoke.

"They don't like to speak unless they have to."

"What do I do, then?" Sarka whispered back.

"They only know one thing," Malffay said, pointing with his head at the bag attached to the saddle. Taking it, Sarka held it in the air.

"For every soldier you have, to obey my orders and fight for me," he shouted, as if the stranger was deaf.

He threw it at the stranger's feet, but he did not bend to pick it up, he didn't even look down at it – instead, he maintained his stare upon Sarka. Then, as if a part of the shadows were becoming detached, another figure emerged, dressed exactly the same as the one standing, but this one appeared to be a woman – Sarka could tell by the curve of her breasts sticking out from the cloth. She bent down and looked in the bag, delved her hand in and pulled a few pure golden coins out, the only other colour in the clearing. She then spoke into the other stranger's ear.

"And there is far more where that came from. All I ask is for your allegiance," reinforced Sarka.

A moment passed as the stranger thought it through. Then, raising a hand up, he clicked his fingers and all around, sparks flew as torches ignited, and hundreds, thousands of torches lit the clearing and deep into the forest. Jumping from trees and crawling out from bushes, the shadows spat out more and more of them. All had either simply a sword or a bow, and were dressed from head to toe in pure navy cloth; only the light from the torches showed that they were there.

***

"Where is he?" hollered Feera, wrenching his sword from a creature's gut before turning his blade on a small bat-like beast, which yelped at him and flew away with only one leg.

The unit descended the volcano on an unmade path. They just worked their own way down by jumping over jagged rocks, as creatures kept flying past them from the sky, and the garrison tried to work their way towards them from the ground. They were all panting heavily, their swords rent, their armour messy and covered in black blood, although some red with nasty gashes to their arms from the bat swarms.

As Havovatch descended, he wrapped a bandage around a nasty lesion to his right arm, caused by a talon from one of the flying creatures. He wouldn't usually do so, but the blood was so thick it was making it difficult for him to grip his sword. Taking a look at his exhausted unit, he wondered, they all wondered, *will we make it out alive?* The attacks from the creatures were relentless and one of their own was missing.

"Who saw him last?"

Panting, they looked at each other and shook their heads.

"Shall we go back for him?" said Hilclop.

"He's gone!" shouted Wrisscrass. "Face it: we all die at some point. He couldn't keep up – he is weak. We need to go now!"

"Maybe where you come from you abandon your friends, but not with us humans. And, if it hasn't occurred to you, he is the mission – he went over to that island, remember!"

Wrisscrass laughed loudly. Havovatch watched on, wanting to say something that would resolve the matter. But he knew that his rank did not affect Wrisscrass, and somehow that made him feel intimidated by him.

"*My* kind look at the situation as it is and act upon it. If your giant was stupid enough to leave us, then that is his problem."

Feera clenched his fists.

"I've killed enough of your kind. I can kill you – it'll make my day!" he said gritting his teeth.

"Just you try, boy."

There was a long pause as they just stared at each other.

"Enough!" shouted Havovatch, as he swung his sword at another flying creature daring to get near. They didn't seem to want to attack any more, but he kept an eye on them.

"He's right," said Havovatch after a moment.

Feera shot him a look of horror.

"We don't know where he is, the land behind us is swarming with creatures and we need to get out of here! He can take care of himself."

"Sir?" said Hilclop, trying to make them aware of something, but he was ignored.

"You cannot forgo Buskull!" shouted Feera.

"Sir?" protested Hilclop, but again he was ignored.

Feera just stared at Havovatch, his teeth gritting together. "Has death made you mad?"

"Feera! Remember your place! Now, move – that's an order!"

"Sir!" shouted Hilclop, who, for good measure, also shoved Havovatch in the shoulder.

Suddenly, everyone looked at him, recognising the fear in his voice. He wasn't staring at them but over their heads, and raising a hand up he pointed to the volcano's highest peak. They followed his point, and above them steam was venting out of the rock. The ground kept opening up as sudden vents appeared, letting white steam gush out as it would from a saucepan with a lid on. The volcanos, which had appeared dormant, were now very much alive.

"Oh, crap!" said Wrisscrass.

"What?" shouted Havovatch.

Wrisscrass pointed to the creature, tall with its arms aloft, a yellow glow emanating from its face. In its hand it held what appeared to be a severed head.

"What's that?"

Wrisscrass didn't take his eyes off it, but just stared on.

"Death."

"What should we do?"

"Run!"

The unit sprinted towards the mist, with their backs to the winged bats. The creatures descended upon them, only to be held back by their swinging weapons. Wrisscrass threw a few knives at them, causing them to fly away again.

Havovatch looked back, he couldn't see clearly what was in its hand, he just hoped it wasn't. He couldn't even bear to think of it.

"Wait!" a shout came from behind them.

They looked back to see Buskull running down towards them, covered in black blood as if he had almost fought to his end and survived. He also seemed fatigued as he took huge, deep breaths.

Instantly, the unit's hearts were relieved, after thinking of all the possibilities of what could have happened to him – now he was there in the flesh.

"Where have you been?" said Feera, who paced forward and punched him in the chest. But Buskull did not answer. Bowing his head, his chest heaving for breath, he just looked at the floor.

"It's not important now. Let's just get out of here," said Havovatch, looking at the creatures coming their way from either side. The ground started to tremble as well, and the volcanos became explosive, with giant rocks being spat out and lava spewing. The sides of the volcanos appeared to be exploding, with the creature above seeming to orchestrate it. Whatever was in its hand was now glowing; like a mystic ball. Suddenly, the flying creatures disappeared in all directions as the steam surged into the air. The slimy demons with turquoise scales scattered in all directions leaving the unit alone on the bleak rock.

"We need to run!" shouted Wrisscrass, with his gaze still upon the demon on the peak.

Surprisingly, he grabbed hold of Hilclop and disappeared into the mist. Feera held the back of Buskull's belt and followed, their bodies quickly consumed by the dense fog. Havovatch, though, stood for a moment, looking at the area around them. He kept looking at the terrain – it seemed to hold such pain, such desolation, it was as if it held memories, and from these he felt great despair. It was strange to be there, but it was almost exciting, as if he was pushing beyond his limits of control to stay somewhere so dangerous, every second seeming like an hour. But he kind of felt he had to stay there, so that he could tell others of what he saw.

Suddenly, he found himself looking up at the sky as he lay on his back, soot and dust covering him. He had fallen to the floor as the ground around him had rumbled and fallen apart. He didn't cough or have to rub his eyes though, for the fabric of his helmet kept it all away. As he sat up, he saw deep caverns open up in the earth, orange glows coming from deep within. He pulled himself to his feet, somewhat sluggishly. The world really was exploding around him as rocks flew into the air, and the entire mountainside fell like a disturbed scree. As he looked up at the creature that appeared to be controlling the apocalyptic event, it stood with its legs apart, its arms outstretched, as the mountain collapsed around it.

Havovatch turned and sprinted into the mist, running as fast as he could. The cloud was so dense that he could only hear the thunderous noise behind him, but that made everything worse for he could not see what was happening. Rocks fell around him, some smouldering white-hot and glowing enough to create their own light. Havovatch heard the noise behind him, which could only be described as a thunderstorm echoing in a canyon. Exhaustion was not on his mind – he just ran as the giant, smouldering rocks appeared to be evaporating the mist, and his heart jumped into his mouth as he looked back and saw the mountain falling towards him, huge mounds of black smoke falling at a colossal speed as if it had weight. Looking up, he gasped as the smoke appeared to be falling on top of him, like a building in an earthquake. The storm cloud was so dark it was as if night was creeping up on him, but it was very much daytime.

Sprinting, he forgot about any injuries he had, for he was desperate to live, to find his unit and get out of this world.

But as he ran, unbeknownst to him, a white orb appeared above his head and a sphere of light surrounded him; any rocks that came his way in that moment rebounded off.

It took a while to get back across the mist, but, unlike when he had cautiously walked alone through it to find his unit following their tracks, Havovatch was running for his life, and before he knew it, he came to the base of the wall. The footprints on the ground showed that the others had turned left, and so he followed.

The noise of the flow started to diminish behind him, yet he heard the rumbles of the mountain's echo across the land. As he looked left, slowly out of the mist came a tidal wave of hot ash, its momentum fading. Stopping mere inches from his feet was just black rock, steaming away. If he were anywhere else he would have fallen to his knees in relief, but he kept running to find his unit. And soon, their silhouettes appeared, as they panted heavily before the base of the hill, which led up to the wall. They all stood watching the smouldering ash before them.

"It's good to see you, General," said Buskull.

"What just happened? And how aren't we buried and burnt to a crisp?"

"The mountains exploded," sobbed Hilclop, as if the reality of coming so close to death really shook him, and he had been spared. "I saw a white light." He continued looking into space.

Wrisscrass rubbed his hair. "Bless 'im, he's seeing things."

"What did it?" Havovatch asked Wrisscrass.

"We call it the Goola, that creature on top of the mountains. Vile thing, even by our standards," he said, smiling. "We are the only things to have escaped its grasp, I bet – he will know we've survived and will now hunt us down."

"Well, we did," said Feera, relieved.

"Yes, and I'm sure he knows. So let's get going, because he will not stop now until we're dead."

They proceeded up the hill and, as they ascended, they heard voices above them. And as they appeared out of the mist, the white orb vanished from around their heads, although no one noticed. Emerging, they saw Xot standing with three Ninsks. As Xot looked down, he froze, and almost choked on the wine he was drinking. The Ninsks went to guard.

"Didn't expect to see us, did ya, chum?" said Wrisscrass as he strutted forward. Angrily, he grabbed the scruff of Xot's clothing and rammed his forehead into his face so hard that it knocked him out cold. The Ninsks started making a strange buzzing noise from behind their helmets and went to parry forward, but the rest of the unit held their swords towards them as they passed.

"Buskull, bring him with us!" demanded Havovatch.

He bent down, picked up Xot's limp and unconscious body and threw him over his shoulder.

"If you or any others follow us, he dies!" said Havovatch, and they made their way over the wall and off into the desert.

Havovatch ordered the unit to stop briefly, as Buskull stitched their wounds from the flying bats. Wrisscrass stitched his own, leaving neat lines of crosses on his grey skin. The mystery of how he had stitched his jerkin together so neatly had now been answered.

"Anything following us?" Havovatch asked Buskull before they set off.

"They are around, but nowhere near, General."

"Good, let's find somewhere to rest."

They had walked for most of the night, and dawn was starting to creep up as the sand dunes became visible around them, spreading long, dark shadows westwards. The unit were shattered, sleep-deprived for three days; and, after the amount of fighting and running they had had to endure, they were reeling on the last of their energy.

"How will we know where to go?" whined Hilclop, as he dragged his feet, creating long grooves from his trail in the sand.

"General Drorkon said he will find us," replied Havovatch.

It was then that he saw a small, rocky outcrop, out of the way of the wind, where they could hide.

As they entered the confined space, Buskull lowered Xot onto the floor in the centre of the outcrop; he groaned slightly but was still unconscious. Taking a huge, deep breath, Buskull went and sat alone near the entrance, looking out in case anything came. His eyes, though, were distant, not looking at the landscape but playing back troubled memories in his head from a long, long time ago.

The rest of the unit sat down, tired.

"Thing!" said Havovatch to Wrisscrass, who looked up and smiled, for insults washed over him. "You want to prove yourself? Then you take the first watch!"

"Very well, *General*," he said, with a mocking salute.

"You two, get some sleep."

Hilclop and Feera were glad for it, and nuzzled into their cloaks; they were out as soon as they had closed their eyes.

Xot's body jolted slightly as he dreamed in his painful slumber, the smash of Wrisscrass's skull playing with his nightmares. It certainly showed, with a bruise the size of a saucepan appearing over his face.

Havovatch knew he would not wake for some time, and looking up at Buskull, he approached him, for he could finally have a private word with him.

Buskull sat in the darkness on his own. He was not like Havovatch had ever seen him before. Almost rocking back and forth, he sat looking into space as if trying to understand something.

"Where did you go, Buskull?" He didn't realise it, but behind his tone was a strong sense of authority, for he wanted to know, he demanded to know.

Buskull did not turn to look at him – he felt too depressed to answer.

"Buskull, I asked you a question!"

"I saw something," he said quietly, not looking up.

"What did you see that was so important to desert this unit?!"

Buskull didn't answer. Havovatch was getting fed up with the mystery. He needed to know what was going on, what from his past had made him the man he was?

"You deserted your unit, your friends! Now, I will have an answer."

Buskull faced him directly, but his eyes kept flickering about as if he didn't know where to start.

"Eighteen years ago," he began...

It was a warm, muggy morning on a bright summer's day. Buskull snored loudly as he lay sprawled across his bed, but his nostrils twitched as smoke passed by. The slits of his eyes opened slightly and all he saw was a blur before his eyes. But he couldn't ignore the smell of smoke. He groaned as he pulled himself up and rubbed his face – he couldn't help but grin, knowing that Ellisiot had let him sleep in again, although he had asked her not to. Sitting up, he frowned at the amount of smoke in the room.

"Kids!" he said to himself, annoyed that his son and daughter had burned too much again. Pacing through the house, he stumbled as he trod on a wooden toy lying idle on the floor. He winced, shook his head and navigated across the room, which was strewn with wooden toys, ready for him to tread on.

"Ellisiot!" he grumbled as he walked across the room.

But there was no reply. He walked over to a long trough they used to wash themselves with, hunched over and splashed water over his face. He stared at his reflection as the water dropped down from his nose and chiselled jaw. "A Warrior?" he said to himself. But he shrugged it off – he was happy with the life he had.

He grabbed a vest from the rail and put it on, the tight shirt pulling against his large, muscular frame.

"Ellisiot, where are you? The kids are burning weeds again – there's smoke everywhere."

But he heard no reply. He was starting to get angry; the smell of smoke would linger in the house for days if he didn't put it out.

He stomped downstairs and saw a haze, as the smoke was thicker, so thick that it tickled the back of his throat.

"For crying out loud, Ellisiot!" he bellowed.

But there was still no reply.

He walked across the room to the veranda, and only then did he realise that something was very wrong. He couldn't see across the valley, for the smoke was so dense he could barely see the ground, and it was moving fast, as if a furnace had got out of control.

Buskull ran outside and covered his mouth with his vest, with one arm outstretched in case he walked into anything. Then, just through the smoke, he saw a glow, which flickered at him. As he pushed forward, the glow intensified until he realised what it was. Fire! His cornfield was alight, with much of it destroyed, the dried plants near the end of their harvest fuelling the ferocious blaze. And, above the noise of the flames, he heard a scream. Running forward, he looked to a rise in the plantation. And there, tied to a pole, was his wife, being burned alive.

"No!" he shouted, not quite believing it.

Seeing the fence post he had created lining the plantation, he knew that to his left was the pigsty, which sloped into a stream. He ran and sure enough the stream was there with a line of troughs for the pigs. Grabbing one, he turned and realised that all the pigs lay slaughtered by his feet. He threw the trough into the stream and then threw the water at the flames. Gallons sprayed over the fire, causing it to dull down. He wasted no time in throwing the trough back in, and repeated the process. Above his valiant attempts to gain control, Ellisiot screamed as the fire consumed her.

"I'm coming, my love!" he bellowed.

Running to and from the stream, throwing gallon after gallon of water, Buskull eventually created a path through the flames. With the last trough of water, he ran through the fire as his legs burned, and threw the water over his wife, covering Ellisiot's body as it steamed. With her head slumped forward, she wasn't present to anything around her.

Gently, Buskull lifted her face so he could look into her eyes, tears welling up in his own.

"Ellisiot, my love," he said gently, not truly believing what had just happened. All he could see in her eyes was suffering, and, cradling her head against his chest, he brought his right hand up and snapped her neck. Her body slumped forward into his grasp; she stopped suffering.

Carrying her wilting body in his arms, he paced back the way he had come. The wind took the smoke behind him and he stepped into the clearing. He slowed his pace and fell to his knees, as he saw another shock that stopped his heart, an image that would forever burn into his memory. Before him, his son and his daughter lay dead, their eyes closed. In his son's grasp was one of the knives they used for cutting meat, smothered in black blood. He lowered Ellisiot's body to the ground, then picked his children up and cradled them in his arms, his head jolting as he cried incessantly, trying to understand what had happened, who could have done this.

"My girl ... my boy," he whimpered.

But, as he looked up, he saw something – a creature, as tall as him, looking on with piercing, yellow eyes. Upon Buskull noticing it, it turned and hobbled into the woods.

As much as Buskull wanted to launch up and chase it down, he sat there, with his family before him, holding them one last time.

Standing over the ground with the churned-up earth, Buskull looked down at the grave, knowing that his family were at peace as the children cuddled their mother.

The fire had grown out of control, and his house was starting to be consumed by the blaze. Kneeling down, he kissed the ends of his fingers and placed them on top of the churned-up earth.

"I love you," he said quietly.

Then, as he stood up, a gentle man left him, almost as if his soul had vanished and been replaced by a new one – although it wasn't so new: it was a man he once was but gave up for love. The furrows of his eyebrows frowned deeply, and his chest started to heave as he stared at the location where the creature had been.

As part of his house fell apart, he ran into the flames, not caring for the embers that landed upon his skin. With his fist brought up high, he punched down hard through the thick, wooden floorboards, and started pulling. Beneath was another yard to the ground, where he delved in and started scraping away the earth with his giant hands. Then, he found it. His axe was covered in wet, sticky mud, but he pulled it free and picked up an old sack hanging on the wall, then left the house as it fell in on itself. Entering the forest, he didn't look back as his life was taken away from him.

Havovatch sat in silence, tears running down his cheeks but his mouth firmly shut, as he wished with all his power for retribution for his friend. He stood beside Buskull and placed a hand on his shoulder. "I'm sorry." He croaked.

Buskull nodded but said nothing; he just looked at the ground.

"Listen – if you need to go back out there, you have my backing, but I need to get back to General Drorkon."

But Buskull looked at the end of his axe handle, just seeing a blue glow emanating from around the edge of the seal. "No – we have a mission to complete. But I am sure that, one day, we will meet again."

Seeing a unit of cavalry riding their way, Havovatch smiled as he held up his hand to his forehead, shading the dawn sun from his eyes, to make sure they were friendly.

"They're here," he shouted to the others, as he recognised the banner of the Two-Twenty-Eighth.

Xot was still unconscious and lay slumped over Buskull's shoulder, drooling from his mouth, leaving a wet patch on Buskull's vest. But Wrisscrass caught his eye again, and walked alongside Feera as if they were friends – although Feera's body language suggested otherwise. He couldn't help but wonder why a savage creature such as he was really there, for just switching sides so casually didn't seem to add up.

They carried on walking as the war riders approached, forty in total. Drorkon had clearly taken all the necessary precautions to make sure that the unit of forty horses and riders did all that was necessary to find them and get them back to Shila. The men and horses were well equipped and covered in armour. Five other horses with no owners were being trailed behind. Gwerob, one of Drorkon's seconds, approached, his hand in the air in greeting.

"It's good to see you, Commander."

"And you, General. You got what was required, I trust?" he said looking at Buskull.

Havovatch looked at Buskull, who gave a nod. Havovatch grew curious as to what was going on.

"Very well. However, I must point out that the whole west side of Ezazeruth has been overrun. We must be fast and stay together."

"Overrun? By what?"

Gwerob gave him a long and confused look.

"I thought you knew, General?"

Havovatch blinked at him.

"The Golesh from beyond the Rogan Defence Line. They've reached as far as Ambenol, and overrun everything in their path."

Havovatch stared on blankly – he had several thoughts hit him at once.

"Ambenol? Is Undrea OK?"

"Yes! She's fine – we got there just in time."

"Oh, no!" he said, looking east.

"General?" Gwerob said.

"I need a horse!"

"Very well. We have one for each of you, but my orders are to bring you to Shila!"

Havovatch mounted with precision, something that was starting to come naturally to him.

"With respect, Commander, I need to do this. I will be two days behind you!" Without a second word, he turned and galloped off east as the others stared at each other, not understanding what was going on.

"We need to follow him," said Feera, quickly mounting one of the other horses.

"We need to report to the general," said Buskull, not taking his eyes off Havovatch, his conscience battling between duty and losing his friend again.

"I'll go!" offered Wrisscrass.

"Ha! Fat chance. We're not letting you out of our sight!" spat Hilclop.

Wrisscrass turned to Buskull.

"You know I am the only one. If I go with you I'll most likely be killed. I can protect him from my kind – I know how they think and how they behave!"

Buskull still had not taken his eyes off Havovatch, and, with a very slight nod, Wrisscrass mounted a horse, dug his heels into its sides, and galloped after him.

"What did you just do?!" shouted Feera.

Buskull watched, on not saying a word, knowing that many more could perish if he did not get to General Drorkon quickly.

Smoke, ash and bonfire was all Havovatch smelt and saw when he reached Haval. The entire town was decimated: not a building was standing, not even the carcass of one. It was just one giant black circle on the ground, as if the Black were leaving their marker.

After a day's hard riding, Havovatch dismounted and stepped slowly through the horror, with his bottom lip trembling. He saw no bodies, no armour, but for all he knew the townspeople could have been thrown into the barn and burned alive. He wished so much that he had ordered the Three-Thirty-Third to stay put; he was filled with so much regret of his own decisions that his hands were trembling, and he needed to vent his frustrations on something.

He fell to his knees at the spot he knew where Lord Kweethos's giant villa had once stood; soot puffed into the air around him.

"You're a hard man to catch up with!" came a cruel voice from behind him. Wrisscrass dismounted and rubbed his groin from the ache of hard riding.

Havovatch said nothing as he looked down, his eyes closed and thinking back to the cathartic feeling of falling asleep on Kweethos's porch after their discussion.

"Ha!" said Wrisscrass. "Right there: that's where your giant threw me through a building."

Havovatch ripped his Kopis from his scabbard, and, launching to his feet, grabbed Wrisscrass by his jerkin and laced the blade across his throat.

"What are you doing here?!"

Wrisscrass, for the first time, did not smile – he just stared and shrugged.

"To protect you," he said softly.

Havovatch gritted his teeth. "I don't need protecting – I'm a Knight Hawk!"

"Look around, human. You think you could have stopped what did this single-handed?"

Havovatch pursed his lips, fury building up inside him. He pulled the blade away, walked off and looked around at the terrain, hoping to see a Golesh, to kill it.

"I would say I'm sorry about your friends," Wrisscrass added, "but you need to coordinate your efforts —"

"Shut up! I don't need *you* telling me what I need to do!" Havovatch said, pointing with his blade.

"You humans really annoy me."

"Get over it."

Wrisscrass smiled.

"What do you want, beast? What do you want from us? Why are you here?"

There was a pause as Wrisscrass stared on, clenching his fists.

"OK – there is a reason. My mission was to kill you, and as soon as I failed, my master killed my brother. He has killed most of my kind, so many that there are just a few of us left. I want to live so that my kind don't get wiped from this earth."

"Genocide? Yet you'll happily kill other things? Creatures? Beasts? Humans?"

"Survival of the strongest, really."

Havovatch cocked his jaw, trying to figure Wrisscrass out.

"What exactly are you?"

"Something terrible," he smiled.

"Can't you take anything seriously?"

Wrisscrass again shrugged. "I want to live, and I want retribution."

"Fine!"

There was a long pause between them.

"You know these beasts from the south?" said Havovatch after a while.

"I do."

"Where have they gone?"

"Some have gone south, but most have gone north."

"Len Seror?"

"Perhaps. I don't know your cities, but judging by the tracks, a majority have gone north."

Havovatch walked to his horse and mounted.

"Fine. You want to prove yourself: help me hunt them down, and when we find them …"

Wrisscrass looked up. "… Yes?"

"Well, we'll see." Havovatch did not want to tell him of his plan; he still did not trust him, but he did have premonitions of slicing his throat.

They both rode north, following the trail of churned-up earth from the army that had laid it.

It took all night to get to Len Seror, but, dismounting a couple of leagues before, Wrisscrass led the way on foot towards the city, leaving the horses to graze after the fierce ride. Havovatch could already tell there was something terrible happening; in the dawn sunrise stood five huge towers beyond the hills, shooting so high into the air that the tops were brushing against the clouds, evening sunlight reflecting off thousands of stained-glass windows up and down them. But, circling the towers was black smoke. So thick and large were the clouds, they created darkness below. Where the smoke was coming from, though, was hidden on the other side of the hill before them.

On their stomachs, they crawled along the ground, using bushes as cover, and they soon made their way up the hill. There were Golesh sentries about, and Havovatch had no doubt that Len Seror was being laid siege to. Without warning, Wrisscrass flicked a knife from his belt and threw it at one that had just appeared. It was doing its trousers up after urinating in the bushes, but was struck on the side of the head and fell. Moving quickly, Wrisscrass pulled the body into the foliage and turned to Havovatch.

"Keep quiet – these things have keen senses and will hear you."

"They sound more like animals than humans."

"Maybe they're perfected humans?" said Wrisscrass smiling.

Havovatch ignored him and looked over the brow of the hill, keen to get over it and find out what was going on. As they crawled up, they came to the top, with bushes spaced out sporadically over the ridge. Keeping low and using the shrubbery for cover, they were unlikely to be seen, and sat peering at a sight of horror before them. Havovatch's eyes went wide; Wrisscrass just managed to cock an eyebrow.

"It appears you're right, fella! The city is in trouble."

Firstly, it struck him how big the five towers inside the city were. As big as the Acropolis of Cam, they shot up into the air. Just as the Acropolis was a symbol of Cam's magnificence, these towers meant the same for Len Seror. And draped all the way down each of their sides were the Lorian banners, as if saying: *We are not defeated, and we will not be defeated.* And surrounding the city was just black: creatures' corpses littered the ground, black blood saturating it; most of the wall was heavily damaged, with blackened areas from blood-like dried waterfalls running down. Carcasses of burnt-out siege engines and ladders lay before the walls, but the defenders had held out well. There were flags still flying (some appeared new, made of patchwork sheets and cloth) and garrisons lining the walls, shouting mockingly down at the creatures as they started retreating from another uneventful attack. As Havovatch squinted, he was sure he could see a group of men wearing cream and burgundy, a broad man amongst them glittering in his burnished armour. And a hopeful smile appeared on his face.

"We need to move," Havovatch said, turning; he knew they needed his help, but he needed his army.

But as he turned, he met a knife at his throat, and, looking along his arm, he saw Wrisscrass sitting there, smiling at him.

Chapter Twenty
Release of State

Andreas wasn't bound; he walked officially between the two lines, as if he were a soldier marching to see his senior officer, his arms marching in time with his gait. But Pausanias knew something was wrong – he had been stripped of his weapons but walked with a clear purpose. *Maybe he was just putting on a show of defiance?*

The line met with the perimeter fence, where one of the generals spoke to the line leader. Other officers approached and clustered around him, asking all sorts of questions and looking back at Andreas. One approached him and started patting him down quite methodically. Once finished, he gave a nod to the others. They all went to one side and talked for a moment, constantly looking back at him, but Andreas stood there, returning their gaze with his chin up.

Eventually, one of the generals returned and escorted Andreas by his arm inside the building, the others dismissing the units with some belligerence. The unit were taken aback by their generals' hostility, and moved away even more quickly when the generals drew their swords. The generals laughed as they watched them scutter away.

Pausanias drew a breath and agitatedly ran his fingers through his hair. He knew that if he was going to do something, he had to do it now. So, he did the one thing he was good at. Delving deep into his satchel, he pulled out the only thing that was inside: his Hawk helm.

He looked at it, knowing that it put fear into so many, and now he was going to kill and scare some of his own. But he knew the generals were now traitors – they had to be brought down.

"You can do this," he kept telling himself out loud, and started muttering his family's word with his eyes closed. In that moment, he felt strength flow through him as if his father were there by his side; whilst a purple apparition appeared next to him.

Holding up his helm in both hands, he stood up and placed it on his head, firmly and with purpose. He held his swords outstretched either side of him and walked slowly towards the picketed line, showing that he was definitely a threat – a clear symbol of strength.

There were about sixteen higher-ranking officers within the picket fence, all milling about. They were so confident, they did not even realise that Pausanias was there, until one, as he lit his pipe and blew out a long puff of smoke, casually glanced his way. His eyes went wide, and his hand froze with the pipe in his grasp, for not only did he know he was staring at a Knight Hawk, he also knew that the man before him was a far better fighter than any of them, and he knew why he was there.

"To guard," he spluttered as he coughed up smoke, dropping his pipe and drawing back as he hoped that someone else would attack him. But, as he shouted, all who looked immediately felt the same: FEAR.

The first attacker was a colonel, a young man. As he sprinted forward, sword raised, Pausanias merely stepped out of its way, spun round and cut through the back of his neck. Still walking, he pressed on towards the others, his arms still held outstretched, blood dripping from one of his swords.

"Attack him at once! He can't take us all on!" another shouted.

"YES-I-CAN!!" Pausanias roared like a dying boar; his voice bellowed with a rage they would never understand, and he charged.

The officers could not take it, and, dropping their weapons, they all fled.

***

"So, all this time you were a traitor?" said Havovatch, with his hands behind his head, his fingers interlocked with each other, as they walked towards the sieging Golesh.

Wrisscrass grunted a laugh but said nothing.

"I should have had Buskull kill you when I had the chance —"

"Shup!" Wrisscrass said, shoving him hard.

As Havovatch approached the camp, he was gripped by a fear he had never experienced. He had a feeling running down his spine of vulnerability, fear, no control, dread. He tried to feel anger, the one emotion that usually helped in times like this, but looking at the sea of black surrounding Len Seror, he felt nothing but pure fear – *what's going to happen to me?*

Wrisscrass folded his bottom lip and let out a high-pitched whistle, and the creatures turned to see them. They shrieked with joy and charged his way, shouting. After all the defeats they'd had, preying on a single individual brought much delight – a chance for them to take their frustrations out on someone. Surrounding Havovatch, they snarled as they assessed his helmet and armour, wondering why they couldn't see his face, but relishing his obvious discomfort. Havovatch said nothing – he couldn't – he was frozen solid, his hands trembling uncontrollably, his eyes wide, and his mind telling him to fight but his arms not moving. Lowering his head, he looked at the ground like a scared dog.

One of the creatures ripped the helmet from his head and held it in the air as if holding a trophy. Others started pulling at his clothing, removing his weapons and trying to pull off his armour. Eventually, after many punches and kicks, Havovatch lay on the floor, half-naked, whilst the creatures cleared a space around him, looking down at his humiliation. Havovatch curled up into a ball, covering his head with his hands. He was kicked so much he felt numb in places, but, looking up with one eye as the other was swollen over, he saw they were just looking at him; the one thing he saw more of than anything else was lots of teeth.

"Oi, g'off, he's mine!" Havovatch heard the familiar voice of Wrisscrass shouting. Being pulled to his feet, Havovatch stood swaying from the ordeal as Wrisscrass propped him up. He could barely see the tall, fat, sweaty creature that approached, with piercings all over its face. Its skin was green, with two yellow eyes, like those of a big cat, sunken into its skull; yet its attention was not on Havovatch but on Wrisscrass.

"Strange!" it said, sniffing around him like a hound. The horde went quiet and visibly trembled in the presence of the green monster. "I don't sense your thoughts, your emotions, almost … as if … you're an outcast?"

Wrisscrass sneered; Havovatch thought he heard him growling.

"You betta' watch your filthy mouth, scum!" he said with venomous intent.

Havovatch thought the green monster should be scared by the way Wrisscrass spoke – *he* was – but it didn't seem to show any emotion, apart from anger. And, lifting its large heavy sword, it touched the tip against Wrisscrass's chin. The ugly beast smiled.

"Ha, ha! Did the Black Lord have no need for a filthy maggot like you? I knew your race would come to an end."

But every Golesh around them jumped, as Wrisscrass let go of Havovatch and stuck his fangerlore straight through the beast's skull. Pulling the creature's face towards his, with the blade through its head, he looked deep into its eyes and growled again as he watched the creature's life leave its body, like sending a message to its dead soul saying that it shouldn't have insulted him, and should prepare to meet him again in the Shadow World.

As the creature fell heavily to the ground with a thud, Wrisscrass looked at the cowering creatures, who now feared *him*.

"I have killed your leader! You're now mine, now sod off back to your duties or I'll rip ya guts out!"

They all moved as one, as they tried desperately to get away from their new chief, most tripping over each other.

"And those who took my captive's equipment, I claim it! Have it brought to my tent!" he bellowed at the retreating creatures.

Wrisscrass stood tall and serious, his arms by his sides, but tense, with black blood dripping thickly like tar from his crude weapon. An empty scene surrounded him, with Havovatch by his feet; then he burst out laughing.

"These vermin are so dumb – they fear whoever their leader is," Wrisscrass said casually to Havovatch, who lay on the ground, trembling. Bending down, Wrisscrass heaved him up, dragging him along the ground. He aimed for a tent ahead of him, telling the guards to "sod off" before he entered.

Once inside, Wrisscrass threw Havovatch to the floor. Havovatch's armour and weapons were sprawled out everywhere, as the creatures had thrown them in and run off. Havovatch did not get up but lay there, traumatised, looking up at Wrisscrass, wondering what he was going to do next.

Looking at the swelling blocking Havovatch's left eye, Wrisscrass bent down, drew a knife and went to cut across it, but Havovatch threw his arm out, catching his. He deflected the blade away and punched him in the face, hard enough to send him backwards. Havovatch grabbed one of his knives lying next to him and stood up, swaying.

"Ow!" Wrisscrass moaned, sitting up and holding his head. "What's that for?"

Havovatch said nothing as he kept shaking his head, trying to regain full consciousness. Wrisscrass went to get up, but Havovatch launched forward with his knee to his face, sending him back down, but it was too much and, feeling dizzy again, Havovatch fell backwards and dropped the knife. The world spun before him; he was only conscious by his will.

"Argh!" Wrisscrass groaned as he lay on the floor. His foot twitched and he looked up at Havovatch. "I was going to cut that ball on your face so you can see." He pulled himself up to his feet and stood over Havovatch.

Havovatch just sat there looking up at him.

"Fine. If you don't want me to help you, I won't."

He turned and started shuffling through the contents of the tent for anything he could use, whilst holding his head from the knock. Panting hard and holding the wound on his face, Havovatch looked up at him.

"So, it was all an act?" he puffed.

Wrisscrass turned and smiled. "When did you work it out?"

"I wasn't sure until now, but I suspected it when you picked me up. I have seen your lot – they attack until the death and start shredding limbs off their kill. You wouldn't let them. Either you wanted me alive for something, or you were acting?"

"Very smart. I'm starting to change my mind about you."

"You could have told me!" Havovatch clutched his ribs and winced as he got up.

"When we were in the bushes, I noticed a group of scouts saw us and started heading our way, I had to take you in or they would have known I was with you. Your wounds will heal. You're lucky it was just Golesh that attacked you! If it were my lot you'd be dead a lot sooner, but in far more pain," he said, turning with a grin.

"Comforting. So, who're your lot you keep referring too? Are you not a Golesh?"

Peering through the flaps outside, Wrisscrass's grin broadened but said nothing.

"So, what now?" said Havovatch as he started collecting his knives and armour together in a pile on the floor, his right arm still caressing his ribs.

Wrisscrass saw a bowl of red blood on top of a small table. He paced over to it, cupped his hands and splashed it over his mouth and forearms.

"We wait until nightfall, then we leave. Stay here for a moment. I won't be long."

Before Havovatch could protest, Wrisscrass left through the tent flaps.

Perched at the end of the bed, Havovatch winced as he reached around to do up the last strap on his armour, by his hip. Now fully armed, he drew his new blade and looked at it as if trying to work it out – what was its name, how would he use it? He ran a spit stone along the edges so he could take care of it as he waited for Wrisscrass to return. But as much as he held it, he was not used to it; he preferred his Kopis.

As he sat there, he was fighting an uncontrollable urge to go out and fight till the death. He would have the element of surprise and was sure he could bring down twenty, maybe thirty ... hell, he even thought about killing a hundred of them with the anger flowing through him. He felt unsettled, though – he could hear the creatures outside, their howling, and the sound of boulders crashing into the walls of Len Seror, the smell of fire as it wafted past the tent. He needed the Knight Hawks. He needed the Knights of Ezazeruth. And so he just sat there, with his eyes wandering off with his thoughts as he slowly ran the stone against the edge of the blade.

But, catching him off guard, the tent flap suddenly lifted and in walked a creature. It didn't notice Havovatch's presence as it strolled over to the table opposite him with a tray of metal cases. The creature set down the tray and placed one of the cases on the table, and then began to tidy the cups and plates up. Havovatch sat frozen with his mouth hanging open, not daring to breathe. Yet, with the creature's back to him, he knew this was his moment – he couldn't risk waiting for it to turn. Havovatch got up slowly and made his way towards it, his Hawk sword outstretched, ready to strike. As he approached, though, he realised he should have drawn a knife, but putting the blade down would make a noise; so he stood for a moment, wondering what he should do, but, shaking his head, he carried on.

He held his left hand out, ready to cover its mouth, and his right arm up back to force the sword into its back. But he didn't see the basin sitting on the stand, and, as he knocked into it with his hip, it fell with a loud clatter. The creature turned sharply and dropped the tray, with the scroll cases and plates spilling out onto the floor. It drew its own sword and stood defensively. Havovatch didn't want to engage with metal upon metal, in fear of other creatures hearing and entering. But, in the small tent, the large beast charged at him. Sidestepping out the way of the heavy blade, Havovatch went to parry, but winced. He had forgotten the pain in his ribs and doubled over as he put pressure on them. The creature was strong and quickly brought the blade back around. Havovatch dodged and ducked every thrust, battling through the pains in his chest and trying to focus through his right eye. As the sword passed over his head he dropped his own and smacked the creature in the side of the face. Crouching low, he spun around and back-kicked the creature in the side, making it fall to the floor.

Jumping on top of it, he grasped its neck hard and strangled it, pushing all the force he had into his arms. Saliva spat out as he gasped and tried to use all the force and strength he had, his confidence very much back. But the creature was far stronger. It grabbed Havovatch's forearms and parted them out of the way, as he gritted his teeth and tried to resist. Then, launching itself up, it headbutted Havovatch in the face. He fell backwards holding his nose, his eye watering from the knock. He felt the beast pull him up by his armour, and again it headbutted him in the face. Havovatch groaned at the second knock and almost passed out, although he reeled hard to try to stay conscious. His toes were off the floor, but he had enough consciousness to bring his knee up hard into the creature's groin. The creature doubled over, with Havovatch landing on his feet but staggering to stay up.

Taking in gasps of air and wiping the tears from his eye and blood from his nose, he turned on the creature, knowing that if he didn't control the situation soon, he'd be dead. Kicking it in the stomach as hard as he could, he took in another breath to feed his body, and again kicked it in the face, sending it to the floor. Then he started repeatedly stamping on its head, as hard as he could. The sound of the bone breaking did not make him shudder one bit, and, drawing his Kopis, he went to cut its throat. But, remarkably, the creature pulled itself up and tried to get to the tent flaps. Havovatch jumped through the air and struck his sword through its leg, which stuck into the ground, stopping the creature from getting to the tent flaps; it howled in pain. He jumped on top of it, wrapped his arm around its neck and pulled hard. Just then, two huge hands appeared and gripped around the creature's mouth as Wrisscrass stopped its screams. Havovatch finished it off – in one quick motion he jerked and felt the creature's neck break and its body slump.

Havovatch fell backwards, panting heavily. "Where have you been?" he said, blood gushing from his nose.

"To get you these!" he said, holding up a Golesh helmet and poncho. The helmet would cover most of his face, not allowing anything to see him. "We need to get out of here, now!"

"Why the rush?"

"Because every moment that thing is not reporting to its master, we have a problem."

"Fine!" he said, still gasping for air.

"But remember," he said, turning sharply, "some of the Golesh can sense each other. They will see emptiness in us, so keep your head down, grunt, match how they walk, give them no reason to look at you. And when we get to the sentries, we need to kill them. Wait for my move."

Havovatch nodded. He wiped away the blood from his face on the front of the poncho, and placed it on. He put his Hawk helmet into his satchel, slung his Malorga over his shoulder and looked at the stinking helmet Wrisscrass had given him – dreading what must have worn it, as he saw flakes of possibly skin and long strands of white hair inside.

Wrisscrass peered out of the tent. "OK – now is our moment. C'mon!" He vanished into the evening air.

As he stepped out, Havovatch tried to keep his eye on the floor, but couldn't help but look around. He was surprised by how well organised the creatures were. They appeared to have halted their siege for the day, as most were walking back from the city, their posture very negative as they dragged their weapons along the ground and slumped their heads after another day's defeat. There was a tremendous cheer from the battlements as the besieged threw their weapons into the air, taunting their foe. He couldn't help but smile behind his helmet at the tenacious efforts from the Lorians.

But he felt a shove as Wrisscrass stood there, irritated that he was not paying attention. Nodding, he gestured for Wrisscrass to lead the way.

As they strolled along the plains to the outskirts of the battlefield, Havovatch did everything that Wrisscrass had told him, matching how the other Golesh walked. With his swollen eye, he found he was having to turn his head right around to see; he began to understand how his uncle Verdrey felt, being blind in one eye and tripping up all the time.

Seeing a helmet sitting idle on the floor, he kicked like a stroppy child to help his masquerade. Getting through the camp proved fairly easy; nothing stopped them or got in their way. In fact, as Havovatch took a quick look around, nothing was looking at them at all. When he thought about it, he wouldn't look at all his men if they were in armour; nothing out here knew who they really were, but the fact that he knew who they were made him fearful that he could be caught.

Soon, they came to the perimeter and walked out into the open plains. On the other side of the hill there were creatures sporadically milling about; one was digging up the earth as it burrowed for a rabbit, but with little luck.

Wrisscrass just walked through them. He was huge in comparison. One looked up and sniffed him like a curious dog, but stood well back, too scared to get close.

Before long, they were well away from the creatures and Wrisscrass turned to Havovatch.

"You can take that off now."

Havovatch threw the helmet and poncho away and rubbed his hand through his hair, shaking out flakes of something he did not wish to identify. Whilst Wrisscrass let out a crude whistle, Havovatch looked around, wondering what he was doing.

"We need to get back to your men."

"Why do you care?"

"Because that city won't hold out for much longer."

"OK – how?"

"Them!" he said, nodding at their horses as they came cantering towards them.

"You have some mysterious gifts, creature."

Wrisscrass let out a grunt and mounted, and they both set off northwards, leaving behind them the Golesh, the smoke, and the courage of the Lorians hanging by a thread.

***

"I understand you have some information for me?" Imara said as she lay on her side on an elegant couch, dangling grapes above her mouth and biting some off the bottom of the bunch.

Andreas looked around; behind him stood one of the generals, and sitting in the corner on a rickety bench was Lord Fennel.

"Yes, my Lady."

She stared at him expectantly.

"Well?"

Andreas stammered, not really knowing what to say. He had been hoping it would just be him and her – how wrong he was. He wasn't as good a fighter as his brother was in hand-to-hand combat. But he knew why he was there.

"I understand." She smiled and stood up, tossing the rest of the grapes over to Lord Fennel, as if he was only good enough to eat her scraps.

"You do?" he said incredulously, wondering if she knew something he didn't.

"Yes. You are a young man, you have heard of the rumours, so let me put your mind at ease."

Andreas stood perfectly still, only his fingers moving as he wondered who she thought he was.

"We will be leaving soon, very soon," she said. "The only people who will be going will be you, me, a few generals, and this man," – she waved a dismissive hand at Fennel, who smiled slightly, glad that he had been recognised – "as my own personal guard."

"And where will we be going?"

"Leno Dania. We will take our wealth there."

She then stood in front of Andreas. This was his moment. He only wished he had his sword. Could he kill someone with his bare hands? He hadn't done yet. He knew how, from training, although reality was a different thing – but he was readying himself to do so, his fingers twitching. But Imara sighed heavily, walked across the room and began pouring wine from a jug.

Andreas huffed – he had missed his chance.

"I am not a patient woman. Tell me what you have come here to tell me, or my officers will force it out of you."

Andreas's mouth hung open. He wanted to kill her, he knew what she had done, he knew what his mission was, he had to do this, but he couldn't – not like this. She was a woman; she was unarmed.

"Well, another time-waster." She raised her eyebrows at the general, but he did not move.

"General!" she said sternly, as if the act of ignoring her was forbidden. But he remained still.

Suddenly, there came a tremendous crash from the hallway behind the doors; then the doors flew open and two assassins landed on their backs, with nasty wounds to their guts and arms.

"What the ...!" Imara shouted, pulling up her dress so she could stagger backwards against the wall. "Fennel, do something!" she screeched to her waiting puppy. But he clung to his bench in fear, not knowing what to do.

Out of the shadows of the hall, all the candles and torches had been blown out, as if Shadow Demons sensed the anger about to enter the room. Then, in walked a Knight Hawk, red blood covering his front, his bare arms and his swords. Everything about him, his movement, his faceless helmet, personified his hatred.

"I can you make you rich!" Imara said hurriedly as she retreated into a corner, thinking that wealth could buy off any man. She kept looking between the general and the Hawk, hoping the general would do something. But the Hawk stopped next to Andreas, then fell forward, giving him a very tight and relieved hug.

"DO SOMETHING!" she shouted at the general, who still stood where he was.

The brothers parted and Pausanias looked at the motionless general, sensing that there was no threat in him, none at all.

Then, the general paced towards the door, pulled the bodies through and closed it, barring them inside the room. Fortunately for them, Imara had made the place almost impregnable – no one was getting in quickly. He then stood next to the Hawk and removed his helmet, revealing himself to be Fandorazz.

"You!" she shouted, aghast.

"Yes – me," he said, plainly.

"But you're just an architect. You're supposed to be mad!"

"Maybe I am?" he said casually as he walked towards her. Just then, Fennel went to stand up, but Pausanias pointed his sword at him, telling him to sit back down.

"I will ask you one question, woman, and if you answer honestly, I will not kill you." Her mouth quivered. "Did you arrange for the death of my family?"

For a moment she was still, looking at him as she tried to think of how she could get out of this, but realised she couldn't. She broke down, bringing her hand to her mouth and falling to the floor. She began to sob uncontrollably.

"I won't repeat myself," he said, brandishing a dagger from his belt.

"Please – it's not what you think!"

"Is it not?"

"No, no, it's him – he made me do it," she said, pointing desperately at Fennel, who suddenly went very alert, looking between her and the others, his mouth hanging open but not knowing what to say.

"What? Me? No! I don't even know what you're talking about," he said innocently.

They all returned their gaze to Imara.

"HELP!!" she screamed at the door, but there was no sound from the other side.

"It appears you have no one left to protect you," said Pausanias, still pointing his sword at Fennel.

Her blubbering increased, her tears making track marks through her thick make-up.

"I don't want to die!" she begged.

Fandorazz knelt down. "Neither did my family," he said calmly, almost sinisterly, "neither did those soldiers who tried to get back to their families, neither did those innocent people who you kicked out of the forest."

Imara said nothing. She knew of the atrocities she had committed. Greed had consumed her. She was willing to let everyone around her rot and die for her own gain, and it had all come undone.

"You do not deserve to be on this planet any more!" Fandorazz brought his fist up, holding the dagger downwards. She screwed her eyes shut; he forced it down.

Andreas gasped.

Fennel vomited.

Behind his helm, Pausanias cocked an eyebrow.

Imara opened one eye to see the dagger stuck in the wooden wall next to her face. She then looked at Fandorazz. His jaw was locked tight with fury, and his eyebrows were frowning deeply, but he was also welling up with tears.

"I'm not a killer – not like this, anyway," Fandorazz said. He reached round to his parchment bag, drew out a scroll and unrolled it.

"Care to hold this for me, my good fellow?" he asked Andreas, holding up an inkpot. His voice was wobbling as he tried to sound chirpy, but was full of emotion. Pausanias holstered his sword and heaved Imara to her feet. He placed her firmly on a bench in front of the table, and then stood confidently behind her.

Fandorazz placed the parchment before her. "Sign this!" He held out a quill he had just dipped into the inkpot; she took it and looked down at the document titled:

Release of State

"You can't. This will be everything I own."

Fandorazz stood on the other side of the desk, staring intently at her, his arms behind his back, his chin in the air. Her hand shook uncontrollably as she stared down at the parchment.

She scanned the main titles:

Release of the Camion military
Release of everything I own
Release of King Colomune ...

At the very bottom:

To the good of the Camion people.

"Listen – I have a lot of money, we can do a —"

Suddenly, her hair was pulled back and the edge of a sword appeared at her throat.

"Sign it, or see your head parted from your shoulders. Either way, we get what we want," said Pausanias between gritted teeth, and grabbing her hair tighter for good measure.

She trembled, then bowed down and signed her name to the parchment quicker than she had ever done before.

"Get out!" Fandorazz said to Fennel, and watched jumped up and scuttered towards the door. Andreas pulled the beam up and he ran out.

Fandorazz then rolled up the parchment and approached Pausanias.

"Knight Hawk, I don't know of your name, but your timing is impeccable. Can I suggest you take this to whoever is in charge, and tell them that they are liberated from this tyrant?"

"What will happen to me?" whimpered Imara.

"That is for the committee to decide."

A slight smile appeared over her face, knowing that they were within her grasp.

"I wouldn't smile, my dear. Don't you remember? You have expelled most of the Camion socialites from this forest, all despise you; and a new committee, which will be made up of people from all backgrounds and walks of life, will judge you, fairly."

With a respectful bow of his head as if he were addressing any woman in the street, Fandorazz then walked out of the room with his hands behind his back, tears streaming down his face and the small portrait of his family in his grasp.

Andreas stood looking at her, a picture of shock wrought over her face. Moments earlier she had been safe – she had had it all. Now she had nothing, and her mind couldn't process it.

"Yeah!" he said, pointing after Fandorazz. "Yeah, that's what you get!"

"Subtle," said Pausanias, mockingly.

They both went for the door, but Pausanias turned to Imara.

"If I'd had it my way, I'd have killed you, slowly."

Her jaw quivered, and she fell to the floor and rolled herself up into a ball.

Pausanias placed his arm over Andreas's shoulders, and the brothers walked back outside.

As Pausanias and Andreas stepped out into the open, they were met by a wall of bronze, as hundreds stood before them. They were from all battalions and ranks, some on horseback and others with shields and spears. All wearing the same expression – that of expectation.

Before them were the senior officers who had fled; they had been stripped of their weapons and made to kneel down with their hands behind their backs, some of the lower officers standing next to them with a spear or sword pointing at them. To the other side were a group of differently dressed soldiers. Pausanias knew they were the assassins, and had been rounded up in a pen. They looked grim as they knew what their fate was to be.

He held up the parchment and shouted, "We're free men – let's go home."

There was an almighty cheer from everyone and, almost instantly, most turned and left to find their friends, brothers, fathers, whoever they were with, so that they could inform them that they could go back to Cam. But just then, a horse could be heard cantering through the crowd towards them – it was the messenger from the Two-Twenty-Eighth.

"Who's in charge?" he bellowed.

Pausanias looked around; the sergeants and corporals gave a nod – it was he. With pretty much all the senior officers arrested, he was the only one who had the experience and confidence to take charge of the army.

The messenger dismounted.

"I am from the Two-Twenty-Eighth. I have been ordered to send you all to the Defences, now!"

"These men haven't seen their loved ones in months," said Pausanias. "Let them go back to Cam first."

The messenger shook his head frantically.

"Apologies, but that is not the case. Cam has been overrun by Emiros. If anyone goes near it, whoever's left in the city will surely be slaughtered."

Pausanias grabbed the messenger by his arm and took him to one side. "Lower your tone, soldier!"

"Apologies. The general said that the Knights of Ezazeruth will deal with them."

"Who?"

"Another army, but he said you must get to the Defences – there is no one there."

Pausanias thought long and hard. He preferred being a soldier, not an officer; he was not one for making decisions.

"When will this army be here?"

"A matter of days, but the Defences are abandoned. If the Black arrive, they will land unopposed."

Pausanias sighed. He knew they needed to get home, but unfortunately they were the only defence Ezazeruth had. The terrible thought would be that these men would die before seeing their families again, but Drorkon was right – they needed to get there, fast, otherwise any tactical advantage they could have would be lost.

"Sergeant?" he asked the closest one.

"Kutain."

"Sergeant Kutain, I see you're from one of the cavalry regiments?"

"Two-Seventy-Ninth," he said proudly.

"You're now acting general to all cavalry regiments. Take every horse we have, and, with haste, head to the Defences and secure them."

"Right you are, Sir," he said, saluting. He ripped the helmet and insignia from one of the crouching cavalry generals, and paced off.

"You!" Pausanias said to a lieutenant.

"Meliss, Sir."

"Infantry?"

"Yes, Sir, Three-Thirty-Sixth."

"Same: you're in charge of all scouting, light and heavy infantry units. Get them to the Defences as soon as possible."

Again, pulling the rank from the appropriate general, he made off to make it so. Not because he wanted to be a general, but because he knew full well the situation, and it was best just to obey orders first and resolve the situation later.

"The rest of you," Pausanias addressed the men around him, "go with them to confirm their story. If you find any lackeys or engineers, make them ready. We need to get food and water there now!"

Suddenly, all around was movement – eager movement, as if they had all sat down for too long and had to move their aching joints.

"Every man must work. Everything that can be made use of, use it!" Pausanias bellowed after them.

But, seeing two battlefield surgeons pass, he placed a hand up to stop them. "Gents, there is a colonel in the woods just behind you. Please treat his body with respect, I would not be here now if it were not for him."

They nodded, and went to follow his instructions.

Looking around at the movement within the forest, Pausanias saw the generals all being penned in with the assassins and spies. He eyed them with contempt. A vision played before him of entering with his swords. They could all have a go, until he was dead or they all were. The thoughts became so vivid that he found himself pacing forward and reaching for the grips on his swords, when someone called out to him.

"Hawk?"

He turned to see Fandorazz walking next to Atken, who was limping. He had stripped off his general's masquerade and wore light clothing, with a small sack thrown over his shoulder and a parchment in his hand. Atken shook hands and left to find the King.

"Well done in there – you did the right thing. If I'd done it, it would have got messy."

"I did what needed doing, although I wish I had seen what you would have done to her. I thought you may have struck me down first, though."

They both grinned, for he was right, but the outcome was still good.

"Tell me," Pausanias asked, "What was the young lad going to say to her?"

"The officers found him wandering around outside the forest. When they confronted him, he said he had information about a plot to assassinate her. He was brought straight here. The generals were going to have him killed, but I persuaded them to let him meet Imara, for I would have a chance to meet her in person. She wouldn't want many people knowing about the possible plot, and would have told everyone to get out. But when she spoke with him, he remained defiant and said nothing, although I wondered if he was trying to bring himself to do something that he didn't think he could do. But then, you entered."

Pausanias looked at his little brother talking to friends from his old archery regiment, the Four-Eighty-Second, and grinned, for he was a good man.

"Thank you. I needed to hear that."

"You're most welcome."

"What about you? You look a little adventurous. Will you be coming with us to the Defences? We could use someone with your talent for authority."

"Alas, I have a dear friend who is on a mission without me – I must catch up with him."

"Where are you going?"

Fandorazz sighed and rubbed his head as he tried to remember where Groga said this place was.

"The Forgone Pass?"

Pausanias frowned. "The Forbidden Passage?"

"Yes, that's it," he said, clicking his fingers.

Pausanias shook his head. "No, no – people don't go there."

"I need to."

"Why?"

"My friend is of the belief that there are people there that could defend the Defences, for they were all we had when the Camions left."

Pausanias sighed. "You think it will make a difference?"

"Right now, we have an army going to the Defences. I just need to find my friend."

"Can you ride a horse?"

"Ha! I don't think there is anyone in the upper class who doesn't know that skill." Fandorazz reached out to shake Pausanias's hand, and they did so with much admiration for each other, but in doing so Pausanias felt something more tangible. "I hope we meet again, Hawk." As Fandorazz walked away to find a horse, Pausanias looked down at a small respect knife with a beautiful blue handle within his grasp.

Chapter Twenty-One
The Curse

"Will you stop pacing around? You're starting to irritate me!" Garvelia barked at Avron. With her feet up on the desk in an unladylike fashion, she was strangely calm under the circumstances.

Avron sighed. "In case you haven't noticed, we're going to die in a few hours. The sun has almost set. And we're not going up to the clouds, nor even down to the Shadow World – we will become ... nothing!" He sighed heavily by puffing his cheeks, leant on his chair and bowed his head.

She threw her arms into the air. "What did you expect? You know what he's like. Besides, I didn't think you believed in an afterlife. Maybe there is just nothing?"

Avron sat down and stroked his face.

"I thought, after all this time, I thought that there might be some hope?"

"... so did I."

There was a sudden knock at the door, which silenced them both.

"Come!" Avron said expectantly, frozen against the chair.

A guard entered the room, but his body language said it all before he spoke. But the commanders said nothing and just stared, nodding in anticipation of good news.

The guard just shook his head.

Avron sighed heavily. "Fine – thank you," he said. The guard left without saying anything.

"It appears that we will become nothing to the wind?" sighed Avron.

"You know? I never thought it would end like this," said Garvelia distantly, as she stared at a crack in the wall as if it held all the answers. "I thought about dying in battle, or old-aged with a loved one?"

"With Duruck?" Avron interjected, looking at her sharply, as if he knew a secret she tried poorly to conceal.

"You knew?"

"My young lady, everyone knows."

She had a face of disbelief, feeling rather foolish.

"How do you feel about him now? Leaving you like this?"

She shook her head as if she didn't know what to think.

"Love is a powerful thing – it makes us do things we don't mean to. It clouds our judgement, even after two thousand years."

"You know ... Duruck and I have met a couple of times."

Avron looked very serious for a moment; the furrows of his brow deepened as if she had just revealed a shocking crime. Then, he burst out laughing. "Ha, ha! We all have, young lady."

"You met him as well?" she said, aghast.

"Of course! The amount of time he and I just met up for a drink, fishing trip, hunting, just to take the burden of being commanders off us for a while."

She smiled with her radiant set of white teeth, and brushed her hair out of her face and tucked it around the back of her ear.

"I'm glad," she said. "I worried about you – I thought you'd go mad being cooped up for that long in your tropical paradise."

"That is exactly why I left to meet him."

"How long was the last time?"

"Five years."

"Five!"

"Well, how long did you?"

She bit her lips. "Seven."

"Liar!"

"Well, I couldn't help it. I needed to see him."

"He told me he got married though, a few times."

"There were some centuries we didn't see each other."

There was quiet after that, as Garvelia reminisced.

"What did the young captain say to you to make you change your mind?" Avron said, changing the subject.

"He said nothing ..."

She looked at the ground as if she were about to confess to something.

"Garvelia?"

"I watched him leave my forest. I stood there watching him, wanting to run out to him, to tell him that we would accept our oaths. But after all this time, I felt like I was not in control of my body, so I just stood there, tears running down my face."

"What happened?"

"They were attacked by a sortie of Golesh. You should have seen him fight – so fluid, so strong, so brave."

247

"Him?"

"What?" she said, as if she had just come out of a trance.

"You didn't refer to *them* – they were a unit. You said *him*!"

Garvelia looked at the ground, not really knowing what to say.

"The last time I heard you speak like that you were talking about Duruck."

She grinned. "Do you think he'd like me?"

"Probably. All young men are into older women these days, even two-thousand-year-olds. Something to do with experience or something?"

She gave him a shove.

"Come on, though, get to the point. What happened to make you change your mind?" Avron pushed.

Garvelia bowed her head again. "His friend was injured and fell; one of the rekons cut off his head. Havovatch tried to get to him, but ..." she sighed, "that young man could have been here today if I had told my men to fire at them, but my oath held me back, and I just thought, how many more will die? He then threw his sword into the woods and it landed just before my feet – it nearly cut me into two, but I just watched it fall. I didn't even flinch, either, and I realised that it was time to stop hiding and come out and fight for what was right."

"Hmmm." Avron looked at the floor, fearing the worst. "Do you think Duruck killed him?"

Garvelia maintained her stare at the floor, but her eyes began to water, hoping that it was not true, although knowing that it was. It was Duruck's way.

There was a long and quiet moment between the two, as they stared into space with their own thoughts. So long passed that if it had been night, it would certainly be day by now.

The silence was broken, though, when Avron pushed his chair back and took in a deep breath.

"Come – we have a lot of brave men and women out there; we'd better go and address them."

Garvelia nodded. Sniffling, she stood up and composed herself.

"Before we go, how long has it *actually* been since you last saw Duruck?"

"Eighty-two years."

"Why so long?" he said, frowning.

She shrugged. "We just drifted apart. I tried writing to him but he didn't reply."

"The stubbornness of Duruck: the only thing stronger than his sword."

Looking in a giant mirror, they fixed themselves up to make sure they looked the part in front of their regiments. But there was a roar from within the tunnel, which echoed, causing dust to fall from the ceiling. Garvelia and Avron glanced at each other before rushing out of the door.

Appearing on the balcony, they looked at the labyrinth of Shila, with blue cloaks all around as the Xiphos exchanged greetings with the Oistos and Ippikós. Standing at the centre on a raised stone platform, Duruck looked around; then he saw Avron and Garvelia. He did not wave or say anything, but gave a slight nod as if greeting a companion he had already seen that day. They made their way down through the tunnels and into the open chasm. The soldiers parted the way for them. She jumped up as thirty thousand pairs of eyes were on them. And the first thing she did was slap him across the face, followed by raucous laugher from all around. Duruck held his cheek, confused.

"You didn't write back!" she screamed.

Avron grinned. "You're a brave man to suffer the fury of a woman," he said before stepping forward and bear-hugging his friend, as Duruck still felt the rawness of his cheek. Slowly, as if accepting it, Duruck hugged him back, yet it was clearly not his style.

A guard of Avron's brought a goblet up for Duruck; he took it and held it into the air.

"To the amazing archers of Oistos!" he bellowed.

There was a thunderous cheer as ten thousand men and women threw their tankards and goblets into the air in celebration of his announcement.

"To the mighty horse lords!"

Again, ten thousand red-coated men and women splashed their drinks with delight.

"And to the terrific, unbeatable, wondrous, amazing, blue coats of the north!" he bellowed with biased mockery.

There was much louder applause from his own as the others gestured dismissive waves at them. And, even louder, as he threw his drink into the air, "... and the old gits that lead 'em!"

The place erupted with the joyous celebration of the thirty thousand warriors clapping into the air. The labyrinth echoed and vibrated, with dust falling from the ceilings.

Duruck took a long, deep gulp from his goblet and tipped it upside down to show that it was empty, much to the delight of everyone around him. It wasn't his way, but it appeared clear he knew how to inspire those around him; a natural leader.

He put his arms in the air, appealing for silence.

"My brothers, my sisters, it has been too long since we have lusted for blood, we have lusted for death. And now, we shall have it. We have an oath to fulfil! You have all done so well to live this long and not give in to darkness, and for that, I am grateful." He looked down at Garvelia and Avron, who looked up at him in admiration. "I still remember the sound of the Black's drums. The tales said that the Black is the darkness. Well, I think we have been through far worse. When we march out of this haven, we march on the Black, and it shall be they who quiver, for them, maybe the darkness, but we shall be the light!"

Shila again erupted with thunderous applause and jubilation, as the Knights of Ezazeruth's hearts were lifted.

He turned to his commanders and stepped down.

"Come – we have much to discuss."

As he passed, Avron looked at his chin as if he had seen something new.

"What?"

"Oh, nothing ... just realised that you've learnt how to shave."

Duruck at first tried to give him a long and distasteful stare, but then they both burst out laughing, and, throwing their arms over each other's shoulders, they stepped down into the crowd of men and women, giving handshakes as if they were celebrities..

Soon, the commanders stepped into the office in the heart of the canyon and sat comfortably around the triangular desk. There was a long silence as Duruck got some paper and a quill out, ignoring their intent stares upon him, for they had many questions.

"Duruck?" Avron said after a while.

"Yes?" he said, not looking up.

"What made you come back?"

"My father!" he said plainly.

Avron and Garvelia looked at each other, sitting up in their seats.

"You what?" said Avron, tensing up, his knuckles cracking as he clenched his fists.

"Look," said Duruck, taking in a breath, "we can talk all about this later. Right now we need to discuss the here and now! Agreed?"

There wasn't even a nod from them, but they remained quiet.

"What intelligence do we have?"

A voice came from the doorway. "The Golesh have risen from beyond the Rogan Defence Line." Leaning against the frame was Drorkon, with his arms folded.

"This is no place for someone like you!" said Garvelia, jumping to her feet, as did Avron.

"Sit!" Duruck said firmly.

"But —"

Pointing at her chair and raising his eyebrows, he said nothing, and slowly, she settled back into her seat, looking long and hard at Drorkon, still in the doorway.

Duruck clasped his hands together and leant forward on the triangular table. "Listen – we are at war. Need I remind you how close the Black nearly came to defeating us last time? We need to be ready and better prepared, but once again, we are short on time and resources. It also appears that we are dealing with two forces: the Black of old and the Black of new."

Drorkon entered the room feeling slightly confident. "I've had a scouting party go beyond the Rogan Defence Line. They report the place is nearly deserted – the lands have cleared out as the Golesh of old march across Ezazeruth. When the unit returned, they brought with them one of the commanders from the walls. During a very brief interrogation, he informed me that Chieftain Framlar appeared in person one day, and ordered him to let the creatures beyond, to march north across the wall unchallenged, and to carry on posing as if there were no issues."

"Where's this Framlar now?" said Duruck, as he wrote down notes in his own language, with light flickers of thin lines spread across the page that only he could decipher.

"The unit reports seeing a man like him in a strange form beyond the wall. The commander of the unit also said that the Chieftain did not appear to be himself, and after speaking with them, he casually walked into the mist ... alone. He has not seen him again."

Stopping, Duruck looked up at him. "This form – do you know what it was?" There was a tone of fear to his voice.

"They said they found a verdant area with statues of what appeared to be stone creatures. A man matching his description was amongst them, but not yet fully turned grey."

Duruck looked at Avron, who also showed his concern.

"What?" said Garvelia, noticing their attention. "You two know something?"

"It's not important now. Let's focus on the current threat. Firstly, how far have the Black got?"

"They were thwarted at the borders of Camia and Viror, but there are still large portions missing. I have sent my scouts out to find them, but my guess is they're spread out across the south."

"More or less!" came another voice at the door. And standing there, huffing with exhaustion and his left eye swollen over, was Havovatch. "They are attacking Len Seror, tens of thousands of them!" he said, panting. "The city has nearly fallen."

Avron rose to his feet. "That's my homeland. We need to get to there, now!" He began pacing to the door.

"And we will," Duruck said, waving a hand at him to sit down. "Patience, my friend." Avron did so with some reluctance. "Right, this is what we're going to do. Father," – Drorkon looked down at him, surprised – "you go with Avron, and take your Knight Hawks, General," he directed at Havovatch, "stop the siege. I will take the Oistos and the Xiphos to Camia via the northern route and down, clearing any contact with the Black of old." He looked up at Avron. "Avron, once you have finished at Len Seror, proceed across the southern route towards Cam, and wipe out everything in your path. Don't leave one Golesh with a beating heart – we can't deal with stragglers or prisoners!"

Avron nodded and got up to walk out of the door. Just as he passed Duruck, he bent down and whispered into his ear. "We need to talk; come and find me." Duruck acknowledged the request, but said nothing.

Havovatch gave a nod at Garvelia, who smiled sweetly back. It sent a light, fuzzy feeling through him, and, with a goofy and uncomfortable grin, he turned and left. Drorkon placed a hand of gratitude on Duruck's shoulder, but he pretended nothing untoward had happened.

Drorkon smiled at Garvelia, who just gave him a long and resentful stare.

"Buskull!" said Havovatch, as he saw his giant silhouette further down the tunnel, outlined by the blue gems in the ceiling.

"What happened to you?" he said, startled, and looking at Havovatch's swollen eye under the dim light.

"I'm fine."

Buskull looked up at Wrisscrass, who stood against the wall eyeing the Xiphos soldiers; he seemed fascinated by them, or at least by their weaponry. He went to push towards him before Havovatch put a hand against his stomach.

"No! This wasn't his doing. Well, it was, but he had his reasons."

Buskull's face could not have shown more confusion.

"General Havovatch," came Drorkon's voice. "May I please have your sword?" he said, pointing to his Hawk blade.

Havovatch reached over his shoulder and drew it, a loud ringing hissing out into the tunnel. "Thank you. I'll be back shortly."

He left into another room as Havovatch watched on, wondering what he was doing with it.

"I'm confused. Wrisscrass beat you up, but he had his reasons?"

"No – he had other creatures beat me up, but it was because we were about to be captured and he had to put up a cover. Anyway, I'm fine. I've had worse beatings in my life." He actually hadn't, but thought it made him look tougher.

"Thank you, General," said Drorkon behind him, as he gave him back his blade.

"Thank you, Sir. Can I ask what you did with it?"

"Just checking it was sharp enough was all. Now, we must get going."

Havovatch examined his blade, but he couldn't see anything different. Unbeknownst to him, though, Buskull and Drorkon exchanged a cautious look, wondering if they should tell him of the raw power of the gem within.

"So, we failed?" said Avron, as Duruck and Garvelia stepped out of the office. Duruck looked around to make sure they were alone.

"It appears so."

"Are you going to tell me what's going on now? I didn't think we kept secrets," said Garvelia with her arms folded.

Duruck looked to Avron. They both seemed uncomfortable, as if a past they wished would stay hidden was going to be revealed.

"We cannot talk about this. Not here, anyway – there's too much at stake and we're short on time."

"I want to know what's going on!"

"And you will."

Duruck was glad to hear his father's voice, giving him a distraction.

"Commander Duruck …"

He turned to Garvelia. "When we get to Cam, we'll talk about this more." Turning, he met his father. "Yes, Sir?"

"Can I please introduce you to Commander Thiamos?"

Thiamos was much bigger than Duruck, but they exchanged a firm shake of hands. Wanting to be nowhere near Drorkon, Garvelia and Avron turned and left the tunnel in separate directions.

"Thiamos is the longest-reigning commander of the entire Camion military," beamed Drorkon, "and my dear friend."

"Really? So how many men are under your command?" Duruck asked casually, as if that were the true measure of a good commander.

"Close to a hundred thousand," he beamed, pleased with his result, and knowing that no one to date had had a bigger force.

"Impressive. I look forward to seeing what they can do."

"Commander," interjected Drorkon, "I must take my leave, but could I ask that Commander Thiamos make his way back to Cam with you? He'll be an asset with the ensuing battles – he has much experience."

Duruck nodded. "Agreed. You can update me on the ways of this world. I look forward to fighting alongside you, Commander."

"As I with you," Thiamos grinned.

Drorkon patted Thiamos on the back. He was pleased with how well they were getting on, and, walking down the tunnel, they started many long conversations, which they would be continuing all the way to Cam.

Chapter Twenty-Two
Rid the Land

Hewing the creature from the parapet, Lord Kweethos stumbled back. "I'm getting too old for this," he said quietly to himself.

One of the novices – now a veteran soldier, with the recent experiences he had been through – gave him a quizzical look.

"Manner of speaking. Now go and kill something."

The young soldier grinned.

The battle at Len Seror was drawing to a close for that day, and his men were throwing the dead Golesh bodies off the wall. The number of bodies littering the floor by the base of the wall had grown impressively, with all the Black's siege towers destroyed, leaving charred and burnt-out frames of wood. The Golesh resorted to using crude ladders, which they could get aplenty from the local forests, yet their catapults had given the city a continual battering; the tenacity of the Lorians, though, held out.

Lord Kweethos pulled a flask from within his breastplate and downed the whisky. As much as he felt alive and young from the activities he was sharing with his lads from Haval, he was feeling age creeping up on him. He looked along the wall again at his boys – he had had eighty-eight, but now he had less than half that. Most had been injured and were now unable to fight, but he had lost one or two, and with a heavy heart he regretted their deaths deeply, yet wrath fuelled him and he used it.

"My Lord?" offered one of his boys, holding up a canteen of water. He took it and smiled, although he wanted something much stronger and his whisky flask would only last so long.

"Chin up, lads – they're not beating us."

He received a few happy grins, but he knew that his words were losing their meaning with each passing day. But as he watched on, a deep voice broke him from his trance.

"My Lord," – looking up, he saw two of the Bastion Guards – "you're summoned by the commanders of the city."

The first thing he noticed about them was how clean and polished their armour was. He sneered at them, for they were strong and battle trained, more so than any other man on the walls, and instead of fighting on the walls they sat safely at the centre of the city; an ancient law not letting them leave their posts to fight anywhere else.

"Very well," he said quietly.

Without a word, they turned and walked away. "I'll be back soon, lads," he said to the novices with a jovial tone. They toasted after him with their metal mugs.

He arrived there in no time at all – the headquarters were not far for him to walk, being very near his section of the wall. It was a building much like his own back at Haval, although several storeys taller. Like his, it was white with picturesque stained-glass windows lining the walls on every side, each telling a story of old, so that their history would always be remembered. This was the Lorians' way – every window they put into any building across the city told a story. True art had gone into making them, with the artists becoming very rich indeed.

As Kweethos stomped up the steps and onto the veranda, two tired servants held the doors open for him, and he made his way exhaustedly up the long staircase to the top floor. But as he ascended, he heard shouting – two people were really having a go at each other and one of the voices sounded familiar to him.

"I think you should let me do my job and stop interfering!" bellowed one of the voices. They sounded authoritative and spoke of experience.

"All I'm explaining is a different point of view!" replied the other voice, who sounded more aristocratic. "I mean a peace deal may be the only way forward."

"Yeah? Go out there and tell them that. They'll stick several arrows into you before you can get twenty paces!"

"I'm merely making a suggestion. Don't expect me to see that through – that's your job!"

"Well, it won't be me going out there!"

"It's the only way!"

"Not necessarily," said Kweethos as he hobbled in and collapsed into the first chair he could find. "The walls are still being defended, and the Golesh are losing more soldiers than we are." But one of the generals in the room grunted.

Kweethos looked at the man who had been defending his actions. It was the commander of Len Seror's defences, and his old friend, Terram. To say he was battle-hardened would be an understatement; his body was riddled with scars, which some said formed a secret map to buried treasure! He was tall and strong despite his age, which was at least ten years ahead of Kweethos; he was fitter and more able too. But he just stood there with his jaw hanging open, as if about to admit something, "... three sections of the wall were overrun today. We got them back, but at a cost – it has shown a weakness. We suspect that they will throw an all-out assault tomorrow."

"Exactly," cut in the irritating lord, who felt his place needed to be that of deciding matters of the defences, despite having no experience of them. "You said you would hold the walls; you have not, so it is now time for a diplomatic solution, and that means letting me take over. We must have something here that they want, something we can use for trade or a deal?"

"They don't want gold or valuables, you rekon, they want blood – THEY-WANT-US-TO-DIE!" Lord Kweethos shouted, thumping his fist on the desk.

"Lord Kweethos," began the aristocrat as he approached, looking down at him, "an old man who doesn't know his place." He looked on mockingly as if he knew of Kweethos's past.

"He has more of a place here than you!" Terram interjected.

"Watch who you insult – I pay your wages!" spat the aristocrat, pacing over to him and getting close to his face.

"You won't be for much longer with your suggestions on fighting!" Terram said, staring him down.

There was a long pause as they continued their staring contest.

"Gentlemen, please," said a colonel. "We are not Camions – we don't let our rich make decisions for us. I think it would be prudent to have this individual removed." He appeared tired, as did the others, and wished to get on with the meeting. There was thumping on the desks all around from the captains and generals who wanted him gone. The aristocrat packed up his books, held them under his arm and left abruptly.

"Thank you, Colonel Talon," said Terram. "Of course you are correct. I believe everyone is here now, so let's talk about what is going on."

Terram nodded at the guards, who shut the doors from the outside, locking in just the higher-ranking officers of Len Seror.

"I'm not interested in lengthy debates today, gentlemen. Let me tell you how it is, and we'll go with the best option presented to us."

There were nods of agreement from all in the room.

"Our defences have collapsed. Tomorrow, the Golesh will attack the city, and we have no more reserves to hold them off. Our arrows are spent, we have improvised everything we can … suggestions?"

For the first time in that room since the siege had begun, it was deathly silent, as all knew their fate.

"I think it is obvious," said a captain in the corner. "We're all going to die."

"Hang on," said Kweethos, holding up his hand to the captain. "Did you find the entrance I told you about?" he said, addressing Terram.

"Yes, we did. It was found this morning, and we have a scouting party heading down the tunnel now."

"It is the only choice. Get all the women and children down there with one hundred of our finest men —"

"That'll be the Bastion Guards!" chided a sergeant.

"Please, not now!" said Terram, waving a dismissive hand at him as if it were a petty argument he could no longer bear to have.

"Well, throughout this conflict, where have they been? Safe and sound —"

"This is not the place for this discussion," Kweethos interrupted, again trying to get the key facts down. He agreed with him, though – the sergeant had just found out that his family had been killed a few days previously, due to a part of the wall being poorly defended – he had nothing to live for now.

"Tonight, let's get the men fed well and watered. Let them have a good night's sleep, and tomorrow, we spread our forces thinly, but prepare for a glorious battle. We give ourselves much time for the Queen, women and children to get to Camia!"

Terram could see others also wanted to make suggestions, but he knew that Kweethos's suggestion was not the best idea – it was the only idea.

"Very well. Are all in agreement?" Terram asked the room.

There was a nodding of heads from most of them with a few others thumping the desks.

"Good. I'll come by each section at dusk, to explain what is happening and to inspire the men. You never know, some of us may get out of his."

There were murmurs of laughter, although none knew why.

"Make everything so. Good luck, gentlemen."

Terram gave a coded knock on the door; the guards opened it and he stepped out, followed by the officers.

"Terram!" Kweethos shouted. "A quick word?"

Terram waited for the officers to leave before re-entering.

"What is it, old friend?"

"These escorts? Send my boys – they're young and strong, they have their whole lives ahead of them. Don't forsake them to the walls."

"Do you not think that every officer in here would want me to do that for their own men?"

"You know me – I have *never* used our friendship or my position to gain favour ... until now. The rest of this garrison are old warriors, men who are due to die anyway. Forgive me for being blunt, but these times call upon blunt actions! Don't let it be these boys who die. I implore you!"

Terram looked at Kweethos for a long moment; then, sucking in a breath, said, "I will see what I can do."

He walked out, leaving Kweethos sitting alone, not believing his words. He gazed at where Terram had stood, in deep reflection. He needed another army – he needed someone's help – but there was none. He did not think he could predict the future, but sometimes in the past he had just known his time was not yet up; even when things had been as bad as they could be, he had known that his life was to continue. But this time he felt empty, as if that sense within him saw only bleakness. In a way he was happy with the thought, for it gave him purpose not to fear, and to kill as many of those beasts as possible; he just hoped that his boys would be OK.

"Lads, to your feet!" bellowed Kweethos as he saw Terram approaching along the battlements. His forty-two brave young men lined up perfectly on the stone wall with their chests out and chins up. Terram came cantering along on a beautiful white stallion. He had had the horse especially groomed to look its best, to help inspire the garrison.

"My, my!" he said, admiring the well-equipped Haval Knights standing to attention. "I've heard some good things about some regiments upon the walls, but I've heard staggering things about this section." Kweethos couldn't help but notice that he seemed to have rehearsed the way he was speaking – he had probably said the same thing to every unit along the walls.

"Lads, tomorrow will be a day in history for this city, a time for a new window on our walls, and you will chisel the writing by your actions. I won't lie to you – there will be an all-out assault tomorrow, but I know you can hold. You must hold! It will be a glorious fight, and if you open your eyes to the Shadow World or the light of the sky above, you will have done this country proud, you will have done me proud." He didn't receive as much laughter as he had done from other units on the walls who embraced death so easily. But these were younger men, and still had expectations they wanted to see through. "I hope to see you all after the battle tomorrow, lads. Good luck."

Kweethos saluted Terram as he passed, but observed him scornfully, annoyed that he had not sent these young, fit men to escort the women and children through the tunnel to safety, but instead left them to die on a forsaken parapet. But Terram didn't see, keeping his eyes straight ahead – he could not look at Kweethos.

When he had gone, Kweethos turned to his knights, who had clustered together and were talking about Terram's words.

"It's gonna be a fight till the death – can't you lot see that?"

"He didn't say that at all. He just said there will be an all-out assault."

"What brain fuzz have you been drinking? Tomorrow, we're going to die!"

"Maybe," said Kweethos, getting amongst them. They parted out of the way, and listened to him in respectful silence. "You're no idiots, I know that, and in all the battles I have fought in, all the conflicts I have been a part of, you young men are the finest I've fought with. Tomorrow may be the end of us," – he gripped the shoulder of one of the lads – "or it can be the beginning. It is up to you if you die or not, so choose not to. Now, get some sleep – you'll need it."

Without question, they turned in for the night, pulling their burlap sacks tight against them, but they did not fall asleep quickly. Finding it strange that this could be their last day on earth, they silently looked up at the stars with their hands behind their heads, trying to work out why life had been so short.

Kweethos sighed heavily, and sat on part of a broken house which a boulder had smashed through. Looking out into the darkness, which was just littered with fires from the Golesh camps like fireflies buzzing in the night, and slight howls and screams ringing out as the Golesh fought amongst themselves or taunted the Lorians, he wondered what he could do. *Shall I desert my post and find the tunnel with my men?* he thought. *Probably not – they would have barricaded the entrance anyway by now.*

He started to feel the tingling sensation in his head as sleep crept up on him, but he tried to stay awake and keep watch, just so his boys could sleep for one more night, so that they might have one more dream before the chaos of reality would happen on the morrow.

"Estia!"

Her beautiful face looked up at him; she grinned.

"Estia, come to me, my love!"

She reached out but could not get any closer. She looked more like a picture than a real presence – a picture of pure worry.

Kweethos lay on his belly with his arms over the cliff face. He did not realise the staggering height, but focused on his wife.

"Estia, listen to me! You-need-to-give-me-your-hand!" he started to *whimper, as he realised it was hopeless but refused to give up.*

"No," she said softly. *"Be safe, my love."*

BONG!

"Estia!"

"Look after our son."

BONG!

"Estia, please!"

"Goodbye, my love," she said gently, and smiled again.

BONG!

She let go, and fell; it happened in slow motion, so much so that he kept his eyes on her until she was a dot falling to the ground.

BONG!

"Estia," he said softly, and closing his eyes he sank his chin into his chest.

BONG!

Kweethos started as he awoke, opening his eyes to a dazzlingly bright day, with the hills shrouded in black armour as the creatures prepared for their final assault. His head throbbed to the beat of the continual bongs from drums beating out across the land.

"They're not messing about!" said a voice next to him. Terram sat there quietly.

"How long have you been here?" he said, sitting up and rubbing his eyes. He had more-or-less slept in the same position he had been in before nodding off.

"About an hour."

"What do you want?!" he said sharply, clearly conveying his annoyance with what he had done. Terram sighed and looked down at the stone floor, with black patches running along the brickwork, some of it still wet. The troops were still asleep, lying in strange positions upon the stone floor, but he could not bear to look at them.

"I thought I should come and explain to you what happened and why … to your face."

Kweethos didn't look at him; they both looked out to the death before them.

"You asked me for a favour, but it was the favour of another man I had to fulfil."

"What was it? Did he clean your shoes once? Lend you money? Give you —"

"He saved my daughter!" Terram interrupted. Kweethos stayed quiet. "It was a few years ago now. She was kidnapped, and I had to keep it hush-hush or she was going to be killed. Lord Arum – at the time he was commander of the Secret Guard – he found her and killed the perpetrators."

Kweethos said nothing – what *could* he say? Instead, he fished around in his breastplate for his pipe, as did Terram. He pulled out a small, reddish-brown box, with a hammer and anvil etched on the top.

"I received this many years ago from a friend from a distant land. This small piece of tobacco is worth more than the treasure caves of Esha … apparently."

He opened the lid and gave some of the dried root to Terram, who started a spark onto a piece of kindling and ignited their pipes. The smoke they blew out was far denser than what they usually smoked. And silently, they sat puffing, looking out.

"Kweethos?"

"Yep?"

"This tobacco is disgusting ..."

Kweethos tried not to smile, but eventually he could hold it no longer, and they both burst out laughing, coughing from the awful taste in their mouths.

"Did you say 'friend' or 'fiend'?"

"Just wait until I get my hands around his neck."

Although their stomachs were tense and their jaws ached, they felt rather calm despite the situation.

"I can't believe our mighty city has but a few soldiers surrounding its walls, soon to be ..." He couldn't finish the sentence.

"Aye, dark times."

"Indeed."

Suddenly, a loud horn rang out from the sieging army, and, as one, the Golesh converged on the city. The green of the ground was covered by black. No boulders came hurtling their way – every Golesh was being sent forth, even the reserves, and it looked as if all the killing the Lorians had done was for nothing, for they had barely created a dent in the Black's ranks.

"Where are you fighting?" Kweethos asked, as they both got up and stretched.

"Here. I let a friend down last night, but today I'd rather die by his side."

Kweethos put his hand on his shoulder.

"You sure this is wise? Shouldn't you go with the women, the children, the injured?"

"No – they're far away now, and hopefully safe. I have distributed the rest of the commanders around the city. There's nowhere I want to be other than here."

They grinned at each other. In the background the Black charged but the old friends shared a moment, a moment of so many good memories, so many experiences which were etched into several windows around the city, and soon, on that day, it was all to end.

"Battle stations!" they both yelled, kicking the burlap sacks as the boys scrambled out, rubbing their eyes, yawning and trying to fasten the straps on their helmets.

"Come on, you maggots, get up!" bellowed Kweethos.

"There's swordplay that needs attending to. Get up or you'll be flogged!" shouted Terram.

Soon, they were arranged in a long, neat line, weapons drawn in their right hands, their shields brought to their chests. Waving from their armour were flaps of their own tunics; they were tainted with blood and gore and dishevelled, and no one would have guessed that they were new, made by their mothers only a few months earlier.

Soon, the clonking of wood came as the ladders hit the parapet.

"Gentlemen," Kweethos bellowed into the air, "prepare to defend yourselves, prepare to defend your city!"

Terram and the young men threw their weapons into the air, and just as a Golesh appeared, its head was carved in two by Kweethos's broadsword. The Golesh that followed met a bloody end from the Knights of Haval. But the flow continued, and soon they were overwhelmed.

***

"Murderous rekons!" Avron gasped as he looked at the Golesh attacking the city of Len Seror. They were within the city as they flew their flags from the towers and steeples, and all anyone knew, as they gazed out, was that the city was well and truly overrun. With the base of the wall covered in burnt-out carcasses of siege towers and copious amounts of the Black, death seemed to be ubiquitous. The Knights of Ezazeruth stood on a hill watching from the west, as fires erupted uncontrollably. There were echoing screams from men as they were mutilated within the city. Avron turned to his officers, Drorkon and Havovatch, looking very anxious.

"Bam, take your unit and attack from the south." Bam left instantly. "Farek, take two companies, go around Bam's and cover their escape from the east." He too left at a gallop, the horse's hooves a song of metal as he pushed his mount on. Avron looked to the rest of his officers. "I will lead the main body of men. Our duty is to get anyone out who is still alive and kill every Golesh we find. Take no quarter – they all *die*!"

With a salute, his officers made their way to their regiments, all keen to do their duty. Avron turned to Drorkon and stared down at him from his mount, as if he were a mere vagrant before him. "We have this covered. Help as you wish. Just don't get in the way!"

Drorkon's regiment and the Knight Hawks stood aimlessly to one side, eager for battle, as they gazed on at the giant smoke plumes coming from within the city.

"He means it, you know. Best to stay put for the minute!" said Drorkon to Havovatch as they stared out over the city. Havovatch kept rocking on the balls of his feet; he watched the city in ruin, keen to get there and find Lord Kweethos. In his other hand he held the small token knife Kweethos had given him. He couldn't believe, after all the riding and hoping he had done, that he was finally there with an army, but could do nothing to help them.

Avron had assembled what was left of his men – four thousand men and their horses standing in long, superbly neat lines behind a hill. Then he stood up high on his stirrups and waved his helmet from side to side, signalling for everyone to move as one.

"The five pillars of the city," said Drorkon as he gazed on, depression personified over his face. "One for justice, one for faith, one for reason, one for health and the last for strength."

Havovatch looked at him, not really knowing what to say.

"All about to become nothing …"

"But we can save them?" he said hopefully.

But this time Drorkon said nothing, and just looked on as if the millions of stories that the towers told were about to become unknown, and as if any tradition the Camions kept would be erased from memory.

The Ippikós began their advance. There were no horn blasts, and no bells rang out, as the front rows of the Ippikós started ahead at a canter, with the next rows joining and so forth. It was highly disciplined. Avron did not want to give away their position to the Golesh, in fear of them turning and creating a rearguard, and so the charge began, as the red-cloaked knights, with their dark, heavy armour, and their long, red banners twisting in the wind, rode out as silently as they could to charge down the Black horde. And, the first battle for the Knights of Ezazeruth in over two thousand years had begun.

"Die, you filthy rekon, die, die, die, die, dieeeee!!" Havovatch screamed as he kept striking his sword vertically down into the creature. It jolted with every stab and was long since dead, but with one of the bolts from his Malorga protruding from its heart, it kept twitching.

Standing up straight, panting heavily, Havovatch paced through the streets to find something else to vent his frustrations on.

The Ippikós had slaughtered the Golesh, but they had decided that they had saved everyone and everything they could save, and for their own safety they left and regrouped outside the city. In the streets, though, the bodies of the Lorians were scattered everywhere amongst the Golesh, as they made their last stand. Most had been killed with multiple wounds all over their bodies as they were hacked away at. Some buildings had been barricaded to help the wounded, but as the Golesh broke in, they attacked the helpless Lorians as they lay in their beds. Some had been dragged out into the streets to be butchered.

With Havovatch feeling like the only person alone in a giant city that was shrouded in a blanket of smoke as the battle subsided and the fire spread quickly, he tried in vain to find his friends. The ancient city of Len Seror was no more, with its population unaccounted for, and its garrison down to a handful of men who were sitting on the plains outside in shock, watching as their home became ash.

Havovatch, though, kept searching through the streets for the Haval Knights.

"Kweethos!" he bellowed, but heard nothing.

Just then, another creature appeared, looking stricken and terrified, looking each way and wondering where to go, as if it were lost.

Havovatch threw a knife at its leg, making it fall to one knee. Then, running at it, with one clean swoop he carved through its neck, letting the head roll into the doorway of a burning shop. As he looked down at the body, he couldn't help but cry in despair, as he tried to think of what to do. *What would the smartest person in the world do?* The smartest people he knew were his parents. He tried for a moment to think how they would react, what would they do. Standing still and squeezing his eyes shut, he thought hard, but every scenario he conjured led back to the same thing: *GET OUT!*

"General!" came a voice from behind him.

Slowly, he opened his eyes, the feeling of giving up apparent. He turned to see Buskull, and, pursing his lips, he just shook his head as tears formed in his eyes.

"General, we need to get out, now!" Buskull instructed.

Havovatch turned and looked down the empty streets, filled with nothing but smoke and ash, which was becoming thicker as the fire enveloped the city. As he stared, he said nothing, as if a moral bond held him there.

"General," he heard again as Buskull placed his giant hand on his shoulder. Havovatch closed his eyes and looked at the floor, finally giving up.

"We're gonna make them pay, Buskull. By my blood and the loss of these souls, we will make them pay!" he whimpered.

Suddenly, behind them a house collapsed, blocking their way back. Havovatch stared at it, the sense of defeat clear in his eyes; his shoulders dropped.

"Then let's get out of here, before we become one of those souls," Buskull said softly. Havovatch nodded gently, then took one last despairing look around. "You said to me only a few days ago to concentrate on our mission," Buskull continued. "Now I am saying it to you – we need to go."

He looked up at the tall, bald giant staring down sympathetically at him. The first thought in that moment was that the smoke and fire didn't seem to bother him any more. Yet he had too heavy a heart to ask why. Turning down the street, away from the furnace of flames, they headed towards blue sky in the distance, just appearing through the smoke.

They didn't rush as they made their way to the wall, despite flames flaring up around them, sparks falling upon their skin, and collapsed houses behind them. They just walked quietly, as if out for a stroll after finding out bad news.

When they finally came to the walls, they had no need to climb up and over, for it was the part that had been repeatedly bombarded by boulders from the Golesh catapults, and left open with many dead on the floor. It had been the epicentre of the fighting, with the Lorians battling tenaciously as hundreds of Golesh corpses littered the ground. There were so many that the two Camions had to climb over them.

Once out, they walked away from the smoke and into the clean air, as the last part of Len Seror was consumed by flames behind them – it was almost as if something had been shielding them from the fire, and now behind them was just a mixture of white and orange flames from the inferno and black smoke.

They joined the Knight Hawks, who all stared on solemnly at the city, as the base of the mighty towers soaring high into the air began to become engulfed in flames, and the dense, black cloud consumed the lower level. The flames were so fierce, they swept through the city as quickly as the wind blew them, with smoke of every kind ascending, some of it like small stems flying lightly into the air, others billowing out from the tightly packed windows as the gases of the fire forced the smoke out. The wisps of smoke all circled the huge black cloud from the centre as it flew higher and higher, roaring from the furnace of the city within, the wind taking it west. For dozens of leagues, it could have been seen, almost as if the Golesh had planned it to be a banner of the Black. If one looked closely, one could see faces in the smoke – either the souls that had been consumed by the fire or the black creatures that had started it.

It was nothing like Havovatch had ever seen; it was like a bad dream, as if it were winter and the clouds were about to snow, but instead of snow, ash billowed out from them – there was nothing natural about it.

"A city ..." he said despairingly, seeing what the Black could do, and thinking that Cam may see a repeat of this.

No one said anything as they gazed on. To turn away seemed like an insult to those who had suffered. Those who had perished would have no burial; they wouldn't have a prayer read out or a song sung over their graves. Their bodies would be consumed by the fire, turning their corpse and whatever was around them into ash, dead to the wind in the last pose they left upon this world. It would suffice to say that anger was all around, yet all Havovatch could feel was sadness and regret, burning deep to his core.

Suddenly, there was a terrible crash, as one of the giant towers gave way and fell in on itself. As if they were in a bad dream that they wanted to wake up from, all anyone could do was watch.

"How many survivors are there?" said Avron as he sat behind a yew-tree desk in his tent. Standing around him were two of his senior officers, General Drorkon and Havovatch, and one of his men standing to attention before him.

"One hundred and twenty-eight Lorian Guards, three hundred Bastion Knights, two Golesh captured, minor casualties to the Ippikós, no injuries to the Two-Twenty-Eighth, no injuries to the Knight Hawks," said the Ippikós officer, reading clearly and with a deliberate tone from the parchment in front of him.

"If I remember correctly, my orders were for *no* Golesh to be captured?"

"Your orders were clear, Commander. However, we found these two trying to flee from the city; they have just been brought here."

"Fine. Have the regiment make camp, the horses well fed and watered. Slaughter the two remaining creatures." Avron spoke with such malicious intent that Havovatch felt uncomfortable. He supposed that after two thousand years, he wouldn't have much feeling for the creatures that had started all of this.

Avron turned to General Drorkon.

"I believe you now have your own mission to attend to? With this threat now dealt with, I don't feel the need for your services!" he said plainly, and looked down at his desk, conveying his repulsion for him.

Drorkon turned and pushed his way out of the tent flaps without a word. Avron then looked up and nodded to Havovatch, who did likewise.

Outside, Havovatch donned his helmet and tried to keep pace with General Drorkon, who seemed more than irritated. Drorkon suddenly stopped and turned, placing a firm hand before him.

"I don't mean to be rude, General, but please leave me alone," he said bluntly, before pacing off in no particular direction.

Havovatch started at the sudden belligerence, not expecting it from a man he had known to be so pleasant and calm under any circumstance. He felt awkward. After the story Drorkon had told him of his past and what he had to do, the only thing Havovatch could think of was that he was forced to do what he did, and did not like the fact that the knights hated him so much for it.

He stood on the spot looking around. Len Seror was still burning, but was now little more than debris, with only the one last tower standing, and that for not much longer. He heard echoes like thunder ring out across the land as the foundations started to crumble, but the building remained standing as if it were making a defiant attempt not to fall.

He could no longer look at the city, and so, taking in a breath, he turned to face what was around him. He looked at the Ippikós soldiers;

he had thought the Two-Twenty-Eighth were the most disciplined regiment he had ever seen, but these were on a whole different level. The Two-Twenty-Eighth spent their time relaxing when not working, and fulfilling their duties to the fullest when they were. But the Ippikós were all working non-stop. Changing horseshoes, checking their horses' reins and saddles, cleaning them, sharpening swords, lining up to be registered and accounted for, and everyone else was training with their trade. Lancers charged at targets held up by their brethren, swordsmen practised riding whilst swinging their blades, and archers shot at targets thrown into the air by their comrades; they laughed and jeered as they did so. He thought it was strange that they would act in this manner under the circumstances. Others, such as the Ippikós physicians, were tending to the wounded of the Lorians. The entire camp was alive, with not one of them resting – all were making sure that everything that needed to be done, was done.

But he felt a physical pain of suffering when he looked over at the garrison of the city. Most were sitting down, some standing up with their hands on their heads or walking about aimlessly, wanting to do something. They had all been given food, but had pushed it away with no appetite, as their homes lay destroyed before them and nothing they could do about it. With nothing to do, he decided to approach them. *Maybe there is something I can say...* he thought. But as he approached, something caught his eye; in the centre of the group was a young lad standing up, wearing cream and burgundy, although it was tarnished by black and red blood.

Havovatch almost sprinted over to him, pushing through some of the others. As he got closer, he saw another lad, and another, and there, sitting with a pipe in his mouth and looking angry, was Lord Kweethos.

"My Lord!" Havovatch shouted with delight, forgetting his surroundings. A lot of heads turned to see who was so cheerful in this grim scene. Lord Kweethos looked up and frowned at the Knight Hawk before him. Havovatch, with his helmet still on and the black fabric covering his mouth and eyes, realised that Kweethos could not have known who was there, and so he took it off.

Kweethos showed as much of a smile as he could under the circumstances, and rose. The young lads cheered up as well, and gathered around Havovatch, patting him on the shoulder. He didn't know any of their names or recognise their faces, but he hugged the closest one to him.

Lord Kweethos limped up, and, with his mighty arms out wide, he gripped him tightly.

"My friend, 'tis good to see you."

"I've been looking everywhere for you, my Lord. I feared you had perished."

"We nearly did." He turned and looked at the Ippikós. "Did you bring them?"

"Yes, my Lord – we came as soon as we could. I'm just sorry it was not soon enough."

"It was when it was. Come, walk with me."

He gave a nod at his lads, who sat down, a little bit more cheerful than they had been.

"How many have you lost?" Havovatch asked as they walked along the side of a creek.

Kweethos knelt down and splashed water over his face, cleaning soot off. "Well, half were taken with the sick and injured, and twenty died this morning in the city as we pulled back, so a few."

"Good men!"

"That they were, very good men. My friend died there as well – Commander Terram, bravest man I ever knew."

Havovatch frowned. "I know that name."

"So you should. He is … was, master of the Lorian military."

"May the Grey Knight of the soul help guide him to the everlasting light."

"May it!" said Kweethos bitterly.

"It must have been a terrible ordeal, my Lord?" Havovatch said, facing his back.

"Clearly," Kweethos said with a hint of sarcasm.

"Apologies, my Lord. I don't really know what to say."

"You're a young man, Captain Havovatch, but a good one."

"Erm, General now, my Lord," Havovatch corrected.

Kweethos stood up and looked him over. Only then did he realise that his armour was not the bronze with a blue crest as he had seen before – it was now black with three rust-coloured crests.

"Found a better regiment?"

Havovatch could see it in his eyes, as he sought in his mind to find out which one he was from.

"Ha! No – I got promoted. I'm now General of the Knight Hawks."

Kweethos looked at the red-eyed hawk hilt of his new sword hanging behind his shoulder.

"Well, you are full of surprises."

Havovatch grinned at the remark.

"So, who're these horse lords? They don't look anything like Camion military, nor Virorian, nor Leno Danian?"

"They are the Ippikós – the red window of your villa, my Lord."

He smiled. "I knew it – just wanted you to confirm it. So you succeeded?"

"With difficulty, my Lord." Havovatch absent-mindedly rubbed his chest at the memory. "I made one decision I wish I could reverse, though."

"That you left the Three-Thirty-Third at Haval?" he guessed.

Havovatch nodded.

"You didn't know this would happen, and you certainly could not have left a Camion military unit in Loria. You made the right decision!"

Havovatch looked back at the city and took in a sharp breath.

Just then, the last tower consumed by flames to the very top gave way, and fell, sending ash, smoke and a thunderous noise far and wide.

A tear appeared in Kweethos's eye as they watched it fall. It was so tall, it appeared to happen in slow motion. "I stole my first kiss up there …"

Havovatch let him have his moment.

Eventually, Kweethos turned his back on the city, and they walked along the creek in silence.

"What became of your son, my Lord?"

"I sent him away. A couple of weeks ago, one of the novices shouted out that the dwarf mercenaries were running this way from the south. I ran out to meet them and they said that a dark horde was heading this way; they barely stopped, and then kept going. Off in the distance I saw the dark shadow on the hills, as if a dense cloud passed above. So, I got everyone out of there, and then we marched for Len Seror."

"Did you all make it OK?"

"Yes – just in time to raise the alarm. A few days later we were under siege, but ready … well, as ready as we could be. Before that, though, a party of monks was leaving the city, keen to get away from the fighting. I gave all the coin I had for them to take Rembon with them – I just hope he's OK!"

"I'm sure he is, my Lord. The armies left the Rogan Defence Line. One force went to Minta in the north; the rest came here."

Kweethos sighed. "Thank you, General. I needed to know that. With any luck he should have slipped away." He then frowned. "Hang on – did you say that the Golesh came from beyond the Rogan Defence Line?"

"Yes, my Lord. The Ninsks betrayed us."

"I doubt it was the Ninsks – they're cantankerous rekons with no emotion, but they obey their leaders. If they had been told to let the Golesh cross the line, they would have done. If not, they would have fought that lot till the death; there are many of them there, and the Golesh wouldn't have crossed unless they could have done unopposed, otherwise they would have tried much sooner."

Havovatch looked at the ground, as he knew exactly who it was.

"Well, I am aware that Xat and Xot were behind it."

"The X brothers? Hardly. I've heard that their grip is tightened by Chieftain Framlar of Santamaz."

Havovatch said nothing at the remark.

"So, what of you next, General?" said Kweethos, changing the subject.

"I am to command the Knight Hawks to the Black Lands, and kill Agorath."

"Argh, a wise move!"

"What of you, my Lord – what will you do?"

"Well, I doubt there is much of Haval left. So I can't go there. I suppose the only place will be the ports, or maybe your city of Cam."

"Will the ports still be there, my Lord?"

"Oh, yes. They're well defended – nothing would get through them. They're packed in better than the crack of a dung beetle."

Havovatch grinned. Seeing the Two-Twenty-Eighth preparing themselves as well as the Knight Hawks, Havovatch turned and held his hand out to Kweethos.

"I must take my leave, my Lord."

Kweethos took his hand in both of his warmly and smiled. "I don't know what the rest of your life holds for you, but I wish it full of luck."

Havovatch grinned again and nodded, and turned to make his way towards his regiment.

General Drorkon on his mount came cantering towards him. Everywhere he went, his cohorts followed close by.

"General, I trust you're OK?" Drorkon asked kindly, as if he regretted the berating he had given him earlier.

"Yes, thank you, General." Havovatch looked over at what was left of Len Seror. "I can't believe this has happened, though. What if that is Cam in a few weeks?"

"Then, we must make sure that it isn't."

"What now?"

"I think it's best that you go ahead with your unit. Go to the Port of Beror and commandeer a ship; once you have done that, come back and find us. I will lead the Two-Twenty-Eighth and your Hawks there, but it will take longer with more of us."

"Yes, Sir. I will see you in a few days."

Havovatch made his way to Buskull and the others. It wasn't difficult – he just looked for a man standing above the rest. And there, in the thick of the crowd, was Buskull trying to keep the Lorian spirits up as he helped patch wounds. Finding their mounts, the unit left the goings-on of the Ippikós behind them and rode south whilst the black cloud of what was left of Len Seror consumed the sky behind them.

Chapter Twenty-Three
The Shipmen

After two days of hard riding, the unit arrived at a smoky port. What they found was not pretty, but it could have been so much worse. At the base of the cream, stone walls surrounding the town were copious amounts of dead bodies of the Black. It was clear that they had given the town a beating, but the town's guard had held out well. There were small plumes of smoke rising into the air from the houses that had been destroyed just behind the wall; the smoke was thinning out and grey, as if it were being extinguished. Outside the wall, the town's guard were out in force, piling the corpses into wagons after stripping them of their armour, which was being loaded into carts and fed back into the town.

"Oh, no," sighed Buskull as he looked down at the guards.

"What?" said Havovatch, trying to follow his gaze and work out what he was seeing.

"The Averchi."

"Who?"

"The Averchi. They're part of an ancient order, but sell their soldiers for hire. That's why they're the richest order in the known world. You hire as many or as few as you need. They're a stubborn, cantankerous bunch."

"Mercenaries held out here?" said Feera, not quite believing it.

"They get paid well, and their training is certainly not for the faint-hearted. When money is involved, they'll do everything they can to protect their assets."

"What are they doing now, with the bodies?" said Hilclop.

"I'd imagine they're taking their spoils from their kills as rewards. My bet is the town's blacksmiths will melt the metal down, use it for their own purposes and give a portion of the proceeds to the mercenaries."

"They were lucky to have mercenaries here. If they had Lorian soldiers, they would have been called up to the Banners, leaving them defenceless," said Feera.

"And lost to the sea," added Havovatch.

"Well, they can't be as hard as the rest of ya from what I've seen," said Wrisscrass, as he dug his boot into his horse's side and started moving down the hill.

"Wrisscrass, I wouldn't!" said Havovatch.

He stopped and looked back at them. "Wha'?"

"It will take too long to explain to them why you're here. I suggest you go and hide in the bushes over there," he said, pointing to a large group of shrubs lining the hill.

"Wow! A few hours without Wrisscrass – I'm gonna miss him." said Hilclop with a cheesy grin, waving a finger at him mockingly.

Wrisscrass stayed put; he almost appeared to be sulking.

"As soon as you walk towards that lot, you'll be one of those corpses, and your weapons will have a new owner," said Buskull bluntly.

Mumbling under his breath, Wrisscrass slumped down from his mount and aimlessly wandered over the crest of the hill. They just saw his head disappear as he slumped into the bush.

"We'll come and find you when we're done. Just stay there," Havovatch shouted after him. But a hand appeared with a gesture that made Buskull grimace.

Buskull took the reins of Wrisscrass's horse and they slowly made their way down the hill towards the gate, which had clearly taken more of a battering than the walls, with scorch marks along the stone and heavy damage exposing the inner brickwork. One of the gates was so badly damaged that the Averchi had nailed a cart to it to try to give it some added strength. Arrows were embedded everywhere, and surrounding the portcullis (which appeared to be jammed because it hadn't been used in decades) were thick, black stalactites of hardened tar, which had been thrown over the gatehouse onto the besiegers.

As Havovatch approached, he studied the men around him, for he was starting to recall bloodthirsty stories of the Averchi; from what he had heard, they did not seem human. But now they were in front of him, there was nothing to indicate that they were anything else. No one seemed to regard him, though – most were too busy looting the corpses or testing the weapons by swinging them in mid-air. Havovatch didn't like it, it seemed too immoral; he was a soldier and couldn't go through a human corpse's property, nor that of a creature, for that matter, to look for signs of profit. But he forgot that these were mercenaries – everything they did was for profit. They would probably defend their own wealth better than an army of loyal soldiers. *Which, come to think of it, is probably why they were hired to protect the town – because of its trade.*

"Stop!" came an ominous shout from their right.

Stomping purposefully towards them was a very large man by human standards, yet Buskull still towered above him. He was dressed like all the other mercenaries – a black cloak with a red inner lining, a dark silver cuirass with the pattern of the Averchi upon its breastplate – a large "A" with a cross behind it. From head to foot he had chainmail and a charcoal-black tunic, a broadsword sat by his thigh, and there was a collection of daggers about his person. He had a bald head and a very long scar running down his face through where his left eye had once been.

"Who're you? What you want?" he bellowed. To try to make him more intimidating, several of his cohorts strutted forward and stood behind him, brandishing their weapons confidently with grins on their faces. Havovatch couldn't help but feel it had been rehearsed.

"I am General Havovatch of Camia. We are here to secure a ship. We mean no harm."

The bald man held out his hands at the scene around them. "Well, it might not be apparent to you, *General*, but we're a tad busy right now!"

"Oh, don't mind us. You carry on. We just want to get into the town and speak with some captains," said Havovatch a little sarcastically – he didn't mean to, but his feeling for them had got the better of him.

The bald man cocked his jaw as he looked up at him.

"I don't like your tone, *General*. And how old are you? You're a mere child!"

He got several laughs from his men.

"To some," Havovatch responded quietly. Then, as quick as a flash, he drew his Kopis and pointed the tip at the bald man's chin. A slight push and it would have cut him, but Havovatch had controlled and aimed it well. "But just as fast as an adult."

The man held his hands aloft and took a step back from the blade.

"Well ... I don't believe you're a general, and I don't believe you're from Camia," he swallowed. Clearly it had shaken him. "Just shove off!"

By now the mercenaries had started to edge forward, and more had gathered behind their commander.

Sensing the hostility, the one thing Havovatch knew about the Averchi was that they feared the Knight Hawks, greatly. Pulling the flap up from his satchel, he dug his hand in, pulled his Hawk's helmet from within and placed it on.

"Recognise this?" he shouted to the gathering crowd, and pulled up his Malorga. The commander clearly did, his eyes wide and looking slightly fearful. Knight Hawks dealt more with mercenaries than with any other soldiers, as it was usually criminals of wealth who hired the mercenaries to do their bidding, and so they greatly feared the Hawks. Hawks had probably killed more of the Averchi than any other army, order or country had done.

"I am General of the Knight Hawks, and I have more beyond the rise of that hill. So, we can argue about this or you can take my word that there will be no trouble, and let us in. One way or another, I'm not turning away, Commander!" He didn't realise it, but the confidence he got from wearing his helmet had made his voice more hoarse and full of conviction.

The commander ground his teeth as he thought. He didn't want them to enter, yet he couldn't show weakness in front of his men.

"Al'right," – he jabbed a long, scarred finger at him – "but if I get so much as a whisker of trouble from you lot, you'll be thrown out, and stripped of your weapons, you 'ear?"

"Understood," said Havovatch, as he tried to sound serious, but clearly was not. He dug his stirrup into his mount and they proceeded through the gate.

Hilclop sat there grinning, like the smallest boy in a large group of thugs, but feeling just as strong as the big boys, which clearly added to the mercenaries' anger. Feera and Buskull, on the other hand, acted more professionally and kept their eyes straight.

"I thought Hawks had to don their helmets all the time in public?" whispered Buskull as they went through the gate.

"Really? News to me," said Havovatch, removing his and placing it back in his satchel.

"Yes – it's one of their mysteries, for people do not think they're human."

"You seem to know a lot about them?"

"Aye, I've been on many missions, General."

"Really? Why not join the Hawks? You'd be perfect."

"Narr ..." he said dismissively.

Havovatch couldn't help but feel there was another story there, yet it was not the time to hear it.

On the inside of the port, the place was a mess. Every house before them had been flattened or burnt down, leaving just the charred remains of the frames. There were red patches on the ground where some of the mercenaries had been killed (well, the unit hoped they were mercenaries and not the townspeople). There was little movement from within – the mercenaries seemed keener on getting their loot from the Golesh than on sorting out the houses, which made Havovatch sigh even more at their greed. He remembered in his training that if such a disaster had arisen in Cam, the order would be for him to set about rebuilding what was damaged to get the city working again. For every day it wasn't, the city lost money.

They proceeded down the path towards the quay. They were still high up and looking left and right, Havovatch saw the town clearly. Sloping downwards like half a bowl, from east to west, were the high points, with the town descending towards the sea – like a large arena, but filled with houses and shops instead of ascending steps. And, instead of a gladiatorial sandpit at the bottom, there was a port with jetties and piers stretching out beyond the horizon, with one very long pier to their right.

As Havovatch looked upon the skyline, he could see the glittery reflection of the sun upon the wavy ocean; it was very tranquil.

The harbour was where most of the activity was going on. Like the branches on a tree, quays stretched out into the water with ships of every size moored up alongside them. Beside the larger ships were wooden cranes, their large ropes hauling pallets from within the holds of the ships, being pulled by a long line of large men, as if they were in some massive tug-of-war. Countless sacks or crates emerged from within the holds and were laid onto carts. It was all clearly done so often that the stevedores knew how to work quickly and efficiently.

As for the town, it was a blur of movement and colours in the narrow streets, with loud chanting sounding everywhere as wealthy barons and shopkeepers traded.

He pushed his horse on down the cobbled street. Although every country was at war, and the Port of Beror had just had its first taste of it, the town was still alive with the sights, sounds and smells of its burgeoning trade. Blacksmiths were hammering away on their anvils, heat billowing from their forges as the unit passed by the doors. The strong smell of fish was tangible as they passed fishmongers, their counters displaying creatures from the deep that he'd never seen before; and there were cloth stalls selling exquisite pieces of linen, in assortments of colours and shades he hadn't even known existed. It reminded Havovatch of the Busy City, but everything seemed to be of a much higher quality.

There were also several large warehouses being loaded and then locked up, with one of the mercenaries putting the key on a chain around his neck and tucking it under his armour. As he left, the Averchi stood to attention all the way around it, like a human wall. They looked threatening, scanning their gaze over anyone who came near. Yet the locals appeared to be accustomed to them and just walked on by. Havovatch pushed on. Every shop, no matter what was being sold, had crowds around it, with people haggling for the best buy; it didn't seem to occur to them that the town had been under siege or that masses of dead creatures lay at their doorstep. Most of these people were not from Ezazeruth, though, but further regions beyond the sea, sailing for weeks before any land would appear.

After a while of asking politely for people to move out of the way and admiring the shops around them, the unit eventually came to what they were looking for – a rusty silhouette of a ship swinging above a door with the words *Tavern* inscribed into it.

"I may as well enter on my own – I don't want to draw too much attention to us. Stay with the horses, but listen up: if I call you, come running!" said Havovatch as he donned a very large cloak that covered his armour.

"But you're a Knight Hawk!" jibed Feera. "You can take on anything!"

"Hmmm," mused Havovatch, before entering.

Havovatch entered the tavern and was instantly struck by what felt like a scented wall of tobacco. The room was filled with a dull mist, with the wind taking most of it out as he opened the doors, but it left a stale aroma of foul air. The room was dark, with a bar at the centre and small, round tables spread along the walls. All the windows were covered with drapes, as if to hide the goings-on inside. The only source of light came from candles lining the room, with some on the table as thick as his forearm. It was a warm afternoon outside, so he got several strange looks from people in the bar with his heavy attire covering his body armour – he was starting to think that he should have taken his armour off instead.

Quickly shutting the double doors, he made his way to the bar, examining the people around him, looking intently for someone he could trust; but from the merchants, barons and seamen (and what he thought may be cutmen) he received nothing but hateful stares.

He approached the barman who was drying a glass and throwing an inquisitive look in his direction.

"Yes? How can I help?" he said bluntly.

"Greetings, I am … Therma, from the north. I seek a ship and a captain."

"Well, you have come to the right place, *Therma* of the north," he said, with a tone that suggested he didn't quite believe him. He pointed with his head to a man sitting idle in a dark corner of the tavern. His face was barely lit up by the embers of his pipe; his eyes were dark and seemed to hold many vicious stories. He had a long, trimmed beard and neat clothes, and his fingers glittered from the candlelight, he had so much jewellery on, but his henchmen sitting around him were not so elegantly dressed. Clearly he liked to spend money lavishly on himself rather than pay an equal share to his crew. The man stared intently towards him, blowing smoke and waiting for him to approach. But Havovatch did not favour him, with the ill look he possessed. He wished for someone he could control … and trust – if such a person existed in this part of the world? He turned back to the barman. "I don't think he is the sort I am looking for. I am looking to sail to an uncharted land, and I need someone who is not part of a trade and can go off course for a couple of months."

"There will only be one man who can help you in this town, laddie. I dare say he will not be the best choice for you, though."

"Very well. Where can I find him?"

The barman looked to the other side of the room. Havovatch noticed that this part of the tavern was nearly deserted, with just a scruffy old man hunched up in the dark corner, gazing into a candle flame as if it held all the answers he sought. He looked like a vagrant, with long, grey, matted hair, long fingernails, and food and beer stains down his beard.

Havovatch turned back to the barman with a quizzical look.

"I told you, he will not be the best choice."

"But you said that he is the only man?"

"Then there you go."

The barman tired of this stranger's questions, threw the towel onto the bar and went out the back.

Havovatch cleared his throat. Feeling slightly apprehensive, he made his way towards the man. Standing in front of him, Havovatch grunted. But the man did not look up, too engrossed in the candlelight to be interested in who the stranger was before him. He mumbled as if trying to remember what he had seen in the candle.

"Excuse me. I believe you can help me?"

The man did not answer, nor did he move. Havovatch was being watched by all in the tavern now, curious as to who he was and what he wanted.

Havovatch pulled up a chair and sat down, looking at the man. "Excuse me, sailor?"

The man looked upon him with soft, compassionate eyes, as though Havovatch was the only person ever to call him a sailor and mean it.

"I need a captain and a crew; I'm told you are the best person to help me?"

The man stuttered and looked Havovatch up and down incredulously, as if he were a figment of his imagination. Recognising his confusion, Havovatch drew closer and lowered his voice so others could not hear.

"Listen – I am a general in the Camion military. I need to travel to a place few know of. It's a long way away, but you will be well paid."

The vagrant's eyes narrowed, then he boomed with laughter and slapped the table. Shaking his head, he returned his attention back to staring into the candlelight.

Havovatch looked at him for a long minute, then reached over and took his hand.

"If I were not real, could I touch your arm?"

The man didn't withdraw, but kept looking at Havovatch's grasp, then back at his eyes.

"I told you, I need the help of a good captain and a good ship."

"Where is this land?" the man asked hoarsely, as if he had not spoken in years, and his mouth was trying to learn how to do it all over again.

"East, far across the sea of Azure. But it is fraught with danger and I doubt that I will be coming back. We just need to get there."

"No, there's nothing across those seas, laddie. No sailor in his right or wrong mind would dare sail that far – it's too dangerous."

"What do you mean?"

"Ships go missing that way, laddie. We only ever sail south."

Havovatch let go of his arm. In one way he felt glad, because it was a sign that they were going in the right direction.

"We can pay, handsomely."

The vagrant shook his head and continued to look into the candle.

"What do you want, then?"

The man looked up sharply. "To die."

"You want to die?"

"Yes – I have my reasons. Why do you want to go to this land?"

"I want to go to this land so that others may live. And if I and my army perish, it doesn't matter as long as we succeed."

"Then … maybe, I can help you," said the stranger with a curt grin.

"Thank you." Havovatch raised his hand to shake that of the stranger's over the table; after a moment's hesitation, he took it softly, surprised by the friendly manner. After the constant mocking he had received, he was not used to kindness. They shook for a long moment as he enjoyed the human interaction.

"I am General Havovatch of the Knight Hawks," he said quietly, trying not to let his voice be heard by unwanted ears.

"My name is … my name is …" The man looked down at the flame again as if that held the answer.

Havovatch looked at him, concerned. The man looked confused and hurt, as if he could not remember the simplest things, even his name.

"My name is …" he kept repeating, as if he knew the answer then forgot it.

"How about I give you a name … until you remember yours?"

The man nodded vacantly.

Havovatch frowned. It was actually quite hard – what name could he think of? For some reason Rembon kept surfacing but he didn't like the idea of calling him that. But then he had a good one.

"How about Mercury? A good name for a good man, after an old friend of mine."

"Mercury?" the man said with a grin, looking down at the table with some nobility.

"Do you want to talk here? Or go somewhere else?"

"How about a pie and a pint, and we'll talk about this ... quest of yours."

Havovatch realised that he had no money on him. Hesitantly, he got up and went to the bar. The barman had been watching in astonishment.

"Impressive," the barman said, looking confused.

"How so?"

"That old codger has not spoken to anyone in years. He doesn't go anywhere. He just sits there day after day."

Havovatch looked back at him; he just sat there, looking at him feebly. Havovatch couldn't help but pity him.

"Why is he this way?"

"No one knows. He used to be a fine tradesman – came from a cutman background but turned good. One day he went out, unfortunately during the great storm of Pera nearly twelve years ago. Very few returned. He did, though, but he was the only one. All his ship's crew died, and he kept talking about some nonsense of fighting creatures of some sort. Of course, everyone thought it was baloney, that the sea had turned him mad. So, he gave me his entire fortune and said he wished to just stay in the bar. Of course, at the time, with the amount he was going to give me, I couldn't say no, but he has sat there ever since, getting worse by the day. The irony for me was that I lost all the money gambling the very next night."

"He has been there for twelve years?" said Havovatch, not quite believing it.

The barman just nodded.

Havovatch could not believe that the old man had been in the bar longer than he could remember in his own life – he barely knew what had happened before he had enlisted.

"He asked for a pie and pint."

The barman poured him two large ales. "The pies will be out shortly. Don't worry about the cost – I guess these are on him."

The barman sighed heavily in regret at the fortune he'd lost.

"Thank you."

Sitting down, Havovatch gave Mercury the pint. He pulled it to the edge of the table and tilted it towards himself and sipped the foamy nectar.

"Now, tell me where we're going."

"Mercury … I have just been speaking to the barman. Did you fight creatures? Beings of untold stories, grey skin, unpleasant teeth, shaggy white hair?"

"You're mistaken, laddie. I thought I had, but as it turns out, I went mad with the storm."

"What if I were to tell you that you didn't go mad, and the thoughts you possessed were those of real events – in fact, I could show you several thousand of those creatures right now if you come for a walk with me?"

"Then I would be telling you that *you* are the crazy one, and to go home and not end up like me. A feeble old wreck, constantly mocked."

Havovatch took his hand. "*I* believe you, Mercury." He stared into his eyes and showed his conviction. "Tell me what happened to you."

Mercury glanced around at the bar, but, knowing that someone for once wanted to hear his story, he remembered the images as if they had happened just the day before.

Many years ago, I took my crew of thirteen out – good, strong men, hearts of the sea and gills of the serpents within it – I was proud to sail with them. But we were struck by a storm few would ever live to know nor see nor hear about, the worst I had ever been in. Yet my brothers knew what they were doing and everyone went to their positions. We managed to sail through it, but we ended up in dark times, and away from any familiar setting, that we did.

After three days of scaling large waves and the constant rain pouring down upon us, the sea calmed and the serpent stirring it left, but the ship was battered and needed repair, so we sought out some land.

We had been gone for five weeks before the storm hit us, and after it we were severely knocked off course. We had no idea where we were, but we sailed in one direction, in the hope of finding land, and land we found. It was a bleak rock on the horizon, but after the altercation with the sea, it lifted the morale of the men, though it was not a land we knew of. Dark clouds loomed above and as we drew nearer it turned into a barren wasteland, a country of rock and little life. We went on nevertheless, and, finding a cove, we slipped in and secured the ship. The first night, we decided to have a good meal and then to set off in the morning to find timber, and that was what we did. Armed with axes, ten of us climbed the rock face.

Once at the top, we set up a pulley system and set off to find some timber. We were gone half the day, and eventually found something that resembled a tree; we cut it down and we towed it back. But there was something in the air that sent a chill through the bones of all men, and a noise in the background, a noise that struck fear into us all. We tried to ignore it – being on a strange land we just wanted to get our repairs done and leave as soon as possible, and that we did. Five days we were there, and the ship was ready, but on the fifth morning, we awoke to hard times. Getting up, I heard shouting ... and fighting, I took my cutlass and ran up on deck, and there, on board MY ship, were these ravenous dogs duelling with my men. They were disgusting, harsh and cruel beasts. I know not what they were but they were not friendly, so we fought them. We won the battle, and, with the ship ready, I shouted to raise the anchor and get ourselves out of there. I lost seven men in the fight, and the rest of us made to get away, but as we went to leave the cove, a black ship blocked our path.

"RAM IT!" I shouted, seeing the death of my brothers, who were lying on deck. I wanted vengeance. The ship was long and narrow and not of a size to stop us, but the wind was not in our favour and we hit into it too gently, though we pushed it out of the way. The creatures from the ship boarded and I stayed at the helm to get us out of there. The last of my men risked their lives so that I may live, and I stayed at the helm, turning the boat into the wind whilst they sacrificed themselves, and there was nothing I could do. I wished I had gone down with them – it was either stay at the helm or we all died. I just thought some of them would have made it.

One beast was left when we got away. The wind in the sails pushed us on, and two more dark ships appeared, but they could not gain, and, tacking, I had the advantage, so I drew my cutlass, and with one hefty swipe, I killed the foul creature.

After that, I sailed for six long weeks in no particular direction. I buried my men at sea as they deserved, and cast the creatures off my ship, the most regrettable thing I have ever done. But then I came into sight of familiar land. I pulled up into the Port of Beror and I rushed to this tavern, found my old sea friends and I begged and pleaded for them to help me. But they refused, and said that I had gone mad with the wet, the rain and the waves. And that my men died during the storm and everything I had experienced was nothing more than a mere dream.

Soon, my friends became enemies and all I held so dear and trusted became no more, so I gave my wealth to the barman of this tavern and drank myself into a stupor every day, desperately trying to work out if it were a dream or if it had really happened.

Havovatch looked at him for a long moment as Mercury returned his gaze to the candle.

"I can tell you it did," his voice breaking with emotion. He was overcome by this story – the story of a good man being treated so poorly. "The creatures you fought are called Golesh, they are from an empire known as the Black, and they are trying to invade Ezazeruth as we speak. I am going to stop them, but my men need a ship to get us there. Can you do this?"

Mercury, incredulous at hearing the words of this stranger, incredulous that he was finally believed, incredulous that his years of wondering were finally over, looked long and hard at Havovatch, before nodding firmly. "Aye, oh aye, on one condition."

"What?"

"When we get there, let me fight alongside you. Those filthy rekons took my men and my life from me; it's about time I repaid them the favour."

Smiling, they took each other in a sailors' grip, clutching each other's forearms tightly, and they got up to leave. But as Havovatch turned, he almost stepped into the finely dressed captain, who had been sitting at the other end of the bar, now standing in front of him with his ruffians behind him. Havovatch was so engrossed in the story he had not even heard them approach.

"Can I help you?" Havovatch said, unamused.

"Who're you?" the captain spat.

"I don't think that is any of your business."

"I ask again, who are you?"

"I could repeat myself, as well you know!" Havovatch said harshly, showing that he was not intimidated by the man. "But playing games like this, I feel, is best left to children."

"You speak very confidently, man of the north? Listen here – I am the richest and most powerful tradesman in these waters, and I like to know *everything* that is going on, especially if there is profit in it, so, sit, tell me of this conquest."

"My matters are no concern of yours, so get out of my way, before I remove you."

The captain's face turned scarlet. "I am a captain of a fleet of ships, peasant!"

Havovatch tensed up; he clenched his fist, grabbed the side of his robe and removed it in one sweep, revealing his uniform. "And I am a general of the elite army of shadow warriors!"

The men drew back on seeing that he had solid armour on, and a decent-looking sword. He looked so intimidating that they pulled knives from their belts as they retreated.

"Listen, *General*," the captain said, as if it were a dirty word, "you may have a small army of shadow warriors, but at the moment you are just one to my twelve."

"BUSKULL!"

The doors suddenly flung open as if the God of the Mighty Winds had told them to, and standing there, silhouetted by the darkness from the room, and – just by chance – with a thunderclap behind him, Buskull strolled in slowly, holding his axe. The lightning showed his face for a moment, staring on sternly. The other patrons in the bar quickly made for the door and left behind him, leaving the twelve shipmen, a few holding curved daggers. Buskull walked over to them, purposefully stomping on the ground as he did so, his footsteps echoing in the room and the floorboards creaking.

"Is there a problem?" he boomed over the men, who clearly had never seen a man so large on their travels.

"I don't know – is there?" Havovatch directed at the captain.

The captain was quivering, but keen not to step back from this, he pointed at Buskull. "He is but a giant – we still outmatch him."

Buskull's knuckles cracked.

"Yeah? Why don't you test that theory?" said Havovatch.

The captain looked back up at Buskull, but said nothing.

Havovatch pushed past him, with a firm grasp on Mercury's arm, and they made their way to the door. Hooding himself up again, he pulled Mercury out into the sunlight.

Buskull waited until they had left, and, lowering his axe, he growled with one last look of malice at the group, to make sure they did not follow.

"We will meet again, giant!" spat the captain.

And upon hearing the word, Buskull stopped, then turned and walked back in.

The unit heard the sound of chairs and tables being thrown about, along with the noise of someone punching a body and the wind being knocked out of them; the noise continued for some time.

"So, how did it go in there?" asked Feera casually, eyeing up their new companion as the brawl continued behind them.

"Very well, thanks. This is Mercury."

Mercury held his hands up to shield his eyes – it appeared he had not seen the sunlight in so long that his eyes couldn't adjust.

Just then, one of the sailors came flying backwards out of the bar doors and landed on the other side of the street. Back inside, there were more chaotic sounds of fighting.

"Soooo … is he going to help us or something?" said Hilclop, as he pulled at Mercury's jacket with a sneer, as if he were some sort of filthy tramp (which wasn't exactly incorrect).

"Our new friend here has had a rare coincidence. He has possibly been to the Black Lands before."

Mercury started to whimper, as if the mention of it brought back some bad memories.

"I'll fill you in later," whispered Havovatch to the others.

Just then, a chair came flying out of the door, just missing the unit. They didn't flinch, but carried on their nonchalant discussion of what had happened inside.

Soon, the bar fell quiet, and with almost a spring in his step, Buskull emerged. He had barely a mark on him – he was as clean and as dignified as he had been when he'd entered.

Chapter Twenty-Four
The Wreck

Havovatch guided Mercury by his arm as they paced through the streets. He was now their most valuable asset, and he was keen to protect him. To make a point, Havovatch had donned his Hawk helmet to create some intimidation in the crowd, and it worked, with everyone around them keeping away, giving long, interested, but fearful looks.

Mercury was shuffling along with short footsteps, his head bowed and hands together. He had a smile behind his huge, unkempt beard, like an expectant child on their way to their favourite play park.

"How much further?" whispered Havovatch.

"Not far," croaked Mercury.

Havovatch huffed. He didn't like the streets they were walking through – everyone was watching them, and gangs of kids were running around, and upon seeing them, they beamed with interest and kept murmuring behind their hands to each other. The streets were very narrow and dark, with the second-storey buildings closer together, letting very little light through. There weren't any shops any more, but there were what appeared to be houses. The worn, cobbled streets were covered in straw and dirt, brown stains smudging the ground. Some were so thick that Havovatch could feel the hump through the soles of his boots.

Steadily, he wrapped his hand around his Kopis in case he needed to draw it. But he stopped upon hearing Buskull. "General!" Turning, he saw a group of shady-looking figures surreptitiously milling about in the shadows behind them. They were trying to keep pace with them, their heads momentarily looking up, then back down again, trying their best but failing to act nonchalantly. They were big, strong men as well, broad-shouldered and long-armed; they were clearly a threat.

"Do you know who they are?" he asked Buskull.

Sensing the threat, Feera and Hilclop donned their helmets and gripped their swords in their scabbards, ready to use them.

"Yes," he said with a sigh. "Cutmen."

"What will they want with us?"

"Anything. I suggest we just keep moving."

"Agreed."

They upped their pace as they made their way to wherever Mercury was taking them, but as Havovatch turned, he saw the captain from the tavern quickly hide behind a wall, a very large bruise starting to appear over his left eye.

"How much further?" he pressed Mercury.

"Almost there," he said cheerfully, completely unaware of the situation around them.

"I hope so," Havovatch said under his breath.

As he glanced around, he saw more appearing, as if a silent call had gone out. There were sixteen now: three behind, four to their right, seven to their left and two ahead, with possibly more on the way.

"Buskull," Havovatch called over his shoulder. Buskull approached and walked by his side.

"Yes, General?"

"I don't like this. They're clearly stalking us."

"I agree. We should not let them know where we're going."

Havovatch looked around at the tightly packed streets, then back at the horses, and a smile appeared on his face. "On my mark," he whispered, "mount up."

Buskull looked back at Feera and gave hand signals for *mount on mark*.

Feera responded with a flat hand to his shoulder, as did Hilclop, who had learnt more than he had let on.

Havovatch pulled Mercury back towards Buskull, who swapped his axe into his other hand. But the cutmen knew something was amiss and started to approach. With a shout, Havovatch sprang up into his saddle as if it were a natural ability he had, and the others followed suit. He held the reins tightly and dug his heels into his mount's side, and the horse sprang forward. Two cutmen dashed towards Havovatch and tried to grab him, but, with a swift kick of his heel, he broke one's nose and punched down hard on the other. Buskull lurched up onto his horse, pulling Mercury up with him and holding him in front; they looked like a father and child on the mount, albeit a child with a rather big beard.

The attack happened so quickly, the cutmen around them had little time to act, running forward and trying desperately to draw their cutlasses as they slashed away at the unit. Everyone in the street pushed themselves back against the walls, ran into houses or hid in the alcoves of buildings, as if a stampede of bulls were charging their way. Strangely, despite his frail state and the violent jolting of the horse, Mercury had a huge grin plastered across his face as Buskull held one arm across him.

Havovatch had one plan as they galloped – putting distance and confusion between him and the cutmen as quickly as possible, and turning down every alley that was wide enough to fit them, they galloped hard, zigzagging until they got away.

Eventually, they came to a quiet part of the docks, an area where there was nothing but abandoned warehouses and broken piers jutting out into the calm, turquoise water. The area was deserted, apart from the occasional rat scuttering along the ground.

"We're here," Mercury said joyfully and slid down from the horse.

"Are we?" said Havovatch, looking around and stepping down. "And where exactly is here?"

"Come on, quick!" Mercury said, shuffling down the abandoned road, zigzagging around debris of collapsed houses and timber on the quay.

"Were we followed?" he asked Feera, as they made their way behind Mercury.

"No – we left them way back. We gave a few a beating, though – they tried to keep up, but the crowd joined back up behind us, wondering who we were, stopping them from seeing us."

"Good ... I guess we go this way," Havovatch said, leading his horse after Mercury.

Mercury was like a little child in a toy shop. Almost skipping (as much as his weak body would allow him), he followed the path as if the way had been unchanged since he was last there, leading towards a corner of the quay, with a very long, thin pier leading out to a solitary warehouse on stilts, sitting idle in the ocean. It was more than an arrow's shot away, and the pier was in ruin, with most planks missing; the ones that were there were corroded, mouldy or broken.

Mercury didn't slow down as he approached the pier. Havovatch's heart almost launched into his mouth as he leapt forward to grab him, as Mercury jumped forward onto the planks. But Mercury didn't fall – he jumped from one to the next, as if playing hopscotch, as if he knew the planks that would hold him. Havovatch wasn't sure, but he thought he could hear the old man singing as he danced along the pier, the words and chorus matching the steps he made, as if the song held the puzzle to the planks that were strong. The unit exchanged a quizzical look.

"He's nuts," said Hilclop.

"Nuts or not, he's helping to save the world."

Havovatch went to proceed forward, trying to figure out which plank was the safest. Gently, he put his foot on the first one; it looked sturdy enough. But as he placed his weight on it, it gave way underneath him. He turned and managed to grab hold of the quay, but Buskull was there and bent down with one arm to lift him back up. Havovatch dusted himself off. "This is ridiculous. We can't go that way – we'd be better off swimming."

"I wouldn't advise it, General – look at the water."

As they looked down into the turquoise ocean, they saw columns of old pieces of wood in varying heights in the water, as if this whole area was once just a big dock of piers, but was now little more than a graveyard of them. Some tipped just above the surface of the water, but most were below the surface, with rusty nails sticking out.

"It's too deep to wade through," Buskull said, "and it's too dangerous to swim."

"So, we get a few cuts. I bet the water's perfect," said Hilclop, edging forward and starting to remove the clasps on his armour.

Buskull shot out a hand to stop him.

"I wouldn't do that if I were you, laddie. *You* may only get a few cuts, but that will attract unwanted creatures within the shadows of the bed of the sea."

Hilclop looked down, trying to see the sea creatures. Although he could see the bottom, most of it was cast in shadow from the coral, and a shiver ran down his spine as he thought about what could be lurking there, looking up at him.

"Also, any cuts you get from down there will become infected. It's too risky."

They looked up at Mercury. He was almost at the end now, still dancing, his singing even louder as if he finally had found his voice. And, arriving on the platform of the pier next to the giant warehouse, he pulled something from around his neck, which appeared to be a key, because he shoved it into the door and disappeared inside.

"Well, this is dandy. Now what?" said an exasperated Hilclop with his hands on his hips.

Havovatch shot him an irritated look, but as he did so, he looked past Hilclop, and something behind him caught his attention. Walking forward, he pushed past and looked at a pile of beams, spreading ten feet long and about a foot wide. He lifted one up and, despite some slight damp, they were strong.

"Use these. Hilclop, you pass them to Feera; Feera, you pass them to Buskull; and Buskull, you pass them to me. We'll position them along the beams all the way across the pier."

"Can't our friend just come back and teach us the way across?" said Feera, scratching his head.

They all looked back at the warehouse, but there was no sign of him.

"Not right now. C'mon, let's get this done."

By mid-afternoon, the unit had stretched dozens of planks along the jetty. Due to the intense heat and the manual labour, the unit had stripped off their armour; sweat covered them all, with the fabric of their tunics dark and sticking to their bodies, steam evaporating off them. They had left their cuirasses, with the helmets set atop, by the side of the quay, as if two half-men stood looking out to sea; with Hilclop's helmet lying on its side and his shoulder pads slung over a pillar to the jetty. By now, instead of carrying one at a time, Feera and Hilclop found it better to load several planks onto either side of Buskull's shoulders, as he wrapped his giant arms around them and carried them out along the jetty.

Havovatch stood at the end of the line, shouting for Mercury. Despite some loud noises, which appeared to be hammering of some sort, there was no sign of him.

Buskull arrived and Havovatch pulled the first plank down, placing it in front of him. He tested it by placing most of his weight on his back foot and slowly applying pressure onto his front. Some of the short planks underneath fell into the water, but the long plank held firm on the sturdy ones, and they proceeded on. Havovatch would take the next plank from over Buskull's other shoulder, to make sure he was evenly loaded. He knew Buskull could probably cope – he just wanted to show some initiative.

Soon, Havovatch and Buskull had made it across, and stood in the shadow of the warehouse. Feera and Hilclop dragged their armour, with Feera carrying Havovatch's Hawk cuirass and Hilclop his Hawk helmet. They both stared at the Hawk equipment admiringly, for they had always wanted to touch it, to see it up close – they just wished they had their own.

Havovatch approached the door, but instead of opening it – which just seemed weird because he was outside someone else's door – he knocked three times.

The constant hammering stopped. "Who is it?" came a voice, as if they really did not know who was there. The voice echoed, as if there was a lot of room inside.

Havovatch grasped the knob and entered, the unit following. And there before them was a ship sitting out of the water, with about three feet of space between the ship and the sea below it. To their right were huge doors that would allow the ship in and out. Unfortunately, the vessel was clearly not seaworthy, with heavy damage to its hull, a missing mast and several heavy scratches all around.

"Friends!" shouted Mercury, who leant up at the helm, with most of his body hanging over the side as he banged wooden planks against damaged parts.

"Mercury! You said you had a seaworthy ship."

Mercury paused and looked out of the corner of his eye, as if trying to recall the memory. Then, after a moment, he shrugged and carried on banging away.

Looking left and right, they saw plenty of materials neatly stacked alongside the walls, with two giant workbenches meticulously displaying all the tools any engineer could ever want. There was just the one space, with a chalk outline of a hammer missing, which Mercury was using.

The unit looked at the task before them, their mouths open.

"Well, one thing's for sure, it will be big enough to hold everyone," said Hilclop.

"Not with holes in the prow, you twit!" shouted Havovatch.

After placing their equipment down on the workbenches, they all worked their way around the warehouse, looking at the ship. All the while, Mercury carried on repairing the damaged parts, unaware of what the others were doing. They eventually met on the other side.

"General, this is bad, but we do appear to have what we need to repair it," said Buskull as he looked over the workbench for the tools he wanted. He delighted himself in picking up a hammer that was so big, it looked proportionally correct for him in his grasp.

"What could have done this?" said Hilclop.

"By the looks of things," said Buskull with a nail gritted between his teeth, and looking at the damage and heavy scratches, "he crashed head-on at speed."

"Must have been when he got back." Havovatch said to himself.

"Eh?" said Hilclop.

"Nothing. Buskull, have you ever repaired a ship before?"

"A ship? No! But I have helped make several houses and repaired the gates of Ardura."

"Ardura?" asked Hilclop.

"Yes," he said, grabbing a long, heavy plank and holding it up against the side of the hull as if measuring it. "When I was on attachment with the Knight Hawks several years ago," – he began banging a very long nail into the wood; two bangs and it was embedded in tightly – "our job was to secure the gatehouse so that the cavalry could storm the keep. The only problem was, at the first sight of them," *bang! bang!* "the bell would ring and the garrison would flood the walls."

He stood back to make sure his work was the best it could be; it was. So he proceeded to get another long plank, and held it above the one he had just nailed on. "So, to stay out of sight, they were several leagues away. We decided," – *bang! bang!* – "under the cover of darkness of course, to destroy the gates," – *bang! bang!* – "with explosives, then raided the gatehouse and signalled the cavalry to charge." *Bang! bang!* "The next day, we had liberated the townsfolk from the tyrant keeping them hostage, and repaired the gates. Took me and all the engineers they had a solid week, but the gates were stronger than before." He actually smiled. The others looked at each other confused, they had never seen Buskull so … joyous before. As he was usually so serious and collected, it was a strange sight.

As Buskull and Mercury happily worked away at repairing the damage, the rest of the unit closed in together.

"OK – Buskull's gone doolally, and we have a mad captain repairing a ship that may or may not be fit tomorrow morning," said Havovatch, shaking his head, drawing the skin around his mouth with his finger and thumb as he thought.

"What shall we do?" asked Feera.

"Firstly, those cutmen are probably looking for us. We need to take the horses and find some stables; you two go and do that first. When you get back, we will move the planks off the jetty so that no one else can get across."

"What?" shouted Hilclop. "All of them?"

Havovatch thought – it did take them a while to get them all laid out. "OK, fine – we'll move the first dozen or so, enough that no one would notice them."

"What will we use for payment, though?" put in Feera.

"Try to see if we can pay tomorrow – we will deal with it then."

They nodded. Feera strapped his sword around his waist, but left his armour on the workbench, and went back outside.

When they had left, Havovatch looked back at the ship. Surprisingly, Mercury had actually done a lot, although the damage he was mending was not as important as the damage Buskull was mending; but they both worked with huge enthusiasm.

It was at that moment that he noticed the main mast – it was a black trunk, whilst the rest of the boat was in different shades and textures of brown. He could also see that the mast was not the same texture as wood – it was smooth but felt heavy and strong.

Trying to be helpful, Havovatch lifted a huge piece of timber from a pile and dragged it across the floor towards Buskull, gritting his teeth and shuffling his feet as he did so. Almost as if surprised, Buskull looked down at him with a nail held between his teeth. He picked the beam up with ease, placed one hand on it, pressing it against the side of the ship, and banged several more nails into it. By the time he had finished, Havovatch had arrived back with another, with even more sweat covering him than when they had been outside, and although exhaustion was setting in, he nevertheless pressed on.

A few more hours passed, and the warehouse started to become dark as day faded outside. The whole starboard side of the ship was now repaired, with Havovatch collapsed on a stack of wheat bags, trying to get his breath back. Buskull, though, was still working tirelessly on the port side, with Mercury banging away on the deck.

The door suddenly swung open, and in walked Feera and Hilclop.

"Not bad. Thought you would have got more done, though," jibed Hilclop, as if he had been planning on saying it, no matter what.

Havovatch made a gesture that came across as strange to Hilclop, coming from a general. However, Havovatch was still young.

Havovatch sat up and wiped the sweat from his forehead with his arm. Feera sat next to him.

"The horses OK?"

"Yeah – found a sweet old lady who said she would look after 'em."

"Good. How much?"

Feera grinned. "She said if she gets a hug and a kiss from Hilclop, she will do it for free."

They both looked up at Hilclop, who looked less than amused.

"Well, looks like you're gonna take one for the team, then eh?"

"No!" shouted Hilclop, before storming off in a huff.

"Something I said?"

"More or less – she was hideous."

"Well, one way or another, he's doing it!"

They got up and, standing either side of a plank, they lifted it together and took it over to Buskull. It was much easier work with two of them doing it, and they got a good routine going. As they held it up, Buskull banged the nails in. Then they got another beam and did it again. Soon, the holes were repaired and Buskull stood back admiring his handiwork, as Feera and Havovatch were bent over, huffing.

"Where's Hilclop?" said Feera.

"I don't know."

Staggering towards a ramp, as if they were disoriented or drunk, they made their way up onto the deck of the ship.

"I haven't felt like this since training," puffed Havovatch.

Mercury was humming away as he re-attached the rudder chain to the ship's wheel.

"Shall we take a look around?" asked Feera.

But both Havovatch and Buskull hesitated – they had spotted something that brought the turbulent history of this ship into sharp focus. What they observed were large black patches all around them, long since dried but still staining the deck of the ship. Buskull's serious expression had returned as they remembered why they were there. Walking around the deck, they found more stains on it, and on the sides. Two of the three masts had splashes; when they went down below, they even found some down there. It was as if they told a story; they could map out where the creatures had fallen, and it sent a chill down their spines. Having to captain and crew the ship back on his own, Mercury clearly hadn't been able to clean up after them all.

Below deck was fairly neat, with hammocks lying open, ready for someone to climb in. Nets were all piled up neatly. Havovatch started to get a feel for what Mercury had been before he had turned into the man he was now. He clearly appeared to be someone who had cared about his work as well as his crew; the hammocks his men lay in were not cheap, but well made. He began to realise the burden he must have been carrying, and to understand his desire to make things right.

He also noticed that it would be cramped for four hundred Knight Hawks, but they would just about fit.

Going back on deck, they all looked at Mercury. No one had said a word, but they had a different respect for him, and, standing in a line, they looked down at him as he tinkered with his ship. For the first time since setting foot in there, he stopped what he was doing and looked up at the unit. And he sensed the respect they were feeling. No one said a word, and, bowing his head, he started to whimper – not because he felt sad, but because he finally had with him the people who understood his story.

***

The waves lapped gently against the big, round stilts holding up the warehouse. There was the sudden noise of a fish popping its mouth out of the water to consume the crumb of bread that Havovatch had thrown down. The noise of seagulls squawking into the night had dulled, with the main noise just being that of the waves hitting the stilts. He could hear Buskull approaching long before he saw him, as the floor creaked under his heavy gait. He sat down next to him. They faced out into the open sea; the three moons were reflecting off the water, with Segorn half hidden by the curvature of the earth. Segorn was pure white, whereas the other two appeared cream. They were so bright, though, that everything around them seemed illuminated, enough so that it was possible to find one's way around without needing a torch, bumping into something or tripping over.

"What's happening?" asked Havovatch as he kept throwing small pieces of bread into the water.

"Well," answered Buskull, "the warehouse is stocked enough for an army. There is food in there, tools, weapons. Clearly he had money and bought the best before ... well, before what happened."

"How could food keep that long?"

"It's mainly wheat – he has machines in his galley that will help crush it and turn it all into flour."

"Well, that will be good – we have a long journey ahead of us."

"There's something else, General!"

"Go on."

"I found a chest, deep in the bowels of the ship. It was full with coin."

Havovatch looked at him. "We're not robbing him, Buskull."

"No, that's not what I meant. We need more than just wheat. We can use it tomorrow to buy other supplies. We need every available asset on this mission, General, and well-fed Hawks will be a blessing. I've worked with them and they are fierce and mighty; fill their bellies and they'll be unstoppable. But this is war, and we need to make use of every available asset."

Havovatch puffed his cheeks as he breathed out hard. He was happy that Buskull shared his ideas, but someone in his own position should be saying these things; not soldiers under him. He feared that it made him look like a bad leader, or at least an uneducated one. He could now see why those in power needed experience and were not just thrown into that position. Buskull would be perfect, for he had much experience, but there was something about him that suggested that being an officer was just not right for him. It did make Havovatch realise one thing about officers, though, after spending years climbing the ranks, getting bogged down with politics and seeing war from above rather than getting involved – he could see why most of them separated themselves from the fighting.

"Yes, Buskull. That sounds like a good idea. Tomorrow at first light, I will ride out to meet the Hawks and General Drorkon. You get whatever you need ... but let's ask Mercury if he's happy with us taking his money first."

"One thing I have come to realise, General: in war, money doesn't matter. And Mercury clearly hasn't got any ties with it."

"Nevertheless, I would still rather ask him."

"Very good. We'd better go and get Wrisscrass soon."

"Well, bugger me!" came a voice below which made them both jump. "Nice of you ta say so!"

Wrisscrass pulled himself up onto the deck, water draining from his clothes. He huffed and sat leaning against the wall.

"What the ...? I told you to stay put!" said Havovatch, getting to his feet.

Wrisscrass waved a dismissive hand at him. "Yeah, yeah. Those Aveti? Averkay ... whatever they were. They came too close for comfort. Had to kill one of them and donned his cloak. Managed to sniff out ya scent but I just had to swim 'ere!"

"Averchi," said Buskull once he had finished. He didn't say it as if he was trying to be annoying, more just trying to correct someone when they got something hopelessly wrong, like a teacher correcting a student.

"Wrisscrass, there is a man in here; he is terribly disturbed, I think your presence will unnerve him. Whatever you do, do not go inside!"

Wrisscrass started snoring loudly, feigning boredom, but he grunted when Havovatch gave him a swift kick to the side of his leg.

Havovatch turned to Buskull.

"Where are the others?"

"Hilclop's asleep, so's Feera."

"What's Mercury up to?"

There was suddenly a loud banging from within the warehouse, so loud that Hilclop and Feera were probably no longer asleep.

"Never mind."

Chapter Twenty-Five
To the Two-Twenty-Eighth

"Feera!" said Havovatch, approaching from out of the shadows, just illuminated by the dawn sun as it pierced the edges of the doorways and broken panels in the roof. He was fully dressed in his Hawk's attire and held his helmet in his hand. Feera was lying on the wheat bags, his arm slung over his face, his tunic still wet from sweat after he had slaved through the night. Squinting hard, he rose from his slumber.

"Yes, General."

"I'm heading off to meet the Knight Hawks."

"OK. Need me to come with you?"

"No – stay here and look after Mercury. Buskull has gone off to get some supplies."

"Understood," he said, rising to his feet and connecting his belt of swords around him. "Where *is* Mercury?"

There came a sudden clatter of banging, this time from within the ship.

"Never mind. Is there anything else you need, Sir?"

"Yes – where's Hilclop?"

The sky always seemed a brighter shade of blue early in the morning than at any other part of the day, with long lines of clouds forming patterns of their own desires, stretching across the heavens. The land below was brightly illuminated with greens and yellows from the cornfields and meadows, stretching over the rolling hills of Loria. And there, walking through it and looking very much out of place was a line of black, as the Knight Hawks made their way towards the Port of Beror surrounded by three thousand, man and horse.

Havovatch sat on his steed as he looked down at them, a grin appearing behind his helmet.

"And that is my regiment," Havovatch said to himself.

Havovatch dismounted and walked amongst them, keen to get to know the men and women he would be fighting alongside. They all seemed to vary in size and shape, with some slim and short, others massive, not as big as Buskull but still big by human standards. They were very talkative with him – no one moaned or showed distaste towards his leadership. They were told by Thiamos that he wouldn't have given them up lightly, and that his successor must be respected; it was clear that they were willing to give Havovatch a chance.

Drakator marched at the front. He gave Havovatch a friendly pat on the shoulder with his large, muscular arm as he passed – Havovatch thought only Buskull had anything bigger!

To match the others, Drakator had donned a Hawk helmet. Just like Havovatch's, it had the three fins of rusty feathers on the back. He wore no clothing other than a black rag around his waist with a very large belt, and a crisscross of belts over his torso, with several swords and knives of varying lengths attached to his belts. With his raw, powerful physique and broad shoulders, he was a formidable force. Havovatch relaxed somewhat knowing that Drakator was there, for it made him feel that he was not doing this alone, and he would be fighting alongside the man he'd grown up wishing to be.

Soon, Havovatch came across General Drorkon riding on his tall, grey steed at the centre of the group.

"How are we, General?" asked Drorkon.

"Very well, thank you, Sir. We have secured a ship and a captain, as well as supplies." He swallowed, hoping he would not need to go into detail. "We sail as soon as we get there."

"Good! Very good. Things are going our way, it would seem. Let's just hope our luck holds out."

"I couldn't agree more, Sir!"

Havovatch walked alongside him in silence, wondering what to discuss. He was glad that Drorkon's usual persona had returned to him: cool, calm and collected, with a contented grin on his face. It seemed to remove another weight from Havovatch's shoulders, although he was not sure why. *Maybe Drorkon's pain is my pain?* he thought.

Glancing casually around, he assessed what he had. With his Hawks around him, he had never seen so many different weapons in one place. But something caught his eye as he looked at Drakator walking ahead, and he realised something – the sword strapped across his back had a purple tinge to the steel, and suddenly he thought of the three coloured swords held by the Knights of Ezazeruth Commanders. As he looked up at Drorkon he also noticed that he too had the same sword strapped across his hip. Both were long, single-edged blades, much smaller than the broadswords of the commanders.

"Sir," said Havovatch, "on my travels, I came across four stained-glass windows," – Drorkon's face changed upon hearing the words – "and in each of the first three was the commander from the Knights of Ezazeruth, but there was a fourth window, and I think I know who was in it."

Drorkon let out a long sigh, as if a truth he'd rather have kept hidden had just been revealed. "Yes – I'd imagine there were two men?"

"Yes – two men, exactly. Who are they?"

"I have not seen those windows in a very, very long time. I didn't even know they still existed."

Havovatch looked up, keen to find out who the mysterious pair were. "The reason I bring it up, Sir, is that one of them held a sword, a sword I can remember seeing but not where from. Then I looked upon your hip, and saw the one strapped across Drakator's back," he said, looking towards him.

"Very astute."

"So, you and Drakator are the two men in the window?"

"No. Drakator is the one staring out; the other man his is brother."

"Drakator has a brother?" said Havovatch, aghast, a little louder than he had intended, as helmets faced his way and discussions momentarily stopped.

"Yes!" sighed Drorkon, as he stared sternly at them, suggesting they return to their business. "Havovatch, you have to understand something: Drakator is not human, only his body."

"What do you mean?"

"Long, long ago, Agorath took two young boys from this world, and he turned them into monsters, puppets to carry out his business."

"But how can that be? Drakator looks to be in his thirties!"

"Agorath stopped them both from ageing when they got to the prime of their lives – the strongest they could be."

"Why, though? Why two boys, when he could create any creature he wants?"

"I suppose Agorath is fascinated by humans."

"You say that as if you know him?"

"I know him better than anyone else. I have to know him, to outsmart him, to out-think him ..."

Havovatch kept looking at Drakator. He pitied him, for he seemed like just another tool in Drorkon's arsenal. "Surely it would have been more kind to have killed him?"

"And could you have done that to Hilclop?"

The reality of what he had felt when he had found Hilclop dawned on him. And suddenly he knew what Drorkon meant.

"I know it must sound sinister what I have done, Havovatch, but Drakator has proven his worth many times over."

"Fair point."

Havovatch looked down at the floor for a moment, trying to understand it. "So, Agorath taught him not to speak?"

"No, my dear boy ... I took that ability away from him."

Havovatch could tell by the general's solemn face that he did not want to delve into this part of his past, but he knew he would not get another chance, and so pushed on.

"What happened to him?"

Drorkon drew in a sharp breath. Havovatch wondered how much longer he was going to get, for Drorkon was returning to the impatient man he had met at the fall of Len Seror. "During the Battle for Salvation, we managed to capture two grown men fighting for Agorath. It wasn't easy! We seized them and found that they were not mere mortals. They were deformed men, not in their own minds, and we needed to know why. Drakator was the first one I approached, and I looked into his thoughts. I instantly disconnected upon seeing the atrocities he was forced to commit, for no human could go through what he had, and it had warped Drakator's mind beyond human comprehension. In fact, the only human attribute he showed was worry, when he looked to his brother lying next to him. So, I knew there was only one thing I could do. I had to cast a spell upon them which would separate them from Agorath's curse, and allow them to have their free will back, but I overlooked something ..."

"When Drakator came out of his trance, he instantly started screaming, and tried to kill himself. For he could not cope with the acts he had committed and just wanted to die. There were two things I could have done, and I had a split second to do one of them. I could have killed him, but instead I decided to save him. I pulled a scroll case from my bag and a purple jagged gem, stuck the gem into the end of the scroll case and stabbed Drakator in the heart. His eyes, mouth and ears glowed purple as light poured out from within, and a thunderbolt shot from the sky into the gem. Drakator was tensing up, and everyone let go of him as he lay there like a star, his brother shouting at him to fight it. But soon, Drakator relaxed, for he was not the man he had been any more. In the shock, soldiers around me lowered their guard and his brother managed to release himself and ran away; we never saw him again."

"What happened to Drakator?"

"I took his soul and replaced it with something else."

"What?"

"An Ikarion, a god-like species. It attached itself to Drakator, but Drakator's soul left and is now at peace. But the Ikarion still retains his memories – only the Ikarion can cope with them."

"So, Drakator's not human?"

"His body is: he can feel pain, hunger; can cry, bleed; his body operates like yours and mine, but his soul is something different."

"So, why can't he talk?"

"Because the Ikarion's voice is too pure for our understanding. He can only talk when he needs power, and connects with his kin to use it. We said that he was mute to cover this up."

"His kin?"

"Yes – you see, when the Ikarions were captured, Agorath did something … *in a minute!*"

"What?" Havovatch looked up confused.

Drorkon smiled, it was as if he was having another conversation with someone else.

"Is everything OK, General?"

"A friend of yours is communicating with me – she wants to talk to you."

"Undrea?"

"Yes – touch my hand."

Havovatch reached up and held Drorkon's hand – this looked beyond strange to the Knight Hawks, as if a father were walking his child. But as Havovatch connected, he felt that same overpowering sense of peace; his mind fizzled with a tingly sensation.

"*Can he hear me?*" the two generals heard in their minds.

"*He can.*"

"*How are you?*" said Undrea. She was sniffling, as if she had been crying.

"*I'm well, my Princess. I'm sorry that I lost your mother's handkerchief.*"

"*It matters not. Do not burden yourself with worry over these things. You have a mission ahead of you, and you must concentrate on that!*"

"*You know of my mission?*"

"*I informed her,*" cut in Drorkon's voice.

"*You make sure you return, General.*"

"*As long as there's breath in my lungs and a sword in my hand, I will come back.*"

"*Wait!*" said Drorkon.

In the distance, a horn blast rang out.

"*What's going on?*" said Undrea.

Havovatch looked behind him, and saw the cavalry all turning and galloping back up the hill the way they had come.

"*We need to end, Undrea!*" said Drorkon sternly.

"*Goodbye, Havovatch.*"

Hearing her sweet voice again, Havovatch went to say goodbye, but Drorkon let go of his hand and galloped away. The calm feeling Havovatch had felt was replaced by loss and regret. He stood there, watching him go, a slight tear running down his face, wishing he had said goodbye to her.

The scout unit of four rode north, making sure that nothing was approaching the regiment from behind. They were alone, with the other units going south to check the way ahead. Seeing the top of the hill they wanted to get to, they made haste. That was how scouts did it – ride as fast as you could to each peak, carry out a detailed search. See nothing? Carry on to the next and do it again. But it was not to be this time. Riding at the front with three others behind him, the lead scout saw the summit of the hill where he was going to conduct his next watch. But he barely saw the arrow coming his way, striking him in the eye. The horse screamed and reared, but was pulled to the ground by the rider's dead grasp upon its reins. The others reacted instantly and turned their steeds, frantically riding to get back to the column – not for the sake of their own lives, but for the sake of their comrades.

They galloped in a way they had all practised many times over – standing in their stirrups, bent forward, whispering words of encouragement to their mounts. It did not take long for them to come into view of the regiment. Marching on, the Hawks and rest of the Two-Twenty-Eighth were completely unaware of what was behind them. Another arrow came whistling past and struck another one of the scouts. With only two riders left, they each glanced back hurriedly and saw hooded men with bows riding towards them, well within firing range.

"Go, warn them!!" shouted one scout to the other, before pulling his sword free and charging gallantly at their attackers. The other scout kept his head low and dug his stirrups into his horse, feeling a strong surge of speed as he accelerated to the rear of the column. His comrade galloped and hollered as he approached the masked men with three coming into view. The first one was still pulling an arrow from his quiver as he approached, and barely secured it to the string before the scout's sword cut through the bow and deep into the rider's torso. But as he approached the second rider he was struck by two arrows – one to his shoulder, the other to his stomach. But his horse kept going, and he used one last bit of strength to bury his sword into the second rider before he fell, taking the man backwards to the ground with him. His horse turned and galloped back towards the column, joining the other two horses, whose riders had come unsaddled. For instinctively they knew they did not want to be used for the enemy, and would either be killed or go back to their masters.

"ATTACK!! ATTACK!!" the scout shouted, but the wind was against him and none of his words were heard by the marching regiment, not even the watchers who were supposed to be looking behind them every few paces.

Taking a nervous look behind him, he did not see his friend, but a black rider came galloping his way with a spear ready to throw.

Again he shouted, "ATTACK!! ATTACK!!"

At last, one of the watchers turned on hearing him shout, as he desperately waved his red ribbon in the air. He pulled a horn from his belt and blew hard, and all turned to look north.

The scout relaxed, knowing that they were aware; but not before a spear appeared through his chest. He looked down at it, he didn't feel the pain. Shock gripped him and the last conscious thought he had was the ground hurtling his way..

Three unsaddled horses came cantering past Plinth. He looked to the hills from where they had come from and five dark, masked riders wearing no armour, just black cloth around their bodies. They sat in a tight line, watching them quietly, as if they had been there the whole time.

"Captain Hereson! Take twenty men and take them out. Bring one ba—" He was cut short as the landscape before them moved, with more riders emerging.

"Prepare!! PREPARE!!" Plinth roared, to create a rearguard. He spun his horse around and galloped to find General Drorkon.

The three thousand riders spurred their horses, and created a line across the landscape to match their rivals.

"ARITHMOI POSITION!" Plinth shouted to the men, his words carried along the line by the other officers. This meant they would stand together in columns, leaving a space before the next row, making them look far bigger to their opponents. It also meant that if arrows rained down on them, they would not be bunched up to take the hits, but spread out. Plinth knew that tactics covered everything from the start until the end of a battle, and making yourself appear bigger to your enemy could create doubt for them. Doubt can lead to insecurity, insecurity can lead to fear, and fear can lead to retreat.

Plinth approached General Drorkon on the other side of the hill. Seeing the port in the background, his heart relaxed somewhat, knowing that they were closer to their destination.

"Report!"

"We're under attack, Sir. We're very outmatched. Regiment assembled on the other side of the hill, Arithmoi Position!"

"Very good, Plinth. I will be with you shortly. Take my command at the head of the column until I return – I shall not be long!"

"Sir!" Plinth didn't salute – they never did in these circumstances. He spurred his horse and rode back over the hill as his general approached Havovatch.

Looking over the hill, Plinth first assessed his men. They had carried out his instructions with immaculate precision. He thought how they would look to the other side, a disciplined and large force. Looking at the enveloping landscape of his attackers, he was surprised to see that they were not moving. They were looking disorganised, just standing there; groups of foot soldiers and many on horseback, at least six thousand in total. They were over half a mile away, and he could not make out who they were, but one thing was for sure – they vastly outnumbered the Two-Twenty-Eighth.

Standing at the head of the column, Plinth saw a rider stride out from the horde, holding a spear with a white rag blowing on the end. He did not approach – this was a job for his general – but would ride out if he had to, depending on how long it took Drorkon to arrive.

All Hawks stopped as they looked around at the sudden behaviour of the cavalry. After the horn blast, they all turned as one and rode hard towards the rear-guard.

Havovatch stood watching Drorkon who was speaking with Plinth at the top of a hill. It was clear something was going on, as the silhouettes of his riders could be seen frantically riding left and right, and banners were loosened and left waving in the wind.

General Drorkon rode towards Havovatch, who ran to him to shorten his journey.

"General! We're under attack. Get your men to the vessel, now! We will give you as long as we can!"

"Yes, Sir!" he shouted. But he did not turn to leave or direct his men – he stood staring up at his general. "I guess this is it, Sir?"

Despite the haste, General Drorkon looked down at Havovatch … his friend. Removed his gauntlet and held out his hand. "Good luck, Havovatch," he said softly.

Havovatch took his hand firmly, and they looked at each other with heartfelt determination. "Thank you, Sir, for everything."

Drorkon nodded. "Now go – you've got to get out of here!"

"Yes, Sir!"

Drorkon turned and rode off, not looking back.

Havovatch ran forward as he shouted at the Hawks to run to the port.

Drorkon came cantering down the hill. He had fixed his helmet on, which seemed strange to his men as he rarely wore it. He stopped next to Plinth. "By Gods, it's Colonel Sarka!"

"How can you tell?"

"I may be old, but my eyes are young."

"Why is he not charging? He had us on the back foot. Now we're prepared."

"Because, why else would he want to talk to us? He only does it because he wants us to know it is he who's here."

Plinth pursed his lips and let out a heavy sigh. "What are your orders, General?"

"We need to protect the Hawks at all costs – we cannot let them get past us."

"Defensive stance?"

"No. When I give the command we'll charge!"

"Very good, Sir."

General Drorkon rode out to meet the lone rider. With every gallop that took him closer, he felt more certain it was Colonel Sarka; he could see more of his features, and noticed that he was now decorated with the symbol of a general.

He said nothing as he approached and stopped a few yards in front of him.

Sarka stuck his spear into the ground and sat smugly on his white stallion. He sat there as if he expected General Drorkon to admit defeat, but he said nothing.

"Where are the Knight Hawks?" he said plainly.

General Drorkon did not reply.

Sarka shrugged. "Very well. Where is Havovatch?"

Again, General Drorkon said nothing.

Sarka sighed. "Drorkon —"

"Your plan has failed, Sarka."

Sarka grinned broadly and shook his head. He went to speak, but Drorkon cut him short.

"Imara Forest? We have infiltrated it, Imara is no longer in command, and the rest of the Camion army is on its way to the Defences."

The smile on Sarka's face slowly began to fade.

"As for Havovatch and the Knight Hawks, they're a long way away from here – you won't find them."

"I found you."

"You did, and it will be your end."

Sarka chuckled. "You are hopelessly outnumbered."

"Quality is not in the numbers you hold, but in the men you have."

"Very poetic. Move aside, or we'll force you."

Drorkon looked at the ground, as if the reality of what was happening was starting to hit him, and he remembered the image he had with the Phalism link. As he looked along the lines of soldiers on the hill, whilst Sarka watched on looking pleased with himself, Drorkon knew that his men – his loyal men – may die today, and he could think of nothing to stop it. *They shouldn't die like this*, he thought. He could turn away and run. Havovatch and the Hawks wouldn't be far – they would be sure to make it, and he could then join his friends and the rest of the Camion military at the Defences. But it was a big gamble.

"Yes, yes – fear!" said Sarka. "I feel your fear. You don't want your boys to die. You shouldn't have got so attached to them, Drorkon. Then you could use them for whatever means you want to."

Drorkon's eyes narrowed, and he drew in a sharp breath.

"When you look for me upon the battlefield, you'll find me fighting beside my men, as you look on from behind yours."

He then turned and cantered back to his regiment, leaving Sarka standing with his mouth open.

"Ready?" he asked Plinth and drew his sword.

"Yes, Sir."

"The men?"

"We will follow you till the death, Sir … and beyond!"

Drorkon looked at him and smiled.

"How did he know Havovatch is here, Sir? How did he know what he's doing?"

"We'll find out. But, for now, who shall we fight for this time? Your son?"

Plinth smiled. "I hope he will be alright."

"He'll be fine. I made sure of that – he's in Ambenol with his mother."

Plinth said nothing. He sank his chin into his chest as he thought of his last image of his son, his little fingers gripping his giant finger.

"Use it!" said Drorkon, feeling his sorrow.

Plinth raised his head and grunted, clearing his throat.

"For Havovatch, Sir?" Plinth offered, suggestively raising his sword.

"For Camia?"

Plinth looked at him. "Aye, For Camia," he said mournfully with a smile, knowing that would tie all within.

They looked behind him at the lines of cavalry. "Two-Twenty-Eighth, Soldiers of Camia ... my brothers ... my friends ... my family ..." Drorkon let the wind cover the space of his silence. "Kill these filthy rekons!"

There was an almighty cheer as spears and swords were thrust into the air.

Drorkon rode along the line, standing high on his stirrups, his sword raised high into the air.

"TO THE TWO-TWENTY-EIGHTH!!"

"TO THE TWO-TWENTY-EIGHTH!!!" the men cried back, louder.

They charged.

The heaviest and biggest riders were placed at the front, with the scouts at the rear. As one, they moved down the hill towards the valley, with Sarka's army looking on, startled.

Standing on a rock at the top of the other side of the valley, Sarka looked down upon the charging regiment. He turned and looked to Malffay next to him.

"This is a setback. It's the Knight Hawks we need to get to, and it's them we need to destroy. Make quick work of them!"

Malffay smiled and trotted down the slope.

"Send in your mercenaries," he said to Droll.

"Forward!" Droll shouted. And the Silent Walkers started running, pulling their sabres out as they did.

Malffay waited behind them at the head of the Two-Twenty-Sixth. "Let them waste their men and exhaust Drorkon's lot, then we'll charge 'em," he said, smiling at one of his young soldiers.

He looked on uncaringly as the cloth-clad mercenaries ran towards the tenacious charge of the Two-Twenty-Eighth.

Drorkon was ahead and saw what they were planning. As the Silent Walkers ran towards him, he knew they would be easy work, but would also slow his soldiers' advance. Then the light cavalry would charge into them, with their light armour and bursts of speed. There was nothing he could do.

Chapter Twenty-Six
Visions of the Past

Duruck picked up lots of tiny twigs as he walked. Thiamos felt too intimidated to ask why, for, although he was a commander too, to ask what he was doing would make him feel small. Maybe it was for building a fire? But he could not understand why, considering they were trying to be covert.

Soon his arms were full as he hugged the many twigs against his chest.

"We're very near," Thiamos whispered.

Duruck just nodded. The three moons shone down enough light for them to see their way through the trees. They could tell they were close by now, with the orange dots of torches from the city visible through the shrubbery before them.

Thiamos crouched down, and slowly pulled down a branch to see the city.

"We're here," he whispered.

Duruck looked around him. They were surrounded by bushes and trees, with a small space for them to sit down. Thiamos crouched down, leaning against a tree. Then, Duruck started placing the twigs in a semicircle on the ground, behind where they were sitting.

Rubbing his hands together to get the dirt off, he crouched next to Thiamos, who looked more than confused.

"Sorry, I have to ask, but is that some superstition of yours to ward off bad spirits?"

"Hardly. Those are very dry twigs. If anyone steps on them it will make a very loud noise and alert us that someone is approaching from behind."

Thiamos was stunned – it was such a simple and good idea, and he'd never heard of it before.

Duruck crouched on one knee and gently pulled down a branch from the bush. Before looking at the city, he looked left and right, then closed his eyes, listening. After a long moment, when Duruck felt comfortable that there were no surrounding threats, he studied the city of Cam.

"Impregnable, you say?" said Duruck.

"Yes. I know that place inside out – this won't be easy."

"It's very different to how I remember it."

"Really? How so?"

"Well, for starters, it was smaller two thousand years ago. The outer wall was up there," he said, pointing to the second level of the city.

"Really? Did you dwell here?"

"No, but I remember it well. I visited Cam many times. When the knights were established, it was under the agreement that we would stay within Camia. The Xiphos were stationed near the coast, but I visited Cam often." Thiamos noticed a slight twinkle in his eye; he wasn't just studying the city, he was remembering it.

"So, what do you think?"

"Have you ever done any practice assaults on the city?" said Duruck as he chewed his lip.

"Yes, often. A part of our Knight Hawks final test is to infiltrate the city and get to the second level unseen. If they're caught, they fail."

"Sounds harsh."

"We only want the best – that's why the regiment is so small. But it keeps the garrison on their toes and helps us to detect weaknesses."

"Yes, I can see it being effective. What ways have they done it?"

"Well, it's up to the leader of the unit infiltrating the city. One time, they threw up a rope with a lasso onto the battlements. It took a few attempts, but they were eventually successful. Another time, they made a small ladder and climbed up … unfortunately they were not so successful."

"Is that all you know?"

"We don't always know how they do it, so that the garrison are always on their toes – if they knew, they would look for it. They have to expect the unexpected."

"Hmmm," mused Duruck. He had not taken his eyes off the city, and was studying it in great detail.

"So – how're we going to do this, then?" said Thiamos, rubbing his hands together excitedly, as if Duruck was about to reveal an easy plot that would get them in with no problem.

Duruck let out a long sigh. "Well, for starters, the guards – whoever they are – are sloppy and undisciplined. That will give us an advantage. The tricky bit is getting onto the walls. All we need is one man to do that, then loop a rope around the battlements and send my lot up; we'll scale them quickly. As soon as we are on the walls, it will be simple.

We'll take each street bit by bit, taking down every man who stands in our way. A splinter group will attack the gatehouse and open it for us at the same time."

"How are we going to do that?"

"I need to take a closer look."

Thiamos shot him a look. "You mean you're going out there?"

"Yes," he said, pulling a hood over himself and looking up at the sky, just seeing a large cloud covering the moon directly above him. "Stay here. I'll make an owl call when I return."

Before Thiamos could say any more, Duruck pushed through the bush and walked out onto the plains and towards the city. With his thick, dark cloak, he was soon lost, and Thiamos sat looking at his city, keen to reclaim what he had let go.

Six figures could be heard approaching – Thiamos heard them before he saw them. Not marching – just walking as a disorganised rabble. He could see one dragging a spear along the ground, leaving a trail in the grass. He knew they would not be able to see him; he was tucked away in the shadows, hidden from anyone's view unless a light was shone at him. He kept his breathing calm, but his heart was racing more than he was comfortable with. But he held his breath as they passed by. They did not even look his way – why would they? They did not know he was there. But he knew he was there, and thought that, with his luck, they would see him.

Soon they were out of sight, but still audible as they chatted and walked along. Their tone was harsh, and their language showed they were Emiros. He would have spat on the floor in disgust if he could, but he kept quiet and waited for Duruck to return.

When the silence had returned, he made himself comfortable and enjoyed the peace and quiet. It wasn't until a few hours later that he sat there and thought how much he was actually enjoying himself. He had not been a field Hawk for a long time, some thirteen years. Since then, he had been more of a diplomat, tending to matters of the state in the Acropolis. But he sat down in the soft foliage of the ground, with his back against the tree, his legs crossed. Just looking through the gap in the bush giving him a good view of the city and the plains before it.

But then, he heard the sound of a dry twig breaking, followed by the growl of an animal. He had barely got his hand around his sword hilt when, bursting out from the bushes came several broad men covered in animal skins, a large dog leading them as it sniffed out Thiamos's scent.

***

The heat was stifling – it felt different from how Fandorazz knew it. The air was dry, and every time he took in a breath his mouth and lungs seemed to shrivel up as they begged for water. The heat went to the core of his body; with every beat of his heart he felt as though his blood was boiling. The white canyon walls didn't help – they seemed to magnify the heat at him, as if mirrors reflected the light everywhere.

As Fandorazz staggered, pulling his toes through the soft sand, leaving trails behind him, he vacantly tried to push on, with his arms held out for balance. But, after falling against a rock, he coughed and lay on the flat of his back, looking up at the blue sky, his vision tunnelling around his eyes as tiredness and dehydration started to consume him.

After a while, the sun moved, the giant rocks casting shadows over him. He cooled slightly and regained some of his functions. Squinting, he pulled himself upright. He sat, trying to calm his breathing as he watched the floor, but something wasn't right. As he looked down at the markings his fallen body had made, he noticed that something else was there. There were fresh tracks, boot prints, wide and long with a flat sole – someone or something had walked past him. In fact, they hadn't just walked past him, they had stopped to look at him, then carried on walking.

"Grogga," he managed to mouth out in a croaky moan. But nothing came back.

Pushing against the rock, he managed to heave himself to his feet. Almost as if he had a pocket of energy reserved somewhere within him, he lifted his heels and paced around the corner to follow the trail. As he rounded the corner, he looked on and saw that the prints kept going. He followed them, but was so exhausted he didn't notice the shadow above him, as two well-built men looked down at the stranger within their domain.

Fandorazz turned around another corner; again the trail continued and he kept going. More men appeared around him, but his eyes were squarely fixed on the trail.

BANG – came the loud clash of metal upon stone.

Startled, Fandorazz stopped and looked up, but there was nothing there. Sure that his mind was playing tricks on him – after all, it had been doing so for the last couple of years – he ignored the strange noise and carried on following the tracks.

BANG – came another noise, this time from his left. Looking up, he saw nothing.

"Is anyone there?" he yelled.

But there was no response, just an eerie silence upon the valley. Neither wind nor bird, no sounds of nature or life could be heard.

Cautiously, Fandorazz pushed on, as he started to realise that maybe, just maybe, he wasn't alone.

Veering around a corner of the valley, his gaze fixed squarely on the tracks, Fandorazz hurried his pace. But then the tracks just stopped. He looked all over the ground around him, wondering where they had gone. Falling to his knees, he reached out and moved the dirt, as if the tracks had been covered and he wanted to find them. But he realised that there was nothing he could do. The tracks had stopped in the middle of the sandy path.

Sighing heavily, he rolled his head back, closed his eyes and clenched his fists. "ARGH!" he yelled.

The sudden burst of frustration helped, and, eyes still closed, he took in another breath. But as he slowly opened them he saw a scene before him – a scene of destruction, as if the whole valley had imploded in on itself. At the end was a forest. His heart sank, for he knew that he had walked all this way and had not found Groga.

He slumped to the floor and fell back. As he closed his eyes, the heat took hold of him and he passed out. His mind unable to keep him awake any longer, he gave up.

BANG … BANG … BOOM. BANG … BANG … BOOM – came the sound of metal hitting stone, the deep bass of a drum echoing around him, and the sound of men chanting along with the beat.

"Stop!" Fandorazz found himself shouting, more out of habit, with his noble status and his expectation that his orders would be adhered to, than in recognition of his surroundings.

Trying to look around, he saw a blur of swaying shapes.

"Stop!" he shouted again. But the beat continued, like a ritualistic chant.

He did not know it at first, but his mind had drifted back six years into the past, his old arrogance and sense of nobility replacing his newfound love for life.

"I'll have you hung for this!" he bellowed, as he tried to regain full consciousness and clear his mind.

But as he became fully conscious, his former self left him again. As if a ghost had revisited his body, he returned to his usual cowering, nervous self.

In an instant, every recent memory came flooding back to him, and he was very aware of who he was and where he had been. But where he was now, he did not know.

He was standing on a flat piece of rock about twelve feet in diameter, with towers of uneven spirals of rock around him. On the top of each tower of rock was a large man, so large that they were almost as wide as they were tall. Their muscle definition showed how strong they were – as if they had been picking up rocks all day, every day. Sitting on each one's head was a huge helmet made from iron. He could not see their faces, for they were hidden behind the shadow within their helmet. In their grasp was what he could only describe as an axe, longer than the men were tall, with the head bigger than their torso, and with a spike at the top and a boss at the bottom. Yet every single axe appeared slightly different, as if the men had each made their own to reflect their personality. They stood wearing very little apart from a leather belt around their shoulders, holding up a white rag about their waist.

As his senses came to him, Fandorazz realised he could not feel his hands. He was clamped, spread-eagled, to the ground, with ropes strung across from his hands and feet to metal hooks that were embedded in the ground.

Fandorazz was terrified. He looked to the man closest to him, who stepped down onto the ground.

"Hello," he tried to say pleasantly.

The man was holding a large knife, dripping thickly with blood. His heart stopped in realisation that it could be Groga's.

"Please – I am here on a mission of peace," he pleaded.

But the words appeared to fall on deaf ears, as if he were speaking a language they did not understand. As if something was about to happen, the chanting increased and they started beating their wrapped fists against their heavy chests.

"I need your help," he begged. "There is a dark tide coming this way, and it will wipe out Ezazeruth."

Some of the men started laughing, but it did not appear to be at what he was saying, more because of his puny bone structure in comparison to theirs, and his feeble attempts at communicating with them in his whining tone.

Anger boiled up in Fandorazz. He was not going to be mocked, especially by these ruffians.

"That's enough!" he shouted, with a strong voice of authority.

Instantly, the chanting stopped, and again there was that deathly silence from all around him.

"I will not be treated in this way! You! Untie me!" he bellowed at the man with the knife.

The stranger sprang forward apace and cut through his bonds. Fandorazz pulled his arms and legs in, as a rush of feeling flowed through them. Longing for sleep, he got up, knowing that he had them in his grasp – he needed them. Keen not to rub the sores on his wrist in fear that it would show weakness, he placed his hands behind his back and walked around the small arena, assessing the men above him.

"I want to speak to your leader!" he said, with his chin in the air in a show of defiance. He tried to stand on tiptoes to make himself appear bigger.

The strangers, however, looked at each other, some uttering words in a tongue that seemed harsh but simple. The stranger with the knife approached Fandorazz, towering above him in his square and intimidating shape. But Fandorazz refused to yield and maintained his posture and stare.

"Car'ful, Gold Man," came the man's voice. It was so deep that Fandorazz wondered if they were human. He wondered why he had called him *Gold Man*, but then saw his bronze helmet being held by one of the men on the rock.

"My name is Fandorazz. I am here to speak with you, to ask for your help."

The man started laughing. Looking up at the others, he spoke to them, as if repeating what he had just said in his tongue. Suddenly there was raucous laughter as all joined in. Fandorazz's posture changed somewhat, as he realised that maybe he wasn't in as much control as he had first thought.

"Please, please hear me," he said, raising a hand out to reason with them. "I am no threat – you must understand that!"

Suddenly, there was a loud clang of metal as everyone in unison started their chant again, ignoring his pleas for reason.

Turning around, he saw that the large man had gone, and landing in the arena was a smaller man, still larger than himself but smaller than those around him. Behind him there was a clang, and looking down he saw that they had given him one of their weapons. He looked up at the challenger, who was crouching low. He was holding a weapon of similar design, just as heavy, yet held as if it weighed nothing at all.

It was in that moment that Fandorazz knew what was happening and he had to fight to be heard. Pulling himself up, he staggered as he tried to lift the weapon that he had with him, but it was far too heavy. He could only lift up the pole with the giant blade sitting in the dirt.

All around him, the giants lifted their weapons above their heads, showing how easy it should be. "HOO, HOO, HOO," they chanted.

Fandorazz felt it before he saw it – the whoosh of air passing him as his body fell backwards. He wasn't hit, and managed to pull himself away just in time. He looked up, and held his hand up to shield his eyes from the sun. Standing above him was his contender, swinging his weapon around behind him to pull it down and cut him in two. The weapon was so large, he saw the threat coming and managed to roll away as the metal blade cut deep into the ground, splitting the rock.

He didn't know where it came from, but a surge passed through him. He pushed himself up, launched himself at the man and tackled him to the ground. He didn't know how he managed it – he could feel how heavy and strong the man was. But, with his balance in the wrong place, Fandorazz was able to push him over.

Sitting on top of him, he pulled his arm back, clenched his fist and punched as hard as he could, hitting the man's helmet. He wished he had thought that through first, though. He fell back, looked at his broken hand and yelled in pain. Everyone burst out laughing, most hunched over, they found it so funny.

The challenger, feeling foolish – he wasn't sure whether they were laughing at him or at Fandorazz – stood up, leaving his weapon on the ground. He bent down, picked Fandorazz up and held him above his head facing upwards. Fandorazz yelled, but it was dulled down under the wails of their chants.

Holding him up and walking around the little arena, the man presented him to everyone.

"ARRGHH, ARRRGHH," he bellowed.

Then he threw Fandorazz to the other side of the arena, his back landing on a giant stone, his arm bent around behind him. Fandorazz could feel the pain, but it didn't bother him. Closing his eyes, he thought of his family, with his last conscious memories being the image of the man walking towards him and the deafening chant in the background.

***

Undrea gazed into the mirror for the twelfth time that night, fondling with Havovatch's Gracker tooth around her neck. She stood, pondering what to do. Growing up, Undrea had always been good, had done as instructed and had never misbehaved. But now, she was about to do something terribly shrewd indeed. With Havovatch's final words and Drorkon now not speaking, she felt alone; she felt as though she had to do something. She tried to stick to her promise to Drorkon, but looking at the same four walls in her tower was driving her mad. And, as night fell over the land, she saw the fires in the hamlets and the howls of creatures echoing into the night. She could hold it no longer. She had skills she felt were being wasted. And so she pondered over what she should do. But if she was going to do something, she must do it now. For the dawn sunrise would soon appear, with just a hint of orange already on the horizon, and she would have missed her chance.

Placing the last small sacks of powder – which she had Lord Malisten buy more of after Drorkon had taken her last stash – into a bag, she slung it over her shoulder and tied it tightly against her body.

She then placed a note on the table, begging for no one to come looking for her and explaining that she knew what she was doing.

As she paced over to her window, there was a sudden thunderclap, which made her jump. Floating in the air outside her window appeared a man shrouded in a purple haze. He stood with his arms folded into the long sleeves of his robes, and shook his head.

"I need to do this!" she protested.

The man looked at her for a long minute, then disappeared, leaving the image of his disapproving expression burning into her mind. But she still couldn't just sit there whilst the rest of the world fought. And, repeating that to herself several times, she faced south and gazed out at the summit of the tallest hill she could see in the distance. Maintaining her stare, she held her arms aloft and, out loud with a small knife in her grasp with a purple tinge to the blade and spoke. "*Gretara.*"

There was a sudden flash of light. She felt as though she were falling, but didn't panic; she forced herself to be calm and concentrate.

Instantly, the atmosphere had changed. It was warmer, with a low breeze. She crouched to one knee and surveyed the area. Just off in the distance, she could see the Acropolis silhouetted with the navy sky behind it, but she frowned when she noticed that the braziers lining the Acropolis had been extinguished – they were never put out, they burned constantly, but due to her situation, she didn't really think too much of it.

Checking the area around her, she smiled with the surreality of the situation, standing in the open with nothing but her wit and skills of magic to protect her. She knew the road to Cam would be long, but she had to do this.

Keeping low, she started running down the hill, crouching from bush to bush as she made her way south.

But behind her, emerging from the bushes, several creatures appeared and followed her, keeping very quiet.

Chapter Twenty-Seven
The Empire Returns

"So, what are you doing here?" Pausanias asked Ferith as they walked across the flat landscape, the clifftop of the Defences just coming into view before them. Soldiers marched around them in long, neat lines in their regiments, the rhythmic sound of thousands of feet drumming an echo across the terrain.

"I'm in trouble with some people."

"Oh? What for?"

Ferith sucked in a breath, but spoke with pride of a dirty secret. "I slept with another tribe chief's daughter, I betrayed his honour, so he sent men after me."

"There's more to that than you're letting on!"

"No, no – it's true," Ferith said, smirking.

"You're lying!"

Ferith stopped and looked at him. "I have no idea what you mean," he said incredulously.

Pausanias sucked in a long breath, and spoke very candidly, as if he were interrogating someone. "As part of my vast skillset, I know when people are lying. And in all the people I have questioned, I have always got them to talk, most without having to touch them. At the moment, everything about you says that you're lying! So, what're you doing here?"

Ferith went to carry on with his charade, but he knew it was pointless.

"Well, why does it matter to you?"

"Because you are following me, and you nearly put my mission in jeopardy. In these circumstances, I'm authorised to take you out. But, seeing as we have a war coming, you may be of some use."

"Because of my brilliant sword skills?" he asked expectantly with a curt grin.

"Hardly. It's easy to strike anyone when their back is to you. You held your arm too far away from yourself, making your blows cumbersome and slow; your feet were off balance – where did you even learn to fight ... a convent?"

Ferith groaned. "... Trees."

"Trees?"

"Yes. I hit many growing up."

Pausanias shook his head and laughed, and continued walking. "You hit trees and you think you're a warrior?"

Ferith, feeling rather foolish, just smirked and shook his head.

"What're you doing here?" Pausanias asked one final time. And his answer would decide Ferith's fate – he could see Pausanias gripping the hilt of his Seax, which the messenger had returned to him.

"My father got into debt," he said, quickly placing his hands out to stop him. "He sold me off to another tribe, who would use me as a slave. Whilst there, I slept with his daughter, and he went to execute me. So I escaped. But, for my dishonour, he has taken my entire family hostage."

"Why?"

"Because my honour is their honour."

"So, they're suffering as you venture the world?"

Ferith said nothing.

"Can't you go back and fight for your honour?"

"As you said, I am no warrior. But I like what you do. I love the sound of going on missions and fighting with a specialist unit. I want to join you, I can learn, I can become you," he pleaded hurriedly.

"What I do isn't for the faint-hearted, Ferith! If you want to join the military, visit Cam when this is all over and sign up – anyone can. You will do six months of hard training and become a competent solider. Then, maybe, you can become a Hawk two years into your service. But if I'm honest, it won't happen!"

Ferith sulked. Saying nothing, he walked with his hands in his pockets and dragged his toes.

"Not what you wanted to hear?"

"Not exactly."

"Get over it. Now, your family are in trouble. If I were you, I'd go back and save them!"

"You don't understand. This chief ... he's a very powerful man."

"What's his name?"

"Charak."

Pausanias grunted.

"You know him?"

"Of him."

"So, you know what I mean? He's powerful and vicious."

"No! The men who carry out his deeds are powerful and vicious – he's just an ordinary man."

"Well, if I were a Hawk like you, we could all go and save them!" he said, smiling.

Pausanias stopped and faced him directly. Poking hard into his chest with his forefinger, he pushed him back and spoke with a very deliberate tone, sending a shudder down Ferith's spine. "We Hawks do not carry out personal missions. We can be purchased for a time, but we mainly carry out the deeds of our King. Now, enough of this Hawk talk. It's boring me! And as I said, it won't happen. You have got in my way once now, and if you *ever* do anything like that again, I *will* kill you in a heartbeat. People rely on me to do my job, and I *have* killed people like you before. Do *not* test me!"

Ferith swallowed and nodded.

Pausanias stopped and looked around. Taking in a breath he tried to get things back on track.

"Now, a complete family is something I wish I had. You have a chance to get yours back, and therefore you can learn a thing or two from me. And maybe, just maybe, when this is all over, I'll help you get yours back. Until then, don't get in my way again!" Pausanias said sternly, and carried on towards the Defences, leaving Ferith to gaze on and consider his words.

"What did he say?" said Andreas, catching up.

"He's just a wannabe. He'll be with us for a few weeks, though – he may come in handy, as we're going to need every man for the fight to come."

"Fair enough. I might even get to kill something now!" said Andreas, puffing his cheeks out behind his helmet.

"It would be good – I'm fed up with doing all the work."

The two brothers finally came to the end of their long march and reached the top of the cliff overlooking the Defences. Looking down, they could see the whole area where they would be fighting. The land was like a crescent moon, with the wall in the centre. The ground leading to the tips of the cove turned to shards of rock, causing the ships to head to the wall. The water had lines of white foam as the waves met the shore, with long spiked logs sticking out everywhere. Floating in the water was flotsam and jetsam from the Black ships, which had attacked some weeks previously. The mast from the submerged galleon was just visible near the cove's entrance. Beyond, the shoreline was scattered with giant black rocks as far north and south as they could see, with an open ocean glittering in the sunlight. But the image of such beautiful scenery was suddenly shattered by the appearance of a thick black line upon the horizon.

"What!" said Pausanias, with disbelief. The Camion soldiers marching down the slope stopped in stunned silence at the sight before them.

"Al'right you cretins! You've gawped long enough, move along!" bellowed Captain Seer.

The soldiers carried on marching down the hill towards the defences, which bottlenecked from the rise of the cliff, then fanned out towards the wall. Filing into neat lines, their spears upright, they gazed upon their foe. The Black had an enormous fleet, so big it felt as if the Camions had already been defeated. But Pausanias snorted, and, strutting along the clifftop and frowning deeply, he readied himself for the ensuing battle as he summoned feelings of hatred to fuel his veins. He didn't know it but his shoulders were raised and his arms were bent like a body builder. Soldiers looking on admired this new incarnation as the confidence it portrayed buoyed their own.

"Have the men sit down and rest for a bit. The ships will still take a while to get to us – we need to use this time. There can be no mistakes!" Pausanias said to a signaller, who jumped up to the cliff's edge and started waving two white flags to his cohorts on the wall, who stood next to a group of lower-ranked officers. But Andreas noticed something coming from inland towards them. It appeared to be a line of horses. As he squinted, he realised who they were. "Oh great!" he sighed.

Pausanias followed his gaze and saw the unit of horses and riders approaching. They looked different to Camion soldiers, for their uniform was not the same as their standard issue. It flayed out like hooks at the shoulders, the helmet's cheek guards were longer, almost reaching down to the chest, and each guard had a vertical red crest on their helmet, tailing down behind them like that of a Camion general. But they were not riding under a Camion banner, but a red banner with a crest of a roaring bear. And, at the head of the unit, was a finely dressed general.

"So, he's come out of retirement?" said Andreas.

"Well, what did you expect? Every skilled general we had betrayed our country. Thiamos had no choice but to ask for his help."

"But he's an arse! Why couldn't he come himself?" Andreas moaned.

Pausanias looked to his brother and stepped close. "Arse or not, he's in charge of this battle today. And he couldn't, he needs to get our city back. So, let's get one with it."

He turned and beamed a smile behind his face guard at the general. "It's good to see you, Sir."

The small unit slowed to a trot. General Tigrami held the reins with one hand, his posture very square, and looked over the Defences for a long moment as he assessed the terrain.

"Hawk, I will take command from here. Please take your station upon the wall and wait for your orders."

"We haven't long arrived, Sir. The men are tired, so I ordered them to sit and regain their breath," Pausanias told him.

Tigrami removed his helmet and looked at him long and hard; with his gaunt cheeks, sunken eyes and dark lips, he looked ill. "But you hold no authority upon these men. You are but a flag-bearer, a symbol of inspiration. Now go to the wall and be that inspiration," he said quietly, as if he had never shouted in his life. The tone of his voice was all the authority he needed.

"Yes, Sir!" With just a nod, Pausanias began to make his way down the slope, with Andreas following.

"No!" said Tigrami, poking his hand into Andreas's chest. "You have a bow, do you not?"

"Yes, Sir."

"Then you stay put!"

Pausanias stood for a moment looking at his brother, who looked back, wanting some encouragement. After a moment, Pausanias walked forward and pulled Andreas close, hugging him tightly.

"Let's make father proud today. I'll see you afterwards," he whispered into his ear, then handed him his Malorga, "and take care of this for me." Silently, he followed the regiments filing down the hill as Andreas watched him, not taking his eyes off him until he disappeared amongst the ranks positioned on the wall.

On the side of the cliff was a small hut, which leant precariously over the cliff face, just held up by stilts embedded into the rock.

Stepping inside and removing his gauntlets, Tigrami assessed what he had before him. Positioned at the centre of the cliff, he could see the entire cove through the large, open window. In front of the window was a fixed map of the wall, with the rocky land shaped like a crescent moon. As officers arrived, they placed statues of their respective regiments on the map where they were currently positioned. As Tigrami moved the figures into groups, the officers watched over his shoulder so they knew exactly where they needed to be. Lining up some archers along the cliff either side of the shelter, he also placed some in the towers behind the wall. After placing the red statues for the engineers by the catapults, he then put the blue and black statues of the infantry and cavalry regiments on the wall, with the infantry taking up the vanguard and the cavalry either behind them or reinforcing the right and left flanks. When he had finished, he stepped back and placed his hands together, a sign that he had finished his mobilisation so the officers could see where they needed to position themselves.

"Have all horses tethered behind the cliff. There will be no need for them here."

"But, Sir!" protested a young officer. "If we lose the ground, they could swoop down and clear the wall."

The young officer hadn't known it, but he got a bit closer than he'd intended. Stretching across the map, he replaced the black statues at the top of the bottleneck. Tigrami stared at him long and hard, before sticking his face so close to his that the hairs on their noses were almost touching.

"If I want your uneducated and pathetic advice, I'll ask for it. Do not *ever* interrupt me again!" Again he spoke quietly, so quiet that the other officers in the room could barely hear. And the message hit the young man, with his eyes wide, stepping back so far he ended up outside.

"Sir?" said Captain Jadge as he entered with the Camion salute, and placed his statue down on the table.

Tigrami took it and placed it at the base of the bottleneck.

"Position your men there."

"Sir?"

"Those are your orders, Captain."

"But, Sir. We're the best infantry regiment in Camia – we're the only infantry regiment that is still whole. We should be at the vanguard."

Tigrami looked down through the window at them.

"Yes, and a third of your men have sticks and barrel lids for weapons? Stay as you are – those are your orders!"

"Sir, I really must protest —"

Tigrami turned to him with his hands behind his back. "The last I heard, the Three-Thirty-Third had been decimated, and yet here you are. I also heard that the captain of the Three-Thirty-Third was not an experienced officer but a young boy fresh out of the ranks, and yet, you're here! I can't help but think that there is something queer going on. Now, those are your orders, Captain!" Tigrami said sternly.

Jadge swallowed, not because he was intimidated but because he was holding himself back. "Yes, Sir!" He didn't salute; he turned and marched out of the hut as Tigrami glared on.

Sergeant Metiya was standing in front of the regiment, waiting for Jadge to return. When he did, Metiya could tell by his posture as he walked that Jadge was disgruntled.

"Captain, everything OK?"

"No!" he spat, and drew in the skin around his mouth.

Metiya said nothing. After a moment, Jadge took in a sharp breath. "Tell the men to stand guard!"

"Yes, Captain. STAND GUARD!" Metiya bellowed in his booming voice. Pretty much all the novices stood to attention immediately, but the experienced soldiers looked at each other, wondering why they were not a hundred paces further forward.

Jadge stood with his hands on his hips as he looked out. Being on a rise meant he could see over the garrison and just beyond the peaks of the cove; he saw black dots becoming bigger and bigger as the dark ships approached.

"Captain?" said Metiya in a quieter voice.

"We have been told to stand guard, Sergeant."

"Can I ask why?"

"Because the general doesn't trust us."

"Understood, Captain. But, if I may?"

"Yes, Sergeant?" he said, not taking his eyes off the sea.

"When in battle, things often don't go to plan."

Jadge looked at him incredulously. "What do you mean?"

"Just bear it in mind," he said with a nudge and a wink, as if in all his years of experience he had seen many things, and anything could go wrong.

The Black ships drew near, so close they were becoming identifiable. They were far larger than what had attacked the Defences some weeks previously – in fact, they were huge, some as wide and long as the Acropolis of Cam, with creatures hanging off their sides and nets, brandishing their weapons and howling at their gain.

"Stand fast, lads," said a sergeant standing on the battlements of the Defences as he watched them approach, hoping that seeing him calm would inspire them.

The Defences were otherwise quiet. Catapults were being prepped, with the cranking of the metal ringing out as the arms were pulled down and loaded with large rocks. The archers all had arrows notched to their bowstrings, holding them downwards until their targets came into range. Field medics and surgeons stood waiting patiently with small tools or dressings, waiting for the first casualties to be ejected from the back of the phalanx, and knowing that although it may have been quiet for the time being, they would be longing for silence very soon. Otherwise, the entire wall was covered in a blanket of silence as the ships approached them.

"AGY, FE'GA!" bellowed the sergeant; this was followed by a tremendous "HAR" from the regiments, breaking the eerie silence with raucous chanting as the Camions welcomed their foe.

The ships drew into the cove. With their mighty sails, they pushed through the waves and approached the wall fast, the tips of the logs just appearing over the waves of high tide. Again, the Black did not slow down, and ploughed through them, causing chunks of their hull to splinter.

"This is it," Pausanias said quietly to himself. Checking the engineers, who were lighting their shot, he waited for the Black ships to get into range. He didn't have to wait long.

"FIRE!" hollered the captain of the engineers in his drill instructor's voice.

The catapults clunked as the ropes were pulled and the boulders flew through the air, hurtling towards the ships. Some of the boulders were on fire, leaving long, black trails of smoke through the air.

The rocks crashed into the ship's hulls, so heavy that most penetrated the decks, with splashes of water coming up through the holes that they had made. Instantly, this started to create chaos for the Black, their ships started to list forward as water poured into the decks. But the ships that were behind, full of momentum, crashed through their own, and kept coming towards the walls.

"FIRE!" came the captain's voice again, and the air was again filled with flying boulders. The sound of wood breaking as the rocks hit into them was audible all around, and gave a relief to the watching Camions, who knew they were causing heavy damage before the battle had even reached them. But the Black's banner of thick, black smoke rose into the air as their ships started to burn, blocking the Camions' view of what was behind. Yard by yard, the ships gained distance to the wall, as others became consumed by the sea, with just their masts visible. Steam vapour, mixed with the smoke from the smouldering timbers, floated into the air. Any creatures that could reach jumped from their burning vessels and joined the others as they tried to get to the wall. The creatures on all ships stood impatiently on the decks, a strange, high-pitched shrieking noise ringing out from them as if they were all furious at the loss of their kin. But the boulders kept coming and made an unpleasant mess in the cove. Soon the ships came so close to the wall that the catapults could only continue their barrage behind them, as the Camions couldn't risk firing on their garrison.

"PHALANX!!" came Captain Seer's voice.

As one, the infantry regiments lowered their vertical spears from upright to forward. With their shields pulled tightly against their chests, all regiments grunted loudly with each manoeuvre as the disciplined regiments readied themselves.

"COLISTO!!" shouted another sergeant amongst the ranks, again followed by a tremendous "HAR!" from the men around him.

Pausanias walked along the parapet with sword in hand. As he did so, the soldiers on the wall lifted their spears up so that they weren't blocking him. But as he turned on the spot and walked back – seemingly unaware of what they were doing – they again lifted their spears up. He wasn't pacing to inspire the troops – he was trying to calm himself, as he couldn't see his brother. He kept looking up at the top of the cliff, trying to pick him out amongst the thousands of archers standing there. But he heard a rattling that distracted him, and, looking down, he saw a young soldier in the front row, visibly shaking, his spear rattling against his shield.

"You OK, fella?" he asked quizzically.

The young man didn't look up, but focused his gaze on the ships.

Pausanias jumped down and faced him.

"You need to calm down, fella. Imagine that you're fighting any other army – these things *can* be killed," he said, casting an arm back.

"I know," he said shakily. "I've fought them before."

"Then why are you so nervous?"

"Because of last time!"

"What do you mean …?"

In the shelter above, Tigrami was studying the map of the rest of the coastline. Behind him were a handful of officers, mainly those who had enough experience to be there or were too old to fight down below. They all held their tongues amid Tigrami's tense presence - keen not to be spoken to the same way the young officer had been who still stood outside. But the silence was cut short when a lieutenant shouted.

"General!"

As Tigrami looked up, everyone followed his gaze at the garrison marching back away from the wall, like an army of ants; the column moved as if the landscape were moving.

"Who ordered that?" he barked at the officers in the room, but no one answered. "Who ordered that?" he forced, but again, no one knew what to say. "I want answers, now!"

A lieutenant immediately ran out and down the path towards the wall; he was so nervous, he didn't think to jump on his mount, which was tethered just outside.

"You're a mere Hawk! You have no remit over the garrison!" bellowed Captain Seer at Pausanias, but he was ignored as if he were a beggar trying to sell him cheap tat. "Don't ignore me – I outrank you!" he continued. But Pausanias remained patient, and followed the front line as they walked backwards. The Camions showed great discipline as they all fixed their gaze upon him, walking in front of them as he counted twenty paces. When he got there, Pausanias held both his arms into the air and the marching ceased. Captain Seer then stood in front of Pausanias, who turned around to face the incoming army. Seer huffed at getting shown up in front of the thousands of eyes upon him. He stomped around and stood back in front of Pausanias, blocking his view.

"Order them back to the wall, now!" he shouted, getting close.

"I'm making up for past mistakes. Now, to your duties!" Pausanias said calmly behind the fabric of his helmet.

"My duty is here. Now, if you don't order them back, I will take you into custody."

"Last time we fought that army, they rammed the walls and crashed through our phalanx!" he said pointing at the approaching fleet.

"I know, I was there. But our orders are to stand still. If we lose some men then we lose some. That is how it is in battle. Now move them!"

Pausanias stood still. The officer gripped his arm, but instantly regretted it. Pausanias took hold of the officer, spinning him around to face the ships and bringing him down to one knee as he bent his arm behind his body, the officer whining in pain as Pausanias applied pressure.

"You see that? You see it?" he whispered into his ear as the ships came towards the wall.

"Yes," the officer grimaced.

"It's time we started fighting them, and not ourselves," Pausanias said calmly. He let go, and the officer slumped to the floor and looked at his arm as if it were broken.

"Also, touch me again, and you'll see your arm removed!"

The officer pulled himself to his feet and ran off clutching his numbing arm amid the mocking gazes of the infantry, who were glad to see a man take charge of their lives who had some common sense for a change.

Just then, the lieutenant who was sent down by Tigrami approached Pausanias, heaving for breath.

"Hawk ... the general wants ... an explanation ... for the men ... falling back!"

"Have you been in much combat?" Pausanias asked casually, as he checked the sharpness of his blade with his thumb.

"Not much. Why?"

"Then I suggest you get out of here."

The lieutenant didn't need asking twice, as the large ships were almost upon them. Travelling fast, they were like buildings charging their way under some unstoppable curse. Blocking out the light, the ships cast shadows over the infantry.

With the lieutenant's mouth hanging open, he turned and ran back up the hill.

"Right," Pausanias said to himself. He was cleared of trouble and ready for what was to come. He took a quick look at the hut on top of the hill, as a signaller frantically waved his flags at them, yet the sergeants around Pausanias instructed the signallers to either pick up their swords or leave. They opted for the latter.

"This is it," he said to himself. Then he filled his lungs with air and bellowed at the infantry: "MAKE READY!"

Pausanias stepped into the front row of the phalanx and picked up a shield that was handed to him, just resting the tip of his sword along the top as he crouched down with the others.

The ships came charging towards them, not slowing down. He knew they were using the same tactic as before, and were going to drive their vessels up the sloped wall and onto the parapet. He just hoped he had ordered the phalanx back far enough. Three ships came towards them, one heading directly for him. The prow was covered in creatures, waving their weapons at them.

"Don't let it get to you, lads. They can still die!" he said to those around him.

The bottom of the ship creaked as it mounted the stone wall, water gushing from its hull. As it bridged itself on the parapet, the creatures launched themselves off and charged at the phalanx. Pausanias did not hear the order, but the light dimmed as arrows pelted into them. Because of this, few got to the phalanx, and those that did were skewered by the wall of spears.

But more ships arrived, filling the gaps along the wall, some of them wedging themselves between others. The ships behind rammed the back of the ships on the wall, hooking themselves up to those that had already landed, with the Golesh charging across the boats and onto the wall. Chaos ensued as the Camions fought to maintain the lines, and this time, despite the numbers of Golesh, they did.

"This is useless!" said Jadge as he looked on at the battle. He was walking a bare patch into the ground as he kept pacing back and forth, amid the patient gaze of Metiya standing next to him. Hearing the screams of his comrades as they died made him angry; the only thing keeping him there was his oath.

"METIYA!" he shouted, thinking he was far away.

"Captain?" came a voice just behind him.

"Dispatch a messenger to General Tigrami, tell him … tell him … let him know, that I *insist* that we advance."

"With all due respect, Captain, it will mean little."

Jadge turned and faced him.

"Are you disobeying a direct order, Sergeant?"

"Not at all, Captain – merely stating a fact."

Judge looked back at the garrison fighting on the wall. He couldn't see much – just a lot of pushing and shoving as the phalanx fought back the creatures. The Golesh came jumping off the ships in their hundreds, with no signs of relenting.

Jadge huffed and resumed walking back and forth, but stopped when he heard Metiya shout, "Captain!" There was a sense of urgency in his voice.

Turning, Jadge saw what he was seeing – a weakness that all had missed. The Golesh on one of the larger vessels had rowed their vessel to the south side of the crescent moon. It wasn't able to dock, with little rocks keeping it just out of reach of the ground. But the creatures began to lower a gangway, hinged on the side of the ship's hull, onto the ground; and immediately the Golesh on board stampeded off and towards the exposed right flank of cavalry soldiers, who had been completely unaware of their presence.

Jadge looked for the cavalry captain, but he was missing, probably caught up in the melee.

"Right," he said quietly to himself. "Prepare, PREPARE!!" he bellowed as he fixed his helmet.

"PREPARE!!" repeated Metiya as he turned and collected his spear, embedded into the ground with his shield resting against it.

The Three-Thirty-Third lined up perfectly square, as officers ran behind them, ready to advance.

"PHALANX!!"

"HAR!" they all roared as they brought their spears forward.

"FORWARD!!"

Their stomping was audible, as they trudged heavily towards the Black to close the gap.

"TON POLEMO STIN EIRINI!!" yelled Metiya, again followed by a tremendous "HAR!" from everyone around him.

"General!" came the same moan from the officer in the hut, watching on. He pointed towards the advancing Three-Thirty-Third.

"Is everyone disobeying me today? Why on earth am I here?!" he said to his officers.

"He's plugging the gap," added a colonel, seeing the onslaught.

"But he had no orders to!"

"Orders or not, General, his insolence may just have saved the day."

Tigrami went to raise his voice, but as he saw the creatures charging, covering the south crescent in black, he couldn't help but admit that on this occasion, Jadge was right.

Marching forward, the Three-Thirty-Third silently passed the right flank. Just the sound of their feet marching in time was heard, as they headed towards the charging mass of Black, who howled and shrieked. The front row of the Three-Thirty-Third stuck out further turning the rectangle into a triangle, with thick with spears from eight men deep, the sunlight glistening off their spearheads. The creatures came forward. Jadge could see them clearly now, their vile wounds held together with plates and screws embedded into their flesh and bone, the weapons they were going to use, the yellow of their eyes; this was it.

He braced himself. They hit. He didn't hear nor see it. His shield pressed hard up against his helmet making him almost black out, there was a ringing in his ears as swords hammered against his shield. All around him, he felt pressure as the row behind him pressed forward. He tried to hold his spear straight, but with all the tugging, it was ripped from his grasp. Pulling his arm down, he grabbed his sword, but with his shield wedged up against him he could not draw it. Behind him, the phalanx closed together, pinning him between them and the Golesh.

Jadge was now in the thick of it – there was no turning back. Seeing the creatures' faces inches away, he could smell their decaying odour.

But the regiment didn't budge, in-fact, they were pushing forward, their spears jabbing away at the Golesh as they howled in pain. Jadge pressed forward with the front line. His shield continued to receive punishment, but both his helmet and shield protected him well. He dreaded this part of battle – he preferred it when it broke up and he could ditch his spear and draw his sword and fight single-handed; but right now he couldn't move, completely locked in as his men pressed against him from behind and the creatures tried to kill him from in front. One creature tried sticking its head over his shield as it tried to bite him. It howled, showing him its fangs. It looked as though it had bitten its own tongue to show him its thick, black blood. He sneered; still not able to draw his sword, he managed to headbutt it. It fell, and he felt something soft beneath his feet. Stomping as hard as he could, he felt bones breaking.

Despite being vastly outnumbered, the Three-Thirty-Third were more than a match for the Black as they drove the creatures back, leaving a mass of maimed and trampled bodies lying on the floor behind them, not one of them Camion.

Behind them, archers came running their way, sent by Tigrami. Arrows began to rain down on the creatures, and any benefit they had once had was now lost.

"General, I think we're winning?" said the young officer who had now re-entered, staring out of the hut with a big grin.

"Don't get ahead of yourself, boy. We haven't won until the battle is over!" Tigrami leant on the map and gripped his fists, turning his knuckles white; this was supposed to be his victory and others were taking it from him.

In the water below, the boats kept crashing into the ones in front, under the raging bombardment from the archers and catapults. But still the swarm kept coming, as the Black ran over every ship until they jumped down onto the wall, forming a pile as the bodies built up. The Camions fought gallantly, not giving any quarter. Like snow in a blizzard, arrows kept peppering the creatures, with the phalanx not giving way. To Tigrami's right, the Three-Thirty-Third had cleared the right side of the crescent moon, and had returned to their position at the foot of the hill. Before they pulled back they threw torches onto the vessel with the gangway leaving it to burn uncontrollably. Even though the battle did seem to be in their hands, Tigrami knew that something was amiss – it seemed too easy, too perfect. And he kept his eyes on the horizon, trying to figure out what it was. But with no reinforcements, the battle on the ground was now up to the trained soldiers.

***

Andreas stood on the hill, with his first arrow still notched to his bowstring as others around them had to run to carts and refill theirs. He kept pulling it back to fire with each volley, but was distracted as he kept looking for his brother every time he heard a scream, for if he fell, he would be alone in this world.

Pausanias fought valiantly. In a later age, poets and screenwriters would create an image of him standing defiantly on a mountain of bodies, as the rags of his torn clothing blew in the wind. His line had not been broken, and before them was a huge pile of creatures lying in pieces. His sword was smeared in black blood, and, despite the continued barrage from the Golesh, he found himself pushing forward rather than pulling back. The catapults exhausted their loads, with one unit hammering a pickaxe into the cliff face to haul out some rocks. The fire from the ships in the cove started to engulf every ship around it, spreading violently as if the ships' wood were coated in oil. Soon, black smoke billowed east as the furnace was a picture of Len Seror, the vessels becoming ash in the water.

The remaining Golesh could not retreat. One of them seemed to take charge; it quickly climbed the mast of its ship on all fours and howled into the air. This time, though, it seemed different, and all the creatures, as one, charged for the line. Pausanias saw it. He could tell by their body language.

"Death charge!" he gasped.

The creatures' charge was unforgiving, and seemed more dangerous than before. They crashed into the phalanx hard, so hard that Pausanias lost his shield as it was torn away from him. He stabbed his sword into one, but was knocked to the ground as the charge came and several holes opened up along the phalanx. His right arm was pinned down under the fallen creature, and, looking up, he saw a small elf-like Golesh appear, brandishing a dagger. Everyone around him was busy in their skirmishes – he was alone. He shot up his left arm and grabbed its neck, but the creature merely smiled. And, mustering breath into its lungs, it went to stab him in the eye. Pausanias winced.

But nothing came.

Opening one eye, he saw an arrow protruding from the creature's skull.

Shoving it off, he sat up and saw Andreas standing in perfect posture behind the line as he fired. Pausanias gave him a nod, and, grabbing his sword, he jumped up and fought to close the gap.

Andreas pulled another arrow from his quiver and ran towards the Golesh funnelling through the gap. Pulling the string back, he barely had time to aim, but fired it with superior accuracy, striking a creature in the centre of its forehead. Ducking under a blow, he held another arrow and struck with force into its heart, then pulled it out and notched it to his bowstring and fired again. His charge continued and he met his brother, bringing the Golesh down in their scores.

"We're being overrun!" shouted an officer in disbelief, as he held a brooch with the God of War, Grash, on it, praying that they would come to victory.

"Damn!" said Tigrami, as he realised the truth.

"Shall I order a retreat?"

"No. Tell every man to fight till the last."

"But, General, we could lose everyone!"

"We *will* lose everyone if they don't hold their ground."

All the officers exchanged looks.

Tigrami noticed their discomfort. "Their reinforcements are spent. Our men just have to fight them till their last. Signal for all engineers and officers to join the fight – there is little else we can do now," he said, leaning against the windowsill.

But as he gazed out at the ocean, his heart jumped into his mouth, and he turned and ran outside. He jumped onto his mount and galloped inland, as his own guards stood looking at each other. The officers watched him leave. They shrugged, wondering what had driven him to such madness. But, turning, they looked on through the smoke, and saw another fleet approaching, one far larger, with ships bigger than they had ever seen. Hanging from their giant masts were huge, black flags, displaying a yellow serpent wrapped around a red star blowing in the wind.

The deck of the ship creaked under the weight of the creature, if it could be described as that. It was more of a monster, with its fangs dripping with red blood as it snacked on the human slaves below, captured from the armada that had tried to attack their land. The sword in its grasp was big, the blade at the hilt at least four times the width of a normal blade. The creature was wrapped in thick armour, which was dark grey and looked well made and beaten, not shabby and crude like those on the creatures dying in the cove ahead of it. It appeared to be made to measure – made for the best results. Every other creature around it was better equipped and armed than the minions it had sent forth.

As they died in the carnage before them, it smiled, relishing their pitiful wails. But the armoured creatures watched on. They didn't throw their weapons into the air as they advanced, they didn't howl to intimidate their foe – they stood silent, looking on intently. With thousands of ships around it, the real invasion force had arrived.

Chapter Twenty-Eight
Scales of Death

Havovatch rode down the hill towards the port. The Averchi had cleared the land surrounding the walls, leaving black stains of blood on the ground and large patches of burnt grass. He rode hard, waving his arms as the gates were closed. As he approached, one of the gates opened and the commander came storming out with several of his cohort trailing, all armed. They had clearly been waiting for him. Havovatch reined in his mount as he saw several dozen appear on the parapet with crossbows, all aiming at him.

"I told ya, next time I see you, you'll be for it. I suggest you turn now and go. I'll give ya thirty seconds," the commander said with a big grin, happy that he had had the upper hand since his humiliation. He also received several sniggers from his cohorts behind him.

"You really don't know what you're dealing with, do you?" said Havovatch.

The commander could do nothing but smile.

"That creatures that attacked this port – there is a far bigger army coming, and they will take over this world."

The commander held his arms out. "I'm not of your world. I live far away, and will be returning soon," he grinned.

Havovatch sighed. He knew that they didn't care. But, just then, he heard it. He saw the dirt on the ground tremble. He kept his eyes squarely on the commander as his grin vanished, his men quivered and returned inside, leaving him alone, and the mercenaries on the parapet looked at each other uneasily.

Lining the hill behind Havovatch were his Knight Hawks, and, as if a drop of ink had fallen upon the top, they made their way down towards the town.

Havovatch stood straight on his horse.

"How do you fancy your odds now?"

The commander just looked on aghast – he had never seen so many of them together.

"Open the gates and allow my men in, or there will be another battle on these walls, and this time you won't survive."

By now a large horde of Hawks stood behind Havovatch, their faces hidden behind their black helmets, as all of the fierce and renowned warriors in the known world huddled before him.

Reluctantly, and rather sheepishly, the commander stepped back behind the gate and disappeared. A moment passed and the gates were opened fully, and, dismounting his horse and slapping its rear to gallop off, Havovatch led his army into Beror.

On the other side, the townspeople were now everywhere, but pulled away upon seeing the Hawks. The commander was nowhere in sight and had clearly made a quick exit. The Hawks created a clear path in front of them, as the entire street was packed with dark helmets and rusted crests. The Hawks marched confidently, staring straight ahead, with an assortment of weapons that made the Averchi look on with envy.

After a while – and leaving several jaws hanging – Havovatch arrived at the pier leading to the warehouse. Feera was standing at the end in his armour, guarding it.

"Follow the planks," Havovatch instructed.

In one long line, the Hawks obeyed. Havovatch waited at the end, looking at the world he was about to leave. He wished he could have had this farewell moment on land, for as he looked down he realised he was on a stone quay heading out to sea. But as he had this philosophical moment, he realised that this may be the he would spend on Ezazeruth. Then he was distracted as he looked up at the gatehouse, and saw horses charging through.

Havovatch hurried his regiment along. As he turned to have one more look at the world, he was met by a gathering crowd, keen to see where they were going. Standing there was the cutmen's captain from the bar, with several of his men. Hunched over slightly and holding his ribs, he sneered as he looked at him.

Havovatch gave a mocking bow, throwing his arms wide and placing one foot behind the other. He bent low, smiling broadly behind his helmet. As he passed each plank, he kicked it off the pier and into the water.

"Are they in place?" said the captain to his cronies as he kept his eyes on Havovatch.

"Yus, Sir. Those vile dogs aren't going anywhere. We will find out what their prize is!"

"Good," said the captain, as he plotted his redemption.

"Good to see you, General," said Buskull at the other end.

"Everyone aboard?"

"Aye."

"Then let's make our way – I just want to get on with it."

Stepping into the warehouse, Havovatch saw that it was much lighter with the doors open at the front. The ship was leaning forward, with chocks holding it in place. Mercury had a huge grin on his face as he stood on the quarterdeck, staring over at the Knight Hawks. Some said hello to him, to which they received a jittery word of some babble in return.

Havovatch made his way up to him. "Let's go, Mercury."

He found his voice wobbling, as if he was holding back a tear, for he was – he felt he was on his path to death, again.

But Mercury turned to him and reached out his hand as if to give him something. Havovatch held up the flat of his hand and Mercury dropped something into it. As he turned and gripped the rudder wheel, Havovatch looked upon a small respect knife with a wooden handle. He smiled, for he knew that he had Mercury's full trust and respect.

Buskull pulled heavily on a chain hanging from the ceiling. There was a loud noise as pulleys and weights fell. Suddenly, everyone held on to the vessel or fell to the deck, as the ship tipped forward and into the ocean. The sails immediately pulled down, and, instantly catching the wind, the ship sailed out into the open water.

Havovatch stood at the aft of the ship, watching the Port of Beror become smaller and smaller. He felt as though he was digging his toes into the deck to stop himself from jumping overboard and swimming back. For a moment, even if he died, he would rather fight in his homeland than on some black land beyond what he knew as home. But he was bound by his duty, and, with a tear running down his cheek, he just watched.

Unbeknownst to him, his unit were close by (although, Wrisscrass was locked in a cabin so Havovatch could explain his presence later), following his gaze, as were most of the Hawks. Mercury, though, was lost in his own world, smiling. With his long, grey, matted hair twisting in the wind, he held the wheel with confidence as if he had never forgotten how to steer. Glancing up at the sky, he knew exactly where he was going, and pushed on with purpose, longing for his retribution.

As the silent army watched, the only sound being the flapping of the sails and the boat being pushed through the waves by the strong gusts of wind as they sailed into the open sea. Not one moved as the land became smaller. In every direction they could see dots of twinkling lights upon the shore, as night fell and people lit their lanterns, the landscape and hills just visible as a black silhouette below the navy sky. But they could not see the stars until they looked up, and there, like a blanket before them, was the scene of silver dots surrounding the three moons.

Deep down in the dark of the ship, a constant dripping from the damp, murky depths echoed in the long, narrow space. One fracture in the hull, mere inches from the water, would instantly fill the boat. There was no way out, not any more. The hatch in the ceiling was sealed. It was dark and confined – even a sane man with a strong mind could get lost in the bitterness of this world, with the darkness playing pictures before their eyes.

Small trickles of water found their way in, but they could not be seen, dark and black as the Shadow World. There was the loud echo inside from the boat pushing through the waves. No Hawk would know of this, though, for they were all above deck, gazing off to their destinies or looking the other way, wondering if they would ever again see the land they were leaving behind. But back down in the bowels of the ship, where no one needed to venture, was just shadow.

Then, two yellow eyes opened.

If you want to know more about the world of Ezazeruth, check out my website at www.thomasrgaskin.com

You can also follow me on Facebook and Twitter by searching for Thomas R. Gaskin.

Dawn of Darkness

Thomas R. Gaskin

Lightning Source UK Ltd.
Milton Keynes UK
UKOW02f1034120816

280552UK00002B/72/P